BLOOD OF HEAVEN

**Other Books by Bill Myers**

McGee and Me! *(children's video and fiction series)*

Journeys to Fayrah *(children's fantasy series)*

The Incredible World of Wally McDoogle
*(children's comedy series)*

Forbidden Doors *(teen thriller series)*

Hot Topics, Tough Questions *(teen nonfiction)*

Christ, B.C. *(adult devotional)*

# BLOOD OF HEAVEN

## BILL MYERS

Zondervan Publishing House
*Grand Rapids, Michigan*

*A Division of HarperCollins Publishers*

*Blood of Heaven*
Copyright © 1996 by Bill Myers

Requests for information should be addressed to:

### ZondervanPublishingHouse
*Grand Rapids, Michigan 49530*

**Library of Congress Cataloging-in-Publication Data**

Myers, Bill, 1953–
    Blood of heaven / Bill Myers
       p.  cm.
    ISBN: 0-310-20119-5 (pbk.)
    I. Title.
PS3563.Y36B56   1996
813'.54—dc20

                                          96-23358
                                            CIP

Published in association with the literary agency of Alive Communications, 1465 Kelly Johnson Blvd., Suite #320, Colorado Springs, CO 80920

*Interior design by Sue Vandenberg Koppenol*

*Printed in the United States of America*

99 00 01 02 03 04 /❖ DC/ 17

*To Jim Riordan,*
*for his love and friendship*

# ACKNOWLEDGMENTS

Many people have given their time and expertise to help me write this book. I'm sure I've still made a few mistakes, but these folks deserve credit for what I managed to get right. My grateful appreciation to Dr. Dennis Revie and the department of biology at California Lutheran University, Dr. Rick Stead, Dr. Murray Robinson, Dr. Jeff Hutchins, Kristy Woods, Fred Baker, Nebraska State Penitentiary administrative assistant Charles Hohenstein, Hugh and Beth Geisbrecht, my brother, Dale Brown, Marta Fields, Larry and Julie LaFata, Ed Penney, Sue Brower, Lori Walburg, Scott Wanamaker, Frank Peretti, and Angela Hunt. Thanks also to Lissa Halls Johnson, Robin Jones Gunn, Carla Williams, Scott Kennedy, Lynn and Peggy Marzulli, Doug McIntosh, Dorothy Moore, Bill Myers, Bob and Helen West, John Tolle, Bill Burnett, Gary Smith, Tom Kositchek, Cathy Glass, Criz Hibdon, and the rest of my "extended family" for their intercession. Also, to my agent and friend, Greg Johnson, and my editor, Dave Lambert, another friend who first heard me weave this yarn nearly a decade ago. Lastly, always, and most importantly, to Brenda, Nicole, and Mackenzie.

"*For in my inner being I delight in God's law; but I see another law at work in the members of my body, waging war against the law of my mind and making me a prisoner of the law of sin at work within my members. What a wretched man I am! Who will rescue me from this body of death?*"

The Apostle Paul

# PART
# ONE

# CHAPTER 1

"You dis me."

There was no response.

"You hear what I say? You disrespect me."

Michael Coleman didn't have to look up from his Thanksgiving meal of turkey loaf and yams to know who was talking. It was Sweeney. Big, brooding, tattoos across the back of his bald head. As a member of the Aryan Brotherhood, he had been convicted for stabbing a Jew to death during last year's Nazi rally in Omaha. He'd come onto the Row a week ago, and this was his move.

"You hear me, Cole?"

Imperceptibly, Coleman tightened the grip on his spoon. He cursed himself for not slipping a homemade shank into his waistband before coming to mess. He'd known a power play was coming; he just hadn't expected it so soon. Still, if a spoon was all he had, then a spoon would have to do. Already his senses were tightening, sharpening. The contrast between the orange yams and the green fiberglass meal tray grew vivid. The eight other men stopped eating and looked in Coleman's direction. In the sudden silence, the hum from the overhead heating duct grew to a consuming roar.

"Sit down." Coleman's command came strong. He was grateful he didn't have to clear his throat. That would have betrayed weakness, and weakness could spell death.

Sweeney shifted slightly.

Good.

Coleman finally raised his eyes. But not to Sweeney. It was to the inmate sitting across from him. A young black man, almost a boy, who'd made the mistake of hitting a white man one too many times in a bar fight. He wouldn't even have been here if he could have afforded a real lawyer. The kid quickly rose and moved out of the way so Sweeney could take his seat.

This was Coleman's gauntlet. If Sweeney obeyed, if he sat, that meant he honored Coleman's position and really did want to talk. If he didn't, then this was clearly a challenge of Coleman's authority.

Sweeney didn't move.

Coleman wasn't surprised. His heart pounded—but not in fear. This was exhilaration. An exhilaration he would carefully hold in check until the perfect moment.

Again Sweeney shifted, but this time to brace himself for what was coming. "You disrespect Garcia and me."

Hector Garcia was the weakest on the Row, which made him the most vulnerable. A bomb freak, he had inadvertently killed an elderly couple who were in the wrong place at the wrong time. Thanks to Oklahoma City, that put him near the bottom of the prison food chain, barely above a child molester.

Sweeney had come onto the Row and immediately made Garcia his punk. No one seemed to mind, not even when he forced Garcia to shave his legs and start wearing jockey shorts dyed pink from cherry Kool-Aid. But after the boy's third or fourth beating, Coleman finally drew the line. He knew Sweeney had clout: major outside heroin connections. In fact, he'd even heard that Sweeney was supplying one or more of the baton-wielding hacks inside, which would explain why they looked the other way during Garcia's beatings.

Still, enough was enough. Maybe it was the memories of his own childhood, his own father. Coleman wasn't sure. But he had passed word down the chain of command that there would be no more beatings. And now Sweeney stood there, not only challenging his decree, but his position as well.

Coleman had several options. Talk it out, which would be read as weakness, or—well, there was really only one other choice. And by the electricity shooting through his body and the razor-sharp focusing of his senses, he knew there was no time like the present.

Sweeney didn't know what hit him. Coleman's five-foot-eleven frame was off the bench and going at him before the man could move. Deliriously out of control, adrenaline surging, Coleman was a wild man, punching and stabbing and tearing and kicking in a euphoric, overwhelming rush.

He barely noticed the hacks descending on him, pulling him off, doing their own brand of kicking and beating. Nor did he really care—although he couldn't help noticing that at least one of them was Sweeney's client. He saw Sweeney stagger back to his feet, flashing a newly acquired, toothless grin and brandishing a pair of aluminum knuckles. Coleman tried to move, but the hacks held him in place as Sweeney came at him. Apparently the man had more connections than Coleman had thought.

There was some solace that it took two guards to hold him as Sweeney did his work. But even as the punches fell and consciousness slipped away, a plan was forming in Coleman's mind. It would take more than this to oust him from power. This was child's play. An excuse for revenge. And revenge would come swiftly. It always did. For Michael Coleman, revenge was not a dish best served cold, but rather piping hot, full of rage, and in a manner they would never forget. That was Coleman's style. That was what made him great. That's why they feared him.


Dr. Philip O'Brien had a problem. His briefcase was packed with so many papers and files that it left no room for the framed picture of Beth and the kids. Now what? Here he was, CEO of the fastest growing biotech firm in the Pacific Northwest, and his brain was gridlocked over what to take and what to leave behind on a forty-eight-hour business trip. In anger and contempt over his indecision, he pulled the core group's "Toxicity of Epidermal Growth Factor" out of his briefcase, tossed it on his desk, and scooped up the photo.

He turned and headed out of his office toward the elevators. Tall, on the downhill side of his forties (though the gray hair made him appear closer to mid-fifties) he still had a boyish, Jimmy Stewart charm. Except for the quiet padding of his Nikes on the carpet and the occasional brush of blue jeans against his briefcase, the hallway was absolutely silent. Just as it should be. No one worked holidays at Genodyne. Except for Security, and the die-hard kids down in Research, the six-story complex would remain closed until Monday. So would the manufacturing plant a quarter mile away. That was O'Brien's style, his vision from the beginning. Happy employees make relaxed employees make imaginative employees make significant breakthroughs in genetic engineering—a theory spawned in the brain of a Berkeley biochem student back in the early eighties. But after dozens of patents and one, soon to be two, products out on the market, it was a theory that had led to a hundred and seventy-five million dollars' worth of business last year alone.

Biotech companies come and go. Of the fifteen hundred or so that had started, only fourteen had actually placed a product on the market. And for good reason. With the public paranoia over genetic engineering, as well as impossible FDA guidelines and innumerable testings, it cost between one hundred and three hundred million dollars to develop a single drug. But, as Genodyne had proven, once a drug hits the market, it can become a blockbuster overnight.

O'Brien passed on the elevator and took the stairs. So why was he here? Why had he, head of this flourishing, feel-good company, rushed through Thanksgiving dinner, leaving his wife and two kids alone for the remainder of the weekend? O'Brien arrived at the next floor landing, pushed open the door, and beheld his answer.

"Glad you could make it." It was a twenty-four-year-old kid, well built, with black hair that always hung in his face, and, according to Sarah, O'Brien's twelve-year-old daughter, a major babe. "The freezer and lab equipment have already been loaded. The jet's been on the runway half an hour. Where have you been?" It was Kenneth Murkoski. Murkoski the Terrible. Murkoski the Ambitious. Murkoski the Boy Genius.

"I had some pumpkin pie to finish."

The man-child didn't smile. "Got a call from Lincoln. There was an incident on the Row."

"An *incident?*"

"That's what they called it."

"Was our guy involved?"

"Big time. They said we should hold off a few days."

"And?"

"I said, 'No way.'"

"Kenny . . ." He saw Murkoski wince. He knew the kid hated the name, so he used it only when necessary. He'd hand-picked Murkoski right out of M.I.T. almost eighteen months ago. He was the country's brightest, best, and most ambitious. He was also a showboat and publicity hound—a volatile combination, but O'Brien had decided to take the risk. Actually, he hadn't had much choice. Having to continually oversee Research and Development, Manufacturing, Administration,

Sales, Marketing, and Logistics had sapped all of O'Brien's creativity. If the company was to survive, O'Brien needed a blue-skyer, some fresh blood (not to mention fresh brain cells) to run the Gene Therapy Division. In short, he needed someone who would think like O'Brien used to think back when he'd had time to think. Of course, that meant more than the usual amount of fires to put out and ruffled feathers to smooth. (Murkoski's social skills were as underdeveloped as his humility.) It also meant losing control of more and more of the details—details that O'Brien occasionally felt Murkoski deliberately hid from him. Still, despite the risks and frustrations, the kid was worth it. Even now.

"You sure we're not pushing too hard?" O'Brien asked. "What did they say?"

"What *could* they say? They're not playing around with some 'B' league biotech firm anymore. We've got the whole Mom-and-apple-pie U.S. government on our side."

"But if they suggest we wait, what's the hurry?"

Murkoski scowled but was interrupted by the ringing of a phone. He reached into his Italian linen sports coat and pulled out the cellular as he answered O'Brien's question. "By the time we get there, things will settle down. The truth is, it will probably make him more willing to play ball with us." He turned and spoke into the phone with a demanding, "Yeah?" The expression on his face shifted, and he turned to walk away. "So what are you saying?" he asked, lowering his voice. It was obvious the kid wanted some privacy, and O'Brien was happy to oblige. Besides, he wanted to check in on Freddy before they left. So as Murkoski continued his conversation, O'Brien headed down the hall.

A biotech company landing a government contract in gene therapy research was unheard of. So was the amount of money they were throwing around. But this was big. Very big. And, in less than a year, the results had proven staggering. No wonder Murkoski kept pushing. It wasn't because of competition—who was there to compete with? It was simply impatience. What they had uncovered, when it was finally developed and ready for the public, would quite literally change the world.

O'Brien arrived at B–11. He held his wallet containing the mag ID against the little black box. He then entered his six-digit PIN. An electronic bolt snapped back, and he pushed open the door.

The room was twenty by forty. The right end looked like an outdoor playground with swing set, monkey bars, slide, and half a dozen boulders of different sizes scattered about. The walls were painted in cartoon-style trees and hills, and the ground was covered in real grass sod that had to be replaced every six weeks. In the far corner a dead tree with three gnarled limbs was held in place by inch-thick cable. The other side of the room resembled a kitchen: cupboards, counters, stools, several toys, and a child-sized table with four chairs. Everything was painted in bright pinks, blues, purples, and greens.

O'Brien allowed the door to shut behind him, then crossed to a park bench near the center of the room. "Freddy," he called. "Freddy, where are you?"

A three-and-a-half-foot baboon scurried up over the rocks and loped toward him. He weighed sixty-five pounds and had a long snout, dark brown, gray-tipped fur, and eyes so close together they almost looked crossed. The animal kept his tail arched high over his back and put on an affected swagger that was almost comical. This was intentional, a baboon's way of saying, "Hi there, look how goofy I am, I can't possibly be a threat." And for good reason. Even though Freddy weighed less than seventy pounds, baboons can be fierce fighters, with the strength of half a dozen other creatures their size.

O'Brien placed the briefcase on the bench and sat down. "How you doing, boy?"

Freddy hopped up beside him and immediately began exploring the briefcase. His long, black hands, almost human, ran over the textured surface, fingering the brass latches, flipping the handle back and forth, looking for some way inside.

O'Brien chuckled. "Sorry. There's nothing of interest in there. Believe me."

But Freddy would not be put off. Now he was lifting the case, looking under it, checking its sides, searching for some means of entrance.

O'Brien watched in silent amusement. The animal had joined the experiment fifteen weeks ago. He was not the first. There had been two other primates before him. Neither had survived. Too many complications. But Freddy had pulled through. And, like the mice in the earlier experiments, his behavior had dramatically changed.

O'Brien reached over and probed the animal's chest. The fur was coarse and bristly. Freddy stretched out for what he obviously hoped would be a good scratch and rubdown.

"Let's see how that sternum is coming, shall we?" O'Brien adjusted his glasses and carefully studied the shaved section encircling what had been a small needle puncture where they had extracted the bone marrow. There had been a minor infection several weeks ago, but now it was completely healed.

"Looking good, dude."

Freddy's response to O'Brien's kindness was instant; he released the briefcase and wrapped both of his arms around O'Brien's arm. It was an embrace. Common among females in the wild, and even between males and babies. But never between male and male. And never with another species; there was too much fear. Yet here he was—a full-grown male embracing and nuzzling O'Brien as if they were father and son.

This wasn't the first time. Freddy had been embracing for almost a month now. But every time it happened, O'Brien felt his heart swell just a little. This was why they were doing what they were doing. This was why he endured Murkoski, why he left his wife and children during a holiday weekend. They were disappointed about his frequent absences now because they didn't understand. But in a matter of a few years, before his children were grown, they *would* understand, and they would rejoice with him just as he was rejoicing now.

O'Brien began parting Freddy's fur and gently kneading the skin. This was grooming. In the wild he would be searching for fleas or lice or flakes of salt, another sign of affection among baboons. And the more O'Brien kneaded the animal's fur, the more Freddy nuzzled in and hugged his arm.

How odd, O'Brien mused. As a scientist he had been taught that baboons occupied a necessary step in the process of human evolution as they made the transition from swinging in trees to walking the open savannas. And now, once again, these same animals were necessary to make what O'Brien hoped would be an equally astounding leap in evolution. A leap just as important, and perhaps even more necessary for the survival of the human race.

O'Brien thought again of Beth and the children. He would call them. In the car on the way to the plane, he would call and say how much he loved them. But first he needed to sit just a moment longer. To sit, to dream, and to savor Freddy's affection.

Katherine Lyon hated Thanksgiving. For that matter, she wasn't too fond of Christmas, Easter, or the Fourth of July. It wasn't so much the holidays as the memories they brought—along with the blitz of TV and magazine ads: All those perfect little families gathered around their perfect little turkeys, or Christmas trees, or whatever.

Katherine sighed wearily as she ran her hand through her cropped, auburn hair. It wasn't the most flattering cut for her, but she didn't care. She hadn't cared for a long, long time. She crossed to the front of the store, set the alarm, and peered back into the darkened interior. Over on the side wall, past the latest-model boom boxes, stereos, and color TVs, she could see the telltale glow from one of a dozen displayed computer monitors.

"Let's go, Eric, I'm not telling you again."

The blue-green light was instantly extinguished, and the head of a blonde, bespectacled eight-year-old floated above the center display of telephone answering machines. How fiercely she loved this boy. Of course the resemblance to his father brought back other memories and emotions. But whenever she looked at him, those feelings of bitterness and loss mellowed into a dull, longing ache.

The rest of his body emerged from behind the display. Slight, skinny, elbows and knees mostly. He was already the object of ridicule from some of the tougher third graders. She couldn't help thinking how he must have looked like Gary when Gary was that age. Until Gary had grown up and filled out into his impressive six-foot-two frame.

"Come on, let's go." Her hoarseness carried a weary impatience. But what else could she expect at the end of another ten-hour day of complaining customers, salesmen on the make, IRS letters, and threatening landlords.

"Got your homework?" She tried to sound pleasant, but it fell flat.

The boy nodded silently and slipped past her to the outside. She followed, pulled the door shut, and inserted the key into the dead bolt. As usual, it was a fight to get the thing to click into place. And, as usual, she cursed softly and promised to complain to the owners. The way they hassled her over the slightest delay in rent, she was entitled to expect a few things in the building to work.

"Lyon Computer and Electronics" was wedged into a tiny strip mall on old Highway 99. The shops surrounding her included the obligatory video rental store, hair salon, music hangout, and Szechwan restaurant. All were closed for the holiday except the Albertson's supermarket at the far end, its dull blue-and-white glow spilling out into the unlit parking lot.

Katherine glanced to the sky. It was dark gray and hung just above her head like wet cement. Another typical evening in Everett, Washington. How she hated this place. But the city, located on Puget Sound, was the furthest she could get away from Iowa. And "getting away" was something both she and Eric had desperately needed.

As the lock finally clicked in, Katherine grew aware of a presence three doors down. He sat on the sidewalk, back against the building. She didn't look. She didn't have to. She knew he was one of the homeless men who haunted the area at night. It's not that she resented these guys. In fact, more than once, when she and Gary had found the rare opportunity to grab a lunch together, she had begged him to buy an extra Big Mac to share. But that was back when life was kinder, back when she was a devoted wife and the loving mother of a newborn, back when she was naive and weak and didn't know how hard and cold the world could be.

She turned toward the parking lot. Her Datsun, a gray beater with a crease running along its back fender, was parked thirty feet away. "Come on," she said, giving her son a nudge.

Eric slouched forward and obeyed. As they stepped off the curb, Katherine discreetly reached into her purse. Somewhere amid the clutter was her leather-cased pepper spray. A gift to herself last Mother's Day. No bigger than a tube of lipstick, it was supposed to be attached to her key ring, but she'd never found the time to do it.

Then she heard it. The scrape of shoes and the rustle of clothes. He was getting up. She kept her stride even and continued digging into her purse.

"Ma'am?"

She fought the panic. She was halfway to the car. Even if she broke into a run, there was no way she could unlock the door and get both her and the boy inside.

Eric turned to look.

"Don't turn around," she whispered.

"But, Mom—"

"Keep walking."

Eric obeyed.

"Ma'am, excuse me . . ." The sound grew louder. Worn tennis shoes scuffing gravel. They were heading toward her. Katherine picked up her pace. So did he.

She continued digging. *Where is that stupid spray? What's this? Lipstick? No! Mascara? No! Where is it?*

"Excuse me?"

The car was ten feet away, but the footsteps were nearly on top of her. He was so close she could hear his breathing.

There! She found it.

Hand still in the purse, she felt for the little red safety tab and clicked it over to the right. Now it was armed. Let him try what he would—she was ready.

Fingers closed around her arm from behind. This was it. If there was one thing Gary had stressed, it was to never be forced into a defensive position. Always play offense. In one quick move, she spun around, pulled out the spray, and fired the thin orange line directly into the assailant's face.

The young man let out a scream and covered his eyes. "What are you doing?" he yelled, dropping to his knees.

Katherine moved in, continuing to unload the spray on his face. *It'll be a long time before he tries this again,* she thought.

"Are you crazy? What are you doing?" Blindly he pushed at the stream, trying to shove it back with his hands. It was then that she noticed the checkbook he was holding. Her checkbook.

"Are you crazy?" he kept shouting. "Are you crazy?"

"What—"

He coughed and gagged. "You dropped this—back there, you dropped this!"

Katherine released the spray. The man threw the checkbook at her as he remained on the asphalt, coughing and choking.

She stepped back and took a deep, ragged breath. As her fear drained away, so did her strength. She wanted to cry, but she wouldn't. Katherine Lyon had not cried in years.

Coleman's hospital bed was located in the north end of the Nebraska State Penitentiary Administration Building. The long, two-and-a-half-story brick building stood at the front of the prison, overlooking the parking lot. Besides the hospital and medical facilities, it housed all the administration offices, attorney/client conference rooms, and a large general visiting area that seated three hundred people. It also contained the execution chamber with the electric chair and adjacent witness room.

As Coleman lay in the evening's silence, he couldn't help thinking that, should his appeals fail, this would be the same room in which they'd prepare him for execution. In less than seven weeks, should the Supreme Court refuse to hear his case, should the three-person pardons board refuse to offer a stay of execution, this room in which he now lay was the exact room in which they would spruce him up so that he could take the fifty-two steps necessary to reach the execution chamber for his ride on Ol' Sparky.

Coleman turned, trying to push the thought out of his head, and pain shot through his body. He had two cracked ribs, a broken nose, and a mild concussion. Yet when they'd brought him into the hospital tonight, he had refused all painkillers. In fact, even before the X rays and stitches, he had insisted on making a phone call. That was nearly four hours ago. Now Coleman forced himself to remain awake, and to wait.

Forty-five minutes later, his vigilance was rewarded. The wall across from the window began reflecting red-yellow-orange, red-yellow-orange. Coleman didn't have to rise and look out to know that it was an ambulance. Someone else in the prison had been injured, but far worse than he. So badly, in fact, that the assistance of an outside hospital with its bigger and better-equipped ER facility would be needed.

Coleman smiled. His phone call had paid off.

He heard a tray rattling down the hall. They were bringing him food. Here, in the hospital, in the middle of the night. A moment later the overhead fluorescents flickered on. He winced at the light. "What's going on?" he demanded.

"Cook said you'd want this." A trustee in a gold shirt and khaki pants pushed the cart toward Coleman. He removed the lid to reveal an enormous portion of tomorrow morning's sausage and eggs.

Coleman sat up, fought the pain in his head, and reached for the cart. He was starved. "What's the action with the ambulance?"

"Your buddy Sweeney. Guess he dealt some bad dope to one of the hacks. The guy OD'd at home couple hours ago."

"Dead?"

"Coma."

Coleman's appetite quickly increased. He dug into the eggs. "And Sweeney?"

"The other hacks weren't too thrilled about it."

"Too bad," Coleman said, cramming his mouth full of food. "Guess these things happen."

"Guess so. Anything else?"

"Tell the cook thanks."

The trustee nodded.

"Oh, have the guys on the Row take up a collection for Garcia."

"A collection?"

"Yeah. Tell him to burn those jockey shorts and get some real underwear."

The trustee smiled and headed out of the room. Coleman inhaled his food ravenously. Once the rage and aggression were spent, they gave way to an incredible hunger. It had always been that way with Coleman. Ever since he was a little boy.

*"Hey, Hon, McKenney's got me doing paperwork again.*

*Sorry. I'll get home soon as I can. Maybe pick us up a video. Kiss Eric good night for me. Love you guys."*

*Beep.*

Katherine sat on the kitchen floor listening to the answering machine. These were not new messages. They were from an older tape she had saved from seven years ago. A few of the voices belonged to her, or her friends and family, but most were Gary's:

*"If you get this before noon call me, and let's grab some Chinese."*

*Beep.*

The linoleum floor was hard and cold. She leaned against the fridge and felt its vibration against her back. Staring vacantly into her glass, she slowly swirled the Cabernet, watching as the vanishing patina slipped back into the liquid. It had been thirty months since she'd had a drink. The three and a half years before that, the ones immediately following Gary's death, were pretty much a blur. Unfair to Eric and definitely unfair to herself. But with the help of a few friends, she'd gotten back on her feet, changed locale, opened a store, and joined the masses of single parents fighting to keep their heads above the emotional and financial waters.

She usually succeeded. But tonight, with the work hassles, the holiday loneliness, the attack in the parking lot—well, the glow from Albertson's and their acclaimed wine department had been more than she could handle.

*"Don't be mad, Hon, but I just got us this puppy. I know, I know, but a kid needs a dog, right? He's a Black Lab. Eric will go ballistic. Trust me on this. See you soon."*

*Beep.*

Katherine had never seen the dog. Somewhere in the confusion of that evening, then the weeklong vigil at the hospital and the funeral arrangements, the dog was neither seen nor heard of again.

Katherine held the glass closer and stared into the crimson liquid. Finally she raised it to her lips and began to drink.

# CHAPTER 2

**H**arold Steiner loved the Law. There was something pure about it, almost holy. In a world of disorder and impending chaos, it was the only mortar holding civilization together. A stronghold, separating man from the animals.

So, nearly forty years ago, at the tender age of nine, Harold Steiner had pushed up his wire-rimmed glasses, cleared his tiny throat, and announced to the world that he would be a lawyer. By twenty-five he had become the youngest assistant D.A. in the history of Nebraska.

But that was a long time ago. Before his life fell apart. Before Melissa's murder. Oh, he still loved theLaw, but now he knew it to be a double-edged sword, one just as easily wielded by the barbarians, by those who could twist and distort the Law to destroy the Law. Savages like Michael Coleman.

Steiner reached into the glove compartment, pulled out a faded bottle of Tylenol, popped the lid, and tossed his head back to swallow another handful. The headaches usually came three or four days before Melissa's birthday and lasted until a day or two after. Today his daughter would have been twenty-six.

No one was sure how many people Coleman had killed, or in how many states. There were the convenience store clerk and cop in Council Bluffs, the hooker in Omaha, and the half dozen or so unsolved murders that he'd never really copped to. But it had been Melissa's murder that finally nailed him.

Of course they hadn't let Steiner anywhere near the case, not only because of his emotional involvement but also because it had been outside his jurisdiction. He had lived and worked in North Platte, near the southwest corner of the state. Missy had been killed at Creighton College in Omaha. But that hadn't stopped Steiner from investing his own time, unofficially observing the collection and evaluation of evidence, talking daily with the assistant district attorney, helping behind the scenes, at the trial, the appeals, testifying at clemency hearings. In short, every time Coleman tried to exploit the law to his advantage, Steiner was there to help block him.

It was exhausting work. Friends warned that he had crossed the line. Coworkers said he'd become obsessed. But the Law was the Law. Coleman had broken it. He had defied civilization, endangering it. And in the process, he had destroyed everything precious in Steiner's life. For that, Coleman would pay. Regardless of the price, he would pay.

Unfortunately, the cost to Steiner had also been high. Two years after the murder, Theresa had left him. Fourteen months after that, he had lost his job. Not really lost—"indefinite leave of absence" was the term they had used. And still

Coleman's lawyers found loopholes, and still they made their appeals, pleaded for stays, begged for mercy.

Steiner turned off Blondo Street and headed north on 60th. Not one of Omaha's classier neighborhoods, but it was something Theresa could afford. She hadn't returned his last dozen phone calls, and this morning's had been no different. But it should be different. This was Melissa's birthday.

He turned into the driveway of a worn, two-story rental and brought his Volvo to a stop. Checking what was left of his thinning hair (after all, he and Theresa still weren't officially divorced), he stepped out of the car, switched on the alarm, and headed up her walk. Junipers sprawled over the cracked concrete, and some unknown vine encroached upon the steps. Melissa's death had affected Theresa as much as it had him, but in a different way. She had simply quit caring.

He pressed the buzzer, but it didn't work. He opened the sagging screen and knocked.

"Go away," a muffled voice called from inside.

"Theresa?"

"Go away, I said."

"Come on, Therese. It's me. Open up. Come on, Sweetheart."

There was no response.

"Theresa?"

Finally the lock clicked open and a woman appeared in a blue terry-cloth bathrobe. She squinted up at him in the brutal morning light. She'd been an attractive woman once. More handsome than beautiful. She could be still, despite the extra twenty-some pounds she'd put on, and the drawn and weary face from too many late nights at too many bars.

"Theresa?" He frowned. "It's ten-thirty."

"So?"

A smell wafted from the apartment. "Are you smoking again?"

"What do you want, Harry?"

"It's the 26th."

She raised her hand to block the sun. "What?"

"The 26th. Missy's birthday. Don't tell me you forgot."

"Of course I didn't forget."

He could tell she was lying. "So, are you coming?

"Harry . . ."

Steiner stood in silence.

Theresa swore. "Harry, it's been eight years."

"What's that supposed to mean?"

"Harry—"

"Listen." He could hear his voice growing thin and tried his best to stay calm. "It could be eight hundred years. The point is, it's her birthday. We'll never forget her birthday. Right? Come on, Theresa, for crying out loud. After all, it's . . ." The phrase was already dissipating, falling apart before he could finish. ". . . her birthday."

Theresa stood a long moment. "Okay," she finally sighed, "I'll be there. But not right now."

"When?"

"Later, all right? Later."

"Therese—"

"I promise."

"But—"

"Good-bye, Harry." She closed the door.

"I'll wait," he called. "If you want, I can wait."

There was no response.

"Theresa?" Steiner stood a full minute before turning and heading back to his car. He would go to his daughter's graveside by himself. He would wait for Theresa there. Melissa at least deserved that: both of her parents, side by side, together at her grave. On her birthday, Missy at least deserved that.


"This is a joke, right?"

"I assure you, Mr. Coleman," Murkoski said, trying to regain control of the conversation, "this is no joke."

"You come in here with some story about the blood of Christ, and you—"

"No one said we had the blood of—"

"—expect me to be your guinea pig?"

"Please, Mr. Coleman ..." Murkoski swallowed. He appeared to be regrouping, trying to start again. He threw a nervous look at O'Brien, who sat beside him in one of the three fiberglass-molded chairs. They had been in the attorney/client room with Coleman for only thirty minutes, and the killer already had Murkoski on the ropes, looking like a fool.

And not just Murkoski. O'Brien had underestimated the man as well. They had carefully researched him, studied his psychological profile, medical workup, X rays, blood chemistry; they had even run covert EKGs, EEGs, PETs, and a CAT scan on him last summer. Clinically, they knew everything they could know about the man.

But, like most people, they had erred in assuming that multiple killers were ignorant animals with underdeveloped mental skills. After all, here he sat—ribs taped, nose broken, one eye still swollen shut. How could somebody like this possibly be an intellectual equal? Unfortunately, neither of them had taken into account an inmate's worst enemy: time. Next to sleeping, the best killers of time were reading, writing, and learning the skills of fellow prisoners. Whether it was the careful, step-by-step procedure for making a bomb, courtesy of Hector Garcia, or the intricate nuances of the Nebraska legal system, garnered from the books in the prison library, years of reading and listening had sharpened Michael Coleman's intellect to a razor's edge. Then, of course, there was the psychological gamesmanship he'd acquired in running the Row. All this to say, that in less than half an hour, he had reduced Murkoski, the boy genius, into an agitated knot of frustration.

The kid was flailing; O'Brien decided to step in. "Mr. Coleman. Regarding the identity of the blood. We can only say that it is extremely old, and that—"

"'A couple thousand years,' you said."

"Yes, but—"

"So how were you able to keep it from disintegrating? And don't tell me you found it inside some mosquito embalmed in tree sap. I saw that movie, too."

O'Brien took a long breath, but before he could answer, Murkoski jumped back into the fray. The kid never gave up. "The blood was sealed in candle wax. A small section of vine with fragments of bloodstained thorns was encased in the substance. We suspect it was revered as some sort of religious artifact for centuries. Kept on an altar where dripping candles inadvertently covered and sealed a portion of it."

"And what altar would that be?"

"Pardon me?"

"Where?"

"The southern deserts of Egypt. A monastery. The same one that claims to house St. Mark's bones."

"How convenient."

"No, it wasn't convenient. Not at all, Mr. Coleman." Murkoski's voice rose, trembling. "A lot of people risked their lives to bring it to us, and if you're not interested in helping, then we'll find somebody who is. In case you don't know, there are three thousand other inmates on death row."

Coleman opened his hands and closed them quietly. "Three thousand twenty-six. Perhaps you should contact one of them."

Murkoski blinked. Coleman had just called his bluff. Of all the nerve. Murkoski appeared livid, but O'Brien was more impressed than angry. Coleman had no idea how many months they'd researched him, nor the time constraints they were now working under. And yet he'd uncovered Murkoski's vulnerable underside, pressed all his buttons, and taken control of the conversation—in record time. The man was far more clever than they had imagined.

O'Brien cleared his throat and tried again. "Mr. Coleman—whoever's blood it is, and we can't say for certain, we do know that this individual had a genetic makeup slightly different from the rest of us." He could feel Coleman's eyes searching him, looking for a crevice, for a weakness to take hold of. But he held Coleman's stare and kept his voice even as he went into the details. "Human DNA molecules consist of over six billion base pairs. If strung out in a line, that's enough to stretch to the moon and back 16,000 times. In the ancient blood sample we have, most of those have not survived. But what portions we do have, those that have remained intact, have proven quite interesting."

"How?"

This was the hard part. The part O'Brien rarely shared. But it was Coleman's body they were asking to experiment on, and it was certainly his right to know. "As far as we've been able to tell, the blood contains all the usual maternal genes, but there are some fairly unusual genes we've discovered on the male side."

Coleman raised an eyebrow, waiting for more.

Murkoski moved in. "Certainly a man of your intelligence knows about X and Y chromosomes?" It was a patronizing question, and it was met only by Coleman's silence. Murkoski continued. "Two X's together make a female, while an X and Y chromosome determines a male?"

More silence.

"The X chromosome carries up to five thousand genes, while the lowly Y chromosome, that which makes us men, contains only a little over a dozen. So far science has only determined the function of one of those dozen-plus genes, the one that tells the embryo to develop testes instead of ovaries. The remaining male genes appear totally useless."

"Until now," O'Brien corrected. "We don't know how or why, but for some reason the portion of those Y genes that we were able to recover from the blood have a totally different makeup than any other male gene."

"Meaning?"

Murkoski leapt to the punch line. "Whoever's blood this was could not have had a human father."

Silence settled over the room. O'Brien watched Coleman. Not a muscle moved. Murkoski, on the other hand, leaned back in his chair, obviously assured that the playing field had once again been tilted to his advantage.

The silence continued. O'Brien coughed slightly then resumed. "Most of these new genes still appear useless, but one in particular has stood out. When it is introduced into other organisms—when we replicate it in the blood of say, mice, the creatures' behavioral patterns shift dramatically."

Coleman's voice grew strangely quiet. "You've done this with other animals?"

"Yes. Mice first, then more recently primates."

"And?"

"The mortality rate has been higher than we'd like, but for those who have survived, the results have been staggering."

Murkoski continued. "They are no longer concerned with what's best for themselves. Instead of focusing on their own needs, they act in a manner that's best for their community."

Coleman sat motionless. Although he didn't take his eyes off the men, it was obvious that wheels were silently turning.

Unable to endure any silence for too long, Murkoski continued. "And now we're ready to take the next step. To introduce this blood into a human being."

A flicker of a scowl crossed Coleman's face.

Murkoski didn't appear to notice. "There are no promises," he said. "The process could kill you. Or it could turn you into a lunatic or some type of mental vegetable. But if the experiment succeeds, think of the ramifications." His voice rose slightly as his excitement grew. "We would be able to rid our society, our entire race, of its violence and aggression. Our tendency toward evil would be totally eliminated. We would create world peace. Nirvana. Heaven on earth."

Coleman's voice remained quiet. "You're playing God. You're changing how we're made."

Murkoski shook his head. "No. We're merely accelerating the evolutionary process within our species. Some insects are already doing this, bees for instance. Several varieties commit suicide by stinging an intruder to save the community in their hive. Some birds risk their lives by warning if a hawk or other predator is in the area. There's little doubt that our own species has already begun that evolutionary step—elevating the community over the individual. We're merely picking up the pace a little, that's all. Doing in a few months what would take evolution thousands of years to accomplish."

Another pause. "Why me?"

"You're scheduled for execution in six weeks. The Eighth Circuit has already denied your appeal. That just leaves the U.S. Supreme Court and the Appeals Board."

Coleman gave no reply.

Murkoski was once again taking charge. "If you agree to participate, and *if* you survive, you have our guarantee that the governor of the state of Nebraska will commute your sentence to life."

For the first time, Coleman showed expression.

"Mr. Coleman," Murkoski continued, "we have contacts in very high places."

Coleman held Murkoski's gaze. He'd been in the penal system long enough to know that, with enough clout, anything was possible. He sat for nearly a minute. Finally, he rose to his feet. The meeting was over. The decision made.

"No," was all he said.

Murkoski sat stunned. "What do you mean, *no?* We're offering you your only hope."

"Walking the yard as some do-gooder holy man is not hope. I wouldn't last a week. No, if you want my cooperation, the deal is you get me a pardon."

There was no hiding the incredulity in Murkoski's voice. "How do you expect us to do that?"

"You're the hotshot player here. If you've got the power to pull the governor's strings for clemency, you've got the clout to pull a little harder and get me out."

Murkoski rose to his feet. "Listen, pal, we're offering you your life. Who do you think you are, trying to negotiate with us?"

"I'm a nobody, son. But apparently a nobody you need." He turned, rapped on the eight-inch square of bulletproof glass in the door, and a guard instantly appeared. "Thanks for stopping by."

A moment later, Murkoski and O'Brien stood alone in the room, Murkoski in shock, O'Brien in quiet amazement. Coleman wasn't only smart, he was also a high roller. He'd just taken control of the game, upped the ante, and escalated the stakes to double or nothing. The man was either very foolish or very, very fearless. O'Brien suspected the latter. And if they intended on using him, he knew at that moment that they'd better be careful. Very careful.


Katherine had put off the meeting with Eric's teacher for nearly a month. It wasn't due to lack of concern for Eric. He was the most important thing in her life. It didn't even have to do with having to close the store for ninety minutes as she schlepped down to the school and met with the man. No, Katherine didn't like meeting with Eric's teacher, because she didn't like Eric's teacher.

The last meeting with Mr. Paris had not gone well. The first few minutes, discussing Eric's mathematics and computer skills, had gone okay. Eric was impressive on both accounts. It was even okay when Eric's teacher had discussed Eric's need to work on his reading comprehension, physical fitness, and social skills (it seemed lately Eric had become the all-school punching bag). What was not okay was when the man hinted at Eric's need for a good male role model, Katherine's need for a good man, and Mr. Paris's need for a good roll in the hay.

Katherine was quick to spot his moves and draw the line, making it clear that she wasn't interested, which led to Paris's observation that he liked spirited women, which led to his hand gently taking her arm, which led to the outside edge of her shoe scraping down his shin from his knee all the way to his foot, which she stomped good and hard just in case he had missed her point. More training from Gary.

But that incident had taken place over two months ago. And, ever since that little trip to Albertson's, Katherine's attitude had been changing about a lot of things. Maybe she had been overreacting. Maybe it was time to loosen up a bit. At least that's what she was thinking as she sat at a student's desk in the front of Mr. Paris's empty third-grade classroom, burping back the taste of the Cabernet she'd just had for lunch.

Paris, on the other hand, sat behind his oak desk, working hard at sounding professional while reviewing Eric's scores.

As the man droned on, Katherine couldn't help noticing that he was not quite as repulsive as she had remembered. Oh, he was still going for the twentysomething cropped hair look. His pants and neckties may have both been a couple or three inches too short. And somebody should tell him that goatees were better suited for the Brad Pitts of the world. But there was something almost … well, not unattractive about him. Something she couldn't put her finger on. The thought surprised her, and she immediately tried to forget it.

"… even though he's in the ninety-eighth percentile for mathematics, and his computer skills are exceptional—"

"He got that from me."

"Pardon?"

Katherine felt foolish for blurting it out, but she had committed herself, so she explained. "The computer skills. I used to work in computers for the government. He got that from me."

"I see. Actually, that's about the only way Eric and I have been able to connect. I'm a bit of a computer nut myself." He redirected his attention to the printed results in his hand. "In any case, your son is still very far behind in reading comprehension, language arts, social studies—in fact, in nearly *all* the other areas."

Katherine nodded.

Mr. Paris continued staring at the printout. "I don't think it's intellectual. He's proven he can think. I'm afraid much of it has to do with lack of incentive and self-esteem—along, of course, with his lack of social interaction."

"Social interaction?"

"Does Eric have any brothers or sisters?"

Katherine shook her head. "It's just the two of us."

"What about neighborhood kids to play with? He keeps entirely to himself here at school."

Again Katherine shook her head. "He stays with me at the store 'til I close. When we finally get home and eat, it's time for bed."

Mr. Paris frowned. Was it her imagination, or did this man seem legitimately concerned about her son? Whatever the case, this was a much different individual from the one she had seen in action last September. Again she caught herself beginning not to dislike him.

"What about Little League—any kind of sports?"

Katherine almost laughed. "I'm afraid not. Coordination is not one of my kid's specialties. Besides, like I said, we don't have the time." She sensed what she thought to be an expression of disapproval. "Look, I know it's not fair to Eric, but—"

"No, I understand. Believe me. My own mother was a single parent. She was our sole breadwinner. I know how difficult it can be."

Their eyes seemed to connect just a fraction longer than necessary. There was no mistaking it, the man was sincere. Either that or it was the wine. Maybe both.

He glanced away and frowned again, this time tapping at the paper in his hands. "Listen, I coach a soccer team on weekends. Do you think he'd be interested in trying out?"

"He doesn't know the first thing about the game."

"I could give him a few pointers. Besides, as coach," he almost smiled, "I bet I could pull a few strings to get him on the team."

Katherine fought back a rising suspicion. "You'd do that for him?"

"Only if you think it's appropriate."

Again their eyes locked, again perhaps just a little too long.

"Appropriate," she repeated. "Well, I suppose—sure. I mean, let me talk to him first. But if it's okay with him, I guess it would be okay with me."

Mr. Paris finally broke into a smile. It wasn't a bad smile. Not bad at all. "Good," he said. "Good." With that he scooped up the test scores, apparently bringing the conference to a close. "I think we're done for now. Unless you have any further questions."

Katherine shook her head.

"Well, if you do," he said, rising to his feet, "don't hesitate to give me a call. He's a bright, sensitive boy, and I'll do whatever I can to help."

Katherine took the cue and rose from her chair.

They crossed toward the door. "Oh, here," he said, handing her the test scores. "You may want to look these over when you get a chance."

"I wouldn't know where to start," she said as he opened the door for her and they stepped into the hall. At this proximity, she was certain he could smell the wine on her breath, and for some reason that made her feel a little embarrassed.

"It's really not that difficult," he said. "If you'd like, I'd be happy to explain them to you sometime?"

She gave him a look.

He grimaced. "I'm sorry." Already she could see the color rising to his face. "That wasn't supposed to be a come-on."

She held his look, knowing better.

"Well, okay." He shrugged. "Maybe it was, but just a little. The point is—I know we got off to a pretty rocky start last fall, but—I really do find you attractive and, well . . ." He cleared his throat. "What I'm trying to say is, you have every reason not to trust me, but, if you wouldn't mind, maybe we could, you know, have dinner sometime?"

Katherine tried not to smile. It wasn't over his request, but over the delivery. Like a tongue-tied teenager on his first date, he was blushing and fumbling for words. She liked the vulnerability, of course, but it was also nice to know she could still have that type of effect on somebody. In fact, it was so nice that, before she knew it, she heard herself saying, "Sure, why not?" For a second she was as surprised as he was.

"Well, thanks," he said, looking a little startled. "I'll, uh, I'll give you a call, then."

She nodded. Then, without a word, she turned and headed down the hall. She could feel his eyes on her, but she was too busy berating herself to care. What did she think she was doing? The man was a pig. He'd proven that the last time.

Still, people can change, can't they? Doesn't everybody deserve a second chance? He's got a steady job, he's looked up to in the community, and he made it clear that he knows he behaved like an idiot. He says he's interested. Who knows, maybe it's time to get back into the field again. Maybe not all men are dogs. Maybe Gary wasn't the only exception to that rule. She had her doubts. But what would it hurt to step out again, just to see?

It had been seventy-two hours since Harold Steiner had watched the sun set over his daughter's grave. His wife had never shown. He had driven home that evening confused, outraged, and more determined than ever.

Seventy-two hours had passed, and still he couldn't sleep. Oh, there was the occasional hour or so of dozing, filled in by the nonstop drone of CNN, books he couldn't concentrate on, calls to his law office about having the flu, and visits to the Golden Arches at irregular hours. But he had no rest. How could he when the Law was being ignored, when justice was slowly being forgotten, first by the state, and now by his very wife?

It was 1:30 Monday morning when he stepped into the shower. He cranked up the temperature and let the water pound against the back of his neck. The headache had not gone away this time.

Did they think, did they honestly think that seven years of maneuvering, appealing, squirming for a way out—in their wildest imaginings did they think that Michael Coleman's crimes would be *forgotten?* By some, maybe. By those who watched news as entertainment. Those who, after the third or fourth appeal, felt they were watching a rerun and switched over to more current amusement. But for Harold Steiner, this was no amusement. He would not forget. Everyone else could—even his wife, or what was left of her. But he would not. He could not. The Law was the Law. Michael Coleman had broken it, he had been sentenced, and now he must pay. No amount of stalling or exploiting the legal system would cancel that debt. Justice would be served. Steiner owed it to society; he owed it to Missy.

When the shower ran out of hot water, he toweled himself off and slipped into a pair of boxers. A thought had come to mind, and he padded down the hall to the bedroom. The room was neat as a pin. It always was.

He crossed to his desk, snapped on the computer, and logged on to the Internet. With a few clicks of the mouse, he brought up the photograph of Coleman he had previously scanned from a mug shot. It was perfect. Unrepentant, unfeeling, an animal at the peak of savagery. To make sure that the viewer felt no sympathy, Steiner had erased the convict's serial number at the bottom. Today, in its place, he typed two words. Bold, centered, and in caps:

**NEVER FORGET**

A few more clicks of the mouse brought up his e-mail address book—people he'd communicated with over the years. Carefully, one by one, he went down the list, highlighting those who had been involved with the Coleman case: family members, friends, cops, attorneys, judges, relatives of past victims, members of the media, politicians, and the list went on. One hundred fifteen in all.

Once he'd selected them, he brought up the photo of Coleman, dragged the mouse down to the "SEND" box, and clicked it. He sat back and closed his eyes. In a matter of hours, all one hundred fifteen parties would receive a special marker on their computer indicating they had received an e-mail message. They would punch it up and watch as their entire screen filled with the photograph of Michael Coleman and Steiner's admonition: "Never Forget."

Steiner snapped off his computer. Sending that message had helped to ease a little of the pain, but not enough.

# CHAPTER 3

eath Row at Nebraska State Penitentiary in Lincoln is one of the finest in the country. No sweltering, rat-infested cells. No shotgun-toting guards busting heads, no insane droolers clinging to the bars and screaming hysterically through the night. In fact, as far as accommodations go, this Death Row gets four stars. Built in 1981, the cells are air-conditioned and single occupancy, with steel doors to assure a certain amount of privacy and aesthetic value—though no one can figure out why the outside of those doors are painted a ghastly lime green. Each eight-by-twelve-foot, beige, cinder-block cubicle contains a tile floor, bed, toilet without seat (toilet seats can be used as weapons), wash basin, and long (52" by 24") bullet-proof window with two one-and-a-half-inch-thick horizontal bars running through it to prevent any unscheduled leaves of absence.

A centrally located dayroom, a cafeteria, access to show-ers three times a week, two fifteen-minute phone calls a week—not to mention opportunities to visit the law library, to purchase personal goods from the canteen, and to spend up to forty-five minutes a day in the exercise yard—add to the home-away-from-home ambiance for the convicted killer. The only way Coleman could have made out better was if he had been captured and convicted next door in Iowa. There is no death penalty in Iowa.

There are seven two-story housing units at the peni-tentiary. Each is shaped like an X, with four wings. Death Row takes up the top wing in the unit furthest to the north-east. The ten men (actually nine—Sweeney, thanks to Cole-man, was still visiting Lincoln General Hospital) have an entire floor to themselves. They are cut off from the general prison population, forming their own community—eating, socializing, reveling in one another's accomplishments, and walking the exercise yard—all as an elite, fraternal order sentenced to the same fate.

The guards are few. Most of the interaction with inmates is handled by trained case managers and caseworkers with degrees in psychology, sociology, or criminal justice. The bywords for all staff involved with Death Row inmates are *dis-cretion* and *compassion*.

In short, there is no torture on Lincoln's Death Row, except perhaps the torture of time ... and the mind.

For the next five days, Coleman sat in his cell and thought about what he was rejecting. He'd never considered himself a lucky man. In fact, he figured his luck ran out the day he came home from the hospital with his mother, when she was beaten by his father for insinuating that their newborn son, the man's own flesh and blood, may not actually *be* his own flesh and blood.

As time passed, the beatings transferred from Coleman's mother to Coleman himself. He really didn't mind; he figured they helped make him strong. If he could survive his father's explosive outbursts and relentless poundings, while learning to read the man's erratic mood swings and compensate for them, he figured he could survive anything. And for thirty-five years, he had been right.

But this . . .

Five days he sat in his cell, holding to his bluff. He received no phone calls from Murkoski or O'Brien, no more requests for meetings. If they could meet his terms, fine. If not, with less than six weeks to live, his remaining hours were far too valuable to waste on crackpot scientists, no matter how much clout they claimed to wield. Of course, they had insisted that he keep their proposal a secret; they had even threatened to call the whole thing off if he went public. No problem there. Who would believe it? He certainly didn't. At least most of the time.

But there were those other times, the ones that stole up on him when he was the most vulnerable, when he thought that maybe, just maybe, it might be true, that maybe science could pull off something like this, that maybe he could have a second chance.

Like most men on the Row, Coleman seldom thought of the chair. Oh, it was always there—but for the other guy. The chump. Coleman had gotten himself out of too many jams too many times to be worried. And what was Ol' Sparky but just a little bigger jam, requiring just a little more ingenuity. True, every con talked about how they'd go—some bragging that they'd go down fighting to the end, others vowing to take the chair like a man, still others planning to make a long filibuster speech for the media about the injustice of the justice system. But deep inside, no one ever thought they'd die. The same was true with Coleman. He was a hero in his own movie, and heroes never die.

But this ...

What kind of mind game were they playing? It was an impossible hope, it was crazy—so crazy that he couldn't quite shake it. To appeal was one thing; that was a game everybody played. But this teasing of the imagination, this absurd flaunting of impossible hopes that were just crazy enough to be possible—this was inhumane.

The news came with the dawn of the sixth day. O'Brien and Murkoski would meet his demands. It would entail unprecedented maneuvers with the Witness Protection Program, not to mention some clandestine cooperation with the highest state officials and a tiny handful of prison personnel. But, *if* he survived the treatments, and *if* there was the expected shift in his personality, then Coleman had their word that somehow they would remove him from the Row and relocate him in society, a free man.

His head pounded. His suspicions rose. He had offered them impossible terms, and they had accepted. What made them so anxious? What was their angle? They were the ones holding all the cards; why did they fold? Maybe they already knew the experiment would fail, that it would kill him, make him crazy. Still, dying this way might be better than electrocution. And if he went crazy—wasn't being a little crazy for forty more years better than being dead in a few weeks?

Coleman wrestled with these thoughts all morning, then did what he always did when faced with fear and indecision. He acted on instinct. He met these fears like he met every other fear. Head-on and from the gut. If they wanted this deal badly enough to meet his terms, then he would make the deal. He would play the odds, take his chances.

For the second time in a week they shuffled him out of Death Row, his hands and feet fettered with nylon bracelets called flex cuffs. Except for their length and strength, the cuffs were almost identical to the ties used to seal household garbage bags. The symbolism was never lost on Coleman.

The late afternoon air was crisp and clear. The sapphire sky already revealed traces of pink on the horizon, giving promise of a spectacular sunset. But Coleman barely noticed. He seldom did. Beauty was a luxury he had no time for, not even as a child. Beauty was for poets and women, not for a man fighting to survive. In his world, such weakness could spell death. As the hack escorted him across the yard to the administration building, the only thing Coleman noticed was the conflicting thoughts warring inside his head.

When Coleman reentered the upstairs hospital room, he was surprised to see Murkoski alone.

"Dr. O'Brien had to get back," the kid explained. "This is a straightforward procedure; his presence wasn't necessary."

Coleman didn't mind. He didn't like Murkoski, but he knew how to play him. In some ways, he sensed that they were cut from the same cloth. The only difference was that Murkoski loved to talk, to pontificate. Coleman preferred to listen and learn. Knowledge was power. And power was something Coleman could always use.

"Will you sit on this table, please?" Coleman crossed to the metal examining table they had wheeled in. Murkoski nodded to the guard, who removed the flex cuffs and stepped outside. "Take off your sweatshirt."

Coleman obliged, pulling off the hooded sweatshirt they'd loaned him for the walk outside.

"Listen," Murkoski said, "we're going to be spending a lot of time together, and I want you to know right off the bat that, despite my education and position in life, I do not consider myself your superior."

Coleman thought of dropping the punk right there. Instead, he pushed back the impulse and remained silent.

Murkoski opened the Igloo ice chest on the floor near the drug cupboard; a circular biohazard decal was plastered to it. "Also, I do not hold you in contempt for your past."

"Neither do I."

Murkoski looked up. "Seriously?" he asked. "You never feel guilty?"

"Why should I?"

Murkoski looked at him a moment, then nodded and knelt beside the ice chest. "In any case, the only difference I see between you and me is the cards we were dealt."

Coleman sighed and rattled off the rest of the bromide. "And since I'm just the unwitting product of my environment—"

"No, actually, just the opposite." Murkoski lifted a small plastic container from the chest. It was gray, the size of a small cigar case. It had no markings. "We are products of chemistry, Mr. Coleman. No more, no less. Chemistry determines who we are. Everything we say, think, or do is a chemical reaction—electricity firing across neurons, which in turn release chemicals to fire more neurons, racing down our nerves at four hundred feet per second until they reach our brain, which kicks in its own chemical agents. Simply put, you and I are nothing but chemical laboratories."

Coleman frowned. He didn't like being controlled by anything, much less something he didn't understand. "You're saying I'm who I am by how a bunch of chemicals got thrown together?"

Murkoski had opened the plastic case to produce a small vial wrapped in foam. "No, I'm saying you're a product of your mother's and father's chemical factories."

Coleman liked this idea even less. "So why isn't my brother like me?"

"Please, Mr. Coleman. That's like asking why every child of blue-eyed parents doesn't have blue eyes."

Coleman hated the condescending tone. As the kid flashed a syringe from the case, he thought how little effort it would take to change that tone forever. But, of course, there was the guard outside, and the experiment . . .

Murkoski continued his lecture. "You're right, though. Studies of identical twins raised apart, in entirely different environments, usually show they have similar characteristics. Not only in IQ, but in personality traits like boldness, aggressiveness, inhibition. In fact, the Center for Twin and Adoption Research at the University of Minnesota has data on twin brothers separated from birth who actually preferred the same cologne, the same hair cream, even the same imported toothpaste. Then there were the separated twin sisters who counted themselves to sleep in exactly the same manner."

Murkoski produced a milky white pair of latex gloves and snapped them on. "Or the results from the National Institute on Alcohol Abuse and the National Institute for Child Health and Human Development. Through selective breeding, they've managed to create different families of rhesus monkeys with entirely different personalities: some shy, others outgoing, and others aggressive."

Coleman watched with a slight uneasiness as Murkoski inserted the needle into the vial and extracted a small amount of clear liquid. He was supposed to be receiving blood. Why the injection?

"There are dozens of other studies. But the one you'll find most interesting is the Danish family with an abnormal history of violence. One of the brothers raped his sister, then stabbed the warden at his psychiatric prison. Another tried to run over his employer. Another forced his sisters to undress at knifepoint, and two more were arsonists."

"Not exactly the Brady Bunch."

"And the cause?" Murkoski didn't wait for an answer. "An abnormally low level of serotonin."

"Serotonin?"

"Yes." He tapped the bubbles out and carefully inspected the syringe. "It's a chemical, Mr. Coleman. A neurotransmitter that reduces aggression. One, I might point out, that is present in thirty percent lower quantities in men than women—which may explain why nine out of every ten violent crimes are committed by males. It also takes a dip during adolescence, which no doubt accounts for their erratic behavior. Pull up your shirt-sleeve, please."

Coleman obliged, pulling up his government-issued goldenrod shirt while watching Murkoski's every move. "And all of this has been proven?"

"Absolutely. Unusually low amounts of serotonin have been linked to violent criminals, suicides, even arsonists. In fact, one researcher now at Columbia University was able to create a strain of mice lacking fourteen serotonin receptors."

"And?"

Murkoski crossed to the glass-enclosed cupboard of drugs, laid the syringe down on a metal shelf, and reached for a cotton swab and a bottle of rubbing alcohol. "They became wildly impulsive. Incredibly violent. In fact, and you will appreciate this as well, they are often referred to as 'Killer Mice.'" He smiled at his joke.

Coleman didn't bother. "This Danish family, they all have low levels of serotonin?"

"Genetically, all the men lacked monoamine oxidase, MAO, an enzyme directly linked to the production of serotonin. And keep in mind that serotonin is just one of dozens of classical neurotransmitters that we inherit. And who knows how many undiscovered neuro*receptors* we may have." Murkoski stepped back toward him and began swabbing his arm with the alcohol. "We've discovered an 'Obese Gene' that tells us when to stop eating. We've even altered the genes in male fruit flies to make them behave like females."

"Why isn't all this publicized?"

"Oh, it is. But right now genetic behavior, the study of how we act because of our heredity, is a political hot potato. Everyone's afraid to touch it because of the race and bigotry connotations. In fact, the National Institute of Mental Health has yanked funding from at least one study because they're afraid of the repercussions."

"That people will judge others because of their genes instead of who they are."

Murkoski stepped back to the counter, dropped the alcohol swab in the trash can, and picked up the syringe. "You still don't get it, do you? People *are* their genes, Mr. Coleman. You have no choice. You are the result of chemicals received from your parents, who received similar chemicals from their parents, and so on and so forth, all the way back to our primordial ancestors."

"And you're going to change all that?"

Murkoski shrugged and approached with the needle. "We'll soon find out. It's certainly been the case with our mice and with Freddy."

"Freddy?"

"Our baboon. His behavior has dramatically shifted to something much less aggressive. But as far as what he or the mice or any other lab animals actually feel, we have no idea. We can measure their heart rate and blood pressure, but we don't know what they're thinking."

"Enter Michael Coleman."

"Precisely." He took Coleman's arm with his left hand and prepared to insert the needle with his right.

"What's in there?"

"A retrovirus."

"A what?"

"A retrovirus. Like HIV."

"Hold it." Coleman pulled away.

"Relax. All of the harmful elements have been genetically removed."

"You're injecting me with the AIDS virus."

Murkoski laughed. "No, I'm injecting you with a virus that works in a way similar to the AIDS virus. But it has been genetically altered. There's no way it can reproduce itself inside you."

"I thought you were giving me blood. What happened to the blood of Christ?" Coleman looked and sounded like a little boy making excuses not to get his shot, but at the moment he didn't much care.

"For starters there's no guarantee whose blood we've discovered. But for argument's sake let's say it is Christ's. This virus holds the code for one of the genes of his blood. We inserted that code into this virus, so that when the virus attacks your own blood, your T cells, it will infect them with his DNA. And that's the crux of it. For reasons we don't fully understand, this new blood alters the function of certain neurotransmitters and receptors. As a result, we wind up with a brand-new Michael Coleman. Now will you hold still, please."

Coleman hesitated a moment longer before finally submitting. The tiny prick of the needle was barely noticeable. And the burn of five cc's being pumped into his vein was over before it began.

"So you're not giving me his blood, you're changing my blood into his."

Murkoski nodded. "You're receiving part of his genetic code."

"But not all of it."

Again Murkoski nodded. "That's correct. You'll receive one gene in particular, along with the usual junk DNA."

"Junk DNA?"

"Portions of DNA we don't understand. Probably mistakes in nature left over from when we were swinging in the trees as apes."

"When will it start?"

"Start, Mr. Coleman?"

"When will his DNA start infecting me?"

"Why, Mr. Coleman, it's already begun."

# CHAPTER 4

A five-year-old face looks through the rectangular holes of a wire fence. He shivers violently; tears stream down smudged cheeks, leaving tracks through the dirt. He looks like a younger Michael Coleman, but he isn't. He is wearing only his underwear.

"Please," he cries, "please don't leave me here!"

He's outside, and it's winter. There are no colors. Everything is black and gray and white. The rolling hills are covered with hundreds of acres of cornstalks sheered off at their base. It is near Coleman's home.

*"Please, Mikey, don't leave me here. Please!"*

Coleman is there. He's sitting on a thick tree branch fifteen feet above the boy. It's his little brother, Eddie, trapped inside an empty corncrib. The floor is concrete, about twelve feet in diameter, with a wire fence rising high above him and topped by a cone-shaped aluminum roof. Someone has shoved a large log up against the gate. They are the only ones there. The nearest farmhouse is over a mile away. The winter wind howls and bites.

*"Please, Mikey . . ."*

But Coleman doesn't notice the wind as much as he notices the smell. Raw chicken. The disgusting smell of uncooked chicken fat and flesh, an odor Mom can never completely wash from her hands. Some adults have vivid childhood memories of smells: their father's aftershave, the mixture of cut grass and gasoline from mowing the lawn, Grandma's musty basement. Coleman's only memory is the smell of his mother's hands after she has put in eight grueling hours at the Campbell's Soup factory. Like many of the poorer women in Tecumseh, Nebraska, her job is to debone and eviscerate the birds, removing their skeletons and scooping out their guts.

*"Please . . ."*

Coleman looks back down. His brother is small and frail, shivering in the crib. In fact, he looks so helpless that Coleman has to laugh. He can't help himself. It serves Eddie right. If Dad always beats Coleman and lets Eddie go, then this is only fair. Eddie's perfect little world must be shattered from time to time. Of course this isn't Eddie's first wake-up call, nor will it be the last. It is Coleman's self-appointed task to even the score and prepare his sibling for the hardships of the real world, a task in which Coleman revels.

But as he sits in the tree laughing, a cold shiver runs through him—a shiver that has nothing to do with the wind. He isn't sure whether he hears it or senses it. But somebody is there.

*"Mikey, my feet don't got no feeling."*

*He squints into the wind, searching the field. He and Eddie are the only ones there. And yet—there it is again. A cracking sound, below him and behind. He twists around until he can see behind the tree. Nothing. Just a rusting, '58 Ford pickup with one door sprung, the other missing.*

*"Please, Mikey. I won't tell, I promise."*

*There it is again. Twigs snapping. Right below him. He looks underneath.*

*Nothing.*

*Now he hears grunting. Grunting and the sound of heavy boots scraping against bark.*

*"Please, Mikey . . ."*

*It's coming after him. Whoever is there is climbing the tree and coming after him. The grunting grows louder. But Coleman sees no one. He can only hear the scraping bark and the grunting. He panics, scrambling to his feet.*

*"Mikey . . ."*

*He nearly loses his balance and throws himself against the trunk for support. The noise approaches. He frantically searches for a getaway. There is none.*

*Now, all at once, he feels a different cold. Harsher. It's no longer the cold of his fear, but the cold of the wind. Eddie's cold. He shivers violently. The sound is closer. He thinks he hears breathing. His father's breathing. He is certain of it.*

*"Mikey . . ."*

*His teeth chatter. He shivers so hard that he must cling to the tree for balance. He hears clothes flapping in the wind. But not Coleman's clothes. They belong to the father he can neither see nor hear. The cold is intense. Before he knows it, he is also crying.*

*He looks back down at Eddie. Amazing. Their sobs are in perfect synchronization. As his little brother gasps, he gasps. As Eddie sobs, Coleman sobs. He is sharing his brother's fear, his loneliness, and feeling the icy wind—the awful, icy wind that will not stop until—*

Coleman awoke. It took a moment for him to catch his breath and realize that he'd been dreaming. He tried to move, but the blanket had wrapped around him in a knot. Angrily, he untangled it and flung it aside. Throwing his feet over the edge of the bed, he took another deep breath, forcing reality to return.

The incident was real, though he hadn't thought of it in years. Nor had he ever had a dream quite so vivid. Yet what really unnerved him was the empathy, the remorse. Michael Coleman had never felt anything for any of his victims. But now, he had experienced his brother's emotions—the cold, the terror, the unbearable ache of being alone and abandoned.

Coleman ran his hands over his face and noticed something even more startling. His cheeks were wet. But not from sweat. Moisture had filled his eyes and spilled onto his face. And when he swallowed, his throat was tight and constricted.

He rose and stepped across to the window. The moon hung over the horizon. It was full and flooded the yard with a serene stillness. Its stark light glinted off the rolls of razor wire atop the fence and bathed the distant highway in silence. Nearly two miles across the road, grain elevators he had never noticed before glowed in the moonlight. It was the most beautiful thing Coleman had ever seen. The ache in his throat grew stronger.


"Don't tell me you're going like that."

"Why not?" Katherine shifted uncomfortably under the scrutiny of Lisa. The downstairs neighbor was a disgustingly slender twenty-five-year-old, with rich, ebony skin. She stood in the bathroom doorway carefully checking Katherine out. Lisa had agreed to watch Eric while Katherine had her evening on the town with Mr. Paris.

"It's a new world out there, girl. If you want his interest, you've got to advertise."

Katherine turned to check her profile in the bathroom mirror. The moderately cut dress of burgundy crepe hung well, accenting her figure and covering the slightest trace of a pooch she'd been fighting. "It's the best thing I own. Besides, I think it's flattering."

"Flattering?"

"Yeah."

"*Flattering?* Nobody wants flattering. When's the last time you were on the dating scene?"

"I, uh—" Katherine resumed fluffing her cropped hair, trying her best to give it some body. "I grew up pretty sheltered, being a preacher's kid and all."

"Your daddy was a minister?"

Katherine ignored Lisa's surprised tone. "That was long ago and far away."

"I should say so, girl. What about your old man?"

"Gary and I, we met as freshmen in Bible college, so—"

"So you don't know nothing, do you?"

Katherine continued working her hair, pretending not to hear.

Lisa glanced at her watch. "What time are you meeting him?"

"He'll be here at 8:00 to pick me up."

"*Here?*"

"Well, yeah."

"You invited him *here?*"

"It's not like I'm not going to ask him inside."

"Girl, have you ever heard of stalkers, rapists—"

"Sure, but—"

"Muggers, perverts? You think he's going to wait for an invitation if he wants to assault you?"

Katherine reached for the half-empty glass of wine on the counter. Lisa was immediately at her side, removing it from her hands and setting it beside the sink. "And this you save for later. Till you make the decision. Otherwise, you need all your wits about you."

"Lisa—"

"It's a jungle out there, survival of the fittest. And you never let some man know where you live. Not till you check him out. Even then you don't invite him back here. Always go to his place."

"He lives on a boat in the marina."

"I don't care if he lives in a pup tent. You never, never invite a guy to your place. At least not till the second or third date."

"It's a little late now," Katherine said as she reached for her glass. "He's going to be here in fifteen minutes."

Lisa shook her head. "All right, all right." She raised her hands as if making a magnanimous offer. "I'll stay till the two of you leave. That way he'll think I'm baby-sitting here."

"Thanks."

"But that dress . . ."

"The dress is perfect."

"Have it your way. What about that makeup?"

Katherine gave her a look.

Lisa folded her arms and waited for an answer.

"I always use this mascara, and I bought the lipstick special to highlight the dress."

"That's it? Lipstick and mascara?"

"And blush."

"Don't go away, I'll be right back."

Ten minutes later, Lisa finished applying a hasty combination of concealer, foundation cream, powder, blush, eyeliner, lipstick liner, lipstick, and peach, emerald, and almond-roast eye shadows. "Now put your finger in your mouth, wrap your lips around it, and pop it out."

Katherine followed her order, making a little popping sound. "Like this?"

"Perfect."

"What does that do?"

"Keeps the lipstick off your teeth." Finally Lisa stepped back to carefully inspect her work.

"So what do you think?" Katherine asked skeptically.

"See for yourself."

Katherine rose from the edge of the bathtub, crossed to the mirror, and gasped. "I look like a hooker!"

Lisa grinned. "Exactly."

The doorbell rang. Instant panic. "Oh, my gosh, he's here." For the briefest second the two women were fourteen years old again.

"I'll get it," Eric called from the bedroom where he was working on his computer.

"No, sweetheart, let me get that." Dashing into her bedroom, she grabbed her white shawl, threw it on, and spun around to Lisa, who had followed her in. "What do you think?"

Lisa tried to smile while reaching out to adjust the bottom of the shawl. "Well, at least he won't try anything."

"Lisa—"

The doorbell rang again.

Lisa pushed her toward the door. "Go go go."

One last adjustment of the hair, and Katherine headed down the hallway of the apartment, into the living room, and to the front door. "Who is it?"

"Thaddeus Paris."

Katherine threw a forlorn look back at Lisa, mouthing, "Thaddeus?"

Lisa shrugged, and Katherine motioned for her to step back out of sight. Reluctantly, Lisa agreed.

"Hello?" came the voice.

Katherine reached for the dead bolt and slid it back. She could hear her heart pounding in her ears. Then, with a breath to steady herself, she opened the door.

Mr. Paris stood in the hall wearing white Reeboks, designer jeans a couple sizes too small, and a burgundy sweatshirt with *Just Do It* printed across the front. To complete the ensemble, a laptop computer hung from his shoulder.

"Hi." He grinned.

Katherine swallowed back her surprise. "Hi."

"You're all dressed up."

"Uh, yeah."

Suddenly the lights came on. "Oh, I'm sorry. I thought Eric told you."

"Told me what?"

"My new software."

"Software." She sounded like a parrot repeating every phrase, but she was still trying to get her bearings.

"Yeah." He motioned to his computer. "I'm having a dickens of a time with some new software. I thought maybe we could work on it for a while." He flashed what was supposed to be a sexy grin while raising a six-pack of Budweiser in one hand and a bottle of wine in the other. "Then maybe work on some of our own moves."

"Moves?"

"Well, yeah."

Katherine stood a moment, then she reached for the door—

"Hey, wait a min—"

—and shut it, clicking the dead bolt back into place.


"Daddy, Freddy won't share his apple with me."

O'Brien looked up from his picnic lunch—a dripping peanut-butter-and-jelly sandwich, partially baked Tollhouse cookies, chocolate milk, and Snickers bars. The lunch had been packed by Julie, his seven-year-old. Julie was partial to sweets.

Both Julie and Sarah, her twelve-year-old sister, had been playing on the gym set with Freddy while O'Brien and his wife sat on a blanket spread across the newly laid sod. Granted, no one would catch a tan in the artificial environment, but it sure cut down on the flies and ants.

"Daddy." Julie stood with her little hands on her little hips. It was a pose she had learned early from her mother. "Make him share with me."

"Sweetheart." Beth threw a concerned look to O'Brien while addressing her daughter. "I don't think you and Freddy should be sharing food. There's no telling what type of germs he may be carrying."

"Mom—"

"I'm sorry." She reached into the Tupperware and pulled out a carrot stick. "Here, chew on this for a while."

Julie took the carrot with an overly dramatic sigh, then trudged back to her sister and the baboon. The three were playing a game of tag. Of course Freddy didn't completely understand the rules, but it was obvious that he loved chasing and being chased. He also loved the hugs and cuddles that followed each capture.

O'Brien turned to his wife. "Actually, it's the other way around," he explained. "In this environment, Freddy's the one with the fewer germs."

Beth said nothing as she watched their raven-haired beauties play. O'Brien knew she still had some trepidation about Freddy, but that was small potatoes compared to the resentment she harbored. Through the years, their marriage had often hit rocky ground. You don't raise a multimillion-dollar company from nothing without a little stress and a few thousand hours of overtime. Then, just as things were beginning to settle down and the marital stress was starting to mend, along came this new project and, of course, Freddy. Suddenly everything went into hyper speed, with every problem needing to be solved yesterday, and O'Brien's family having to take the farthest seat in the back. The recent eat-and-dash routine at Thanksgiving was the perfect example—an example O'Brien still found himself paying for.

"They'll be okay," he said, rubbing the back of his hand against her arm.

She nodded and tossed her black, shoulder-length hair to the side. It was obvious where the girls inherited their beauty. She had classical Italian features, a strong profile, dark eyes, full lips, and a figure to match. She was also a great mom and wife. Despite their fights over his time spent away, O'Brien knew he needed her as much as the girls did. In fact, if he hadn't had her there, reminding him of home and family, his work would literally and quite completely consume him. She was his tent peg, a reminder of what was really important. That was the purpose of the picnic. If Mohammed wouldn't come to the mountain this Saturday afternoon, then Beth would bring the mountain to him.

For as long as O'Brien could remember, science had been his passion. As a kid, he'd wanted to know how everything worked. Now, as a genetic engineer, he wanted to make everything work better. So far, he and his peers were doing just that. Slowly, of course, but step-by-step, discovery after discovery, they were making progress. Gene therapy had already been used in treating over three hundred people, beating cystic fibrosis, ADA deficiency, hypercholesterolemia, as well as certain forms of anemia. Meanwhile, everyone was hot on the trail of ways to use it to cure breast cancer, sickle-cell anemia, melanoma, attention deficit disorder, schizophrenia, alcoholism, and the list went on. The opportunities were mind-boggling. By current estimates, there are four thousand human diseases caused by malfunctioning genes. That's four thousand opportunities to make the world a better place. Four thousand ways of not only increasing the quality of life, but in many cases actually saving life.

Granted, social problems resulting from improved genetic science were rising almost as quickly as the cures—like employers refusing to hire individuals if they didn't like what showed up on their genetic screening, or health insurance companies dropping clients because genetic tests indicated a high risk. O'Brien still shuddered at the HMO group who'd told an expectant mother of a cystic fibrosis child that they would pay for an abortion—but not for treatments if she chose to give birth.

Still, these were problems to be worked out in the courts, not the laboratory. O'Brien had neither the time nor the interest to deal with people's greed or prejudice—unless, of course, he could find a gene for that, too.

"So what do you think?"

O'Brien turned back to Beth, who waited patiently for an answer. She'd obviously been having another of their conversations without him. His mind raced. What had they been talking about? He was clueless, and she knew it.

"About getting away this winter," she repeated. "Maybe Mazatlán."

"Yeah," he said. "I think that would be good."

"If I could clear it with the schools, maybe we could stay a few weeks."

"Well," he stalled, somehow suspecting that this was a test. "I mean, we don't have to decide that just yet, do we?"

Beth sighed and looked away. It *had* been a test, and he'd just flunked.

Trying to regain lost ground, he continued, "Actually, you're right. A few weeks might do us all some good."

"Fine," she said flatly, without looking back at him. "I'll get the information."

"Great," he said, sounding a little too enthusiastic. "And we can look it over and decide as a family."

Nice try, but still no response.

He gave it another shot. "But you're right, a few weeks would be really good for us." He stared at the back of her head, unable to tell if he'd made any progress. "Real good."

Before she could respond, his beeper went off. He had been careful to switch it to vibrate instead of beep, knowing how Beth hated the sound. He stole a peek at his belt: 3798. That was Wolff, one of Murkoski's assistants. The man never called unless it was important. And since Murkoski was still in Lincoln . . .

"Listen, I, uh—"

"You need to answer that," Beth said, without turning.

He looked at her, surprised. How did she do that? "I shouldn't be long," he said, rising to his feet.

"It's okay, I understand."

"No, really, I won't—"

"I said I understand. And I appreciate your letting us have this time."

He wasn't sure whether she was serious or sarcastic. After fourteen years of marriage, she still had her mysteries. In any case, he bent down and kissed the top of her head. "Thanks." Then, turning to the kids, he shouted, "What does a guy have to do to get a good-bye kiss around here?"

The children ran toward him, shouting "Daddy! Daddy!" and began protesting his leaving. Even Freddy showed some disappointment as he loped up to him, wrapped his arms around one leg, and indicated that he'd be happy to pick off a few lice if O'Brien stayed.

"Sorry, fella," O'Brien chuckled, "duty calls." After another round of hugs and kisses, he left the room. His heart was heavy, but only for a moment. Back in the hall, the thousand-and-one migraine makers of running Genodyne Inc. quickly returned.

How he envied people like Wolff. People completely immersed in research. No worries about funding, no P and L statements, no keeping an antagonistic board of directors satisfied, or disgruntled employees happy, or impossible FDA compliances met—all this while trying to remember why he had started the company in the first place. It was more than one man could handle, and too many things were slipping through the cracks. That's why he'd brought Murkoski on board for the new project. And that's also why he was always having to play catch-up with the kid. He didn't like it much—particularly when it appeared that Murkoski was keeping him out of the loop.

That seemed to be happening more and more lately. Despite O'Brien's efforts to stay informed, Murkoski seemed to be gradually building a wall around the project, slowly turning it into a company within a company. More than once O'Brien had wanted to slow things down, but the pressure they were receiving from the government, coupled with the potential for incredible financial reward, and Murkoski's own brazen ego, made it difficult to find the brakes.

He'd thought they'd hit a barrier when Coleman had made his impossible demand to be removed from Death Row. And yet, in just a few short days, Murkoski had secured permission. "If that's what it takes to do it," Murkoski had said of his government contacts, "then that's what they'll do. This project is too important to balk at details."

O'Brien shook his head as he moved down the hall. Was there nothing the kid couldn't pull off? He was amazing. But just as amazing was how the project had become so complicated. When you get right down to it, gene therapy is anything but complicated. In fact, in its basic form, it's so simple a child can grasp it. Both Sarah and Julie thoroughly understood the concept.

Every living cell contains DNA, that spiral ladder magazines are so fond of drawing. Inside this DNA are genes that we inherit from our parents. These genes tell us whether we're going to be turtles or people, short or tall, die from breast cancer, or live to be a hundred. You'd think such important messengers would be impossibly complex. They're not.

In fact, it all comes down to just four building blocks, four basic chemicals: guanine, adenine, thymine, and cytosine, better known as G, A, T, and C. These are the rungs that hold the strands of the famous spiraling DNA ladder together. That's it, just four chemicals. But it is the way these four chemicals are combined that creates the fifty to one hundred thousand different genes found in the DNA in every human cell.

Genodyne's job is relatively simple. Discover the gene or combinations of genes that creates a specific characteristic (one gene can contain a group of hundreds or even thousands of these chemical rungs), find which rung it begins at and which rung it ends at, snip out that characteristic at the appropriate rungs with chemical scissors called *restriction enzymes*, and replace the old section with the new one. Don't like brown hair? Find those genes, snip them out, and replace them with the genes for blonde hair.

But having one cell in your body that says "I'm a blonde-haired person" when millions of other hair-producing cells are saying, "No way, we're brown," is a losing battle. The trick is to find some way to tell all the cells that influence hair color to change from manufacturing brown hair to blonde. That's where a virus like the one injected into Freddy and Coleman comes in. Since viruses love to multiply by infecting other cells, why not inject the new genes into a virus, and turn the virus loose in the bloodstream to infect the appropriate cells, changing their brown-haired genes into blonde-haired ones.

That's gene therapy in a nutshell. Of course, there are thousands of minor problems, which explains Genodyne's staff of four hundred fifty and counting. Just to find the right gene is a near-impossible task. That's why there are programs like the Human Genome Project discovering new genes every week in the hope of having all 100,000 mapped and labeled by the year 2005.

Once the genes have been discovered, snipped out, and replaced, there's still the problem of making sure they'll really do what they promise they'll do. That's where Wolff's mice come in. Since the DNA rungs in all animals are made up of the same four chemicals, G, A, T, and C, the mouse doesn't know from where it's receiving these snippets of DNA—it could come from anything from humans to insects. (One of O'Brien's favorite stories was the grad student who isolated the genes for making fireflies glow and inserted them into a mouse to see if the mouse would glow. It did. Well, sort of.)

Once the genes from the precious ancient blood sample had been identified and reproduced, they were inserted into the eggs of Wolff's mice. They could have been inserted into the blood of adult mice, but since the gestation period for mice is only twenty days, it's simpler and cleaner to change the creatures before they're even conceived. These genetically altered eggs were then replanted back inside the mouse, where they were fertilized and eventually birthed.

Still, the new generation of mice infected with genes from the ancient blood didn't necessarily show any change of appearance or behavior. Much of genetic research is guesswork, hit and miss, looking for the right combination of genes. So they had repeated the process, again and again, generation after generation, until they were finally able to isolate and identify the "GOD gene." Murkoski had come up with the name—a hangover, he said, from his Catholic school days. By gene standards, it wasn't terribly long, only one thousand and fifty-eight ladder rungs. But when inserted into the mice, the results were astounding. They no longer scrambled for food, but shared it. In fact, the purest strain (the DNA Freddy and Coleman shared) seemed to actually make the mice more concerned about the welfare of their fellow mice than about themselves.

Incredible. But to O'Brien, no more amazing than the fact that the key to the difference in every animal—from flies to mice to baboons to man—is controlled by the combination of those same four chemicals, G, A, T, C. The concept never ceased to amaze him. And, more and more often, as he made entries into his personal lab notebook, he found himself referring to the "Genius" behind it all—spelled not with a small *g*, but with a capital.

O'Brien entered the research wing by shoving his billfold against the five-by-five-inch black box. The magnetic ID card in the wallet buzzed the door. He then entered his six-digit PIN. The door unlocked and he stepped inside to the bottom floor of an impressive, six-story arboretum. Balconies of each of the other floors looked down on him from all sides. Thirty-foot palm trees and assorted flora and fauna stretched toward the frosted skylights. Of course, his board of directors had told him that this was a waste of square footage, but O'Brien, who had spent more than his fair share of time cooped up in a lab, had insisted. Any scientist working in the dozens of labs along the halls that opened up onto the balconies would relish the fresh air and glimpse of nature that the arboretum provided.

He walked past a small trickling waterfall and shoved his billfold against another box, reentering his PIN. The door to the Transgenetic Mice Area clicked open. He moved down the hall and entered a small room where paper gowns and booties were folded neatly on stainless-steel shelves. He unfolded the gown, slipped it over his shirt and jeans, and buttoned it. Next came the paper booties. These were a little trickier. There was a line painted across the floor, dividing the room into two sections. The first half was for street shoes, the second half was for paper booties. One had to balance on one foot on the street-shoe side while slipping the paper bootie over the other foot. When the paper bootie was in place, the papered foot would come down on the bootie side of the floor, and the whole process could begin again with the other foot.

Once O'Brien had suited up, he stepped onto a sticky floor mat to pick up any dirt or organism that may have contaminated his paper booties while he was putting them on. He then opened the other door and entered a hallway.

He crossed to one of the four metal doors with square, viewing portholes in their center and rapped on the glass.

Wolff, an athletic, red-haired surfer type in his late twenties, looked up from dozens of racks. These held the clear Lucite boxes that housed the individual mice. But these were no ordinary mice. They were pampered beyond belief. Not only was the whole gown-and-bootie process for their benefit, but so were the special temperature and humidity controls, the filtered air, the low-fat food, and the vast array of other amenities you would only provide mice that, after months and months of genetic alteration and breeding, cost thousands, sometimes hundreds of thousands of dollars to produce.

Wolff crossed to the door and opened it. O'Brien felt the gentle breeze against his face as the positively pressured room blew any contaminants he may have brought in back outside into the hallway.

"What's up?" O'Brien asked.

Wolff looked grave as he silently escorted O'Brien over to the racks near the far wall. Unlike the other racks, these held larger Lucite boxes containing groups of four to eight mice, housed together to see how they would behave in a community environment.

"This is our last generation," Wolff said, "the same strain we have in your guy back at Lincoln."

"And . . ."

Wolff stooped down to the third shelf. "They were fine this morning, but when I checked them after lunch—well, see for yourself." He pulled out the Lucite container, and O'Brien bent down for a better look.

Five mice were huddled together at one end, some eating, others cleaning and sleeping. They looked and behaved perfectly normal. It was the sixth mouse, at the other end of the box, that made O'Brien catch his breath. The mouse that lay all by itself, perfectly motionless. The mouse whose body had been shredded apart and partially devoured.


At times Coleman thought he was losing his mind. One moment he'd be holding his own, maintaining the mental and emotional steel necessary to run the Row. The next he'd be suddenly distracted by the beauty of the low winter sun striking a brick wall, or the crisp, cold air in the exercise yard, or the soft rustling of pine needles in the tree just outside the fence. These experiences unnerved him. Not only because they were new, but because he wasn't sure when they would come. Lack of control angered him, and when he wasn't marveling over the beauty, he was cursing its intrusion. Frequently he tried to push the thoughts and feelings out of his mind. Sometimes he succeeded. More and more often he did not.

But there was one feeling he could never push away: the terrible loneliness from the dream. It never left. As the days progressed, the ache grew deeper. It was more than his brother's pain. It was his own. A feeling of abandonment. Of emptiness. More than once, it was all he could do to fight back the tears. And when the sense of wonder and beauty surrounding him struck at the same time as the loneliness, it was impossible to hold back the tears.

But it wasn't just *his* loneliness. He started seeing it in others, too. The way their shoulders sagged as they sat. The way they slowly walked the yard when they thought no one was watching.

But mostly he saw it in their eyes.

"Something wrong, Cole?"

Coleman blinked and came to. He was in the showers. Skinner, a big black man who had been on the Row a couple of years longer than he had, stood under an adjacent nozzle. Just as he had learned the details of bomb making from Garcia, Coleman had learned the intricate nuances of lock picking from Skinner. They weren't friends, but after seven years of living together they were definitely comrades.

"You're staring again, man."

Coleman blinked again, then resumed lathering with his bar of soap.

Skinner leaned closer. "What's wrong with you?"

Coleman dropped his head and let the water pelt his forehead and scalp. It was a pleasant sensation: the way the water pounded against his skin, the way it gently massaged the roots of his hair. It's a wonder he'd never noticed it before. He tried not to smile at the pleasure, but didn't quite succeed.

When he came out from under the water, he opened his eyes to see Skinner standing with a quizzical look on his face. "I don't know what's going on with you, man, but you better be careful."

"What do you mean?" Coleman asked.

Skinner lowered his voice, making sure they weren't overheard. "Word has it you're getting soft."

Coleman shook his head and swore.

"No, I'm serious, man. Losing your grip, that's what they're saying. And with Sweeney coming back from the hospital next week ... all I'm saying is you better be smart, man. Just be smart."

Coleman held Skinner's look. He was finding it easier and easier to tell when people were lying, and as far as he could make out, Skinner was shooting straight. He gave a faint nod of acknowledgment. Skinner turned off the shower and walked away. A moment later Coleman followed suit, furious. How could he have been so stupid? It was one thing to feel what he was feeling, but to let others see it? That was insanity. Any weakness on the Row meant trouble, and apparently he had shown that weakness more than once. What was happening?

He crossed the white tile to a metal bench, where he scooped up his towel and began drying off with the other men. No one said a word to him. They knew. Something was coming down. Coleman was losing his touch, and with Sweeney returning, any allegiance to Coleman now could be dangerous. The thought infuriated him.

"All right, men, let's head back." It was McCoy, one of the 9:00 A.M. to 6:00 P.M. hacks. He'd been with them almost four years. A good man, though impossible to con. They obeyed and shuffled into the hall, their thongs flip-flopping as they headed back to their cells.

It was then that Hector Garcia pulled up alongside him. "Listen, Cole, I never got to, you know, say thanks."

Coleman stared straight ahead.

"And if I can ever, you know, show my appreciation ..." He gently let his arm brush against him.

The punk was putting a move on him! Gratitude or not, you never broke protocol by talking to someone of Coleman's status without being spoken to first. And you never, *never* disrespected him by making an offer like this.

The fury over Skinner's comments, the silent betrayal of the men, his own stupidity—it was more than Coleman could contain. His vision grew sharp and narrow. The sound of the men's thongs exploded in his ears. The colors of the beige walls and the lime-green doors burst in vivid contrast. It was time to reestablish his authority.

It took a single blow to double Garcia over, and one double-fisted uppercut to throw the boy's head back and reeling into the wall. Garcia was unconscious before he hit the floor.

McCoy's baton came down hard, but Coleman felt nothing. He never did in this state. He spun around, grabbed the stick from the startled McCoy, and was about to smash his skull when he came up short.

It was the fear in McCoy's eyes that stopped him. The fear that said he had a wife, kids, a mortgage. Fear that said he was only trying to do his job and please, please, don't hurt me. I'm lonely and scared and faking it just like everybody else. Please . . .

The rage began to dissolve. There he was, in front of all the men, standing with the baton in his hand, staring at McCoy and doing nothing. But how could he strike when there was such fear and loneliness in McCoy's eyes? He threw the baton down in disgust and turned back to Garcia. The kid lay on the ground with a trickle of blood running from his nose.

Overwhelmed with empathy, he stooped down to check on the boy. He could feel the other men's eyes, but he no longer cared. He knew he'd already lost their respect by refusing to go after McCoy. And by kneeling to check on Garcia, it was doubtful that he could ever regain it. But that didn't matter. Right now, all that mattered was Garcia's injuries, and the tightness of emotion constricting Coleman's throat.

He was barely aware of the rattling sounds behind him as McCoy retrieved his baton from the floor. There was a sudden, powerful blow to the back of his head. Pain exploded in his brain for a split second before he lost consciousness.

# CHAPTER 5

What do you mean, he's withdrawn his appeal?" Steiner sat up rod-straight in his legal clinic work cubicle. "He can't do that!"

"He can do anything he wants," came the voice at the other end of the line. "It's his life."

"But—" Steiner fumbled for words. "What's his angle?"

"No one knows. Could be he's grown tired of the fight; we've seen that before."

"No. Coleman doesn't get tired. He's a machine, an unfeeling machine."

The silence on the other end did not disagree. "Of course there is the other theory . . ."

The voice hesitated. It belonged to Robert Butterfield, assistant D.A. for Douglas County. The two had worked together on the case since its beginning. Unofficially, of course. Steiner knew Butterfield had caught heat from the press over their alliance and on more than one occasion he had received some questioning memos from his boss. But Steiner also knew Butterfield's respect for professional courtesy. More importantly, he knew the man had a daughter. And whenever Steiner's relentless naggings put an edge to Butterfield's voice, Steiner only had to ask, "What if it had been your daughter, Bob? What if she were the one who was stabbed to death and found with her throat slit?"

"What other theory?" Steiner demanded.

"Rumor has it something's happened on the Row. Coleman's supposedly gone through some sort of change. Moping around his cell, feeling remorseful, that sort of thing."

Steiner scowled. He knew Coleman inside and out. Men like that didn't have remorse. An accidental killer might. Or someone who kills out of passion, sure. But not multiple killers. They never have feelings for their victims; it's simply not in their nature. So what was he up to?

Steiner cleared his throat. "What does his counsel say?"

"They're as puzzled as the rest of us."

"They're playing straight?"

"Whatever scam he's trying to pull, he's pulling alone."

"Maybe he's going for insanity—proving he's not mentally fit for execution because he agrees he should be executed? Others have tried it."

"I don't know, Harold. I'm only telling you what his lawyers say and what I hear from the Row."

Steiner's mind raced. Coleman was clever, crafty. And he was absolutely amoral. What *was* he doing?

"Harold?"

A thought was forming.

"Harold, you still there?"

"Yeah. Listen, Bob. If this is legit, and we know it's not, but if it was—wouldn't the best way for him to prove it to everybody, wouldn't the best way be for him to finally let me visit him?"

"We've been through that a hundred—"

"I know, I know, but think about it. The man claims he's repentant. The father of his victim wants to meet him. What's he going to do, say no? Who would believe him then? Don't you see, he's played right into our hands. If he says yes, I get my meeting. If he says no, I prove he's a fake."

There was a pause on the other end. "It could backfire. He could play the media and turn public opinion around. 'Repentant Killer Begs Forgiveness.'"

"Like Walking Wily in '94?"

"That's right."

"But we still fried him, didn't we?"

"True."

"And with the public so pro-death these days, and this being an election year . . ."

Butterfield finished the thought. "It would be political suicide for the board to pardon him."

"Exactly. Let me take my chances, Bob. Ask Coleman's lawyers to run it past him again. See if you can get me in. Tell them it's a good litmus test to see if he's legit."

"And if they refuse?"

"Then I'll be the one to go to the press. If Coleman wants to play a new game, that's fine with me. He's still not getting away. I won't let him. The Law won't let him."

There was a long pause on the other end. Finally: "I'll get back to you later this afternoon."


*The stench of raw chicken fat is replaced by disinfectant, an overwhelming odor of pine and ammonia that makes Coleman's nose twitch. It's a new smell for the fourteen-year-old, but it's a smell he will grow accustomed to over the years.*

A Ping-Pong ball clacks back and forth. Kids talk, swear, laugh. Boys and girls. A billiard ball cracks. Coleman reaches into his pocket and pulls out a white sweat sock, the same type they issue every day in this juvenile center located behind Douglas County Hospital. White socks, white T-shirts, and blue jeans.

He is waiting for Father Kennedy. He steps back—black, high-top Keds squeaking on yellowing floor tile. He feels the pool table behind him and turns. Discreetly he reaches into the leather-thonged side pocket.

"Get your paws outta there."

He flashes the boy with the cue stick a leer and pulls out a single billiard ball.

Cue Stick Boy momentarily considers making an issue out of it but appears to remember Coleman's reputation and decides otherwise.

"Oh, here you are." It's an older voice with a trace of an Irish accent. Coleman stiffens but does not turn to face Father Kennedy.

"Thanks for meeting me here, son. May I buy you a Coca-Cola?"

Coleman shakes his head.

"Listen," the man says, "I'm sorry if I embarrassed you at chapel."

Coleman slowly opens the sock. His back is still toward the Father.

"I really am quite open to hearing opinions and answering questions."

Cue Stick Boy pretends to line up another shot, but it is obvious he is watching everything.

"Still, there's a time to speak and a time to listen."

Coleman drops the billiard ball into the sock. It stretches the material three or four inches. He raises it so it does not clunk the table.

"And by challenging my authority in front of the group, well, I'm afraid your comments were a little too disruptive. That's why I had to ask you to leave."

Coleman discreetly wraps the long neck of the sock around his right hand one time.

"I hope you understand. No hard feelings?"

He hesitates.

"Now, if you have any questions, I'd be more than happy to discuss them with you."

Coleman spins. His arm flies into the air, whipping the ball, whirling it toward the man's face. It is only then that he recognizes the eyes. They are not Kennedy's eyes. They are his own eyes. He can tell by the emptiness, their aching loneliness.

But it is too late. The ball smashes into Kennedy's left cheekbone. Yet it is Coleman who cries out in pain. The impact is jarring, searing. He feels his own face give way, sees his own eyes staring back at him in pain and confusion and betrayal.

But he cannot stop. He swings the ball again, then again—each time feeling the blow himself. As victor and victim he screams. And still, he continues.

Somebody runs toward him. Construction boots against tile. His father's boots.

He continues swinging. The eyes in the battered face no longer register any expression. Coleman hits his face again, shrieking in pain, weeping at the cruelty.

His father is there. Coleman's eyes are too battered to make out the blurry form of the man, but he can smell the whisky on his breath. He will kill Coleman. The boy begins flailing his arms, but he hits only air. His eyes no longer work. The pain is unbearable, resonating from his skull through his body and into his gut. He doubles over, convulsing. Once, twice, until finally . . .

Coleman woke up vomiting. He rolled onto his side and managed to spew most of it onto the floor. When the convulsions ceased, he sat up and threw his feet over the edge of the bed. He ran his hand over his face. It was covered in sweat and tears.

They were coming every night now. The dreams. Acts of violence he had completely forgotten. Brutality where he becomes his own victims, feeling their pain, screaming their anguish. Each dream ending the same way, with uncontrollable tears of remorse.

As he sat on the edge of the bed, catching his breath, he heard a train's distant and mournful whistle. He paused to savor the sound. Over the years he'd been vaguely aware of it, but never really heard it. It was painful and beautiful. A distant, sorrowful wail that cut through the stillness of the night.

Over the past weeks Coleman had grown accustomed to the beauty surrounding him. It was still just as breathtaking, but it was no longer quite as unnerving. But the other thing—the ache in his chest, the tightening in his throat, the gnawing loneliness—once that pain came, it never left. No matter what he did, no matter how he tried to ignore it, it was always there.

The only thing worse than the loneliness was the look in other people's eyes. The inmates', the guards', the caseworkers'. They seemed so haunted, so full of their own emptiness. They were Coleman's brother's eyes, forsaken and abandoned. They were Kennedy's eyes, full of searching anguish. That was the reason Coleman spent more and more time in his cell, away from the rest of the population. It was their eyes. He simply could not bear to see the loneliness.

Shadows crossed the window of his door, and he stiffened. Somebody was out in the hall. A key slipped into the lock and the door swung open. Glaring light poured in from the hallway, and Coleman squinted as two, three, maybe four forms shuffled inside.

"Who's there?" he demanded.

No answer. The door shut. It was dark again.

"What do you want?"

"Hello, Cole."

A chill swept through his body. He recognized the voice. It had a different diction, thanks to the missing tooth, but there was no mistaking its owner. Sweeney was back. Other silhouettes became distinguishable. Three men from the Row. No hacks. Just inmates. Apparently Sweeney had been busy all afternoon recruiting and convincing them to change their alliance. Coleman wasn't sure, but for a second he even thought he saw Garcia.

"You wouldn't come to my welcome-home party," the voice sneered, "so I thought I'd bring it here."


"That's ridiculous," Murkoski protested. "How can you say I'm pushing too hard?"

O'Brien held the phone against his left shoulder, bending and unbending a paper clip in his hands, trying his best to remain calm. "Kenny, a mouse from the GOD gene colony has been killed by one of its own kind. We've got to slow down. We've got to retrace our steps to see what went wrong."

"I'll tell you what's wrong." Murkoski's voice scoffed over the phone. "Wolff's an incompetent buffoon, that's what's wrong. I've said that from the first day we brought him on board. Did you run a biopsy on other animals in the colony? Run some gels? See if one of them's mutated?"

"No, he suggested we wait until you—"

"See what I mean? Incompetent! The man won't even run a gel without me there. Totally incompetent!"

O'Brien paused a moment to let the conversation cool. "It's not going to hurt us to put off the transplant a few more weeks."

"He's scheduled for execution in thirty days."

"So have your federal guys talk the governor into a stay."

"It's not that simple."

"Kenny, I just don't understand the rush. What would it hurt—"

"Look, if you want to run this thing, then you come back here and run it!"

"Kenn—"

"The guy is off the prison grounds and in a local hospital. His behavior is exactly as we hypothesized. And this latest beating is the perfect alibi to keep him out of circulation for the next several weeks. I'm telling you, the timing couldn't be better."

"Have you checked with him?"

"What do you mean?"

"I remember you conveniently forgetting to mention anything to him about a bone-marrow transplant when I was there."

"He'll go along with us. What other choice does he have? Besides, I've already pulled his stem cells and infected them."

"You've already pulled his marrow?"

"He was unconscious when they brought him in, what better time? The departments here are top rate. X ray has the sophistication to kill the cells, and their isolation ward is good enough to keep out infection until he can regenerate new ones. I'm telling you, it can all be done right here and now."

O'Brien's head spun. He knew that a bone-marrow transplant was necessary, just as it had been with Freddy. It was one thing to give Coleman the virus injection every few days to infect his new blood cells as the old ones died off. But those effects were only temporary. To make them permanent, one had to actually change the way the blood cells were made. And since blood cells are manufactured inside bone marrow, it's necessary to change the marrow.

"It's like a car factory," he had explained to little Julie. "They make red and blue and green cars. But if you want a bunch of polka-dot ones, you can either stand outside the car plant and individually paint each car as it rolls out, or you can install new machinery inside the plant that automatically makes them polka dot." That was the case with Coleman.

They could either change the blood cells one at a time, or change the bone marrow—the blood factory—itself.

A bone-marrow transplant was simple enough. Insert a needle deep into the big bones, such as the pelvic bone. Do this fifteen to twenty times to withdraw an adequate portion of the gooey red bone marrow. This is where the stem cells are located, those tricky, hard-to-find cells that actually produce the white and red blood cells. Once outside the body, the marrow is infected with a virus that instructs the stem cells on how to create the new kind of blood. When these stem cells have been reprogrammed, they are reinjected back into the body. In theory, this would allow Coleman to create the new blood all on his own, permanently.

In theory.

"I'm telling you," Murkoski said, "we're all set here. Just say the word, and we're on our way."

O'Brien was losing control of the situation. It was time to test the waters. "And if I don't give the go-ahead?"

He was not surprised by the pause on the other end. Nor was he particularly shocked at the answer when it finally came. "We're talking about a lot of money here, Phil—not to mention power. A lot of rich, influential people who will be very disappointed in us. In you. For crying out loud," he blurted, "we're about to change the entire course of human history!"

O'Brien said nothing. He suspected there was more. He was right.

"To be honest, I don't think McGovern or Riordan or *any* of your board would be too happy to let this type of money and prestige slip out of our hands . . ."

O'Brien closed his eyes and waited. Here it came.

" . . . slip out of our hands and go someplace else. No, they would not be happy with that at all."

O'Brien took a long, deep breath. Just as he had feared. If he pulled the plug now, Murkoski would go to the board. No question about it. He had the audacity and the ego to do that sort of thing. But that was the best-case scenario. The worst case would be that Murkoski would simply quit and go to another company. The kid would pick up all of his toys (along with all that government funding) and go find a company that was willing to let him continue at his own accelerated pace. It was blackmail, pure and simple. Of course, there would be lawsuits and court battles, but by then it would be too late.

O'Brien stalled, trying to change tack. "What about the execution?"

"We'll be running the GSR as soon as his risk of infection stabilizes and we get back to the penitentiary."

"Will you tell him? About the GSR test?"

"I don't think we can. If he knew what was going on, it would ruin the results."

"That seems rather cruel."

"Of course it does, but can you think of any other way to get an accurate reading?"

O'Brien couldn't.

"I'm also nailing down the other details," Murkoski continued. "The Witness Protection guys are making contact with somebody in our area. Looks like we may have ourselves a little bonus in that department. Also, I'm flying out Hendricks, one of our own electricians, to rewire the chair."

"Everyone back there is sitting tight on this?" O'Brien asked. "Only a few people will know the execution is a fake?"

"Not even the coroner. She's going to get sick that day and will be replaced by an assistant she doesn't even know about."

O'Brien was weakening. "But what about the mice?"

"Have Wolff run the gels and get back to me. I'm sure it was just mishandling, maybe some mislabeling. Typical techie incompetence."

"And Coleman? If something should go wrong with the execution? If he should accidentally . . ." O'Brien searched for the right word. "Expire?"

"Then we'll find someone else."

"Kenny . . ."

"Listen, Phil, it's time you realize that this program is more important than one man's life. Or, for that matter, several."

A dull cold tightened around O'Brien's stomach as his worst fears resurfaced. Did this kid know any boundaries?

"We're talking about changing the human race here. With stakes like that, a few sacrifices, especially like a Michael Coleman, are of little consequence. Not when you look at the big picture. Besides, he's scheduled to die anyway, what's the difference?"

O'Brien's head began to ache. Again, he changed the subject. "If you're successful, if we get him out of there alive and free, how will we convince him to keep working with us?"

"I'm adding a viral leash to the marrow. If he doesn't come to us every five to six days, his body will create such massive quantities of cytokines he's going to feel like he's having the flu five times over."

O'Brien's intercom buzzed. He tried to ignore it, but it continued. He pressed the button and snapped, "I thought I said no interruptions."

"I'm sorry, Dr. O'Brien, it's Mr. Riordan, line two. He insists on talking to you about the epidermal drug."

"Can't he wait?"

"He's pretty insistent."

"I'll be with him in a minute."

"He wants to speak to you *now*."

O'Brien rubbed the back of his neck and spoke into the phone. "Kenny?"

"Yeah, I heard."

"Okay, look, it's your call, but give it another day, all right? Phone me tomorrow and let me know your final decision."

"Phil—"

"Twenty-four hours won't hurt anything. And it will give you an extra day to catch your breath and think through any options. All right?"

Another pause. Then, "All right."

"And please be careful."

"No prob, Phil. Talk to you tomorrow."

Before O'Brien could respond, Murkoski hung up. The CEO of Genodyne Inc. took a long, deep breath. He had done the right thing, he was certain of it. Even though he felt spent and used, at least for now he had done the right thing.

That thought provided little consolation as he reached for line two, preparing for another confrontation with his most demanding board member. Dr. Philip O'Brien did not much care for his job today. And he was caring for it less and less as the day dragged on.

Kenneth Murkoski smiled as he hung up the phone inside the pre-op room. He'd pulled it off without a hitch.

A nurse already in scrubs poked her head into the room. "Dr. Murkoski?"

"Yes?"

"The patient's prepped. We're ready to begin when you are."

"Excellent." He stuffed the cellular into his pants. "I'll be right there."

*"Don't you mock me!"*

*"I wasn't—"*

*"I'm still your mother."*

Katherine's mind replayed the scene again and again. It was a continuous loop. No matter what she did, she couldn't stop the memory of Eric's voice or hers.

" 'Scuse me . . . 'scuse me," she called to the passing bartender. He was a cutey, in his early twenties. "Give me another one of these . . . these, what are they called?"

The bartender grinned. "Surfer on Acid."

"Right." Katherine nodded. "I'll have another . . ." The name had already escaped her. "Another one."

*"Don't you mock me!"*

*"I wasn't—"*

*"I'm still your mother."*

*"I wasn't—"*

*"I demand your respect, do you hear me?"*

Though her brain was fogging, the scene wasn't. It remained as clear as when it had unfolded nearly two hours earlier.

It had been another long and trying week. The IRS was closing in fast, demanding she pay for some honest miscalculations made over three years ago.

"How can I pay what I don't have?" she had pleaded for the umpteenth time over the phone.

"We can work out a payment plan, Mrs. Lyon, but this is the United States government—and you *will* pay."

She'd had a similar conversation with her store's landlord that same afternoon. Same basic threat, same bottom line. Bills were piling up faster than she could keep track. Now she was dumping her mail on the floor at the end of the sofa, refusing even to open it. Not that she had time. With work and shopping and creditors and chauffeuring Eric, she had time for nothing.

Except the booze. And the guilt.

The only daughter of a Baptist minister, Katherine had grown up in a strict, religious home. No one drank in her family. In fact, she had not even tasted beer until she was a senior in high school. Even as an adult, drinking had never been a part of her life. Oh, she and Gary would have an occasional glass of wine during one of those rare and infrequent dinners they couldn't afford, but that had been merely an attempt by the young newlyweds to be sophisticated.

Then Gary had been murdered, and everything went wrong. Her trust in a loving God. Her belief that good people were protected from evil. Her fights with her father. And on one particularly rough evening, the visit by a well-meaning friend with a four-pack of wine coolers to help her get through.

What relief they had brought. What blessed, numbing relief. For seven weeks she had been trying to shut down her mind, to stop the pain. Nothing had worked. But there, in those four little coolers, she had found the switch. Those few hours were the only peace she had known in nearly two months of visiting the hospital, enduring the death and the funeral, pretending to be the strong police officer's widow, the faithful preacher's kid. Those four bottles had given her more comfort than any of the hundreds of well-meaning clichés and spiritual bromides shoved at her by friends and relatives.

It was a comfort she had pursued more and more often until she had slowly lost herself to it. That's when she had taken a stand, sworn it off, allowed her dad to enroll her in AA. He was no longer welcome to speak about his God, but he was welcome to help her kick the booze.

And he had. He'd been there every minute she'd needed him. Until eleven months later, when he'd died of a massive coronary, and whatever vestiges of faith Katherine had were snuffed out. It was then she had moved halfway across the country to get away from the suffocating do-gooding of friends and family, to make a go of it in a world with little compassion and no mercy.

She *could* make a go of it, she was certain. She just had to lessen the pain.

*"I demand respect, do you hear me?"*

*The boy mumbled something she couldn't hear.*

*"What?"*

*"Nothing."*

*"What did you say?"*

*"I said what am I supposed to respect?"*

That's when she had hit him. Tears had immediately sprung to his eyes. Not tears of pain, but of betrayal. He'd tried to fight them back, but couldn't.

It was then, seeing the expression in her son's eyes, realizing what she had done, that she'd called Lisa and asked her to baby-sit. She had to get away, she had to stop the pain.

"Here you go, Ma'am."

She looked up surprised as the bartender placed another drink in front of her. She thanked him and asked, "How much do I owe you?"

"No charge. The gentleman over there sent it."

Katherine followed the boy's gesture and squinted at an oily-looking fellow in a worn suit sitting at a nearby table. He raised his glass to her and smiled.

Katherine turned back to her drink. Her last binge, three years ago, had proven to her that men were pigs, animals waiting to take advantage of another's weakness. She would not fall into that trap again.

"Tell him no thanks," she said, fumbling for her wallet. She may be a drunk, but she wasn't for sale.

# CHAPTER 6

What's going on! What are you doing?"

The two men said nothing as they finished strapping Coleman's left arm and leg to the gurney. They had entered the room while he slept and pinned him down before he had a chance to awaken. Now Coleman fought, but with little success, as they forced down his other side and strapped him in.

"What is this? What are you—"

His shouts were cut short by a roll of gauze shoved into his mouth, then quickly sealed in place with surgical tape. Coleman breathed hard, nostrils flaring, eyes wild. He raised his head, trying to see faces, but was quickly shoved back down onto the gurney.

Three weeks had passed since the bone-marrow transplant. His recovery was on schedule, and just that afternoon he had been transferred back to the prison hospital. He had complained about having to sleep on a hospital gurney for the night, and they'd given him some excuse about a lack of beds. Now Coleman realized—too late—that there had been another reason.

Again he raised his head, this time searching for Murkoski. Lights flickered on, and he squinted into the brightness. Again his head was forced down, and this time it was held in a rigid hammerlock by two muscular arms. He tried to bite the arms, to shred them with his teeth, but the man was a pro. Coleman couldn't move an inch.

Suddenly there was electrical buzzing and a harsh scraping atop his head. They were shaving his hair! Why? The only time they shaved a Death Row inmate's head was ...

Adrenaline surged through Coleman's body. He twisted and strained, but accomplished nothing. The straps and armlock held him firm. Suddenly he heard the distinctive squirting sound of an aerosol can spewing foam and felt cold lather smeared onto his head. Then came more scraping, slower this time, burning and stinging—a razor nicking and cutting his skin.

Shaving the head was the first step in executing a condemned prisoner. It assured the cleanest contact between the skin and the electrodes implanted in the chair's headband. But not now. Not tonight. They were eleven days too early!

Hadn't Murkoski carefully explained it? To keep everyone happy, they would have to stage a mock execution with all of the frills. It would be the only way to convince the public that he was actually dead. And it would have to include everything, the whole nine yards: staged before witnesses, verified by the prison physician, confirmed by the county coroner, extensive coverage by the media, everything to satisfy the folks who wanted to see him fry. But not now. The date had already been set by the courts. He was scheduled for execution January 14. This was January 3!

Now they shaved his left calf, where the second electrode would be placed. The circuitry of the chair was simple. There was a three-and-a-half-foot gap between the chair's head electrode and calf electrode—a three-and-a-half-foot gap that needed one condemned prisoner to slip in and make the circuit complete. That circuit contained 2,450 volts. It would shoot through him, immediately knocking him unconscious and disrupting his heart's electrical pattern.

But not for Coleman. His was to be different. And it was scheduled to be in eleven days, not now.

Unless they were pulling a double-cross.

With their attention on his calf, he was able to raise his head again and look around. Still no Murkoski. Just the two burly men. Coleman might have been able to take them out, if he could move. But he couldn't.

A moment later they smeared a clear, oily gel over the top of his head and then his calf. This was standard procedure to insure maximum contact between the metal electrodes and human flesh.

They pushed open the hospital door and wheeled him out of the room. Coleman's mind raced as they headed down the hall. Seventy-five feet later they arrived at the elevator. Beside it was a blue door and a narrow flight of stairs, the stairs he would have taken if he'd been allowed to walk to his execution. They keyed the elevator, and it opened. They wheeled him in, and the doors closed. As they rode down to the first floor, he tried to read the two men's faces, to make human contact with them. But neither would look at him.

The elevator came to a stop, and the doors rattled opened. He raised his head. He was sweating now, and the tiny rivulets carried the gel down his forehead and into his eyes. It stung fiercely, but he forced himself to keep them open. Directly across from the elevator was the closed door of the execution chamber. To his immediate right was the control room that would hide the humming transformer and the man who would rotate the single dial. The man would be paid around three hundred dollars to stand behind that door and twist the dial on and off four times.

But tonight the door was open. Two men stood inside. One was a stranger, the other Murkoski. Hearing the elevator open, Murkoski turned toward him. Coleman tried to make out his expression, but the sweat and gel blurred his vision.

"I'm sorry to have to do this to you, Mr. Coleman, but there is no other way."

Coleman tried to talk, to plead, to threaten. He shook his head, hoping to signal with his eyes for Murkoski to remove the gauze so he could speak. But Murkoski turned from him and nodded to another large man, who pulled open the door to the execution chamber and went in before them.

It was a nine-by-nine, off-white, cinder-block room. What looked like an old oak throne sat majestically in the center. The chair had been built sometime between 1913 and 1920; it looked like a crude antique. The seat and back were covered with black rubber mats—insulation. Near the top, a small block of wood, which served as a headrest, was also covered with the grooved rubber matting. The four legs, made of four-by-fours, rested on two parallel skids, also made of four-by-fours. They were anchored to the floor by heavy wires threaded through attached ceramic insulators. There wasn't much room to move as the three men unstrapped Coleman from the gurney, carried him across the rubber floor mats, and dumped him into the chair.

Of course Coleman fought, but it served little purpose. These men knew exactly what they were doing.

They began buckling him down with brand-new leather straps, bought expressly for the execution. First the lap strap, then the chest strap, then one for each biceps, one to hold each of his forearms to the armrests, two more to strap his thighs down, and two more around his calves. The purpose of all these straps was not to prevent him from running, but to prevent his body from convulsing and flying out of the chair when they turned on the electricity.

As they attached the electrode to his left calf, Coleman looked ahead at the large rectangular window, not three feet in front of him, covered by a heavy, gold drape. On the other side was the twelve-by-fifteen-foot witness room where the ten chosen witnesses should be watching. But Coleman knew they wouldn't be there. Not tonight. Tonight was eleven days too early.

He turned his head to the left and saw Murkoski standing in the doorway, watching with scientific detachment but avoiding eye contact with Coleman.

The first two men filed out as the last one attached the metal electrodes to Coleman's head, making sure the strap fit snugly. Then he turned and left. Only Murkoski remained, standing in the open doorway between the control room and the execution chamber.

Sweat streamed into Coleman's eyes, continuing to sting them with jelly. But he kept them open. If he'd known how to pray, this would have been the time. He didn't. Instead, he braced himself, preparing for the worst, trying to forget the stories he'd heard. Most of the inmates had speculated that he would feel nothing—"Knock you out before you know what hits you." But Coleman had read an entirely different account from former U.S. Supreme Court Justice Michael Brennan:

> The prisoner's eyeballs sometimes pop out and rest on the cheeks. The prisoner often defecates, urinates, and vomits blood and drool. The body turns bright red as its temperature rises, and the prisoner's flesh swells and his skin stretches to the point of breaking. Sometimes the prisoner catches on fire, particularly if he perspires excessively. Witnesses hear a loud and sustained sound like bacon frying, and the sickly sweet smell of burning flesh permeates the chamber.

Coleman glanced down. Under his left wrist was what looked like a round coffee mug stain. There were plenty of rumors about that stain. Historians believed that it wasn't a coffee stain at all, but the stain from an ink bottle. In the old prison, the execution chamber had also served as the clothing storeroom. The inmates who had run the store used to sit in the chair to write letters.

Coleman was breathing hard now, trying to catch his breath. Again he looked at Murkoski, who turned to the control room and nodded.

And then it hit.

But it was nothing like Coleman had expected. No jolt. No spastic convulsing. No burning. In fact, he barely felt anything, just the slightest tingle across his skin for several seconds, and then it was over.

Had the chair short-circuited? Had they made a mistake?

He turned back to Murkoski, who was still looking into the control room. "Did you get a reading?" Murkoski asked.

"Yes," came the reply.

"Let's do it again, just to make sure."

Again Coleman prepared himself. The first attempt had failed. This time he closed his eyes, preparing for the worst, and felt—

Nothing. Again.

"Got it?" Murkoski asked.

"Yes. Two good responses."

Coleman opened his eyes just in time to see Murkoski turn to him and smile. "Good," he was saying, "very good." He looked over his shoulder and called, "All right, gentlemen, go ahead and release him."

Two of the three men reentered the cubicle, looking far more relaxed. The first thing to go was the surgical-tape-and-gauze gag. But Coleman, who had earlier wanted to shout and swear and scream, said nothing. He could only pant, trying to catch his breath, as he stared at the smiling Murkoski.

"We had to measure your galvanic skin response," Murkoski said.

Coleman still didn't speak. He wasn't sure he could.

Murkoski continued. "If we're going to stage a mock execution, we have to know what type of jolt your body can withstand. By running this test, Hendricks here"—he motioned into the control room—"will be able to install the correct ballast resistor as well as determine the proper voltage, enabling us to stop your heart without frying your brain."

The men finished unstrapping him, and Coleman continued staring, still trying to comprehend.

"Galvanic skin response, or GSR, is a measurement of the electricity your skin conducts. It changes depending upon the amount of stress you are under. That's why it works so well in lie detectors."

Coleman's hands were free, and he wiped the sweat and gel out of his eyes.

Murkoski continued. "If we had told you this was just a test, you'd have been far more relaxed, and we would never have received an accurate reading. To obtain the proper measurements, you had to think it was real. I trust there are no hard feelings."

"Hi, Kate."

Katherine Lyon looked up from the hard disk drive she had been installing in the store's back room, removed her glasses—and saw a face from the past.

"Jimmy!"

James Preston was thirty-seven years old and built like a tank. He barely had time to enter the room before Katherine raced around the worktable and threw her arms around him.

"Jimmy, it's so good to see you! How are you?"

"I'm fine, Kate, just fine."

He seemed a little stiff, a little uneasy. It may have been the years since they'd seen each other, or the presence of his companion, a tall somber man in a dark suit. Either way, it was a reminder that times change and so do people. She couldn't suddenly return to being the person she had been. Nor could he. She pulled away, a bit more reserved. "Come on in," she offered, then called into the store, "Eric! Eric, come here a minute." Turning back to Preston, she said, "He'll flip when he sees you."

Preston smiled.

"So what brings you all the way out here? Don't tell me you've moved."

"No, Kate, I came to see you."

Eric appeared in the doorway.

"Eric, this is your uncle Jimmy."

"Who?"

"Your dad's partner. You remember Uncle Jimmy."

Preston crossed to the boy. He had a pronounced limp. It came with the artificial leg. "Hi, Eric."

"Hi."

Preston spoke gently. "You don't remember me, do you?"

"Yeah, a little." Eric pushed up his glasses.

"I was with your dad on the police force. We were partners."

"Were you with him when he got shot?"

"Yes I was, Eric. It was my life your father saved."

Eric said nothing.

"He was a brave man, Eric."

The boy nodded. "Uh-huh." Then turning to Katherine he asked, "Can I go now? I got somebody on the Internet."

A shade of disappointment crossed Katherine's face. "Sure." She nodded. "Go ahead."

The boy quickly turned and headed back into the store.

"I'm sorry," Katherine said. She ran her hands through her cropped hair. "You two used to be such buddies."

"That was a long time ago, Kate."

"I'll say." She moved behind her table, then motioned to the broken-down sofa across from her. "Please, have a seat."

The men made their way through the cluttered room to the sofa, where they rearranged a few catalogs and electronic odds and ends to find a place to sit.

"Can I interest you fellows in a drink?" she asked as she sat.

She caught Preston's disapproving look at the glass and bottle on her table. "I thought you quit."

She resented the reprimand and purposely reached for the bottle to pour herself a refill. "It's one of the few pleasures

I've got left, Jimmy. That and Eric." She recapped the bottle and set it back on the table. "So, who's your friend?"

The suit was immediately on his feet, extending his hand over the table. "I'm Agent Kevles, Ms. Lyon. Witness Protection Agency."

Katherine shook his hand with less enthusiasm. She took a drink and turned back to Preston. "How's Denise? The kids?"

Preston glanced down. "We've been divorced three years now. She moved back to Vermont eighteen months ago." He continued more quietly. "The shooting took a lot out of us, too."

Katherine said nothing. She was already beginning to dislike the meeting. "So why are you here, Jimmy?"

"Agent Kevles asked me to come with him. The Witness Protection Program has done a lot of research for a special project, and they think you're a prime candidate for the job."

She turned to Kevles. "Job?"

"We have a client we need to place. I can't tell you his name. But I can tell you that he is very, very special. Perhaps the most important placement we have had in years."

"By placement you mean somebody who's informed on somebody else, right? Is he a con?"

Kevles started to respond affirmatively, but Katherine cut him off. "I don't know if Jimmy has filled you in on all the details, but my husband was killed by an ex-convict."

"We are well aware of your history, Ms. Lyon."

"Then you're also aware that I'm not too keen on helping any of the creeps."

"This man is different. I guarantee it."

Katherine said nothing but slowly finished her drink.

Kevles leaned forward more intensely. "I should clarify something. This man is *not* an informer. He's part of an experiment."

"Experiment?"

"Up in Arlington. With a firm called Genodyne."

She waited for more.

"It's a biogenetic company. The project is classified, so I can't give you the details, but I can tell you that we are prepared to pay generously if you would consider hiring this man as your employee."

Katherine held his gaze. "Why me?"

"Well, as I said, you fit the profile—"

"Why me?" she repeated.

Kevles adjusted his glasses, obviously uncomfortable revealing any more information than he had to. But it was also obvious Katherine would settle only for the truth. "Much of this experiment is sociological in nature. And because of your past—your bereavement, your psychological profile, even the fact that you have a seven-year-old son—"

"Eight. My boy's eight."

"Even the fact that you have an eight-year-old son—all of this has strongly influenced our consideration."

"So what does that mean? He's not some kind of pervert, is he? I'm not going to have my kid exposed to—"

"I guarantee you that he is one of the most sensitive, loving people you will ever meet."

"Right. He's still a man, isn't he?"

Kevles appeared unsure how to respond.

"How much?" she asked.

"Pardon me?"

"You said pay was involved. How much?"

She could see the relief cross his face. He was back to familiar territory. "We are prepared to pay eight hundred and fifty dollars a month."

Katherine didn't believe her ears. Eight hundred and fifty dollars a month *plus* free help around the store. But she'd learned much from being on her own, and she knew that the figure had come far too easily for him. She had room to negotiate.

She met his gaze firmly and said, "Twelve fifty."

"Ms. Lyon, twelve hundred and fifty dollars per month seems a bit—"

"Take it or leave it. I have no idea who this creep is. Or what he'll try to pull. You're asking me to spend ten hours a day working beside somebody I don't even know, risk my safety, risk my son's safety, all because you *say* I can trust him. You know, you may have a point: twelve fifty isn't enough. I'd say fifteen hundred is more realistic, wouldn't you, Jimmy?"

Preston stared at her.

Kevles removed his glasses and folded them. "Ms. Lyon, I don't think fifteen hundred dollars is a reasonable—"

"You're right, you're right. I don't know what I was thinking. I'd have to train him, he'd always be underfoot, he'd—"

"All right—"

"There's no telling what he could break or—"

"All right, all right, I understand." Kevles put his glasses back on. "I suppose fifteen hundred dollars isn't all that unreasonable."

Katherine almost smiled. "Good. Of course, I'll have to run it past Eric, but we'll see what we can do."

*Please, take anything you want. Please, but don't—*

"Augh!" Coleman cried, as if he'd been slugged in the gut. But no one had touched him. Not Harold Steiner who stood four feet away in the attorney/client room, not the guard who remained glued to his side. Neither had moved.

It was the picture of Melissa Steiner someone had set on the table that had doubled him over. A pretty girl. Auburn, shoulder-length hair, a smile bordering on mischievous. Coleman leaned on the table with both hands, trying to steady himself.

*I've got a stereo upstairs, take it. Please—*

Cold sweat broke out on his face. He continued breathing deeply, refusing to give in to the nausea and dizziness trying to overtake him. He didn't recognize Melissa's face. Except in his dreams, he never remembered his victims' faces. But there were those eyes. Different in color and shape, yet somehow similar to his brother's and Father Kennedy's.

And her voice. *You're scaring me, please don't*—As clear and real as if she were standing in the room with him. He hoped this was another dream. But he knew it was something new, something stronger.

"What's wrong?" It was Steiner's voice, far away in another world. "What's happening?"

Coleman watched the beads of sweat falling from his face and splattering on the table beside the photograph. He had agreed to meet Steiner, not because he wanted to, but because he had to. He had to tell the man how sorry he was, that he now understood the unfathomable pain he had inflicted.

"Mr. Coleman."

Of course the press would have a field day with it, but this wasn't for the press. It was for Steiner. And, somehow, for himself.

"Mr. Coleman, what is wrong?"

Coleman nodded, but he wasn't okay, not at all. Once again his senses were tightening, focusing. But not tightening and focusing on the present.

*Please, I'll do whatever you want, but please—*

Coleman watched the sweat drip and splatter, drip and splatter. But he could no longer look at the photograph. He no longer had to. Now he could see the eyes without looking at them. Lonely eyes. Begging for mercy.

He felt something in his right hand. It was still the edge of the table, but it wasn't. It was a knife. Her knife. From the kitchen. And that sound. That irritating laughter of a TV sitcom. Mocking him, taunting him.

"Mr. Coleman . . ."

*Please—if you want money—*

He feels his left arm wrapping around her neck. He is standing behind her. His right hand suddenly jerks inward, toward her, hard, again and again. Now the gasping cries. Hysterical. Pleading, like the eyes. And the rage, the uncontrollable rage as his hand continues thrusting inward. But not rage at the girl. Rage at himself.

He continues stabbing, again and again, only now the girl is gone. Now he is stabbing himself. Now he feels each burning penetration of the knife, each slice and tear of his own flesh. Now he is crying out in her pain. He is in the attorney/client room, gripping the table, and he is back at her apartment in Omaha, jabbing the knife, but not into her. Now it is into his own chest, his own abdomen, again and again and again. Gasping in her anguish. Weeping.

Then the footsteps. His father's, he is sure of it. Louder and louder. They thunder in his head. Just before he arrives they dissolve into another sound. Someone rapping on glass—the guard, signaling for assistance. He hears the door unlock, he hears voices, but the gasping cries in his head are too loud, his own weeping too overpowering.

Arms take his shoulders, leading him away. Other voices ask what is wrong. He cannot answer. It takes all of his effort just to breathe, to walk. He is in the hallway, tears blinding his eyes, making it impossible to see. Sobs of unbearable pain and remorse escape from his throat. Someone is swearing. It is Steiner. He can't make out the words, but the man is not happy.

The meeting has been canceled.


"A little to the left. No, left. There you go."

Theodore Wolff, better known as "Teddy" to the handful of women vying for his interest, was grateful for the gym Genodyne had installed. If there was one thing he hated about genetic research, it was the long hours cooped up in the lab. Of course he loved working his mind, but he also loved working his body. In fact, his greatest inspiration often came in the midst of a grueling racquetball session, or tussles with the Universal Gym. And nothing finished off a good workout like a great rubdown.

"Attaboy. A little more. Good. Now to the right just a bit. The right."

Wearing only a sweatshirt and gym shorts, Wolff lay facedown on the sod of B–11 as Freddy walked up and down his back, gleefully kneading the muscles with his handlike feet, while occasionally giving a little jump, just to liven things up.

"Oaff! Come on, Freddy, that's not funny."

But of course it was funny, so Freddy frequently added the little surprise.

"Up a little . . . there you go."

Besides his athletic build and thick, red hair, Wolff was also known for his perfectly trimmed and manicured nails. He wasn't a neat freak; he just preferred things tidy. Even his work station, that five-foot area of personal lab counter each researcher staked out as his or her own, was uncustomarily clean.

He also liked to shower. A couple times a day. "If you knew the mites and microbes crawling around on your skin," he joked, "you'd be showering, too."

Wolff was as fastidious with his research as he was with his personal hygiene. That's why he worked so well with Murkoski. Where Murkoski would race through a study, impatient over the details, Wolff would remain behind, cleaning up, verifying, and triple-checking everything. If there was ever a scientific Odd Couple, it was Wolff's Felix to Murkoski's Oscar.

"Thanks, Freddy." He patted the grass beside him, signaling for Freddy to step down. The animal obeyed, but not before giving one more playful hop.

"All right, you!" Wolff rolled over and tried to catch him, but the animal was too fast. Freddy ran off screaming in mock panic, his mouth opened wide while keeping his teeth covered with his lips. This was the "play expression" for baboons. It made no difference what noise or gesture they made—just as long as those needle-like canines were covered, it was all in play. And Freddy loved to play. The swings, the gym set, the tree, the slide, they were all fine. But baboons are social creatures, and no amount of toys compare to a good game of tag or roll-and-tumble with another animal.

Before Wolff could sit up, Freddy raced in from behind and gave him a good slap in the ribs. Wolff shouted in surprise and lunged for him but missed again. Freddy ran off screaming in delight, obviously hoping Wolff would follow.

"I can't right now," Wolff said, rising to his feet and brushing off the grass. "I've fooled around enough for one day. Maybe I'll stop by for dinner."

Freddy responded by racing at him full tilt, screaming all the way. But instead of ducking or running, Wolff turned back toward him—just in time to catch the animal leaping directly at him. The impact sent Wolff staggering backwards until man and baboon both crashed onto the grass, Freddy hooting in delight, Wolff laughing in spite of himself. "Come on, boy. I'm serious! I've got to go."

But Freddy continued the wrestling and tumbling as long as possible, chortling the whole time.

"Freddy! Come on now, Freddy." At last Wolff was able to untangle himself from the animal and rise to his feet. Once again Freddy raced off, turned, and prepared for another assault until Wolff held out his finger and gave a stern command. "No, Freddy. No."

The animal's countenance sagged as he slowed to a stop. Then, raising his tail over his head, he loped toward Wolff in his favorite goofball fashion.

"I'm sorry, boy, but I really have to go."

Freddy leaned hard against Wolff as the man reached down to give him one last series of pats. "Tonight, before I go home. I promise."

As Wolff turned and headed toward the door, Freddy stayed glued to his side, then raised his arm for the mandatory last hug. Wolff stooped down and held the animal for a moment. "See you in a few," he said. Freddy chortled and seemed almost to sigh as Wolff withdrew and headed out the door.

Wolff's specialty was mice. Transgenetic mice. Once the specific DNA was recognized and isolated, it was his job to oversee the placement of that DNA into the eggs of the mice, creating and raising up each new generation of the animals.

The actual insertion of the DNA into the egg was fairly simple: Remove the egg from the mouse and stick that egg under a stereoscopic microscope. With the left hand, turn the micromanipulator knob that holds a tiny pipette—a microscopic glass rod that uses small amounts of suction to position the egg and hold it in place. Once the egg is in place, move the right micromanipulator knob and insert a hollow needle directly into the egg. Once the membrane of the egg has been penetrated, inject the DNA. It's as simple as that. In fact, a good technician can insert DNA into one egg every twenty seconds.

Once the egg's DNA has been altered, it is surgically reimplanted into the mouse, and just twenty days later, there is a new brand of mice that the world has never seen.

Of course, the obvious question is: Why not do this with human eggs? A good question, and one that provides a field day for dozens of sci-fi writers. But there are drawbacks. First, it is highly illegal. Second, to obtain the desired results, one would have to wait for the fetus to develop, be born, and in some cases grow to adulthood. For humans, that period is at the very minimum nine months, and depending on the characteristic being developed, possibly twenty years or more. For mice, twenty days. And with the competition and breakneck speed of genetic research, every day is like a year.

Wolff suited up in the paper gown and booties, headed down the hall, and entered the pressured room of his mice colonies. It had been nearly three weeks since the malicious slaughter of one of the mice. Quite a shock at the time. And, despite the tests, no one was entirely sure what had happened. Some abnormality, yes. A mutation in one of the mice, of course. But the jury was still out as to how and why.

Wolff reached for the Plexiglas clipboard and double-checked the day's charts. It wasn't until he strolled toward the back of the room that he noticed it. One of the upper Lucite cages had no movement inside. Colony 233. He reached for the container, slid it out, and gasped.

The cage was covered in blood. All six mice were dead.

# CHAPTER 7

Coleman stood silently in the snow, awed by the absolute stillness. He'd seen snow every year of his life, but not like this. Not with this tranquility, this soothing, calming peace. It had fallen steadily all night and had just let up now, a little before sunrise. He scanned the exercise yard. Every harsh edge, every sharp corner was smoothed and rounded by the soft whiteness. The administration building, the picnic tables, the fences with their rolls of razor wire, everything was covered in gentle serenity. The grime and dirt and mud were completely gone. Erased. Even the sounds from the distant highway were cleansed and absorbed by the smooth, chaste blanket. It was as if the snow had removed all evil from the world—softening its hardness, covering its filth, replacing its vulgarity with silent, pristine purity.

The intensity of Coleman's emotions had been leveling off for the past several days. He still marveled at the beauty surrounding him and grieved over the painful loneliness he saw in individuals, but as the days came and went he was able to gain more and more control over his reactions to those feelings.

He took a deep breath of the cold, fresh air. He felt a tingling all the way to his fingers. He was alive. For the first time that he could remember, really alive. By comparison, his past had been a faded, black-and-white photograph. For thirty-five years he had been sleepwalking, barely aware of his surroundings. Now he was awake. Seeing and hearing and feeling everything as if for the very first time.

But with the exhilaration came the other feeling. His own loneliness. It never left. It was a gnawing hunger he could not shake, an ache that the beauty and wonder around him only heightened. It was as if that beauty were part of something greater and grander than he could ever be. It made him feel cut off, like a perpetual outsider—a fleeting shadow dancing over the surface of creation without ever really being able to connect with it. Though he never ceased to marvel at the world's beauty, whether it was the reflection within a drop of water or the intricate designs in the palm of his hand, he knew that something much grander and deeper was calling to him. But calling him to what?

He took another breath. The air bit his nostrils and stung his throat. Today was the day. Actually, tomorrow at one minute after midnight. That's when one of four electrical jolts would shoot through his body. That's when Michael Coleman would finally die.

"Why can't I just fake it?" he had asked.

"Fake electrocution?" Murkoski had scorned. "I don't think so. We'll greatly reduce the other three shocks, but the first will knock you unconscious and stop your heart, so you won't have to worry about faking anything."

"And if you don't revive me in time?"

"We'll revive you. The assistant coroner will actually be one of our people. He'll roll you to the waiting ambulance and restart your heart in there. We have roughly six-and-a-half minutes. It will be close, but we can do it."

Coleman had not been reassured.

"Relax," Murkoski had grinned, "we've been practicing for days. You're too valuable to us to watch you go up in smoke."

Coleman didn't grin back. "No more surprises?" he had asked, looking into Murkoski's eyes, searching for the truth.

"No more surprises," Murkoski had answered solemnly. "We'll run you straight from the prison to Saint John's, where one of the top plastic surgeons in the country will make alterations."

"How much of my face will they change?"

"Enough that you won't be recognized. Might even fix that nose you're so proud of."

Coleman lightly touched his nose. It had been broken two, maybe three times in fights, and had not always been set with the greatest of care. "How long will all this take?"

"You'll be at the hospital a week to ten days. Then we fly you out to Washington State where you're set up with a nice job and an apartment."

They had discussed a thousand and one other details about the continuation of the experiment and what would be required of Coleman. But, in his usual insensitivity, Murkoski brought it down to the bottom line: "You're our guinea pig. We're giving you a second chance, and you owe us big. We won't ask much. Come into the lab once or twice a week for tests. But we're the boss, and whatever we say—"

"What if I get tired of it?" Coleman interrupted. "What if I decide to walk?"

Again Murkoski smiled, a smile Coleman was growing less and less fond of. "First of all, I doubt that a man of your

integrity would double-cross us like that, and second . . ."
Murkoski seemed to hesitate, unsure whether to continue.

Coleman pressed him. "And second?"

"And second, I've included a little chemical leash to insure that we'll always stay in touch."

"Leash?"

"Have you ever had the flu, Mr. Coleman?"

"Of course."

"Remember all those aches and pains? Well, those aches and pains don't really come from the flu virus. They come from your own immune system, from chemicals that your body releases called cytokines."

"What's that got to do—"

"During the bone-marrow transplant I took the liberty of altering your DNA in another area."

Coleman felt his anger rising. "You did *what?*"

"It was the only way to insure that you wouldn't, as you say, 'walk.'"

With effort, Coleman held his anger in check. "What did you do?"

"Actually, it's pretty basic. If you don't come in every five to six days for an injection, your own body will release so many cytokines that it'll make your worst flu experience seem like a picnic."

That conversation had taken place four days ago. And, although Coleman's anger had quickly subsided, his lack of trust for Murkoski had not. The youngster was ruthlessly ambitious.

Back in the yard, the sun was just rising. The bank of clouds resting on the horizon diffused it like a light behind fine china. Snow started falling again. Coleman tilted his head back and felt the cool flakes softly touch his face. Then Michael Coleman did something he had never done in his life. He closed his eyes, opened his mouth, and caught a snowflake on his tongue. It was incredible. Absolutely amazing. Joy spread through his chest, and he had to chuckle. If the boys back on the Row could only see him now.

"Cole?" The voice was quiet and considerate. "Coleman?"

Coleman lowered his head and opened his eyes. It was one of the guards standing in the open doorway to the administration building. "Hour's up. Sorry."

Coleman nodded. He turned and started crunching back through the snow toward the door. "Where to now?" he asked.

"Back to the hospital wing. That's where they'll keep you under observation until . . . well, until tonight."

Coleman nodded again, appreciating the man's sensitivity. He lifted up his face one last time and felt the cool flakes gently brush his cheeks. Then, lowering his head, he stepped back into the building for the very last time.


Sixteen hours later, Harold Steiner stuck his hands deep into his overcoat pockets to fight off the freezing night. It was 11:00 P.M., and despite the cold, he and three hundred other people stood in the prison parking lot, some of them in favor of capital punishment, others opposed. The two factions were separated by a simple snow fence and about a dozen state troopers, heavily armed and wearing riot gear. Michael Coleman had made quite an impression.

Steiner's side was the loudest—and drunkest. Chants went up every few minutes, ending in applause or slowly dying out. Some spectators waved signs and placards with such incredibly witty sayings as "HEY, COLE, IT'S *FRY*-DAY" or "LIGHT UP THEM COLES FOR A BBQ." The atmosphere outraged Steiner. Instead of an equitable and impartial execution of justice, these people were treating it like a sporting event.

The folks on the other side were no better. They cradled their candles and held their flashlights while praying and crying and singing. A mixed lot. Shallow thinkers, mostly. Religious do-gooders and knee-jerk emotionalists, more concerned about saving a diseased killer than preserving society. He knew that at least a dozen had been imported by Amnesty International, and probably that many more by the ACLU.

His side was just as diverse, including anticrime groups, good ol' boys looking for a good ol' time, and women's rights advocates. Yes, indeed. Capital punishment could make for some very strange bedfellows.

Steiner was disappointed that he was not being permitted to actually watch Coleman die. He blamed himself for that. After all, the man had played him like a fool. Coleman's performance at their meeting had quickly leaked out, and the media had had a grand old time. "Incensed Victim Confronts Broken Murderer," "Convicted Killer Has Change of Heart," "Cole Begs Forgiveness." The headlines and articles had all been variations on the same theme. Michael Coleman had finally seen the error of his ways, and now his victims, like Harold Steiner, were suddenly being cast as the guilty aggressors. The gall! Harold Steiner guilty? Of what? Of upholding the Law? Of honoring the only thing holding civilization together? If that was the charge, fine. Consider him guilty. He could think of no higher honor than being accused of maintaining the majesty of the Law.

Of course he'd heard all the arguments . . .

"What about mercy?" some demanded.

Mercy had its place. But no one seemed to remember Missy's own screaming for mercy as she was stabbed to death in her apartment.

"People change," opponents insisted. "The Michael Coleman you are executing today is not the same Michael Coleman who killed seven years ago."

Maybe so. Then again, who knew what type of person Missy would be if she had been allowed to live.

"Public execution does not deter murder."

A nonissue. For Steiner, capital punishment was more principle than practical. A line drawn in the sand that says you may go only so far in your attempts to unravel society, and no further.

Then there were the fringe arguments. The liberal Christians who insisted that the only time Jesus Christ commented on the death penalty was when he released the woman caught in adultery. Or the Jews, with their provisions in the Torah for forgiveness of the repentant. All valid arguments, he was sure. But it was one thing to live in the pristine world of theological theory, quite another to survive in an imperfect world that contained monsters who wanted to destroy it.

TV lights glared suddenly in the parking lot. Steiner craned his neck and caught a glimpse of someone trying to raise a swastika. It was quickly torn down.

The media. It was because of the media that he was out here in the cold instead of inside where he belonged. He'd expected Coleman to pull some sort of theatrics at their meeting; he just hadn't expected anything so extensive. Unfortunately, Coleman's dramatics had thrown Steiner back on the front page of the *World-Herald*—and straight to the bottom of the waiting list of those wanting to see Coleman die.

That was the bad news. The good news was that, no matter what spin the press put on it, or on him, the people of Nebraska were no different from the rest of the seventy-five percent of the nation who endorsed the death penalty. Since its reinstatement by the Supreme Court in 1976, nearly three hundred people had been executed—and that figure was rising quickly. By some estimates, the U.S. would soon be executing one hundred convicted killers a year. Not a lot when, last year alone, twenty-two thousand Americans were murdered (nearly thirteen times the death rate of England). But, again, it was a line in the sand. Some justice was better than no justice.

There was another stir in the crowd. "Look, it's Cole!"

"Isn't that Coleman? Right up there?"

Steiner looked toward the administration building, a hundred yards away. The second-story window to the far right had been lit all night. Rumor had it that this was hospital room 7, Coleman's holding room for the last twenty-four hours. And now, just on the other side of the horizontally barred window, there was the silhouette of a man—the outline of his head round and clean, as if it had been shaved.

Jeers and chants immediately rose from Steiner's side of the parking lot.

Waving candles and prayers from the other.

Steiner glanced at his watch. In fifty minutes, the circus would be over. Unless the three-person Board of Pardons granted last-minute clemency, the craziness of this evening, not to mention Steiner's seven-and-a-half years of suffering, would finally come to an end.

The process had been long and arduous. Nebraska law provides that any death sentence be automatically reviewed by the state supreme court. From there, Coleman had gone to the U.S. Supreme Court—but the justices had had the good sense to refuse to hear him, and the case had been returned to the original court for review. When that appeal failed, Coleman's lawyers once again brought him to the state supreme court, then the U.S. district court, and finally to the Eighth U.S. Circuit Court of Appeals in St. Louis. From there, they had again appealed to the U.S. Supreme Court.

Around and around they went, playing the justice system for every delay they could. Then one day, for whatever the reason, Coleman had suddenly had enough. He had fired his lawyers and refused any more appeals or hearings. Some thought he was trying for an insanity plea. (If you're crazy enough to want to die, you're obviously too crazy to die.) Others, like Steiner, thought he was up to something else. But whatever his plan, it had backfired. Now, unless the governor were suddenly to have a change of heart, unlikely in today's political climate, Coleman would soon be killed by electrocution.

Many states still executed with gas; a few even used firing squads and hanging. But more and more were turning to what was considered the most humane process: lethal injection. No pain. Just sleep. Too bad Missy couldn't have gone that way. Fortunately for her, Nebraska was one of eleven states still using the archaic, sometimes painfully inefficient electric chair.

Another song rose from the other side of the parking lot: "We Shall Overcome." The old Negro spiritual they had used during the civil-rights days. The comparison of civil liberties with the liberties of a convicted murderer filled Steiner with rage. But as the hymn softly rose from the parking lot, Steiner almost caught himself smiling. Let them sing. Let them cry. Let them pray. Michael Coleman would soon be dead. Justice may not be swift, but at least in this case, it would be inevitable.

"We've got a problem."

Murkoski turned from the door of hospital room 7 and looked into the hallway. It was Hendricks, the electrician he'd flown in from Genodyne. "What are you doing up here?" Murkoski asked. "You should be downstairs with the chair."

"We've got ourselves a major problem."

Murkoski frowned. They'd run through every possibility, every permutation, a dozen times. Not only had they recorded Coleman's response earlier that week, but they had continued the fine-tuning by using a fifty-five-gallon drum of water (somewhat similar in resistance to a 180-pound male). The chair had been recalibrated and retested, leaving nothing, absolutely nothing, to chance.

"What do you mean, *problem?*" Murkoski asked.

"See for yourself." Hendricks motioned toward Coleman, who was still standing at the window above the parking lot. "The man is as cool as a cucumber."

"Why shouldn't he be? After what we put him through last week, this is old news."

"It may be old news, but if he's this relaxed, it's going to completely invalidate our GSR measurements."

Murkoski's frown deepened.

Hendricks continued. "In this relaxed state, his body's resistance will be much higher than what we've calibrated the chair for."

"But you can change it, right?"

"If you don't mind guesswork. Here's the problem: If we keep the current as is, with his higher resistance, we may not be able to knock him out, let alone stop his heart."

"And if you increase the current?"

"We could go too far, and you'd have a real execution."

Murkoski nodded and felt a faint trace of coolness on his forehead. He'd just broken into a sweat. He forced himself to relax. The past few weeks had been hard but exhilarating. For the first time in his life, he felt as if he'd actually been able to use all of his mental capabilities. It was like playing several games of chess at once: securing state permissions, running security checks, producing bogus reports, monitoring Coleman's physical and mental state, running the electrical tests—all this under intense secrecy and the mounting pressure from his investors.

His decision was swift. "Increase it thirty percent."

"Thirty percent?" Hendricks whispered. "No, you're overcompensating. That's too much, you'll kill him."

"Thirty percent," Murkoski firmly repeated, then turned and headed for Coleman. Even though Hendricks was sure that the increase in voltage would be too much, Murkoski still wasn't satisfied. He was used to winning at any cost, even if it meant stacking the deck. And he was about to add a few more aces to the game.

He scowled. He hated working with people. Give him cold data, lab findings, clinical results, computer hypotheses. But introduce a human being into the mix, and suddenly the variables skyrocketed. Still, as with everything else in Murkoski's life, he was sure that he could improvise and overcome any surprise.

The most recent improvisation had been just last night. Everyone involved had agreed that, like the electrician, Ms. Irene Lacy, the county coroner, must also be replaced by someone from Genodyne. That replacement would be the one to hustle Coleman's body into the ambulance, revive him, sign the false autopsy report, and supply a John Doe body from the morgue for cremation and burial. Everyone had agreed, that is, except Ms. Irene Lacy. She was in no mood for an unplanned, three-day weekend. And when pressed on the issue, she had become hostile.

To smooth things over, Murkoski had invited her to dinner. Just the two of them. How could she refuse? After all, she was a single female, and he was the young and ever-so-good-looking Dr. Kenneth Murkoski. That she had agreed mostly out of curiosity had barely registered with him.

Over the French onion soup, he had explained how sorry he was that he couldn't divulge the details of this "matter of national security." Lacy had been unimpressed, and over the baked salmon she had questioned the legality of his plan.

He had been planning to wait until dessert to raise the monetary issue—ten thousand dollars tops—but decided early that there would be no point. He already knew her answer. Bullheaded, pragmatic, false sense of morality—people like that often said no and even feigned offense when someone tried to buy them. She might even try to file charges against him for bribery.

Murkoski had no choice. When she rose and excused herself to the lady's room, he reached into his finely tailored suit coat and removed a Visine bottle. Earlier that day, he had rinsed it and replaced its contents. Discreetly, he leaned over and measured out four drops of the new contents into her coffee. It would be undetectable, but the genetically altered botulism would multiply in her digestive tract until she was so sick she would be unable to go to work the following day.

That had been his fallback plan. But, now that he had spent an hour with her in conversation, Murkoski held the Visine bottle in his hand and reconsidered. She was a strong woman. Determined. Four drops would be enough to make her sick, but a die-hard like Lacy might insist on showing up for work anyway.

Murkoski reached over and poured another three drops, hesitated, and then added two more drops into her coffee. The cramps and nausea would be severe. Maybe lethal. Of course, the latter possibility wasn't his preference, but he had to be certain. There was too much riding on this. Regardless of the outcome, the tests would show that she had simply contracted an extreme case of food poisioning.

Murkoski felt little remorse as he watched her drink the coffee. It wasn't his fault that she'd been so uncooperative.

And now to the current problem of Coleman being too relaxed.

The convicted killer stood near the window saying final good-byes to three of his friends who would also serve as witnesses. He had no living relatives, at least no one who cared. And it had been agreed upon that none of these friends would be told the truth. For in reality, they really *were* saying good-bye. The Michael Coleman they knew would soon be dead. Regardless of whether the chair worked as expected or not, in a matter of minutes, this Michael Coleman would no longer exist.

On the other side of the room stood one of the prison physicians, a short, rotund man. Beside him, the remaining witnesses—four from the media and three from legal and law enforcement offices.

Before Murkoski could reach Coleman, he was interrupted by John Hulls, one of the associate wardens. The actual warden had been "called away" on out-of-state business. Hulls had known that something was up for weeks, but he had been instructed to carry out the execution to the letter, no questions asked. Despite the recent changes in personnel and Murkoski's free-reining presence at all the proceedings, Hulls, the prison physician, and the guards had been instructed to run the execution by the book. "Excuse me, ladies and gentlemen," he called. "May I have your attention? Excuse me, please."

The room settled down as Hulls unfolded a single piece of paper. "I have here the death warrant. I'm supposed to read it now."

The room grew even more quiet, and he began:

"To: the Warden of the Nebraska State Penitentiary, Lincoln, Nebraska, from the Supreme Court of Nebraska.

"Whereas, the Nebraska Supreme Court has released its opinion in this matter on January 2, directing the Clerk of the Supreme Court to issue her warrant, under the seal of this Court, to the Warden of the Nebraska State Penitentiary.

"Now, therefore, you are hereby commanded to proceed on Friday, January 14, between the hours of 12:01 A.M. and 11:59 P.M. to carry said sentence of death by electrocution into execution by causing the passage of an electric current through the body of Michael Hutton Coleman, until dead, as provided by law.

"You shall make return hereof of the manner of your execution to this warrant and of your doings thereon to the Clerk of the District Court of Douglas County, Nebraska.

"Signed, Brenda J. Elliott, Clerk of the Supreme Court."

Associate Warden Hulls folded the piece of paper and in a much less official tone added, "It's time to start wrapping up, folks. We'll be needing you witnesses to follow your escort to the observation room while we make final preparations up here."

Murkoski waited as Coleman said his last good-byes to his friends. He was impressed by the tears filling the man's eyes. Amazing. In just six weeks he, Kenneth Murkoski, had turned this killing machine into a compassionate, caring human being. And that was only the beginning. Regardless of whether the chair worked as planned or not, Pandora's box had been opened, and the world would never be the same again.

As Coleman finished his final set of hugs, Murkoski approached. "Excuse me, Mr. Coleman?"

Coleman wiped the tears from his eyes and looked at him. Murkoski was careful not to meet his gaze. Lately, the way the man searched and probed people's eyes, it was almost as if he knew what they were thinking. At this point, that would definitely be a disadvantage. He cleared his throat and continued. "I'm afraid we have a problem."

"A problem?"

"It's the power supply. There's a major glitch." He saw the rhythm of Coleman's breathing change. A good sign.

"What type of glitch?"

"I don't understand it all. It's something to do with switching to another power company. As you know, the local carrier feels it's bad publicity to be killing you with their juice, the same juice that goes on down the line and lights up somebody's home. We had to transfer to another company. But when we did, well, somehow the resistance has changed. I don't know the details, but now our readings are off."

He could feel Coleman's eyes searching him, and he was certain the man knew that he was lying. But that was okay. The details didn't matter, just as long as he thought he was being double-crossed, just as long as he thought he might actually die.

"You gave me your word." There was a faint trembling in Coleman's voice. Mostly anger. Hopefully a little fear. Things were getting better by the minute.

"Cole?" Associate Warden Hulls approached. "I'm afraid it's time."

Coleman's eyes darted to the associate warden, then to Murkoski, then back to the warden again. He was beginning to panic. "You gave me your word!" he repeated.

Murkoski shrugged. "These things happen." Then, turning, he headed for the door.

"You gave me your *word!*"

Murkoski said nothing. The past weeks of observing prison dynamics had taught him something about playing people.

"Murkoski!"

"Please, Mr. Coleman," the associate warden said, trying to calm him.

"Murkoski!"

"Cole—"

*"You gave me your word!"*

Murkoski stepped outside and let the blue metal door slam behind him. He headed down the hall and descended the stairs to the basement. In the control room, he joined Hendricks and William Pederson, the other Genodyne employee, a good-natured Norwegian from their medical staff who would serve as the substitute assistant county coroner.

The ancient transformer that filled most of the room looked like something from an old Frankenstein movie. It had been turned on at 11:15 and now hummed in ominous anticipation. Hendricks brooded over the machine as Pederson stood at the one-way glass, staring past the chair and into the witness room where the ten witnesses were nervously taking their seats. A guard at the door was discreetly offering them small paper bags, a precaution in case anyone got sick.

"Everything on schedule?" Murkoski asked.

Pederson nodded.

Hendricks didn't look up from his tinkering with the transformer. "I think you're making a mistake," was all he said.

"If necessary, can you cut it from a thirty percent increase down to a fifteen?" Murkoski asked.

"What's the point of doing all these tests and rehearsals if we're just going to keep guessing and shooting from the—"

"Can you cut it down to fifteen percent?"

Hendricks returned the curtness. "I can cut it any way you want it."

"Then do it." Without waiting for a reply, Murkoski turned toward Pederson. "Where's your stopwatch?"

Pederson pointed to the sports watch on his wrist.

"You've got six-and-a-half minutes."

Pederson nodded. "The ambulance is running. The defib is inside and charged. A backup is on standby."

"Good."

The elevator doors rattled open. Coleman, two guards, and the rotund prison doctor emerged. Once again Coleman's head was jelled and he was perspiring. Not like last week, but far more than before Murkoski's little lie. Murkoski refused to meet the convict's eyes as they silently escorted Coleman past him and into the execution chamber.

Murkoski and Hendricks joined Pederson at the one-way glass. The guards had closed the gold curtains between the death chamber and the witness room in case there was a struggle from Coleman. But he gave no resistance as they silently and efficiently strapped him in and buckled each of the nine buckles.

Murkoski tried to swallow, but his mouth was bone-dry. "What do you think?"

"What did you say to him?" Hendricks marveled. "He looks a lot worse."

"You think he's nervous enough, then?"

"I think even the fifteen percent could kill him now. Let me cut it back to—"

"No," Murkoski ordered. "Keep it as is."

"But—"

"Keep it as is," Murkoski repeated as he looked back out the window.

When the final strap was buckled, they reopened the curtains. The first row of witnesses sat ten feet from the glass, the second just behind them. Each could clearly see that it was Michael Hutton Coleman who was about to be executed.

Murkoski watched as Coleman looked each of the witnesses in the eye. The man seemed to be trying to comfort and encourage them. Murkoski was stunned. Coleman actually appeared more concerned over what *they* were about to experience than what *he* was about to face. Murkoski swore softly and gave an angry swipe at the sweat trickling down his own temples.

"I strongly recommend we cut it back to what we had," Hendricks said.

Murkoski gave no answer but took a deep breath to steady himself. Through the glass he could hear the associate warden asking whether Coleman had any last words.

"We might fry him," Hendricks warned.

Murkoski took another breath.

"I'm serious. I know what I'm talking about."

Murkoski gave no answer.

Pederson reached for his watch, preparing to start it.

Coleman was saying something to the assistant warden, but Murkoski couldn't hear.

"Come on," Hendricks insisted.

The guards closed the curtains and quickly and efficiently attached the electrodes to Coleman's head and his left calf. When these were secure, they finally placed the leather mask over his face—a crude affair with a V cut out for the nose. But it didn't quite fit, and it flattened the cartilage against Coleman's face. Most thought the mask served as a courtesy for the condemned, allowing them to face their final moment in privacy. Prison officials understood that it was to spare the witnesses from the condemned's expression as 2,400 volts surged through his body.

Hendricks crossed toward the rotary switch at the far end of the transformer. Murkoski felt the man's eyes still on him. "He deserves a break," Hendricks insisted. "After all he's done for us, he deserves a break."

Murkoski continued wrestling with the pros and cons. If the current was too weak, the doctor, the guards, the associate warden, the media, the witnesses—somebody would suspect something was wrong. There would be questions that would have to be answered, questions that might expose either the experiment or Murkoski's superiors.

Too much current, and Coleman would be killed. They would have to start over from scratch.

The curtains reopened and the associate warden stepped out of the execution chamber, closing the door behind him.

"Come on," Hendricks whispered harshly.

Murkoski stared at the masked form, sitting on the other side of the glass, three feet away.

The assistant warden appeared in the doorway and nodded to Hendricks. Hendricks saw him but did nothing as he stared at Murkoski's back, waiting.

Finally Murkoski made his decision. Ever so slowly he shook his head. The answer was no.

Hendricks stared in disbelief.

"Gentlemen?" the associate warden called softly from the doorway.

Hendricks did not move.

"Gentlemen?" the associate warden repeated.

Murkoski turned to Hendricks. Clearly and firmly he whispered, "Keep it as is."

Hendricks scowled, reached for the black rheostat knob, then hesitated.

"Do we have a problem?" the associate warden asked.

"Keep it as is," Murkoski repeated.

Hendricks's grip on the rheostat tightened as he held Murkoski's gaze. Both men were perspiring.

"Come on, boys," Pederson warned, "let's do something here."

At last Hendricks obeyed. Refusing to take his eyes from Murkoski, he turned the knob.

The machine made a dull thud as the electricity surged.

Coleman's body jerked violently, but the straps held him in place. His hands clenched into fists, and his feet pulled back out of his slippers.

Murkoski heard the tiny beep as Pederson set his stop watch. He glanced at his own. It read 12:18.

The first jolt of electricity ended and Coleman's body slumped. There was no movement except for a few drops of sweat falling from his face.

He had stopped breathing.

Thirty seconds later, Hendricks fired a tiny fraction of the first voltage through the body. Another thirty-second pause, followed by another weak charge. And one final pause followed by one last charge.

Murkoski glanced at his watch. 12:20. The process had taken just under two minutes. They had four and a half left.

According to the schedule, the prison doctor was now supposed to move into the chamber, take Coleman's pulse, and declare him dead. Murkoski looked out into the hallway. The doctor stood by the chamber door but was not opening it. "What's the holdup?" Murkoski called.

"I'm not going in yet," the doctor said, waving his hand in front of his nose, indicating that he expected to find the acrid smell of burning flesh inside.

Murkoski threw Pederson a look, and the phony assistant moved to action. "If you're not, I am," he said heading out of the control room and toward the chamber.

"What do you think you're doing?" the doctor complained. "That's *my* job."

"Then do it."

"What's the hurry? He's not going anywhere."

"I am," Pederson said. He had arrived at the chamber door and was reaching for the handle. "I've got work to do, and I don't plan to be up all night."

"All right, all right," the doctor grumbled. He reached for the stethoscope in his pocket. "You're new, aren't you? With that attitude you won't be making many points around here, I can tell you that." Pederson gave no answer as the doctor pushed past him and opened the door.

Murkoski glanced at his watch: 12:21.

Three-and-a-half minutes left. Time was running out, and they hadn't even unstrapped Coleman. He looked back out through the glass. The doctor had entered the chamber and hovered over the body, taking his own sweet time. Putting on a show, no doubt, for the reporters in the witness room. After listening to the chest, he pulled the stethoscope from his ears and nodded to the witnesses. Michael Hutton Coleman was dead.

Murkoski looked to his watch. Another minute and a half had slipped by. That left two.

The doctor stepped out of the room and the two guards moved in, closing the curtain and unstrapping Coleman's dead body. Pederson was right behind, urging them to hurry as they lifted the body, hustled it out of the room, and laid it on the gurney in the hallway.

Fifty-five seconds.

"This is unprecedented!"

Murkoski glanced up. It was the doctor again.

"There's no need for this reckless haste. This is how mistakes are made." He had stopped the gurney, blocking its path with his body. "I don't understand what's going on. What is the hurry? The man is *dead.*"

Murkoski was grateful to see Pederson move into action. The man knew how to take advantage of his considerable Norwegian bulk. He shoved the doctor against the wall. "You did your job," he growled, "now let me do mine." Then, taking the gurney himself, he shoved it onto the elevator, pressed the button, and stood glowering as the doors lumbered shut.

Murkoski glanced at his watch. Twenty seconds.

"Did you see that?" The doctor turned to the others. "Did you see what he did? That was completely unprofessional. There is no excuse for that type of behavior. What is his name? It'll be in my report, I guarantee you that. This sort of thing cannot go unreported. What is his name?"

Murkoski watched and listened—realizing that he would have to invite the good doctor out to a special dinner as well.


Harold Steiner walked the dirt road alongside the prison as he headed toward the Sutherland Lumber parking lot where he and most of the demonstrators had left their cars.

It was over. Finally. All of it. But, unlike the others, he didn't cheer, light firecrackers, or pray. Instead, he was struck by a peculiar emptiness that he didn't understand. Everything he had worked and sweated over for so many years had finally come to pass. He had won. Justice had been served. And yet he felt so hollow, so empty. Probably just exhaustion. Yet, somehow, he suspected that it was more.

An ambulance bounced out of a side gate, spitting gravel as it turned, then raced past him. He watched, puzzled. No doubt, this was the ambulance taking Coleman's body to the mortuary. But what was the hurry? Steiner slowed to a stop and watched as the vehicle slid around another corner and sped out of sight.

Something wasn't right. In a few days, after he'd rested, he'd have to ask. In the meantime, he stuffed his hands back into his overcoat and continued down the road.

# PART
# TWO

# CHAPTER 8

Do you need a hand with that?"

Katherine's response was swift and accurate. Before she had even finished her startled scream, she swung around the garbage can she'd been emptying into the dumpster and struck her assailant hard in the face. His sunglasses flew off, and he staggered backward until he hit the wall of the building. His head struck the bricks with a melonlike thud, and he crumpled unconscious to the alley.

Eric raced out the back entrance of the computer store. "Mom! Mom, are you okay?"

Katherine nodded to reassure him as she tried to catch her breath. The unconscious man wore a crisp white shirt and a designer tie. At the moment, he didn't look much like the mugger she had taken him for.

Eric kept his distance from the motionless form. "Do you . . ." He swallowed hard. "Do you think you killed him?"

Katherine cautiously walked toward the body. "Go to the bathroom and get me some wet paper towels."

Eric didn't move.

"Now."

He backed through the door, unwilling to take his eyes off the man.

Cautiously, she knelt down to investigate. He was a handsome man. Rugged, closely cut dark hair, late thirties. And the way he filled out his shirt and slacks indicated that he definitely knew how to take care of himself. In fact, except for the faint trickle of blood escaping out of the corner of his mouth, he was an excellent specimen of manhood. Another reason for Katherine to mistrust him.

He stirred slightly. She waited and watched. His face was weathered, with a trace of acne scars across the cheekbones. But it was the bruises around both of his eyes that confirmed her suspicions. Either this man was a prizefighter, or he had just undergone plastic surgery. She suspected the latter, and with that suspicion came the dull realization that she had just decked her new employee. The Witness Protection Agency had said that he would arrive around 4:00 that afternoon. She glanced at her watch. It was 3:59.

She swore to herself and shouted back into the store. "What's the holdup? Where are the towels?"

"We're all out."

"Try under the sink."

She had been told his name was William Michaels—an alias, of course—and that she would have no other obligation to him than providing work. Other than that, he was on his own. She hoped so. The less involvement with somebody like this, the better.

Eric raced out the door and handed her several dry paper towels. "Here."

"You didn't soak them?"

"I forgot."

Katherine sighed and took them. She began dabbing the blood off the man's face.

Eric scooted in closer and watched with awe. "You really clobbered him, didn't you?"

"People shouldn't sneak up on other people," she answered. "It's not polite."

At last the man's eyes began to move under his lids. Finally they opened. They were good eyes, so brown they almost looked black. And even in their state of confusion, Katherine could see a gentle sensitivity in them.

"Are you okay?" she asked.

He winced, trying to move. "Yeah." Raising his hand to explore his cheek, he asked, "Was that aluminum or plastic?"

"What?"

"The garbage can. Felt like aluminum."

Katherine almost smiled but was quick to cover with an admonition: "You shouldn't go sneaking up on people like that."

He nodded and rose to one elbow, again wincing in pain. "I think you made that pretty clear." He struggled to sit. Katherine started to help, but caught herself. He glanced around the alley, still trying to get his bearings.

"Are you William Michaels?" she asked.

He frowned, then smiled, remembering. "Right, right, William Michaels. I'm not crazy about the name. And I hate Bill. But Will's okay." With some effort he extended his hand. "Call me Will."

She shook his hand. It was warm and strong. "I'm Katherine Lyon, Mr. Michaels."

"And I'm Eric."

The man looked to his right and managed to smile. "Hi, Eric."

The boy stared at him.

"Giving your mom a hand at the store today?"

"I'm here every day. You know anything about computers?"

"No. I've, uh, I've been out of circulation for a while, but I'm willing to learn."

The boy sounded disappointed. "Oh."

"Maybe you can teach me."

"Sure." Eric shrugged, then rose and quietly headed for the door.

Katherine watched the man watching her son. Again she noticed the eyes. Not only were they sensitive, they were also vulnerable. Just a little too open, just a little too wide. Poor guy. Obviously he hadn't yet experienced the uglier sides of life, the struggling, the taking, the abusing. But he would. No one could escape it forever. The knowledge seemed to sadden her just a little.

"Listen, do you want a glass of water or something?" she asked.

"No, I'll be fine."

"Well," she said, rising to her feet, "if you're sure you're okay."

He took his cue and started to rise.

"It was good of you to stop by. But you're not scheduled to start work till Monday, so go get yourself settled in, and we'll see you then."

He nodded, locking his eyes firmly onto hers. It was an unnerving sensation, almost like he was trying to read her thoughts. She accepted the look as a challenge and rose to the occasion. "I'm your employer, you're my employee. That's it. If you've got personal problems, I don't want to hear about them. As you've probably been told, I'm not crazy about this setup, but the money's good, so there you have it."

"I understand."

She shifted uneasily. What was he looking at? What did he see? "All right, then. You're welcome to come in and clean up, but if you'll excuse me, I've got work to do." She turned and headed toward the door.

"Do you need a hand?"

She turned and faced him.

"I mean for the rest of the day—do you need some help with anything?"

"No, Mr. Michaels, I don't need any help. We have everything under control." With that she headed back into the store. She wasn't sure what about him flustered and irritated her. It didn't matter. She had established the boundaries. And if he had any doubts about the consequences of crossing them, the newly acquired cut on his mouth should serve as a reminder.

"Julie, how come your knapsack is moving?" O'Brien stood in the open doorway of their two-story colonial home, blinking at the knapsack that lay on the entry hall tile. Something was inside it, and by the looks of things it wanted to be outside in the worst possible way. "Julie?"

But Julie didn't hear. She was upstairs with her mother and sister, making frantic, last-minute preparations for the trip. The family's flight to Mazatlán was scheduled to leave Sea-Tac at seven that evening, and at the moment it would be nip and tuck whether they could make the seventy-minute drive to the airport in time.

"Who took my Barbie car?" Julie's voice cried from upstairs. "Where's my Barbie car?"

"You're not taking your Barbie car," Beth called. "There's no room. Sarah, did you brush your teeth? Sarah?"

"They're just going to get dirty again."

"But Sarah's taking her ant farm," Julie whined.

"She's what?"

"You little snitch!"

"You're taking *what?*"

O'Brien looked back at the knapsack. It was growing more frisky. "Uh, guys," he called. "Guys, what's in this backpack?"

By now Julie had broken into tears and Sarah was in her best preteen, nobody's-taking-me-seriously form. "Why *can't*

I take my ant farm? It's science. I need to see if ants act differently in different countries."

O'Brien thought of calling again but knew it would be futile. As with most of these family outings, he was pretty much along just for the ride. Beth was the one in charge. And that was fine with him. Both of them knew that he would never give the family one hundred percent of his attention. Oh, he tried—but his absentmindedness made it clear that part of him was always back at the lab somewhere. It was another sacrifice Beth had made in their marriage; another crack in the widening rift of their relationship.

The knapsack gave a desperate lunge. That was enough. O'Brien reached down and carefully unlaced the string tie. The neighbor's kitten, the one Julie had been adoring for the past week, hopped out of the bag and made a mad dash past him and out the door. O'Brien watched, realizing that it would probably be good to have another talk with his youngest about honesty.

The phone rang. He hesitated. The car was nearly loaded and already warming up in the driveway. In just a few minutes they'd be gone. Three weeks of rest and relaxation and some much-needed time with his family. Better to let the service pick up.

It rang a second time. Julie continued crying, Sarah continued demanding, and Beth was doing her best to deal with both. "Philip, will you answer that?"

"Let it go," he called.

"Mother, are you listening to me?"

A third ring.

"It might be the Wilson boy," Beth shouted. "He's taking care of the animals while we're gone. He was supposed to call back."

It rang a fourth time. Against his better judgment, O'Brien walked to the end table and picked up the receiver.

The answering machine had already kicked in with Beth's cheery and concise message: *"Sorry. We're out, but you're on."* The machine beeped, and O'Brien heard a voice cough slightly on the other end.

"Dr. O'Brien." It was Wolff. O'Brien listened silently. "I'm sorry to call you at home like this, but I wanted to flag you before you left."

"Hi, Wolff."

"Dr. O'Brien, thank God you're still there."

"We're just heading out the door. What's up?"

"I think we've got a problem."

O'Brien closed his eyes. "More dead mice?"

"No. Worse."

"Wolff, I'm on vacation. Murkoski is back. His man Coleman is in the area now. If you have a problem, talk to Murkoski."

There was a pause.

"Wolff?"

"Yeah, uh, I did. About forty-eight hours ago."

"And?"

"I think that's part of our problem. Look, can you come to the lab?"

"Wolff—"

Beth and the kids had clambered down the stairs and were dragging the last of their suitcases past him toward the door when she asked, "Who is it?"

O'Brien rolled his eyes, indicating that he was trying to get rid of the caller.

"I've run some new gels," Wolff was saying. "I've run them several times."

"Who?" she whispered.

"Work," he mouthed.

She sighed heavily, then turned to children. "All right, you two, get in the car, I'll be right there."

Wolff continued. "And I'm getting some bizarre results."

O'Brien covered his free ear to hear over the commotion. "What do you mean, *bizarre?*"

"I'm not certain, but things aren't as they appear."

"And you can't tell Murkoski, because . . ."

"Because I think he's the reason."

O'Brien said nothing. He saw Beth watching, anticipating the worst. Wolff's silence was articulate, insisting there was a crisis that only O'Brien could solve. The back of his neck started to ache. He turned slightly, cutting Beth from his sight.

"Dr. O'Brien? Are you there?"

He could feel Beth's presence, silent, critical.

He closed his eyes.

"Dr. O'Brien?"

"All right." He sighed. "Listen, I'm going to run my family down to the airport and get them on the plane. Then I'm going to come back up. But so help me, Wolff, if this is something Murkoski or someone else could have handled—"

"I don't think it is, Dr. O'Brien. Not this time."

O'Brien rubbed his neck. "All right. I'll see you later this evening. Oh, and call my office, have Debra book me on the next available flight to Mazatlán."

"Right."

"Have her do that immediately." The urgency was for Beth's sake, but he knew it wouldn't help.

"Will do. Thanks, Dr. O'Brien."

"Yeah." O'Brien slowly hung up the phone. Then, even more slowly, he turned to face his wife.


Steiner eased his Volvo into the parking lot of St. John's Hospital. The winter sky was a vivid blue, and the sun hung just low enough to stab into his eyes, heightening his headache and making him wince. He had some serious doubts about this meeting. Gabriel Perez was just an orderly, and he could barely speak English. Still, experience had taught him that occasionally it's the little guy, the one everybody ignores, who becomes the unseen eyes and the forgotten ears. That's what Steiner was banking on now. Maybe lightning would strike here, as it had two days before in the cemetery.

Steiner still wasn't entirely sure why he had visited Coleman's grave. It was partly to assure himself that it was over, that the ordeal could finally be put to rest. But there was something more. He couldn't put his finger on it, but he was searching for a type of peace. Because, as much as he tried to will it, peace would not come. True, some of his pain had been excised on that early January morning, in that nine-by-nine, cinder-block execution chamber. But the death of pain, the absence of hurt, is a far cry from the presence of peace.

It was different with Theresa, his wife. Somehow she had been able to let go, to let the healing begin. Not Steiner.

Of course he had tried. But there was a problem: The harder he tried to push the anger and resentment out of his mind, the more the images of Missy began to slip away. And that was unacceptable. If the two had become that inter-twined, if he couldn't forget the one without forgetting the other, then so be it. If anger and resentment had become the only way he could remember his daughter, then he would hang on to that anger and resentment regardless of the cost.

Those had been his thoughts as he stood in the county burial section of Holben Cemetery—as he stood gazing down at the ten-inch-by-ten-inch plot that held Coleman's ashes. In fact, he had been so preoccupied that he had barely noticed the caretaker's approach.

"Friend o' yours?" the man had asked.

Steiner had looked up, startled. The old-timer was gray and grizzled and immediately began coughing up a large wad of phlegm. When he spit it out, it was nearly the size of a sil-ver dollar. "Sure caused a stir, didn't he?" the man said as he wiped his chin.

Steiner watched with mild disgust but said nothing. He turned back toward the tiny plot, hoping that the old fellow would leave. He didn't. Apparently he was a talker and didn't get much opportunity to do so out in this older section, espe-cially in the middle of winter.

"Even when we put him down. Never seen such commo-tion over a pile o' ashes. Like they thought he was gonna rise from the dead."

Steiner looked at him. "What do you mean?"

"Some big fella from the coroner's office, he was a-hoverin' and a-stewin' over everything."

"Some people like to be thorough."

"S'pose. 'Cept once a fella's dead, he's s'posed to be dead. The coroner folks, they usually just turn the body over to the mortuary, and they take it from there. But not this time. No, sir, this guy hangs around from start to finish, like he can't be sure enough we'll get him in the ground."

That's what had started the wheels turning. That and the rushing ambulance Steiner had seen the night of the execution.

The following day he had visited the prison, but found nothing—though he did hear of the prison doctor's fatal bout with food poisoning, and about the presence of a couple of scientist types who were said to have had a morbid fascination with the execution process. Other than that, nothing unusual.

It was only after Steiner made a call to the coroner's office that his suspicions really began to take on substance.

"I'm sorry," the clerk had said, "we're still a little disorganized after Ms. Lacy's death."

Steiner had read of the death in the *World-Herald* but had given it little thought. "There must be some record," he had insisted. "Whose signature is on the autopsy report?"

"That's just it. I mean the report is all filled out and everything, but . . ."

"But what?"

"Well, none of us recognize the signature."

Images of that racing ambulance came to mind.

After a handful of calls to Lincoln hospitals, Steiner had information on all the emergency admittances during the early morning hours of January 14th. It had been a light night. There had been only three. A gunshot and a passing kidney stone at Lincoln General. And a burn victim here at St. John's.

Steiner pulled his car into an open stall, stepped out, and crossed the hospital's parking lot. The sun continued to glare, and his head continued to pound.

Fifteen minutes later he was sitting in the cafeteria of St. John's, staring hard at the steam rising from his Styrofoam cup. He never drank coffee, he hated it. But it was important for the orderly across the table to feel relaxed, and "Let's grab some coffee" had sounded as informal as anything Steiner could think of.

"What about special treatment?" Steiner asked. "Do you recall anyone who may have been, say, treated differently from other patients?"

Gabriel Perez, a young Nicaraguan, scrunched his thick eyebrows into a furrow of thought.

"No hurry," Steiner encouraged. "We've got plenty of time."

At last Perez cleared his throat. "I, uh—there was one, in the burn wing. They treat him like he was very special."

Steiner looked on, trying to hide his interest.

"No one was allowed in or out. Not even to clean and bring meals."

Steiner leaned forward. "How long was he here?"

"A week, maybe two. I don't remember."

"What about a name? Do you remember a name?"

He shook his head. "No."

"Did you ever see him? Can you describe what he looked like?"

"No, he was a burn victim. His face, it was all bandaged."

"What about visitors? Do you remember anybody?"

"No."

Steiner fought back his frustration. There had to be something. "How'd he get home? Who picked him up?"

"I do not ..." Perez hesitated, scowling at the table, trying to remember. "Some young man. Expensive suit, dark hair."

"Ever hear a name?"

"No."

"What type of car did he drive?"

Another frown. "I am sorry." He looked back up at Steiner. "That is all I remember."

"Are you sure?"

He thought another moment and shrugged. "I am sorry."

Another dead end. Steiner nodded and rose to his feet. "Well, thank you for your time, Mr. Perez. And if anything else should come to mind"—he pulled a card from his jacket—"please, give me a call."

Perez rose, nodded, then turned to leave.

Steiner was disappointed. Of course he would go downstairs and check the hospital records, but he knew he would find nothing there. Either there was nothing to find, or else those obvious tracks would already be covered. He reached for his briefcase. Somewhere, there'd have to be another lead. It couldn't be over yet, not until—

"Excuse me?"

Steiner looked up. Perez stood three tables away.

"The reason I could not remember his car?"

"Yes?"

"It was because he did not have one."

"I'm sorry?"

"He and the man in the expensive suit, they took a taxi." Steiner's eyes sparked to life. "A taxi? Are you sure?"

"Yes. I wheeled him out, and they got into a taxi. That is why I could not remember the car. They took a taxi."

"Which one? Did it have a name—do you remember the name of the company?"

"No, but we have only two taxi companies in this town."

"Thank you, Mr. Perez."

"That is helpful?"

"Yes, more helpful than you can imagine."


Coleman enjoyed Katherine's company. And, though she was careful not to show it, he sensed that she was growing more comfortable with his. He was glad that Genodyne had persuaded him to give in and let her drive him the twenty or so miles from south Everett up I–5 to Arlington. He'd been resistant and defensive when they'd first questioned his driving skills. It was true that he hadn't been behind the wheel of a car for several years, but they were also skeptical of his driving record—a record showing definite signs of irresponsibility and recklessness. "You're just too expensive an investment to end up as roadkill," Murkoski had said. By itself, that argument had carried little weight with Coleman, who hated to rely on anyone and would have preferred to drive himself. But once he'd experienced the dizziness and vertigo that accompanied the treatments, and had considered the prospect of driving home in that condition, Coleman had given in to their demands.

So, with Eric in school, and after some lively negotiating on a price, Katherine had agreed to make the weekly run up to Genodyne for Coleman's checkup and injection to control the viral leash.

Arlington was a picturesque town of five thousand people with a main street seven blocks long and a single stoplight. Nestled at the foot of the Cascades, its east side was surrounded by the mountains, while its west was flanked by dairy farms—creating an interesting population of farmers, lumberjacks, and service industries to support them both. But, like so many small Pacific Northwest towns, the farms were giving way to housing developments, and the loggers were having a harder and harder time finding trees that didn't house spotted owls.

Amidst the sawmills, dairy cows, and newly constructed homes lay the Arlington Municipal Airport. Surrounding the airport was the usual industrial complex with dozens of manufacturers who had fled big-city hassles and big-city bureaucracies for a calmer, more bucolic life. One of these industries was Genodyne, housed in a two-building, six-story complex.

"Why two buildings?" Katherine asked, after Coleman had finished his first checkup and they were receiving a somewhat grandiose tour of the facilities by Murkoski. "Why not put all of this into one?"

"More FDA red tape," Murkoski explained. "They insist that our manufacturing plant, which is a quarter mile away, be completely separate from this, our administration and research division. Guess they're afraid our multimillion-dollar creations from research are going to sneak out and hop into one of our manufacturing vats. Not that you can blame them. When it comes to what the more gifted of us are able to do in biotechnology these days, I suppose just about anything's possible."

Coleman had the distinct impression that the kid was trying to impress Katherine. Of course, that only made her less receptive, which made Murkoski try all the harder, and the cycle continued until the bottom line became apparent to all: The great Murkoski was going down in flames.

Coleman smiled quietly. It was true, he liked Katherine a lot. But it was far more than just her beauty or her in-your-face honesty. Underneath the abrasive, tough facade, he saw a tender, sensitive heart. He wasn't sure what all had happened to her—she was careful to maintain a wall between them—but during his few opportunities to look past the barricade, he was able to see it. There was something rare and precious inside. Something pure. And something terribly, terribly frightened.

This ability to sense a person's thoughts and innermost feelings had rapidly increased since his first treatment back in December. At times it almost made him feel psychic, as he picked up on things no one else seemed to notice. Then again, maybe there was nothing mystical about it at all. Maybe he was simply so alive that he was able to see the details he had previously overlooked—a quiver in the voice, a nervous shift in the eyes, little mannerisms that he had been either too self-absorbed or too frightened to notice before. He didn't understand how it was happening. All he knew was that the ache and loneliness he saw inside other people removed any fear he might have had of them. And without that fear, he felt something he had never felt before the experiment began: compassion.

Coleman, Katherine, and Murkoski walked across the first-floor atrium with its palm trees and waterfall. They took the elevator to the third floor. When the doors opened, they stepped into the hallway and Murkoski motioned somewhat grandly. "These are my labs," he said. "Eight teams of the finest researchers on the West Coast."

He reached for the nearest door and threw it open with a flourish. A handful of researchers, youngsters barely out of grad school, hovered over their cluttered, black Formica workstations. Above their heads were cupboards with glass doors holding a variety of clean, orange-capped tubes and bottles. Beside them were Lucite electrophoresis boxes and power supplies, racks of Eppendorf pipettes, and centrifuges.

"This is where it all happens," Murkoski said. "This is where we rearrange the building blocks of life—changing and fixing creation's blunders." He crossed toward a common household refrigerator and opened the door. Inside were rows and rows of tiny Eppendorf tubes. He took one from the top shelf and held it up to the light for them.

"See that milky white substance? That's what it's all about. That's DNA."

"That's human DNA?" Coleman asked in quiet awe.

Murkoski scoffed. "DNA is DNA. It doesn't matter whether it comes from humans or monkeys or slugs or bacteria. It's always the same four building blocks, regardless of the animal. It's simply a matter of how they are arranged." He replaced the tube and shut the refrigerator door. "And here, in these labs, is where we cut the DNA apart, splice in different sequences, and put it back together again."

"What are these other rooms for?" Katherine asked, pointing to a closed doorway nearby.

Murkoski smiled. Finally she was paying some attention. "Let me show you."

At first Coleman had been surprised at how candid Murkoski had been with Katherine regarding the project. The only secret he had felt necessary to maintain was Coleman's past identity. He had no qualms about her knowing the rest. "After all," he had said, "she's a part of the team now." And then, with a flirtatious smile, he had added, "And a very attractive member at that."

They stepped into a smaller room. There were no people, only the quiet hum of the air-conditioning and a few electronic apparatuses at work. Some were the size of dishwashers, others the size of coffins.

"Once we redesign the DNA, we have to grow it," Murkoski explained. "That's what these little babies are about." He rested his hand on what could almost pass as a large copy machine.

"Bacteria divide, splitting into two every twenty minutes. That's why we use it as our primary workhorse. First we insert the new DNA into the bacteria. Then we put the bacteria into these incubators, where we provide it with the perfect nutrients, temperature, and climate to make it multiply as quickly as possible." He turned to Coleman. "Hard to believe, isn't it? Everything you've become, you owe to microscopic bacteria inside these machines."

Before Coleman could respond, Murkoski turned and escorted them into the next room. "Once we've grown enough of the DNA, we inject it into various organisms to see how they will react. Sometimes we inject it into cells themselves, which we store in these −70-degree freezers here, or into mice, or"—he threw what could be a contemptuous smile in Coleman's direction—"human guinea pigs."

Instead of growing angry, Coleman felt a strange pity for the kid. Was he really that insecure? Was he really that lonely and afraid and—what else? There was something else going on inside Murkoski that Coleman couldn't quite put his finger on. In any case, when their eyes connected, Murkoski's grin faded, and he glanced away.

He turned and escorted them into the next room.

"What are these?" Katherine asked. She pointed to a number of shallow trays with clear Plexiglas covers and red-and-black electrical terminals at either end.

"Those are the gel boxes. This is where we perform what we call electrophoresis." Katherine seemed interested, and Murkoski rushed to offer more. "Each gene is a different size.

When a current of electricity is passed through them, they move through a special gel at different rates according to their size—the gel is more resistant to bigger genes, making them move slower, and less resistant to smaller genes, allowing them to move faster. When electrical current is run through them, they move across the gel at different rates, forming very specific and definitive patterns of bands."

"Those bands, they're what the police use to identify people?" Katherine asked.

"Precisely. Genes have their own distinct banding patterns. You can never mistake one for another. Never."

There was something about the way Murkoski emphasized *never* that caught Coleman's attention. Again, he didn't really understand it, but there was something here, something that upset Murkoski, something that made him uneasy.

"Now, if you don't mind," he said, herding them into the next room, "let me show you something that I think you, especially, Ms. Lyon, will find interesting. You said you worked with computers?"

"Yeah, I worked computers for the defense department. Back in the NORAD days."

"Well, take a look at this." Murkoski motioned to a piece of beige equipment on the counter. It stood three-and-a-half-feet high by two-and-a-half-feet wide. Beside it, a computer screen glowed with row after row of multiple-colored bands. "This is our ABI PRISM 373 DNA Sequencer. In many ways, these are our brains. We have lots of these beauties scattered throughout the complex."

Katherine stepped in for a closer look. "A DNA sequencer?"

"Yes."

"What does it do?"

"Remember those gels in the last room?"

"Yes."

"These automatically read them. They record the bands, label the gene, hold it in memory, then fire it off to our main computer."

Coleman watched as Katherine examined the computer and equipment. For the first time that he could remember, she appeared totally absorbed, at peace—almost happy. She seemed to lose herself as she poked, prodded, and explored the fascinating new machine. And as he watched her face fill with awe, he began to experience her wonder himself. He knew nothing about the equipment she was examining, but it didn't matter. Not only was he able to feel people's pain, he was also able to experience their joy.

Unfortunately, the moment was short-lived.

"Dr. Murkoski!" A young technician burst into the room, a look of urgency on his face.

Murkoski turned, angry at the interruption. "What is it?"

"B–11, we have an emergency."

Murkoski's attitude instantly changed. "It's not Freddy, is it?"

"I tried to beep you, but you didn't—"

Murkoski pulled up his beeper, looked at it, then threw it to the floor in disgust. Without a word, he raced out the door, the technician on his heels.

Coleman and Katherine looked at each other. Neither was sure what to do, but since neither wanted to be abandoned in this labyrinth of labs, they hurried after the other two.

Murkoski moved briskly down the hall. He took the stairs two at a time, then crossed the atrium. Coleman and Katherine managed to keep him in sight down another long hallway until they finally arrived at the open doorway to B–11.

Two paramedics hovered over a body lying on grassy sod. One checked for a pulse while the other squirted goop over the paddles of a heart defibrillator. A handful of Genodyne staff gathered around, watching. In the far corner, clinging to a dead tree and shaking it, a baboon screamed hysterically.

"Who is it?" Murkoski shouted as he raced toward the group. "What happened?"

"It's Wolff," one of the staff called back.

Coleman and Katherine moved closer as the paramedic placed the paddles on the chest and yelled, "Clear!"

There was a faint thud as the body convulsed. The baboon barked and screamed louder. Murkoski scowled at the animal and demanded, "Was Freddy part of this?"

"They were just playing," someone said, "roughhousing, and suddenly Wolff keeled over."

"Cardiac arrest," the first paramedic explained.

Murkoski scoffed, "A heart attack? He's young, he's in great shape—look at him!"

A chill swept over Coleman. There was something about Murkoski's tone. Even over the animal's shrieking and screaming, Coleman could hear a falseness in Murkoski's voice. Something was wrong. Terribly wrong.

"He's back!" the second paramedic shouted.

All heads turned toward Wolff as he began coughing up a clear pink fluid. His eyes fluttered, then opened. He was searching, desperately looking for something. But it lasted only a moment before the eyes quit moving. Now they simply stared. And it was that expression that brought the cold sweat onto Coleman's face, making his mouth fill with salty brine.

"Hey, are you all right?" He looked up and saw Katherine. Though she tried to hide it, there was no missing the concern in her face. "You don't look so hot."

He nodded. "Yeah, I just have to sit down a—" But he was unable to finish the phrase before he doubled over and threw up. He wretched once, twice, three times, spewing vomit onto the freshly lain sod.

"Get him out of here!" the paramedic shouted. "Someone get him out of here!"

He felt Katherine take his arm and direct him toward the door. They had to stop one more time as his stomach contracted with another set of heaves. At last he was able to rise and make it out into the hallway, as the shrieks and screams of the baboon continued to echo inside the room.

# CHAPTER 9

First time you've seen somebody die?" Katherine asked as they headed back down the freeway toward Everett.

Coleman looked out the passenger window. "I've seen a lot of death," he answered quietly. "It wasn't his dying that hit me. It was the expression on his face."

Katherine nodded, thinking she understood. "That *how-could-this-be-happening-to-me* look?"

"No, it wasn't that." Coleman continued to stare out the window. "That wasn't his question."

Katherine glanced at him. "What do you mean—what was it then?"

Coleman slowly turned to face her. "The man was not asking why he was dying. He was asking why he had ever lived."

The statement stunned Katherine. She wanted to respond but couldn't find the words. Instead, she studied the road in silence.

It had been a week since their first run-in, and this was not the first time he had left her speechless. In fact, it was happening more and more often. But it wasn't just his insight into people that silenced her. It was also his lack of self-consciousness. Whether he was waiting on a customer at the store, horsing around with Eric, or trying unsuccessfully to scale the barriers she kept erecting between them, she had never met a person so completely empty of self.

At first she had mistaken this lack of ego as some major self-image problem. But instead of making him weak, it seemed to make him strong. And the more she saw him in action, the more she found herself envying him. By taking himself out of the picture, by having no focus on self, he was completely *free* of himself. That freedom allowed him to be perfectly honest and to focus intently on others. He saw things in people. Deep things. Like with that dying man back at the lab.

Once again, she felt him looking at her. Searching, exploring. She shifted uncomfortably. "You're doing it again," she warned.

"Oh. Sorry." She could almost hear amusement in his voice as he turned and looked ahead.

The man enjoyed her company, she could tell. And, if she were being honest with herself, she'd have to admit she was beginning to accept his.

No, actually, it was more than that. She found his freedom exciting, his concern for others moving. And these emotions set off a quiet trembling somewhere deep inside her. She was starting to feel things again, things she hadn't felt in a long, long time. But she was through with those types of feelings—she'd sworn them off long ago, and she wasn't about to give in to them now.

"So," she said, trying to change the subject. "Do you think this blood stuff is for real?"

"What do you mean?"

"I mean, what does it feel like to have what could be the blood of Jesus Christ running through your veins?"

"I don't know." He shrugged. "To be honest, I really don't know that much about the man."

"You've never read the Bible?"

Coleman smiled sadly. "Guess I was too busy with other things."

"Come on," she insisted, "everybody's read the Bible—at least some of it."

He shook his head. "Sorry." Turning back toward her, he asked, "What about you?" She could feel him probing again.

"Sure," she said. "When I was a kid I used to read it every night." She couldn't resist glancing over to see how that bit of information was received.

But instead of surprise, his face was filled with questioning concern. "I'd like to hear more."

She knew he wasn't talking just about the Bible. He was also talking about her, about what she'd been through. His sensitivity sent a faint quiver through her body. Effortlessly, without even trying, he had reached in and touched her. She suspected that, in time, if she let herself, she would be able to open up to this man. If she wanted, she would eventually be able to talk with him about the Bible, about God's betrayal, about the brutal loss of the only man she'd ever loved. She could speak of the injustice of losing her father, the only man who'd tried to help, who'd loved her even when she was ugly and unlovable. But Katherine would not—could not—give in to that temptation. Instead, she swallowed back the emotion and remained silent.

"I'm sorry," he said, "I didn't mean to pry. I won't do that again."

She wanted to say something clever, something wry and sarcastic. But she wasn't sure she could pull it off. Fortunately, the Mukilteo Interchange was coming up, so she was able to busy herself checking the mirror, changing lanes, and jockeying for position as they left one freeway and entered another that headed west toward Puget Sound.

By the time she had finished the maneuvers, she had managed to partially reerect the wall holding him out. And to ensure that there would be no further assault, she went on the offense. "What about you?" she asked.

"I'm sorry, what?"

"What Murkoski said, doesn't that concern you? That everything you are, that it's all a bunch of chemicals? Doesn't it bother you that you're nothing but some big kid's chemistry experiment?" She saw Coleman wince and immediately hated herself. Why had she said that, just when they were getting so close? But of course, that was her answer. They were getting too close.

He shook his head. "No. That doesn't bother me."

"What does?" she asked. "I mean, there must be something that gets under your skin, something that sets you off. Or did they take that away, too?" It was another poke, and she hated herself even more.

Coleman remained silent a long moment before answering. "I guess ... I guess what really bothers me ... is the pain."

She glanced to him. He was deep in thought. "Pain?" she asked.

"I never knew that people were in such anguish. I never knew there was so much loneliness. Sometimes when I see it in them, I actually *feel* it, right along with them." He hesitated, then continued, almost sadly. "Sometimes I think it would be better to feel nothing at all than to feel that."

"It's true, then." The edge to her voice was softening. "You do sense what other people are feeling."

He nodded. "On the one hand I experience this incredible beauty all around me, things I've seen every day of my life but have never seen—drops of dew on a spiderweb, steam rising from a wooden fence in the early morning sun. On the other hand, I see our inability to connect with that beauty, to be a part of it. I see in every pair of eyes this frustration, this fear that we're nothing but vapor or shadows, that we're skimming across the surface of reality without ever touching it, without connecting to that—that intangible something, that *deepness* that makes all the other beauty possible."

Katherine realized that she was holding her breath and forced herself to exhale.

He continued. "That's what I saw in his eyes this afternoon. It wasn't his fear of death, it was his searching. The realization that he was nothing but a shadow without substance—dancing across creation's surface with no purpose, no reason for being."

Coleman looked back out the window. "I guess that's what bothers me the most. Sensing all that pain. Feeling all their ... hollowness."

Katherine nodded, then quietly quoted, "'A man of sorrows acquainted with grief.'"

"Pardon me?"

"That's one of the descriptions of Jesus in the Scriptures." Coleman turned toward her as she nodded. "Yes, sir, I think we definitely need to get you a Bible."


Steiner's body cried out for sleep, but he wouldn't listen. He stared at the computer screen while throwing another handful of Tylenols into his mouth and washing them down with a Diet Coke. He'd lost track of time. It could be day, it could be night—he didn't care. He only knew that he was close. Very, very close. He clicked the mouse and brought up the names and addresses of the airplane owners he'd requested from the FAA.

The past few days had not been easy. After interviewing the orderly at St. John's, he had tracked down the cabby who had picked up the "burn victim." The driver was a punk, less than cooperative. All he'd remembered was taking two men to the airport on the morning of January 30th.

"There's nothing else you recall?" Steiner had asked.

"Nope."

"Any conversation?"

"Nope."

"Can you describe the bandaged man's voice?"

"Uh-uh."

"Did they say where they were flying?"

"Nope."

The conversation was going nowhere fast. "You don't remember anything?"

"Nope. Just that the guy stiffed me on the tip."

"That, you remember?"

"If a man's got his own plane and he's too cheap to tip you, that you remember."

"They had their own plane? How do you know?"

"I didn't drop them off at the commercial terminal. I dropped them off at the general aviation area."

"Why didn't you tell me?"

"You didn't ask."

Next had come the slow and laborious process of elimination. Steiner knew this was always the most tedious part in any investigation. But he also knew that if you had the time and tenacity, it was the most profitable. Steiner had both.

First he had contacted the Air Route Traffic Control Center in Omaha and asked for all noncommercial flight plans filed on January 30th out of Lincoln Municipal Airport. These records were confidential and it hadn't been easy to get them, but a few well-placed lies about working for the Johnson County D.A.'s office did the trick.

He had thirty-five choices, thirty-five noncommercial flights that had flown out of Lincoln on the 30th. But he quickly cut that number in half by eliminating all flights that had a destination of five hundred miles or less. If Steiner's suspicions were correct, the stakes and the need for secrecy were high; he doubted they would risk being seen in any airport if they could make the journey by land within a day.

Now the number of choices had been reduced to eighteen.

Next Steiner listed the tail ID numbers of each of the eighteen aircraft and pulled strings at the FAA to get the names and addresses of each of the registered owners.

This was the list he now stared at on the screen. Since Lincoln is the state capitol, slightly less than half of the aircraft were government owned, leased, or affiliated. This could, of course, be a government operation, but he had his doubts.

That brought the number down to eleven. Six private, seven corporate. It had to be someone on this list. But who? Steiner rubbed his forehead. His headache was relentless, but so was his determination. There was something here, there had to be. And he wouldn't stop until he found it.

Once again he scanned the column of private owners:

| | |
|---|---|
| N9745B David Buchanan | Lincoln, Nebraska |
| N340E Richard Kaufman | Salt Lake City, Utah |
| N6980 Willa Nixon | Rockford, Illinois |
| N889DG Thomas Piffer | Lincoln, Nebraska |
| N7724B Susan Smoke | Kalispell, Montana |

He ran a cross-check with Coleman's friends, with witnesses of the execution, antideath groups, defense leagues . . .

Nothing.

He popped another Diet Coke, chugged several gulps, and scrutinized the next list; the corporate planes:

| | |
|---|---|
| N395AG American Containers | Lincoln, Nebraska |
| N737BA Genodyne Inc. | Arlington, Washington |
| N349E Johnson Agricultural | Chicago, Illinois |
| N7497B Kellermen Dye Casting | Omaha, Nebraska |
| N983C Moore Hardwoods and Lumber | Hershey, Pennsylvania |
| N5487G Van Owen Seed Company | Des Moines, Iowa |

He stared at the list, hoping to force a pattern, to see something, anything. He saw nothing. Well, almost nothing. That second name, Genodyne, sounded familiar. He'd read something about that company not long ago. *Time* or *Newsweek,* he couldn't remember. Wasn't it some sort of genetics firm?

He studied the address. Arlington, Washington. What were they doing all the way out there? Cattle breeding? Hybrid corn?

He clicked the mouse a few times and popped up his phone directory. Scrolling down, he found the home number for Leonard Patterson, head of security at the penitentiary in Lincoln and one of the few men at the facility Steiner had not completely alienated. He clicked the mouse, let it dial, then reached over to pick up his phone.

It rang five times before someone fumbled with the receiver and a groggy voice mumbled, "Hello?"

"Hi, Leonard. Steiner."

"Harry? What time is it?"

"I don't know. Listen, do you remember those scientists you said were hanging around before Coleman's execution?"

"Harry, it's 4:30 in the morning."

"Yeah. Did you ever hear what area of science they were into?"

"Harry—"

"Just—did you hear a company name or location or anything?"

"No, Harry."

"Why were they so interested? I mean, what were they studying?"

"They took some blood samples and stuff, I don't know ..."

Steiner waited, letting Leonard think.

"They said they wanted to test his genes or something, yeah, they were a couple guys interested in what a murderer's genes were like."

Steiner's eyes shot to the screen:

Genodyne Inc., Arlington, Washington.

Bingo. His head still pounded, but he no longer noticed.


"And Sarah and Julie, how are they? Can you put them on?"

"They're down at the pool right now," Beth answered. Another wave of static washed over the phone, drowning out the sentence but clearing in time for the words: "... and Sarah's turning into this bronze goddess. Oh, Philip, we're having such a good time, I wish you could join us."

"Soon, Hon. I hope, very soon."

"Something happened, didn't it?

"What makes you think—"

"Don't lie to me, Phil. I can tell by your voice. It's something big, isn't it?"

"Beth—"

"You won't tell me when you can come down, you're vague about the reasons. You won't even talk to me over the office phone. Is it Murkoski again? Is it the project?"

O'Brien gave no answer.

"I thought so." There was another barrage of static that ended just in time to hear the words: "... more important, our relationship, or working with some scientist you don't even trust."

O'Brien gave a heavy sigh. "Beth, this is more than just—"

"I'm not angry, Philip. But maybe we should start to seriously—"

"Beth—"

"—reevaluate our priorities. Maybe we should ask ourselves what we really expect out of this rela—"

"Wolff's dead."

"What?"

"Wolff died. Congestive heart failure." There was silence on the other end and another wave of static. "Beth, are you there?"

"How?" came the shaken reply. "He was barely thirty. He was so young, athletic." There was a brief pause. "Do you think ... he wasn't doing drugs, was he?"

Another pause, this time at Philip's end.

"Philip?"

"He's diabetic. The insulin he kept in the refrigerator at work—someone tampered with the vials."

Beth gasped. "Are you sure?"

"One of his colleagues thought they looked suspicious. We ran some tests. Without knowing it, Wolff had been shooting up with a new version of Interleukin."

"Of what?"

"It's an experimental gene used for cancer treatment."

"And it causes heart failure?"

"This type seems to eat into blood vessels, causing them to start leaking."

"Leaking?"

"Like a sieve. The autopsy showed his heart was weak and mushy, like a sixty-year-old who'd had multiple heart attacks. And his lungs were filled with liquid, indicating that the vessels in them had also opened up, filling the lungs with blood."

"Did Wolff have cancer? Could he have been experimenting on himself?"

"No."

"Have you gone to the police?"

"Not yet."

"Phil, what's going—" The rest of her phrase was lost in static.

"Hold it," Murkoski interrupted. "Rewind that last section." He leaned forward toward his desk, ear glued to his receiver, as he heard the whir and whine of voices running backwards. There was a click on the other end and a repeat of the conversation.

" . . . lungs were filled with liquid, indicating that the vessels in them had also opened up, filling the lungs with blood."

"Did Wolff have cancer? Could he have been experimenting on himself?"

"No."

"Have you gone to the police?"

"Not yet."

"All right," Murkoski ordered. The taped conversation stopped. It was 4:50 in the morning. The young man turned to his office window and instinctively checked out the lines of his suit. They were good lines, ones he usually appreciated.

But this morning they gave him little pleasure. "What time did she phone him?"

"Shortly after seven last evening." The voice was heavily accented. Murkoski had never been able to tell what nationality, although he knew it was Asian. "Mr. Murkoski, I am certain you can appreciate our concern, can you not?"

Murkoski ran his hand through his hair. "Yeah—no—I mean, sure, I understand."

"If Mr. O'Brien were to connect your technician's untimely death with our project, I am afraid it could seriously jeopardize our date of delivery."

"I agree."

"The situation is not getting out of hand, is it, Dr. Murkoski? You will be able to meet your deadline, will you not?"

"Of course," Murkoski said, turning back to his desk, trying to hide his irritation.

"Good. Word is spreading. Competition is asking very sensitive questions. You can appreciate our need for haste."

"I'll get on the problem right away."

"We were certain you would. Good morning, Dr. Murkoski."

Before he could respond, the phone disconnected. Murkoski slowly leaned forward and replaced the receiver. Then, even more slowly, he turned to look out his window and into the darkness.


*The crack stings his throat and burns his lungs. He holds it until he must exhale and gasp for breath. The rush is immediate, exhilarating, running through his chest, his arms, into his fingertips.*

*He is it.*

*Unstoppable.*

*He grabs the shotgun from the front seat and steps out of the car. He sees everything. The ice machine out front. The barbecue charcoal display. The neon Budweiser sign in its final stages of flickering out.*

He kicks open the door, a grand entrance that has the desired effect. The clerk, a boy with long hair and earring, is speechless. He won't try anything. He knows Coleman means business.

Coleman heads toward the counter, pumping his gun. The kid's boom box blasts out an oldie, "Hotel California." The guitar licks are intoxicating, making Coleman sail. The crack screams through his body. He is all-powerful.

Omnipotent.

The clerk falters, throws a look at the security camera. With one hand, Coleman lifts the shotgun and blows the intruding eye to smithereens. There is no sound. Only a flash of light and flying glass and plastic. One chamber is still full. He knows it. The clerk knows it.

"Come on! Let's go, let's go!"

The kid hits the cash register. It flies open. Bills are grabbed, stuffed into a Quickie Mart bag. Coleman grabs a Snickers bar, then several more. He knows he'll be hungry.

"Now the safe!"

The kid makes an excuse. A lie.

Coleman points to the floor. He knows where the safe is hidden.

The kid protests.

Coleman levels his gun.

The punk is shouting at him as if volume will prove his sincerity. Coleman's finger wraps around the trigger. He is grinning.

The boy yells at him. Wide-eyed. Terror-stricken.

Coleman's grin broadens.

The boy turns. Coleman thinks it's towards the safe. But it isn't. He's turning back. There's something in his hand. It's a pistol, a .22. The kid is an idiot, one too many Rambo movies. There's nothing Coleman can do now. He squeezes the trigger.

Another silent explosion of light.

A bell rings, keeps ringing. Somehow the kid has tripped the alarm. Coleman reaches for the bag on the counter, then

*hears breathing. It's coming from behind. Wheezing, cough-
ing. He spins around, but no one is there. The aisles are empty.*

*It grows louder, bearing down.*

*Coleman breaks open the gun. With trembling hands he
yanks out the spent casings.*

*The breathing is louder, roaring in his head.*

*Coleman backs up, shoving his hands into his sweat-
shirt, fumbling for two more shells.*

*He smells the breath now. Alcohol. His father's. It's all
around. Coming from all sides.*

*He turns, stumbling toward the door, but it is locked. He
bangs on it, desperate to get out.*

*"Michael!" It's his father's voice shouting, swearing.
"Michael!"*

*Coleman doesn't look back. He pounds on the glass, try-
ing to break it, but it won't give.*

*"Michael!"*

*He continues to bang, but it is no longer glass, it is
wood. And it is no longer his father's voice. It is a child's. "Mr.
Michaels? Mr. Michaels, are you okay?" The banging continues.*

Coleman awoke with a start, cowering, preparing for the
blows. But none came. His father wasn't there. The breathing
had disappeared. The dream was gone. Only the knocking
remained—and Eric's voice. "Mr. Michaels? Mr. Michaels!"


The picnic had been Katherine's idea. Another week had
passed, and it was time to make the trek back up to Arlington.
Since they were paying her good money to take the day off,
and since Eric had never really been up into the mountains,
she figured—why not take advantage of the situation and go
on a little outing.

She glanced at Coleman as she drove. He was in the passenger seat, poring over the Bible she'd given him. In the days
since their last trip, he'd been true to his word. He hadn't

pried. He hadn't said another word about her past. For that she was both pleased and disappointed. A week ago, it had taken so little effort for him to reach through her barriers and touch her. And now, as the days passed, as she saw his goodness, and as her trust built, she knew it would take even less effort for him to reach in and move her even more deeply. But he respected her; he would not abuse his power. And it was this combination of restrained power and tenderness that made her start finding excuses to spend time with him.

Her walls were crumbling. She could tell by the way she stood at the closet trying to decide what to wear, by the stirring inside when she heard him arrive at the store. She could tell by the way her body began to take on a softness when they talked, becoming curves instead of rigid lines.

Then there was the drinking. She hadn't quit, but when sobriety came, it didn't carry the piercing sharpness it once had. She was beginning to experience a different high.

She glanced into the rearview mirror. Eric was reading. Another miracle. No Game Boy in his hand, no laptop computer. Just a book, a real book.

"You'll like it," Coleman had said when he had tossed it at him. "I got it at the bookstore down the street. It's called *The Last of the Mohicans,* and it's all about Indians and survival in the wilderness and stuff."

Eric hadn't stopped reading it since he'd first opened it.

They'd been on the road forty-five minutes, heading up the Getchel Highway and into the Cascades. Once again she glanced at Coleman. But this time his face was wet with tears. "What's wrong?" she asked, concerned. "Are you okay?"

He glanced up, a little embarrassed. When he spoke, his voice was thick with feeling. "I never knew what ..." He searched for the word. "Wisdom ..."

Katherine smiled. One of the other things she enjoyed about this man was his childlike wonder, his sense of awe, sometimes over the simplest things. She didn't always understand why it happened, but this time she did.

"This ache I have," he was saying, "this emptiness. It's like he understands—like somehow, he's able to meet that hunger and, and ..."

"Help ease it?" she asked.

He nodded and looked up at her in quiet amazement.

"I guess that's why he called himself the 'Bread of Life.'"

"He called himself that?"

"Oh, yeah."

Coleman was dumbstruck. "And people—people know this?"

She couldn't help laughing at his astonishment. "A few."

Coleman looked back down to the page, then up again. "And you?"

The question caught her off guard. "Me?"

"Do you believe it?"

Katherine took a long, slow breath. "I don't know. When I was a kid, that was all I heard about. Then, as an adult, I had a long stint with AA. When everything else failed, my faith was the only thing that kept me sober, that pulled me through. But now—" She took another deep breath and let it out. "I don't know. I guess I just don't see it anymore."

"And seeing is believing."

"It is for me." She sighed wearily.

She could feel him looking at her a long moment before returning to his Bible. She was grateful to be off the hook. Grateful and disturbed. This man was stirring other things inside her as well; deeper things, long-forgotten.

A half-hour later they were at Granite Falls, a huge rocky formation deep in the foothills with towering cliffs and an angry Stillaguamish River that dropped nearly a hundred feet, thundering and crashing into gigantic boulders before slamming, swirling, and crashing into a dozen more.

"Wow!" Eric cried over the roar. "This is so cool!"

"Don't get too close," Katherine shouted, doing her best not to sound like a mother and failing miserably. But neither boy nor man seemed to notice. She watched as, instinctively,

Coleman rested his hands on her son's shoulder. The unconscious act of kindness brought a tightness to her throat. She
turned, fighting back the moisture welling up in her eyes, pretending to notice something downriver. Eric had missed so
many things in his little life. At the store, day in and day out,
with only the computers and people on the Internet as his
playmates. What type of existence was that? No interaction
with others. No men to model after. How could she have been
so insensitive, so selfish, not to see this?

They hiked downstream a quarter of a mile for lunch.
Banter and teasing came easy between Coleman and Eric, and
Katherine was grateful to feel like the third wheel as she
watched their friendship grow. She'd seen it at the store, this
male camaraderie thing, but it had always been on Eric's turf.
Now Coleman was able to take charge, showing her son how
to skip rocks, how to sneak through dense undergrowth so
quietly that even crows could not hear and sound the alarm.

Later, she watched as the two studied an animal's track
in the mud beside the river.

"Looks like a deer."

"How can you tell?"

"See here, this V."

"Oh, yeah. Cool."

"Look at the size. It's a buck. Probably a big one."

Then there were Coleman's Indian stories. How they survived, what they ate in the wild, how they fought. Some of the
details were a little too gruesome for Katherine's taste, but the
facts seemed to thrill her son.

"How come you know so much about Indians?" Eric
asked.

"You don't grow up in Tecumseh without knowing your
Indians."

"Tecumseh? Where's that?"

"Little town in Nebraska. Named after Tecumseh, a
Shawnee. His name meant 'Panther in the Sky.' He was the
greatest Indian ever."

"Oh, yeah? What about Chief Seattle?"

"He was okay for a Northwesterner. But the real Indians, like the Shawnee, they were back in the Midwest."

"Says who?"

"It's common knowledge."

"Oh, yeah?"

"Yeah."

"Yeah?"

"Yeah."

And so the sparring continued, along with the macho challenges, races, and leaps from rock to rock (with more than one slip and crash into the water). But wet clothes and bruised bodies were only a preliminary to the end of their little outing. As they headed back up to the car, they spotted an overgrown path, a shortcut that was clearly only for the stronghearted.

Immediately they began goading each other to take it. And, of course, they both rose to the challenge. Just before entering the tangled pathway, Eric turned back to his mom. "Aren't you coming?"

Katherine peered into the dense undergrowth. "No, I think I'll stick to the path here."

"Come on, Mom."

"No—too much testosterone in this one for me. You boys go ahead."

She watched as they began plowing through the brush, sometimes racing, shouting, always inciting the other to continue. But in less than a minute their outlook had changed.

"Ow!"

"Ouch!"

"Yeow!"

"What's wrong?" she shouted.

"Blackberry bushes," Coleman called.

"They must be twenty feet high," Eric yelled.

"Maybe you better turn around and come out," Katherine suggested.

"No way!" Eric shouted. "I'm not afraid of a few black-berry bushes. Are you?" he called to Coleman.

"Not me," Coleman shouted back.

"Me, neither. Ouch! We'll be fine, Mom. Don't worry 'bout us."

"I wouldn't dream of it," she shouted back.

Twenty minutes later she arrived at the car, but they weren't there. It took an additional half hour for them to finally emerge from the bushes, their arms, hands, even their faces scratched and bleeding.

"You guys look awful!" she cried. "What happened?"

"A few more blackberries than we anticipated," Coleman said.

"It's not that bad," Eric insisted. "Just a few scratches."

"A few," Coleman had to laugh. He held up Eric's bleeding arm. "You've got scratches on top of scratches."

"Oh yeah," Eric retorted, grabbing Coleman's other hand and raising it up. "What about you? You got scratches on top of scratches on top of scratches."

"Guys," Katherine protested, "look at you, you're getting blood all over each other."

They looked at their hands. It was true. Both had smeared their own blood onto the other.

"Cool," Eric said staring at his palm.

"You know," Coleman said, "some Indians believed that the soul of man resided in his blood. That's why they mixed their blood together to become blood brothers."

"That may be true," Katherine said, pulling her son toward her and trying to wipe some of the blood from his face with a tissue.

"Mom—"

"But in this day of AIDS and every other blood disease imaginable, I think that's one ritual we can live without."

"Too late," Eric said, reexamining his palm.

Katherine glanced at Coleman, who was looking at his own hand.

"I'm afraid he's right, Katherine. Looks like we've become official, honest-to-goodness blood brothers."

Eric looked up and beamed. But Katherine barely noticed. It was the sound of her name that had caught her off guard, that had made her legs a little weak, her hands a little less sure of themselves. This was the first time he had spoken her name out loud, and she quite literally had to catch her breath. The walls were crumbling again. If Coleman had looked into her eyes at that moment, he would have known everything she was, understood all that she was feeling.

But something else had caught his attention. "Look at that!"

Katherine turned to see that he was pointing toward a giant cedar.

"What?" Eric demanded.

"That."

"It's just a tree."

"No, past that. Look."

A huge, pale moon was rising behind it.

"It's just the moon."

"You're not seeing it. Look at it."

"What?" Eric repeated.

"Look!"

Katherine continued to stare with them. And, as she looked she began to see something else. The way the cedar stretched out toward the sky, its limbs graceful and drooping, with the full, glowing orb rising behind it. There was a silent splendor here. A quiet strength.

"Don't be stupid," Eric said. He pulled open the back door of the car and climbed in. "It's just the moon. You see it lots of times in the day."

Katherine turned slowly to watch Coleman, who was still staring, transfixed. Then she looked back to the tree. She couldn't find the words, but she was beginning to understand. There was something about this moment, this tiny detail of life, that seemed bigger and more powerful than all of the grandiose plans and accomplishments of her own noisy, scampering little life. For the briefest second she too felt like a shadow dancing across the surface of something far deeper, far more eternal than she could ever be. She tried to swallow and found a lump in her throat. It had nothing to do with pain and everything to do with joy. Katherine Lyon was happy. Happier than she'd been in a long, long time.

The ride down the mountain was full of more Indian tales, bantering, and laughter. It took nearly an hour to reach Genodyne, but it seemed like minutes. The trembling inside Katherine ebbed and flowed, but it never disappeared. It wasn't until they entered Genodyne's lobby that the joy started to fade. First there was the problem of taking Eric onto the grounds.

"I'm sorry," the receptionist explained. "No children allowed in the laboratory area."

"But he's my friend," Coleman insisted.

"I'm sorry, the rules are specific. He may visit the offices or our cafeteria, but he won't be admitted to the labs. No children are."

"Call Dr. Murkoski, let me talk to him."

"Dr. Murkoski is unavailable, but if you'll have a seat, I'm sure—"

Suddenly Katherine saw Coleman's expression change. It was more than concern. It was fear. She followed his gaze to the front door, where a man was just entering the lobby and approaching the desk. He was short, in his fifties, with wire-rim glasses and thinning, brown hair.

When he glanced up, the man seemed equally surprised by Coleman's expression. "I'm sorry," he said, "have we met?"

Coleman did his best to recover. "No. I don't think so."

But the man's interest had been piqued. "Are you certain?"

Coleman shook his head.

The man extended his hand. "My name is Steiner. Harold Steiner."

Coleman took it. "William Michaels."

Noticing the scratches on Coleman's arms and then Eric's, Steiner said, "Looks like you two had quite a tussle."

"Yeah." Eric grinned. "And the blackberries won."

The smiles lasted a fraction longer than necessary before Steiner again asked, "Are you sure we've not met?"

Coleman shook his head. "I'm sure." Then, resting his hand on Eric's shoulder, he quickly brought the meeting to an end. "Well, if you'll excuse us."

"Certainly."

Coleman nodded and turned Eric toward the door.

"Wait a minute," Eric protested, "I thought we were—"

"Plans have changed."

"But—"

"Let's go."

"But—"

"Plans have changed." The sternness in Coleman's voice surprised Eric, and he allowed himself to be moved toward the exit.

"Excuse me, Mr. Michaels?" It was the receptionist. "Don't you want to wait and see—"

"We'll be back later," Coleman said over his shoulder. "Tell him something has come up, we'll be back a little later."

Katherine hadn't missed a thing, and she had the good sense to play along. After a parting nod to Steiner, she turned and accompanied Coleman and Eric out the door. But as she walked out, she knew that Steiner was still watching.

# CHAPTER 10

O'Brien hadn't run an electrophoresis gel since grad school. Although there had been some changes in chemicals and hardware, the process remained essentially the same. It was also the same process Wolff had undertaken seventy-two hours earlier. The one he had called O'Brien about. The one that O'Brien now suspected led to his death.

It was a little after ten in the evening when he quietly slipped into the lab on the third floor. If Wolff had found a problem while running a gel, that must have meant he was getting different identification bands on the DNA. There were only three possible explanations for that. The first was that Wolff had made a mistake, an unlikely option given his meticulous attention to detail. This left only two other possibilities. Either the GOD gene had mutated on its own—or someone had deliberately altered it.

There was only one way to tell. Double-check the gene's fingerprint. Run another gel.

The procedure was fairly simple. First O'Brien pulled out a sample of the GOD gene from the freezer. From this sample he would need to cut out the specific section they'd been focusing on. But instead of cutting with mechanical knives or scissors, they used chemical ones called restriction enzymes. There were hundreds of these enzymes to choose from, but in this case they had been using *Eco*RI, a distant cousin to the deadly E. coli bacteria that had endeared itself to the fast-food chains a while back.

By mixing the DNA with the chemical scissors and then incubating it in an Eppendorf tube for an hour in 37 degrees C water, O'Brien was able to cut open the DNA molecule and remove and dissect the precise section of the GOD gene he wanted.

Next he melted a clear, blue, Jello-like substance in the microwave. He poured this hot liquid into the five-inch-by-eleven-inch electrophoresis gel box. Carefully he inserted a serrated piece of Plexiglas, which looked like a thick comb, into the liquid at one end. He waited patiently as the gel hardened, then removed the comb, leaving several small holes, or wells, where the teeth had been.

It was tedious work, but O'Brien loved it. Being back at a lab bench, working the front lines, was a far cry from the paperwork and politics he was daily subjected to. And, though he appreciated the money and prestige, a large part of him missed the good old days when he and Beth were first starting out. When she had thought him a hero. When he was breaking new ground. The work had been hard, but at least it had carried a sense of accomplishment. For the past several months, he hadn't been so sure *what* he was accomplishing.

He glanced at the clock—11:15. So far there had been no interruptions, no late-night insomniacs swinging by to see how his or her particular batch of DNA-laced bacteria was breeding. And more importantly, no head of the gene therapy division showing up, demanding to know what he was up to.

Once again, O'Brien scolded himself for giving Murkoski so much power. Of course he had his excuses—trying to keep a multimillion-dollar biotech company on course creates a few distractions. Besides, everyone told him that a real leader must delegate, delegate, and delegate. Well, he had delegated, all right. And now something was wrong. Not only had Murkoski refused to return his calls or show up at the office, but the government contacts he knew to be involved in the project were also strangely unavailable. Yes, indeed, something was very wrong.

As O'Brien continued to work, allowing his thoughts to drift, the silence of the lab began to play tricks on him. Whenever the air-conditioning kicked on or the refrigerators turned over, he was certain that someone had entered the lab. It's not that he didn't enjoy returning to his laboratory roots. He just would have enjoyed it more if he didn't suspect that his life was in danger.

Was he being paranoid? Probably. But he had grown so out of touch with the project, and Murkoski had such a raging ego—who knew *what* the kid was up to.

His mind drifted to his children and to Beth. How he missed them. But, until this mess was straightened out, it wouldn't hurt for them to stay in Mexico. At least there they would be safe.

He crossed to the small D.C. transformer and attached the wires to the gel box. The black wire to the black terminal on the left, the red wire to the red terminal on the right. Running a gel was a fairly simple procedure. Since every gene is a different size and moves through the gel at its own rate, he would place the DNA in the little wells he had made and run 100 volts of direct current over them from one end of the gel box to the other. Then, after a prescribed period of time, he would be able to see how far each section of gene had traveled along the current as it pushed its way through the gel. Wherever the sections stopped and congregated, a band would be created. And it was the pattern of these bands that gave the precise length and identification of the gene they were testing. If there was the slightest discrepancy between the bands in the batch he was now running and the benchmarks they had established in their earlier identification and testing of the GOD gene, he would know.

He reached for a small beaker of electrophoresis buffer and poured it over the hardened gel. This was to ensure electrical contact between the two terminals at each end of the box. As he poured it, he couldn't help noticing the beaker shaking in his hands.

Next he mixed a fluorescent dye called ethidium bromide into the DNA. This would allow him to clearly see the pattern of the bands when they were viewed under ultraviolet light.

Now came the hard part. He grabbed an electronic pipette, a measuring device about the size of a small turkey baster. He adjusted it to ten microliters and with a trembling hand sucked up some of the DNA and placed it into the little wells he had made. It was embarrassing how his hand shook, but it served as a clear reminder of just how nervous he really was. It took all of his concentration and willpower just to drop the DNA into the tiny wells.

Then he heard it. The whine of the elevator. He was only two doors down from the elevator, and the lab's door was wide open. He froze and listened.

It stopped. Someone had brought it down to the lobby.

A moment later it started up again. He tried to picture it moving up the elevator shaft, guessing the time it would take to pass each floor. It had passed the second and was heading toward the third. With any luck it would continue right on up to the fourth or even the—

It sighed to a stop. It was on the third floor. His floor. He could not hear the doors open, but he knew that someone was stepping out. He watched the lab door, angry at himself for leaving it open. Quickly he scanned the bench area in front of him. It would be impossible to disguise what he was doing. Anyone looking in would know he was running a gel. He strained, listening for footsteps, but the air-conditioning made it impossible to hear.

He stepped to the right, behind the cupboard, just out of sight. With eight other labs on the floor, the odds were unlikely that whoever had come up in the elevator was heading into this one.

Unless, of course, they were coming for him.

He saw the brief flicker of a shadow on the tiled floor as a form passed the door and continued down the hall. He closed his eyes and let out a quiet sigh. Then he heard:

"Hello? Anybody in here?"

Relieved that it was a woman's voice and not Murkoski's, O'Brien stepped into view.

She was beautiful. Mid-twenties, long dark hair, jade-green eyes. She had a lean yet sensual figure and didn't seem shy about showing it off with the help of a snug knit top and a short, tweed skirt. In some ways, she reminded him of Beth in her younger days. Before the children. When they were helplessly in love. When she still admired him.

"Oh, Dr. O'Brien. I saw the door open and was wondering ..." She stopped as she saw the gel box and beakers in front of him.

He flashed a boyish, self-conscious grin. "Just brushing up on my lab technique," he lied. "I really miss rolling up the old sleeves and getting my hands dirty."

"I see." She smiled. Was it his imagination or was she flirting with him? The thought both excited him and set off tiny little alarms.

He cleared his throat. "I'm sorry. I, uh—I don't know your name. Are you new?"

She moved toward him, extending her hand, not taking her eyes off him. "Yes, I'm Youngren. Tisha Youngren." They shook hands. Hers was warm and firm.

"Philip O'Brien."

"I know."

He smiled. "Yes, I suppose so."

She stood a moment, unmoving. She seemed to sense the effect she was having on him, and she clearly enjoyed it.

"Well, uh . . ." He motioned to the counter, indicating his work.

"Of course," she said, "I've got plenty to do, myself. It was a pleasure to finally meet you, Dr. O'Brien."

"Thanks. Me, too."

There was that smile again. She turned and glided toward the door. O'Brien couldn't help staring. When she arrived at the door she turned one last time. "Oh, Dr. O'Brien. The next time you're running a gel?"

"Yes?"

"You really should wear gloves."

"Why's that?"

"The ethidium bromide you're using there"—she pointed to a beaker on the counter—"it's a carcinogen."

"Oh, right." O'Brien glanced at his hands, hoping he hadn't spilled any. "It's been a while."

She smiled one last time. "I can tell." Then, without a word, she turned and disappeared out the door.

O'Brien relaxed, thinking again of how much the woman had looked like Beth in their younger days. So attractive. So young and alive. With the thought came the guilt. What did he think he was doing? He had no business flirting with anyone, much less an employee, no matter how beautiful.

Still, with Beth gone . . .

He angrily pushed the thought out of his mind and walked to the gel box. It would take another hour for the bands to migrate and establish their patterns.

"You sure I can't talk you into some wine?" Katherine asked as she crossed to the kitchen counter and poured herself another glass.

"Thanks, but no," Coleman said.

"Come on," she teased, "word has it that even your genetic forerunner tipped a few."

Coleman smiled and shook his head.

As she raised her third glass to her lips, she could see the concern in his eyes. Yet at the same time she knew he wasn't judging her. He never judged her.

The day had been too perfect to end, and she had asked whether he wanted to join her and Eric for dinner. Nothing special, just some leftover chicken reheated in the microwave, a little salad, and anything else she could rummage from the cupboard. Cooking had never been her specialty.

Coleman had gratefully accepted, and the dinner had been as enjoyable as the day. It was late now, but Katherine still didn't want it to end. The more time she spent with this man, the more time she wanted—and the stronger the trembling inside her grew. Whether it was about her son, her life, even her forgotten faith—whatever they talked about, this man seemed to make everything inside her come alive again. And now all she wanted was to do the same. To touch some part of him where no one else had been, someplace deep inside, someplace she could call her own.

She had sent Eric to bed (which probably meant lights off, but computer on) and had spent the past hour and a half in deep conversation with Coleman. They had covered their likes, dislikes, pet peeves, fears, vulnerabilities. Maybe it was the wine, maybe it was Coleman, maybe it was everything, but it had been a long time since she'd been able to talk so open-ly and so deeply.

Still, there were the secrets. Most of them his.

"There's just no way you'll tell me who that man was, will you?" she said as she crossed to the sofa and sat beside him.

Coleman shook his head. "Somebody from another life."

"More like a ghost, by the expression on your face."

Coleman nodded and rubbed the top of his shoulder.

"You okay?"

"Yeah. It's just Murkoski's little reminder that I should have gone in for my checkup."

"That chemical leash thing?"

Coleman tried to smile. "'Having the flu times ten,' I think is how he put it. When he returns my call, I need to set up another place for the checkups."

"Why?"

"That man we saw today. He could prove a real threat to the experiment."

"But you won't tell me why."

"It's the past, Katherine."

There was her name again. And each time she heard it, it took just a little longer to recover. "And there's no way you will talk about your past?"

He shook his head. "That part of me is dead, that man is no longer alive."

Once again, Katherine felt a mixture of warmth, weak-ness, and buoyancy. "You're a person of many mysteries, William Michaels—or whatever your name is."

He smiled, then gently turned the tables on her. "What about you? It seems to me you have your own share of mysteries."

"But women are supposed to be mysterious. It makes us more alluring." The phrase came out sexier than she had intended, but that was okay.

He looked at the carpet, almost embarrassed, which made him even more attractive. She changed the subject.

"What about your childhood?" she asked. "You said you grew up in Nebraska?"

"Tecumseh."

"Named after some Indian chief."

"That's right. Population 1,702. Not much to say, really. We were dirt poor, lived in a little trailer." He shrugged. "But we managed."

"Your family? Brothers, sisters?"

"I had a dad who beat me, a brother who overdosed on heroin, and a mother who killed herself trying to hold us all together."

Katherine's heart swelled in sympathy. "I'm sorry."

He nodded.

"Is that why . . ." She searched for the phrase. "I mean, you did serve some time in prison, right?"

"That man is dead. He was very evil, very violent, and now he is very, very gone."

"And you're a brand, spanking new creature."

Coleman shrugged, then nodded. "I guess so."

For some reason, another Bible verse came to mind. Katherine had heard it dozens of times as a child, but she had long since forgotten it. Until now. What was it about this man that stirred so many things inside of her?

He saw her expression and asked, "What?"

She shook her head.

"No, tell me."

She looked up to him, then took a breath and quoted: "'Therefore if any man be in Christ, he is a new creature: old things are passed away; behold, all things are become new.'"

Coleman looked surprised. "Is that . . .?" He motioned toward the coffee table where the Bible she'd given him lay.

"Yeah, it's in there. Though I suppose it has more to do with a person's faith than his DNA structure, wouldn't you?"

Coleman nodded, though it was obvious he was still mulling over the concept. They both sat in silence, thinking. Finally he turned to her. "I know I promised not to ask, but . . ."

She looked to him.

"What about you?" He held her gaze, looking so deep into her that she fought back a shiver. "I get the feeling that you've been through a lot."

A weakness spread through her body, but she didn't want to look away. She tried to swallow, but her mouth was dry. She took another sip of wine. He waited silently, his eyes full of compassion.

Finally she began. At first the story came out matter-of-factly. Her sheltered childhood, her preacher daddy, preacher-wife mommy. Bible college. Meeting the man of her dreams. Married right out of college. The perfect couple, who within a year were adoring their perfect newborn.

And then the tragedies. Anguish and sorrows that no twenty-three-year-old should ever be forced to face.

Gary's shooting. Her pretended strength. The days of ceaseless prayers and their obvious futility. The suffocating love and spiritual formulas from family and church. Her discovery of alcohol and its ability to numb the pain. The bingeing. The bad-girl reputation. Her father's persistent love regardless of the tongue waggers.

But Katherine could go no further. Somewhere, deep inside, the shudders began. Deep sobs from inside that made it impossible to speak. She tried to stop, but couldn't. She hadn't cried like this since her father's death. A moment later she felt his arms about her shoulders. A gentle embrace, an attempt to comfort. She turned and buried her face against his chest. And to her amazement, she felt his own body shuddering. He was also crying, sharing her pain. And if he shared such deep things with her, was it possible that he might share other feelings as well?

For days, she'd been searching almost unconsciously for a sign. But he was always so considerate, so tender, it was impossible to tell how he felt about her. She looked up at him through her tears. Moisture streamed down his own cheeks. It was so touching, so moving. Before she knew it, she had raised her head toward his mouth. He lowered his. Their lips found one another. The kiss was delicately tender, the salt of his tears mixed with hers. The passion grew. She could feel him trembling, struggling to restrain himself. And it was at that moment that she knew he could be trusted, that she could give herself fully to him without reservation and without fear of being hurt. He had touched her innermost being, her very soul, and she had touched his.

Their embrace grew. But as the kiss reached its height of passion, she felt him hesitate. She kissed him harder, encouraging him. But instead of complying, he started to pull away.

"It's okay," she murmured, pressing in, "it's okay—"

"No," he whispered.

She opened her eyes. He gently pulled back and looked at her, searching. "I'm sorry," he whispered hoarsely, "it's—it's not right."

She moved in again, closing her eyes, reaching for his mouth. "Of course it is."

"Katherine."

She looked at him again. The depth of his gaze was unnerving. "This isn't right. Not now. Not for you."

She frowned. Who was he to tell her what was right and wrong?

"I'm sorry." He shook his head.

She pulled back, trying to understand. Hurt and rejection flooded in. "Sure," she said, trying to regain her dignity, "of course." But the anger and humiliation continued to pour into her. Already she could feel herself shutting down, closing off. "I don't know what I was thinking." She pulled back and sat on the couch, straightening her clothes.

"Katherine ..."

"After all, you're part God now, right? I mean, what would happen if—"

"That's not it." He searched for words.

She took her glass from the coffee table and rose unsteadily to her feet. "No, you're right. Besides, it's late, and we've both got work in the morning."

"Katherine." He rose toward her.

She held up her hand, bringing him to a stop. "I said you're right, this isn't what I want. I don't know what I was thinking."

"I didn't mean to—"

"Listen, maybe you should go. All right?"

He looked at her a long moment. She held his gaze, refusing to back down. She didn't care what he saw inside now. If it was her anger, fine. Her humiliation, so what?

Finally he nodded. He turned and crossed the room to retrieve his coat. "I didn't want—"

"It's not your fault," she said. "I don't know what came over me." She wanted to say more, but the anger and embarrassment kept her from continuing.

"Thank you for dinner, Katherine. I had a terrific day."

"Right, terrific."

"Will you tell Eric—"

"Tell him yourself," she interrupted. "He's still up, working on his computer."

"That would be okay?"

"I just said so, didn't I?" She turned on him. "He deserves at least that much, don't you think? For you to at least say good night to him. He at least deserves that." She wasn't sure what she meant, but she suspected that somehow he'd know.

At last he nodded and walked past her into the hallway.

Katherine stood, still smarting. Then, seeing the dinner dishes piled on the counter, she moved toward them, grateful to find something to do.

A weary O'Brien headed out of the research building of Genodyne Inc. and into the parking lot. The night air helped a little to clear his head, but not enough. He was both relieved and puzzled. The bands from the gel had proven to be exactly the same as the GOD gene. It had not mutated, it had not been changed. It was the identical pattern Murkoski, Wolff, and the team had been using for months. So what was the problem? Why had Wolff called him at home? More importantly, why had he died?

There was one other thought: the mice. What had happened to that one mouse, then to the entire community of six? And why only to them and not the others? And what did this have to do with the gels and Wolff's fate?

O'Brien was so deep in thought that he barely noticed arriving at his BMW. He was practically inside the car before he heard the girl's shouts.

"Excuse me! Excuse me, Dr. O'Brien?"

He turned to see Tisha Youngren approach. She looked as good under the glow of mercury vapors as she had in the lab.

"Ms. Youngren. Is . . . everything okay?"

"Yeah," she said, arriving just a little breathless. "I left my keys in the car."

"Ah . . ."

"Boy, do I feel stupid." She gave a helpless little-girl smile.

"It happens to the best of us."

"I suppose."

He reached for his cellular. "Let me give Security a call. They have one of those flat metal things to jimmy it open."

"Oh, don't bother them."

O'Brien looked up.

She stuck her hands in her coat pockets and boldly held his eyes. "I've got an extra set at home. I just live a mile away, over at Smoky Point. Since it's on your way, I thought maybe you could drop me off."

He looked at her. "Uh, actually it would probably be better just to call Security. I mean, they've got the metal thingie and all."

"Better for who?" There was that smile again.

He stared at her, feeling his face flush slightly.

She tilted her head, waiting for his answer.

For the briefest second he forgot the question. She was so young, so lovely, and it was becoming very apparent what she had in mind.

"Listen, Ms.—uh, Youngren—"

"Tisha," she said, her smile growing more coy.

"Yes, uh, Tisha—"

"It would only take a few minutes." She took a tentative step toward him. Now they were less than two feet apart, plumes of white breath rising above their heads. "And if you wanted, I could fix you something to eat or something. I mean, with you being alone and everything, and it being so late."

More color rose to O'Brien's face. An indefinable rush of excitement spread in his chest. It had been a long time since someone so beautiful had shown such interest. Oh, there were the occasional flirtings, but nothing like this. This girl seemed truly impressed by him. Unlike Beth, who grew more critical each year, this girl seemed so accepting. No put-downs, or reminders of clay feet. Just a beautiful girl, half his age, who seemed to really admire him.

He wondered how she knew he was alone, then realized that she was part of another generation, a smart generation who knew how to go after what they wanted. He was both flattered and cautious. But why the caution? Other execs did this all the time, didn't they? Wasn't this one of the perks of power? The stress, the worry, the anxiety—didn't these call for special benefits? Didn't this come with the territory? No one appreciated the pressure men like him were under, certainly not their wives. And this girl seemed so willing. How many times had he been faithful at the hotels, the conventions, the international meetings—with no one there to pat him on the back for his integrity. And he was so stressed, and she was so lovely, and there was no one at home waiting.

He took a step toward her. The plumes of their breath intermixed. She reached out and touched the lapel of his top-coat. "You won't be disappointed."

He was glad to hear that her voice carried a trace of ner-vousness. This wasn't something she did every day. She was putting herself on the line, taking a risk, and all for him. Once again he was struck by her deep, jade-green eyes. So inviting. And he was so alone. He reached up to his coat and placed his hands over hers. She moved closer. No one would know. And she was so young and beautiful and she admired him and no one was at home waiting.

She rose up on her toes and they kissed. It grew passion-ate, full of hunger, a foretaste of what the night could hold. He pulled her closer, drawing her into himself. She surrendered, but at the same time pushed against him, as if trying to turn him. He was too caught up in the moment to notice. She pushed harder until he stumbled, shifting his feet, and turned slightly. It was then that he opened his eyes and saw it.

In the distance, directly ahead. A van.

Tisha pulled back his topcoat, pressing herself into him. O'Brien closed his eyes, trying to lose himself again, but the image of the van would not go away. He reopened his eyes. This time he saw movement inside the van, silhouetted by one of the parking lot lights. Someone was behind the wheel, watching.

Sensing his distraction, Tisha's kisses grew more demanding. He tried to pull from her, but she clung to him. At last his insistence prevailed and they separated.

"What's wrong?" she asked, almost breathless.

He motioned behind her, and she turned to look.

Suddenly the van's engine turned over and its lights blared on. Tisha shielded her eyes from the glare. "What—"

The van's wheels spun, throwing gravel as it lurched for-ward. It was heading directly for them.

With memories of Wolff fresh in his mind, O'Brien sus-pected the worst. Perhaps Murkoski was thinking of another way to silence his questions.

He looked around. They could run for it, but the building was too far away and the van was picking up speed.

"Get behind the car," he ordered.

"What?"

"The car! Get behind the car!"

She started to back away from him.

"Tisha!"

The van roared closer.

"Get behind the car!"

She turned and started running.

"Tisha!"

The van accelerated. It was less than fifty yards away when it veered to the right, and O'Brien realized the sickening truth: It was not heading toward him, it was heading toward her!

"No, Tisha!" He started for her.

The van closed in. Twenty yards from the girl. Fifteen.

It kept Tisha in the center of its headlights.

O'Brien was running now, pushing his legs for all they were worth. "Tisha!"

She threw a frightened look over her shoulder. The vehicle bore down.

Five yards.

*"TISH—"*

Adrenaline pumped through his body. He was flying—but he was too late. The van would hit her long before he arrived.

Ten feet. Five.

Then, just as it was about to strike, the van suddenly swerved to the left. The passenger door flew open and the van slowed its speed to match the girl's. Now she was running parallel, directly beside it. To O'Brien's amazement, she turned and leaped inside, tumbling into the darkness of the open vehicle.

The van accelerated and roared for the exit.

O'Brien slowed to a stop and watched as the vehicle smashed through the security gate, fishtailed a turn, and raced down the perimeter road. He bent over and propped his hands against his knees, gasping for breath, plumes of white vapor rising above him.

And there, alone, bent over in the parking lot, Philip O'Brien realized that Murkoski didn't need to resort to murder. He could find other means of securing people's cooperation.

Coleman headed down the hallway toward Eric's room. He felt terrible. He had humiliated and betrayed Katherine. And he had no idea how to make it right. Maybe he couldn't. That thought made his heart even heavier as he knocked on Eric's door.

"Who is it?" Eric asked. "I'm asleep."

"It's me, can I come in?"

"Sure."

Coleman opened the door and saw the eight-year-old sitting at his desk in the dark, his face bathed by the blue-green glow of a computer screen.

"Hey, Eric."

The boy didn't look up but continued working the keyboard and mouse. "You're not going to sleep with her, are you?" he asked.

Coleman joined him. "How does somebody your age know about that stuff?"

The boy shrugged. "We get cable."

"What are you doing?"

"That guy at the laboratory today?"

"Yeah."

"He said his name was Steiner?"

"Something like that."

Eric clicked his computer mouse twice more and a picture slowly started to scan, from the top of the monitor down.

"It's going to take a little bit of time, since my equipment is like from the Dark Ages. But there's this guy on the Internet, a real nutzoid. Mom doesn't like for me to read anything he writes."

"So, of course, you do."

"All the time. I've been downloading his stuff into my general file folder forever."

The scanning lines had already revealed dark, closely cut hair and a forehead. Now they were defining the slightly crooked bridge of a nose.

"His name is Steiner, too. Anyway, he's always writing these weird letters and sending these pictures telling us not to forget about the man who murdered his daughter."

Eric's voice grew fainter as Coleman watched the monitor. A knot twisted in his stomach as he stared at the emerging eyes.

"And Steiner," Coleman heard himself ask. "He sends this stuff out to everybody on the Net?"

The rest of the nose was forming.

"Nah, just to a few of us."

"Why you, Eric?" His voice was faint now, unsteady. "Why does he send this stuff to you?"

The mouth slowly appeared, followed by the chin. Next, two words in block letters began to form at the bottom of the screen.

"That's easy." Eric answered, his voice was coming from another world.

"Why, Eric?"

" 'Cause the man who killed his daughter killed my dad."

The picture of executed killer Michael Coleman was now complete. And directly below it, in large printed letters, were two words:

**NEVER FORGET**

# CHAPTER 11

Coleman closed Eric's door and somehow made it down the hall. The walls blurred as he stared at the threadbare carpet passing under his feet. He was the one responsible. For their struggles, their pain. He was the one.

He passed the kitchen and heard Katherine scraping the dinner plates. She was eight feet away, but he didn't look up, didn't speak. He had to get out.

He reached the front door and opened it. The knob was tarnished, loose, and like everything else in this impoverished apartment, ready to fall apart. And he was the reason they were here.

Everything would have been different. Katherine would be back in Council Bluffs, in a real home. She'd be a different person, full of the tenderness and innocence he had been able to see inside her. She'd be in her kitchen loading her dishwasher, preparing to join her husband on the sofa to watch TV, or maybe talk about their dreams, their kids, how to swing payments on that new minivan.

But thanks to him, she had no future. Thanks to him she had no life.

He closed the door, headed down the hall, and took the elevator to the lobby.

He had stepped out and was headed toward the main door when, not eighteen inches from his head, he heard the distinctive click of a revolver's hammer being cocked. He froze. Had he been more alert, he might have seen the shadow that had approached from behind.

"Good evening, Mr. Coleman."

He didn't have to turn to know it was Steiner holding the gun. The voice quivered, trying to control its fear and rage. For the first time in months, Coleman felt a trace of anger. Didn't this twit know how easily he could remove the gun from his hands, how he could break his fingers, or just as easily break his neck? The thought startled Coleman almost as much as Steiner's presence.

"I don't know what happened or what's going on," the voice was saying, "but I think it's time the two of us had a good long talk."

Coleman nodded, his anger turning to empathy over the man's fear and confusion. "You're right, there's a lot we need to talk about."

He could sense Steiner wavering a moment, unsure what to do. He took the opportunity to slowly turn and face him. Steiner was blinking hard, as the gun, which trembled slightly in his hands, remained leveled in Coleman's face.

Coleman kept his gaze fixed on the man's eyes and spoke quietly and calmly. "It would be better for both of us if you took a couple steps backward and loosened your grip on the gun a little."

Steiner dug in, bracing himself, refusing to budge.

"That way it won't accidentally go off in your hand. But if I tried to jump you, you'd still have time to shoot."

Steiner remained unmoving.

Coleman understood. The man was so frightened and full of emotion that he could barely hear what was being said, let alone act on it.

"Do you want me to go with you somewhere?" Coleman asked. "Is that what you have in mind?"

For a second Steiner appeared lost. Then, summoning up all of his concentration, he answered. "Yes, that is exactly what I want."

Coleman continued looking into him. The man was completely out of his element, functioning on raw fear and hate. That's all that drove him, pushing him to do things he normally wouldn't, or couldn't, do. But that mixture was a dangerous combination, and Coleman had to try to keep him calm. "Where would you like to go?"

"Outside." Steiner shoved the gun closer to his face. Coleman nodded, then turned and moved through the deserted lobby. Steiner followed directly behind and to the right, never letting the gun drift more than a few inches from the back of Coleman's head.

They passed the mailboxes on the wall and arrived at the glass door. Coleman started to push it open when Steiner suddenly ordered, "Stop."

Coleman obeyed.

Steiner motioned across the street, over to two men who sat inside a gray Audi, drinking coffee. He swore. "They've been following me ever since I left Genodyne." He grabbed Coleman by the jacket and pulled him back out of sight before they were spotted. "Looks like we're staying here for a while," he said. "Let's go pay that lady friend of yours a call."

The words sounded tough, but Coleman knew the man was terrified. He turned. "Listen, I don't think—"

Steiner shoved him forward and took several steps back. "Move!"

Now, even if he wanted to, Coleman could not disarm him. He was too far away. The man was a fast learner.

Reluctantly, Coleman obeyed.


"Hello?"

"Hi, Connie, this is Dr. O'Brien."

"Dr. O'Brien?" The voice grew clearer.

"I'm sorry to be calling so late."

"No, it's okay, I, uh . . ." There was a pause. O'Brien could imagine her turning on her light, trying to force the grogginess from her mind. "I really haven't been able to sleep that much anyway."

"I understand. Wolff was a good man. He's going to be missed by all of us." It was O'Brien's turn to pause. He picked at the rubber molding around what had once been Wolff's desk. He stared at the empty corkboard, the vacant shelves. After the incident in the parking lot, he'd known that he wouldn't be able to get any sleep, so he had gone back. Now he was in Wolff's office.

"Listen, uh—" He cleared his throat. "Wolff's personal belongings, his notes and so forth . . ."

"Yeah, they're all here. They couldn't find any next of kin, so they figured I'm like the closest."

O'Brien had guessed as much. Although Wolff had pretended to be a free agent, it had been obvious since last year's company picnic that he and Connie were becoming an item. Company policy scowled at such relationships, but what are you going to do? It was love. Besides, she was all the way over in accounting.

"Did they give you his lab book?" he asked.

"Yeah, it's right over here on the dresser."

"Connie, I know my timing stinks, but I wouldn't be calling if it weren't important."

"Is there something you want from it?"

O'Brien sighed gratefully. She was making it easier for him than he had hoped. "Yes. His last few entries."

He heard her moving, getting up. "Hang on. Here we go." Pages were flipping. "That's weird."

"What's that?"

"The last page. He ripped out the last page."

"Are you certain?"

"Yeah. Looks like he was in a hurry."

"How can you tell?"

"It's not in his usual, neat-freak style. It was just torn out any ol' way. In fact . . . oh, that explains it."

"Explains what?"

"Here it is."

"Here what is? What are you doing, Connie?"

"They found a piece of paper stuffed in his pants pocket."

"And?"

"Well, I've got it right here, and it looks like the piece he ripped out of the notebook. Now, why would he do that?"

O'Brien's heart began to race. "What's it say, Connie—what did he write on it?"

"Nothing. It's completely empty. There's nothing—well, except up here at the top."

"What's it say, Connie?"

"It's just some name with a Roman numeral after it."

"Some name?"

"Yeah. *Hind*. *Hind*III."

O'Brien stopped breathing. *Hind*III was another restriction enzyme—another chemical used to cut and identify genes. Whatever Wolff had discovered, he had discovered by running the gel with the *Hind*III enzyme instead of the *Eco*RI that they had been using since the GOD gene's discovery.

He glanced at his watch. 2:18 A.M. It looked like it was time to run a few more gels.

"You're not telling me anything new," Katherine growled. She was outraged, and had a right to be. Busting into her apartment and holding a gun on Coleman and herself was not a way to win her cooperation. "I know he's got a past," she continued, "I know he's served time. But people change. Can't you see that? He's not the same man who—"

"Men like him don't change!" Steiner brandished the gun toward Coleman, whom he had ordered to sit on the sofa. Earlier, Eric had stumbled down the hall to check out the commotion and had been immediately sent back to his room with orders not to come out. That had been fifteen minutes ago. Now Katherine and Steiner hovered over Coleman, who remained strangely quiet. She thought it odd that since they had entered her apartment, he had not looked at her. Not once.

"Of *course* they can change," she insisted. "Old things can pass away, all things can become new." It was obvious that Steiner didn't understand the reference, so she continued. "This man, he's the kindest, most sensitive person I've ever—"

"You don't know what he's done!"

"I don't *care* what he's done!" she yelled back. Then, regaining control, she tried again. "Look, I don't know how he hurt you, or how he may have wronged you. But you have to understand, he's changed. He's not the same man. Where's your sense of mercy, your compassion?"

"Mercy?"

"Yeah."

"Compassion? You want compassion? This man is a murderer!"

Katherine blinked. She showed no other emotion, but inside she felt as if someone had smashed a baseball bat into her gut. She took half a step back and found an armchair to lean against. Her eyes darted from Coleman to Steiner, then back to Coleman. "That's not true."

Neither man answered.

She repeated her statement, but this time it was a demand: "That's not true!"

Coleman stared at his hands.

She waited, forever.

Then, ever so slowly, he began to nod. "Yeah." His voice was a raspy whisper. "I, uh," he coughed, then with obvious effort forced out the words, "I killed his daughter."

Katherine closed her eyes. She eased herself down into the armchair.

"And who else?" Steiner's voice quivered with rage and triumph. "Tell her who else you've killed!"

Coleman continued to look down. He took a deep breath then shook his head. "I don't know."

"Oh, really? Let's see if I can help. There was that prostitute in Des Moines . . ."

Coleman kept his head down.

"The convenience store clerk in Council Bluffs."

Katherine stiffened. "Council Bluffs? You killed somebody in Council Bluffs?"

Steiner answered for him. "Of course, none of these can be proven."

Coleman stared at the floor, unmoving.

"Then there was the cop."

"You shot a cop?" Suddenly Katherine's head felt very, very light, as if it were trying to float off her body. "When? When did you shoot a cop?"

Coleman gave no answer.

Now she was on her feet, unthinkable suspicions rising. "Was he a patrolman? Did you shoot a patrolman?"

At last Coleman looked up. His cheeks were wet with tears. "Yes," he croaked. "I . . . think so."

"What's your name?" Blood surged through her body. She was floating high above the scene, somewhere else. "Who are you?"

Coleman held her eyes, confronting her glare. "My name is Coleman. Michael Coleman."

Katherine's head exploded. She barely heard the rest.

"I murdered Mr. Steiner's daughter. I may have murdered your husband, too. I . . ." His eyes faltered. "I don't remember."

"You don't remember?"

He didn't respond.

She moved toward him. "You don't remember!"

He shook his head and looked down. That's when she attacked him. She leaped at him, arms flying, hitting him with everything she had, venting her fury, pounding on his chest, his shoulders, his arms.

"You destroy my life, and you don't even have the decency to *remember?*"

Coleman made no move to protect himself as she flailed and swore, calling him every name she could think of, hitting him so hard her hands were bruising.

It was Steiner who finally pulled her off. "Stop it. That's enough. That's enough, now. Stop it!"

She managed to land several more blows before her anger spent itself into exhaustion and Steiner was able to drag her off and back to the armchair. She was crying now, gut-wrenching sobs. But even then, over the tears, she could hear Steiner's gloating words:

"So much for mercy and compassion."

O'Brien placed the new gel under the UV light so that he could study its bands. He had run it several times, thinking he'd made a mistake. After all, it had been a long time since he'd worked in the lab like this. He'd even cut the gene with enzymes that were different from Wolff's suggested *Hind*III.

But the mistake was not at his end. Something else was wrong. The bands were entirely different. And yet, as he studied them, as he compared their lengths and added them together, he found them to be exactly the same gene.

What he had before him was the GOD gene, and yet, somehow, it wasn't. A cold dread took residence somewhere deep in his chest.

He photographed each gel with the overhead black-and-white Polaroid, then gathered the pictures and headed back to the offices.

The dread grew stronger as he studied the conflicting patterns, and as he remembered the mice ...

He could understand the effects of the experiment breaking down and wearing off. With all of the unknowns they had to deal with, it was possible—in fact, quite common—for some unforeseen element to arise, causing the tests to fail and allowing the mice to revert back to their old behavior. But these mice had not reverted. They had attacked and murdered each other. That was not old behavior. That was totally new. Lab mice wouldn't attack and destroy each other, not like that.

Not only was it new behavior, but—and this is what terrified him the most—it was exactly the opposite behavior of what the GOD gene produced. Instead of a compassionate community working together, those animals had completely obliterated themselves.

An unspeakable suspicion had now risen to the surface of O'Brien's mind. He had been trying to push it aside, but now he knew he must pursue it.

He arrived outside Murkoski's office. The locked door was made of quality oak. Fortunately, the quality of the vertical window running along the side of the door wasn't nearly as high. Still, it took three attempts with the receptionist's chair before he managed to break out the glass. Then there was the matter of reaching through the gaping hole and around to the door handle. He succeeded, but not without sustaining a sizable gash in his left forearm from one of the remaining shards of glass.

He decided not to turn on the lights; instead, he used the glow from the large saltwater aquarium against the wall to help him find the computer. He slipped behind the screen, turned it on, and breathed a silent prayer that Murkoski's arrogance and impatience had led him to forego using a password.

His prayer was answered.

Now came the painstaking process of going through file after file after file. It was the only way. If Murkoski was working a different pattern, he would have it recorded somewhere.

But O'Brien got lucky. The files were listed alphabetically, and he only had to go as far as the "D's" to find it. It was under "Diable.gne."

When he brought the file to the screen and studied the patterns, he could only close his eyes and sink into the chair. Now there was no doubt. O'Brien's worst fears had become reality.

"This is too strange," Steiner said. He was pacing in front of the sofa where Coleman sat. Katherine remained in the armchair. Several minutes had passed since she had attacked Coleman, but neither had completely recovered.

Steiner continued to think out loud. "Of all the people to put together, why you two? Why team up a convicted killer with his victim's own wife? It doesn't make sense. Surely they knew you two would eventually find out."

"Unless . . ." Katherine spoke slowly, her voice dull and lifeless. "Unless that's what they wanted."

"For you to find out?"

She nodded.

"But why?"

No one had an answer.

"And this Dr. Murkoski." He turned to Coleman. "You said he was bragging about all of his big-time government connections?"

Coleman nodded. "Wore them like a badge."

Steiner shook his head. "If this was the federal government, they wouldn't mess with a state prison like Nebraska. They'd go directly to a federal pen. Someplace like Leavenworth. Fewer people, fewer chances of leaks. I'm not saying officials weren't involved, but there's more power being wielded here than the government's. Two people have been killed, maybe more."

Coleman looked up. "More people have been killed?"

Steiner glanced to him, then almost seemed to revel in providing the information. "The county coroner and a doctor from the prison were killed. Both to protect you."

A numbness crawled through Coleman.

"There's no short-circuiting justice. Someone always has to pay. In this case, it was two lives for one."

The numbness spread into Coleman's mind. How much more pain was he responsible for? How much more destruction?

"You said there's more power here than the government's?" Katherine asked.

Steiner nodded.

"What could be more powerful than the federal government?"

Steiner looked at her. "Greed, of course. There's money involved here, Mrs. Lyon. Lots of it."

"But whose? And what type of sadist would throw the two of us together?"

The sudden knock at the front door startled them.

Katherine was the first to speak. "Is that the guys out front?" she whispered.

Neither man answered.

More knocking. Harder.

Steiner motioned her to her feet with the gun. She obeyed. Coleman also started to rise, but Steiner ordered, "You stay put."

Reluctantly, Coleman obliged and watched as they crossed to the door.

"Find out who it is," Steiner whispered. "Tell them to go away."

More knocking.

"All right, all right," Katherine called. "It's four in the morning, who is it?"

"Sorry to disturb you, Ma'am." The voice from the other side sounded young. "FBI. We have an urgent matter we need to discuss with you."

All three exchanged glances. Steiner whispered. "Ask to see their ID."

Katherine nodded, shoving her face toward the peep hole. "You guys got badges?"

Despite Steiner's orders, Coleman rose to his feet and cautiously approached. Steiner was getting nervous with the gun again, and Coleman didn't want him doing anything stupid with Katherine so close.

"What do you see?" Steiner whispered.

"They look real to me," Katherine answered.

He turned, anxiously searching the room. "Do you have a back door, another exit?"

"Just the bedroom windows."

Steiner looked down the hall nervously, then pointed the gun at Coleman. "You come with me."

Coleman shook his head. "We're on the third story."

Beads of perspiration appeared on Steiner's forehead.

Coleman stood quietly, watching. He was beginning to experience the familiar sharpening of his senses, the focusing of vision.

More knocking. "Mrs. Lyon?"

Steiner was in a panic. "What do we do? What do we—"

"Open it," Coleman ordered as he stepped forward.

"What?"

Katherine looked up at him.

"It's okay," he said. "There's no place we can go. Open it."

Katherine turned to Steiner, who was wiping the sweat from his forehead. He glanced at them both, then took a step behind the door. He cocked his pistol and nodded. With Coleman at her side, Katherine unbolted the lock and swung the door open.

Two men stood before them. A pretty twentysomething on the left, a pudgier man in his forties on the right.

"Mrs. Lyon?" Twentysomething asked.

"Yes."

"I'm Special Agent Briner, this is Agent Irving." Without giving her time to answer, he looked to Coleman. "And you must be William Michaels or"—he almost smiled—"should I say, Michael Coleman."

Coleman gave no answer. He was too busy looking into the boy's eyes, evaluating his clothes, the posturing of his body—and all the time, his senses continued to focus and tighten.

"May we come in?"

"What's this about?" Katherine asked.

"I think it would be better if we came inside."

"What's this about?" she repeated, holding her ground.

Finally, Pudgy Man spoke. "We have reason to believe that a Mr. Harold Steiner is in the area and that he may be planning to jeopardize the—"

Coleman lunged at the youngest first, throwing the bulk of his left shoulder into the boy's chest, while sweeping out his right hand and breaking Pudgy Man's nose with his fist. The boy staggered and fell under Coleman's weight, and his partner was too busy grabbing his nose to be of much assistance.

Coleman had taken Twentysomething's head into his hands, and it was only Katherine's scream that prevented him from breaking the kid's neck. He settled for hitting him squarely in the face and knocking him unconscious.

By now Pudgy Man was fumbling for his gun. Coleman sprang up and delivered a single punch to the man's stomach and one to the jaw, dropping him to the floor to join his partner.

The flurry had ended as quickly at it had begun. Except for Coleman's heavy breathing, silence filled the hallway. He stood over his handiwork just outside the apartment door, stunned, trying to understand what had happened. The old exhilaration, the thrill, had momentarily surfaced. It had come and gone in seconds, but it left Coleman deeply shaken.

"What did you do that for?" Katherine demanded.

Coleman looked up, trying to get his bearings.

Steiner stepped out from behind the door and gasped. "What did you do?"

"They're not FBI," Coleman said.

"How can you be sure?" Katherine asked.

"Look at their suits. Feds can't afford quality like that."

Katherine and Steiner continued to stare.

Coleman knelt next to the older man and pulled aside the suit coat to reveal a holstered, shiny new .40 caliber Smith and Wesson. He removed the gun, pocketed the clip, and tossed the piece into the apartment.

"Why . . ." Steiner asked, his voice unsteady. "What were they after?"

Katherine shook her head. "I don't think *what* is the right question."

Steiner began to tremble more noticeably. "But—why? What did I do?"

Coleman pulled back Twentysomething's coat. Same holster, but a Colt Mustang .380. "You said they already killed two people?"

Steiner nodded as Coleman removed the gun and popped out the magazine. He checked the other pocket and pulled out a small, round silencer.

"Looks like they wanted to make it three."

Steiner leaned against the door frame to steady himself.

"You going to be okay?" Katherine asked.

He nodded, but it was obviously a lie.

Coleman remained standing over the bodies, still haunted by his actions. Finally he turned to Katherine. "Do you have any antiseptic? Some cloths and cold water?"

She looked up at him, not entirely hearing.

"Katherine?"

Coming to, she nodded. "Yeah, sure." She headed back into the apartment.

Coleman knelt to inspect Pudgy Man while addressing Steiner. "Give me a hand with these two. Let's get them into the apartment where we can—"

He heard the click of the revolver and looked up to see Steiner raising his gun at him.

"What are you doing?" Coleman asked, more irritated than concerned.

"I think we'll let the police handle it from here."

"You're not serious."

"Mrs. Lyon," Steiner called to Katherine, who was inside the apartment at the kitchen sink. "Please call 911. Tell them we have two injured men here and an escaped convict."

"*What?*"

"You heard me."

As Coleman rose, Steiner backed up several steps to keep a safe distance.

"The man just saved your life," Katherine said.

"And for that I am grateful. But he's still a convicted killer, and I think it's about time we—"

"Steiner, be reasonable," Coleman said.

"Oh, I'm very reasonable, Mr. Coleman."

"Do you honestly think that the police are going to stop guys like this? These guys make a living by—"

"If you'll toss that gun in here with the other and step inside, please. And Mrs. Lyon, will you please make that call?"

"Come on, Steiner," she protested.

Coleman looked at the clip in his hand. He felt its weight, its smooth, hard corners. He ran his thumb over the top cartridge, the next one to be thrust into the firing chamber. Its nickel casing was cool to the touch, the copper coating over the bullet smooth and sleek. Only the nose had texture. It was a hollow point, its tip serrated into a six-pointed star designed to flatten upon impact, destroying as much flesh and bone as possible. So much power here. So much potential. In its own way, its ability to destroy was as awesomely beautiful as any morning mist, or setting sun.

Coleman knew it would be risky, but he could shove the clip into the gun and fire a round or two into Steiner. Of course, he might take a couple of hits himself, but considering Steiner's fear and his inexperience with guns, the odds were in Coleman's favor.

"Drop the gun, Mr. Coleman." The voice was high and quivering.

Coleman looked up and was surprised to see something he had never seen before. In the man's eyes was more than the usual fear and questioning. There was something harder, colder. Something was consuming him, controlling him. Here was a man lost and empty, yet at the same time utterly consumed. The helplessness touched Coleman. He wanted to reach out, to somehow comfort the man. He glanced back at his gun. A hastily fired round into Steiner's body would neither kill what consumed him, nor fill his emptiness.

"I'm not telling you again. Drop the gun."

Coleman slowly lowered the gun and tossed it into the living room.

"Now step inside. And Mrs. Lyon, if you don't make that phone call, I will."

Coleman stepped into the apartment as Katherine began to dial. "I can't believe you're doing this," she said angrily.

"Believe it, Mrs. Lyon. The Law is the Law. And in the end, justice will prevail."

"And justice, that's all that matters?" Coleman asked.

"Justice is all that we have."

"Uh-oh."

The men turned to see Katherine, receiver in hand, looking out the living-room window.

"What's the problem?" Steiner demanded.

Katherine motioned toward the street. "Looks like we've got more company."

# CHAPTER 12

It was Lisa, the downstairs neighbor, who helped Coleman and Steiner escape. After some hasty explanations from Katherine—plus the additional motivation of Steiner's waving gun—she escorted the two men to her back bedroom window, where they climbed out and dropped the ten feet to the pavement.

There was no need for Katherine to come too. No one was after her. But to be safe, she grabbed Eric, had him throw on his all-purpose, purple-and-gold University of Washington sweatshirt, left some cold cloths for the men in her hallway, and asked Lisa if she and her son could hang out at her place for the rest of the evening. There was no telling what those men would do once they regained consciousness—or what the new arrivals Katherine had seen waiting outside had in mind.

"No problem," a wide-eyed Lisa had answered. "But if this is how you've adjusted to the dating scene, we've got some serious talking to do."

It was 4:15 in the morning. Outside, a heavy drizzle fell as Coleman and Steiner quickly crossed the street behind the building, Coleman in front, Steiner behind him with the gun.

When they reached Steiner's rental, a white Taurus, Steiner tossed Coleman the keys. "You drive."

"I don't think that's such a good idea. It's been a while."

Steiner referred to his gun. "I can't drive and hold this, too."

"Then let me take it. You drive and I'll hold the gun."

Steiner gave him a look. "Get in."

Coleman had barely turned over the ignition when the first shot shattered the right rear window. Both men ducked. When they rose and turned they saw a tall man just rounding the building and racing toward them. His hair was long and blonde. He wore a gray topcoat and was re-aiming his .357.

"Get us out of here!" Steiner shouted.

Coleman tromped on the gas. Unfortunately, he'd dropped it into the wrong gear. They shot backwards into a jarring, glass-shattering crash, devastating the front end of someone's new Blazer.

Another shot. The gunman was good; he hit Steiner's window, missing his head by mere inches.

"Let's go! Let's go!"

Coleman shifted, punched the accelerator, and they spun out as a third round hit somewhere to the rear of Steiner's door.

Coleman glanced into the mirror. Headlights zipped around the corner, momentarily slowing for the blonde man to climb in. "Where to?" Coleman shouted.

"The police."

Coleman threw him a look. "You never give up, do you?" The lights in the mirror picked up speed, and Coleman accelerated. "The police can't offer the protection you need—not from these guys."

"What do you care?" Steiner said, looking out the back. "They want me, not you."

Suddenly the rear window shattered into a million fragments.

"I don't think they're too concerned about making that distinction right now," Coleman yelled. He turned to Steiner, whose eyes suddenly widened in fear.

"Look out!"

Coleman looked back just in time to see a street sweeper filling his vision. He cranked the wheel hard to the left, then straightened it out. But the inertia and the slick street threw them into a skid.

"What are you doing!" Steiner shouted.

"I told you—I'm a little rusty!"

He managed to pull it out of the skid as another bullet sparked off the left fender. Coleman checked the mirror. Through the shattered glass he could see the headlights closing in.

"There!" Steiner pointed.

"What?"

"The freeway entrance. Right there!"

By the time Coleman saw the ramp they were almost past it. He pulled the wheel to the right. Again the car slid into a skid, this time taking out a road sign before bouncing up the landscaped incline and finally making it onto the ramp. Steiner was still shouting as Coleman accelerated and headed for the freeway.

Katherine had collapsed onto Lisa's sofa. She was past exhaustion. So many emotions raged inside her: hate, love, betrayal, worry, fear. She wanted to scream, to shout, to beat the wall, but she was too numb to even cry.

She feared for Coleman's life, yet she hated him with such fury and such a sense of betrayal that her head pounded in anger. This was the man who had killed her Gary, who had destroyed everything. There was no forgiving such a monster.

But that monster had died months ago. *Old things are passed away.* The monster was gone, and in its place was a man who had reached in and touched her heart, who was so kind and sweet and caring that he had refused to have sex with her because it was not the right thing—for her. She trembled with both weakness and rage. She had never seen such sensitivity, such innocence—

*NO!*

He is not innocent. He is a murderer! The murderer of my husband.

*All things are become new.*

NO! He is a killer. The killer of everything I had, of everything I was!

The thoughts warred inside her head, back and forth, until finally, with what little strength she had left, she took hold of the door he had opened inside of her and with the greatest effort forced it closed. It slammed with such power that she could feel the reverberation deep into her soul. She had made a mistake. She had started to feel. She had let someone inside. She would not allow that again. Never. Now everything would return to its place, just as it had been, just as it should be. Everything but the tears, which had finally started and which she could not stop.

"Mom?"

She looked up to see Eric's worried face hovering over her. Lisa had tried putting him to bed, but he was up and kneeling over her. "It's okay, Mom." She felt his arms around her shoulders, clumsily patting her, trying to comfort. "We'll find a way to help him."

The tears came faster. Not only had the monster opened her up and touched her heart, he had touched her son as well. "It's okay," he repeated. "Honest. We'll get him back, I promise."

She reached out and drew him to her. But instead of protesting as he usually did, Eric allowed himself to be pulled into the embrace.

Suddenly, the door exploded.

Katherine screamed and leaped up just as Twentysomething and Pudgy Man raced into the room.


They had turned off the Mukilteo Freeway and were heading north on Interstate 5.

"How fast are we going?"

Coleman glanced at the speedometer. "A little over ninety."

Steiner scanned the roadway. "Where's a good cop when you need one?"

Coleman glanced into the mirror. Their pursuers had initially missed the on-ramp. That had put them about thirty seconds behind. But in the distance he could see their lights slowly gaining. Coleman had the accelerator pegged to the floor, but minute by minute the other car was closing the gap.

"Maybe there's some other way to beat these guys," he suggested.

"You'd like that, wouldn't you?" Steiner said. "Take the Law into your own hands. Maybe kill a few extra people along the way."

Coleman fought back the irritation. "People change."

"The Law doesn't."

"You keep saying that, but what about mercy? What about forgiveness?"

"Aberrations. A human invention."

Coleman nearly laughed. "You're not serious?"

"I'm not? Ask yourself, what holds the universe together?"

"You tell me."

"Laws. The laws of physics, the law of gravity, of ther- modynamics—all these laws are what hold the stars, the plan- ets, even the atoms in place. Without these laws, everything would fly apart and turn to chaos."

"But we're not planets, we're human beings."

"And that makes us exempt?"

Coleman had no answer.

"Civilization must have rules. If you break a law any- where else in the universe, you pay the consequences. You jump off a building, you fall. You split an atom, you vaporize."

"You kill a man, you die."

"Exactly. Cause and effect. Since the beginning of time, the equation has been the same. If you break that equation, and do not seek justice, a part of our civilization unravels, exactly as the universe would."

"But *people change*. There has to be forgiveness. There has to be some compassion."

"The Law is the Law."

Coleman glanced in the mirror. The car was two hundred yards away. "I don't want to be petty here, but didn't I just save your rear back at the apartment? Doesn't that count for some- thing in your 'cosmic equation'?"

"Not my decision to make. That's why we have authorities."

"Listen—we have to do something. They'll be here any second."

Steiner looked over his shoulder, then turned forward to search the freeway. An approaching sign read: BROADWAY 1/2 MILE. "There." He pointed. "Take that."

But Coleman had other plans. About a hundred yards ahead he spotted an old plumbing van ambling down the third lane from the median. Instead of pulling to the right and heading for the exit, Coleman crossed to the far left lane.

"What are you doing?"

Coleman gave no answer but began to decelerate.

"What are you doing?" Steiner demanded.

A second later the car was on their tail.

"Coleman!" Steiner shouted. "Turn to the right! Take the exit. Take the exit!"

Before Coleman could respond, the other car swerved to their right and pulled up beside them. He glanced at the speedometer. They were doing seventy-five. He looked over to the car. The driver was motioning for them to slow down and pull over. On the passenger side, the blonde was emphasizing the point with his leveled gun.

The plumbing van was twenty-five yards ahead and two lanes over.

"Get us out of here!" Steiner demanded. "Now!"

"Hang on," Coleman warned.

Steiner barely had time to brace himself before Coleman swung the car hard to the right and slammed into the other vehicle.

The startled driver swerved into the next lane.

"What are you doing?" Steiner shouted.

There was no time to answer as Coleman hit the brakes and they lurched forward. In the other car, the driver and the blonde snapped their heads back, watching Coleman's car in bewilderment as they raced past. But that was only their first surprise. The second came an instant later when they slammed into the back of the plumbing van.

Coleman swerved sharply, making a beeline for the exit. He had gained some time, but not a lot. They sped down the Broadway off-ramp, made a hard left, scooted up a few streets, then made another right. It was a major thoroughfare but completely deserted this time of morning. Malls and stores sped past, slightly obscured by a fog that increased as they approached the river.

Cresting a small hill, Coleman and Steiner saw the flashing lights at the same time.

"What is it?"

"A drawbridge."

Steiner swore, then spotted a side street, off to the left. "There, take that!"

Coleman turned the wheel, but this time his luck did not prevail. They skidded through the slick intersection until their wheels broadsided the traffic island on the other end and the car flipped. Coleman flew hard into Steiner and the passenger door, then slammed up into the roof. The sound of twisting, screeching metal filled his ears as glass exploded, pelting him from all sides. The car's roll flung Coleman down into the steering wheel and dash, then back onto the roof again. There was no pain, the pain would come later, only crazy, out-of-control tumbling amid flying glass and crushing steel.

And then it stopped, as suddenly as it had begun.

Everything was deathly silent. Only the ringing of the drawbridge bell sixty feet away cut through the stillness.

Coleman opened his eyes. He lay on the roof. The car rested upside down. No fire, no explosions. Just the bridge's ringing bell and its flashing red lights.

He tried to move. Pain shot through his left arm. He heard a groan from the other side of the car and twisted to look. In the flashing light he could see Steiner, his face bloodied and his leg crushed by a large piece of metal.

"Steiner? Steiner!"

The man's eyes opened.

"We've got to get out of here."

Steiner tried to answer, but it came out a gurgle. He coughed, then spat a mouthful of blood.

Coleman pushed at his driver-side door. With a little coaxing, it creaked open. He reached across the car to Steiner and grabbed him around the chest. As he began to pull, Steiner cried out in pain. The crumpled metal kept his leg pinned. Coleman tried again, harder, but Steiner could not be budged.

Steiner coughed, spattering blood. "It's no use."

Coleman raised his feet toward Steiner's door and began kicking the metal.

"Leave," Steiner gurgled. "It's what you—" He coughed violently. "It's what you want." He managed to glare in Coleman's direction. "Go ahead, leave me."

The accusation angered Coleman, and he used the emotion to kick the door harder—five, six, seven times—until the metal finally started to bend. After another half-dozen kicks, there was enough room to pull Steiner free. Coleman grabbed him around the ribs again and pulled him across the inside of the roof until they reached his open door. Then, with one final heave, they both tumbled out and onto the pavement.

Coleman lay a second, catching his breath. The bell continued to ring. The light continued to flash. He rose to a sitting position and looked behind them for the pursuing car.

Nothing yet.

He heard a scraping of gravel and turned to see Steiner trying to reach back into the car. For a moment he was confused, then he saw the reason. The gun. It lay just inside, on the roof.

Coleman staggered to his feet and easily cut Steiner off. He reached into the car and scooped up the weapon. He was surprised at how pleasant its weight felt in his hands. It was good to experience that type of power again. And with that power came the anger. It bubbled up from somewhere deep inside. How dare this twisted little man threaten him. How dare he come back and ruin his new life.

Coleman turned toward him. The look of fear he saw in Steiner's eyes said the man knew exactly what Coleman was thinking. The expression made Coleman grin. "What's the matter?" he asked. "Afraid of a little justice?"

Steiner tried to answer but couldn't find his voice. That was fine with Coleman. He'd heard enough of Steiner's lectures, endured enough of his abuse. Now it was payback time. His heart pounded; exhilaration spread through his body. It was just like old times, and it felt good. Very, very good. He raised the revolver until it pointed directly at Steiner's forehead.

But instead of horror, Steiner's expression shifted to contempt. "Go ahead," he coughed. "We both know it's—" More coughing. "... this is who you are. Go ahead. Go ahead!"

Happy to oblige, Coleman pulled back the hammer. His senses sharpened. He could no longer hear the ringing of the drawbridge bell nor see its flashing light. Now there was only Steiner and his ragged breathing.

The man went into another coughing fit and Coleman waited patiently. He wanted to make sure he had the man's undivided attention before blowing him away.

Steiner finished, then glared back up at him. "Go ahead," he coughed. "What are you waiting for?"

Coleman wasn't sure. The rage inside him was beginning to waver. It was losing its strength, no longer supplying him with its power. And the longer he looked into Steiner's eyes, the weaker it became.

"Go ahead," Steiner taunted. "It's what you want! Go ahead!"

Coleman's hand began to tremble—not with fear, but with indecision. It was as if compassion was somehow fighting for control, struggling to resurface.

"Shoot me!" Steiner demanded. "Shoot me!"

Now, once again, Coleman was seeing into the man's heart. Understanding the terrible, searching loneliness. The consuming, controlling rage. But there was something else. Like the moon rising in the cedars, the snow glistening in the prison yard, or the distant wail of the freight train, there was something of beauty in this man, something of value. Despite his ugliness, he, too, bore the fingerprint of creation. Something of eternity dwelt in him, something of eternity searching for the eternal.

"Kill me! Kill me!"

Coleman slowly lowered the gun.

Steiner swore. "You're a coward. A coward!"

Coleman released the hammer, uncocking the pistol. He gave an involuntary shudder at what had nearly taken place, then threw the weapon as far into the bushes as he could. He reached down and pulled the shocked Steiner to his feet. "Come on," he ordered. "Let's go."

"Where is he?" Twentysomething shouted.

"I don't—"

"MOM!"

Katherine lunged for Eric, but Pudgy Man was already pulling him away.

"Let him go!" She was on her feet, leaping at him. "Let him—"

Pudgy Man caught her and threw her back onto the sofa with such force that it knocked the wind out of her.

Lisa stormed out of her bedroom, looking as angry as she was frightened. "Who are—what—"

Twentysomething dropped her with a brutal slam of his fist into her temple.

"Lisa!"

"Where are they?" Pudgy Man demanded.

"I don't know!"

"Mom!"

He threw Eric over to Twentysomething and turned on Katherine. "Where did they go!"

"I don't know! They didn't say!"

He grabbed a handful of hair on both sides of her head and pulled her to her feet. She wanted to claw out his eyes, to snap his knee with her foot. But he knew the moves before she could make them.

"Mom!"

"Shut up!" Twentysomething shouted.

Now Pudgy Man held her face directly in front of his, spittle flying. "I'm asking you one last time!"

"I don't know!" she screamed, "I don't know, I don't—"

Again she was flying across the room. This time into the wall. Her head hit hard. She slumped to the floor, trying to hang on to consciousness.

"Mom . . ." Eric's voice grew faint. "Mom . . ." She thought he might come to her, but he didn't. She hoped he would understand why she couldn't come to him.

The men were talking, but far away, from another planet. ". . . Mom . . ."

She tried to move, but her body wouldn't obey.

Now a face was talking at her. Pudgy Man. ". . . if you cooperate. Keep your mouth shut, and he'll be returned in twenty-four hours. Got that? Twenty-four hours. No cops and you'll see your kid again. You got that?"

She tried to nod and must have succeeded because the face disappeared.

"Mom . . . *Mom!*" Eric's voice faded. With concentrated effort, Katherine managed to raise her head. But the men and boy were already gone.


The bridge remained deserted as Coleman helped Steiner under the wooden traffic barrier, then supported the hobbling man as they headed out toward the center. Unlike your typical storybook drawbridges, this bridge did not operate by tilting up. Instead the entire midsection, about sixty feet of asphalt and steel, was on a counterweight system that raised it straight into the air like an elevator.

Now it was dropping back into place, slowly, silently.

Forty feet below, amid the swirling fog, a red-and-white barge piled high with cedar chips was being towed down the Snohomish River toward Puget Sound.

Coleman again looked for the pursuing car. Nothing. He hoped they'd lost them. In any case, the sooner they crossed this bridge out of the city and disappeared into the miles of foggy marshland on the other side, the better.

Unfortunately, Steiner was not making it a team effort.

"Why are you fighting me?" Coleman shouted as he half-carried, half-dragged the man along.

"I didn't ask for your help."

"So maybe I should just leave you here for them."

Steiner tried to answer but broke into another fit of coughing. They reached the end of the roadway, and Coleman leaned him against the pedestrian handrail. He looked up at the towering piece of iron and pavement, the center of the bridge. It was twenty-five feet above them, continuing its approach as it lowered into place. Soon the steel tongue-and-groove end of the bridge would lock perfectly into the tongue-and-groove of the roadway.

Power and precision.

Coleman walked to the edge, a few feet from where Steiner stood, and looked down through the fog at the river below. The wake of the passing tug and barge lapped silently against the pylons.

Steiner coughed again, only this time he doubled over, gagging and spitting blood.

Coleman walked back to him. "Here, sit down." Steiner tried to push him away, but Coleman didn't give up. "Take my arm here and sit—"

"No!" The cry was part wounded animal, part human rage. And with it came the strength to shove Coleman so hard that he staggered backwards, nearly losing his balance over the edge.

Steiner half rose and shouted, spraying more blood and spittle. "You—" But he broke into more coughing.

Again Coleman approached to help.

But Steiner would have none of it. Angrily, he lunged at Coleman. The impact knocked Coleman off balance, but he was able to recover. Steiner wasn't so lucky. His momentum carried him to the edge. For a brief second he teetered, eyes wide in realization.

Then he fell.

Coleman dove forward, managing to catch one arm. But the force of Steiner's falling body pulled him down, slamming him hard onto the roadway. Now Steiner was dangling over the bridge, clinging to Coleman, his weight pulling Coleman's arm into the roadway's steel teeth.

"Hang on!" Coleman cried. "Hang on!"

He looked up at the descending section of bridge. It was fifteen feet above him and closing fast.

Steiner screamed, trying to pull himself back up, but each tug and jerk dug the steel teeth more deeply into Coleman's arm. He couldn't hold Steiner, not with one hand. He inched himself closer to the edge and reached out his other arm. "Take my hand!"

Steiner looked up, terrified. He coughed again, and the force weakened their grip.

"Take my hand!" Coleman shouted. "Take it!"

At last Steiner began reaching. Coleman strained downward against the harsh steel teeth. They made several lunges for each other, and each time the movement lessened their grip. But finally they touched—first their fingers, then their palms, until they were able to grab each other's wrists.

Steiner looked past Coleman to the approaching bridge. Coleman craned his head to see.

It was ten feet away.

He turned back. The steel teeth continued gouging into his chest and arms. "Pull," he shouted. "Pull!"

But Steiner did not pull. He had stopped.

"What are you doing?"

Steiner gave no response, made no movement.

"You've got to help me!" Coleman turned to look up.

The bridge was six feet away.

He turned back to Steiner. Suddenly he understood. "No!" he shouted, "I'm not letting go! Do you hear me? I'm not letting go! Pull! *Pull!*"

But Steiner simply hung, a dead weight. The bridge was nearly on top of them. Coleman could sense it closing in, hear the difference in the sound, feel the air pressure. "I won't let go," Coleman cried. "You hear me? I won't let go!"

He looked into Steiner's eyes—and saw the spite, the contempt. Steiner would not let Coleman win. He had lived a lifetime proving the perfection of Law. Coleman was wrong. His ways must not prevail. There was no room for mercy. The Law was supreme. Absolute. Not Coleman's mercy. Not his compassion. The Law!

An eerie smile flickered across Steiner's face.

"No!" Coleman cried.

It broadened. He would not allow Coleman to win.

"No . . . no!"

And then, with determination, Steiner released his grip. Their hands slipped apart. And he fell silently, victoriously, into the fog and water.

Coleman rolled out of the way, feeling the steel brush his cheek as the bridge came together, the tongue-and-groove teeth interlocking in silent precision.

It was dawn when O'Brien entered B–11 to visit Freddy. The baboon showed mild curiosity at his entrance, but little else—no enthusiastic welcome, no leaning hard against him to be patted or groomed. He simply loped over to see whether O'Brien had any food; when he saw that he didn't, he headed back to the gym set to play.

Freddy's behavior saddened O'Brien as he slowly sat on the park bench to watch. Something had happened. The baboon's personality had changed. He was no longer the loving and affectionate Freddy he had become since the transplant.

O'Brien sat there numb, barely thinking, until he heard the door to B–11 buzz and click open.

"Well, lookie here."

He was not surprised to hear Murkoski's voice. He had been expecting it.

"Rumor has it you've been burning the midnight oil," Murkoski said as he crossed toward O'Brien.

O'Brien gave his answer without looking. "How much money are they paying you, Kenny?"

"They say you've been brushing up on your lab technique."

"How much?" O'Brien repeated.

"More than you or I have ever seen."

O'Brien nodded. The answer was fair. So was O'Brien's next question. "Is it the Defense Department?"

"Not ours."

For the first time he turned to look at Murkoski.

The kid tossed down the satchel he'd been carrying and smiled. "Some Asian cartel. You've never heard of them."

O'Brien frowned, not understanding.

Murkoski scoffed at the man's ignorance and stretched out on the grass before him. "Empires are no longer defined by geographical borders, Phil. You know that." He picked a blade of grass and began chewing on it. "These days, corporations are the kingdoms. Big multinational corporations." Then, growing more serious, he asked. "How much do you know?"

"I know you're a liar, a cheat, and probably a murderer."

Murkoski shrugged. "Perhaps. But I'm talking about the project, Phil. How much do you know?"

"I know we thought we were working on one side of the DNA molecule, the sense side, when in reality you turned it around and had us working on the antisense."

"That's the beauty of the double helix, isn't it? While one side of the ladder is designed to code for one gene, the other side is designed exactly the opposite, completely neutralizing that gene's effects while coding for another."

"And since both sides are the same length, the gels could not detect the new gene until Wolff started cutting with another enzyme outside the coding region."

"Very good."

"So while you had us thinking we were designing a compassionate, nonaggression gene—"

"I had created the opposite. A gene that removes all inhibition towards aggression."

O'Brien closed his eyes. He had known the answer for the past hour, but hearing it verbalized carried an impact he still wasn't prepared for. Finally he asked the inevitable. "Why?"

Murkoski spat out the grass he was chewing. "Can you imagine what the arms market would pay for something like that?"

"What are you talking about?"

"Come on, Phil, think. In today's world of techno-wars, we have the capability to kill thousands, millions if we wanted, right?"

O'Brien didn't answer.

"So what's the one thing we're missing? What are we lacking?" He didn't wait for an answer. "The will, Phil. We're lacking the men and women with will. We have the buttons, but we don't have people willing to press them. Our technology is capable, but *we're* not. Until now."

O'Brien began to understand. "So instead of compassionate, caring individuals, you're creating killing machines with no conscience."

Murkoski grinned. "Armies select specific personnel. They inject the gene, let them wreak whatever havoc is necessary, and when their time is up, they remove it. Unless, of course there are a few die-hard generals or weapon designers who choose to live with it."

"God help us."

"Too late for that, Phil. He's already been replaced."

"But the mice. I don't understand. There were only six or seven that turned into killers."

"I couldn't very well go around turning everybody into killing machines, now could I? Not unless I wanted to raise a lot of unwanted questions and risk having the project shut down. And why bother? It's the same gene, just reversed. The biological effects will be the same, so why not study them in passive, easy-to-control individuals, instead of killers?"

O'Brien gestured toward the baboon swinging from the gym set. "What about Freddy? His behavior is changing."

"Best I can figure, he's gone into some sort of regression."

O'Brien looked at him.

Murkoski shrugged. "I suspect it has something to do with the junk DNA we introduced. He's gradually reverting to his original state."

O'Brien sadly turned back to the baboon. "And Coleman?"

"He's regressing, too. Of course, it won't be stopping there."

"What do you mean?"

"Wolff noticed it first. There's something about emotional trauma that stops the process. Once they've been exposed to extreme emotional stress, degeneration rapidly sets in. As it progresses, it neutralizes any normal anti-aggression chemistry they may have."

"Meaning . . ."

"Freddy and Coleman are both on their way to becoming far more aggressive than they've ever been."

O'Brien could only stare. *Emotional stress?*

"Probably some sort of defense mechanism of the body's. I guess if you have your teeth busted in enough, it's time to stop hugging and to start fighting. I saw it coming, though. In fact that's why I set up Coleman with one of his victim's wives. See how far we could push him."

"You did *what?*"

"Sure. It was a bonus to find her, but you know me, always the opportunist. Once that little bombshell explodes, it should be enough to push him over the edge. Truth is, my sources say he's already started regression."

"So we've released a multiple murderer back into society who will become worse than he was?"

"Relax, Phil. He's being taken care of. Even as we speak."

O'Brien eyed the kid, afraid to ask exactly what he meant. "And Freddy? What caused him to revert? What was his trauma?"

"Wolff's death, of course. I'm sure it wasn't easy for this poor creature to see his best friend die before his very eyes."

O'Brien had heard enough. He reached into his pocket for his cellular.

Murkoski made no move to prevent him. "And now you're going to put a stop to it all by calling the authorities, right?"

"That's right."

"I don't think so, Phil." Murkoski unbuckled his satchel. "I mean, seeing as you're such a family man and all."

O'Brien's eyes narrowed, his voice suddenly steel hard. "If you've done something to my family, if you've so much as touched—"

"Oh, not me, Phil, not me." He pulled a pile of 8 x 10 black-and-whites from the satchel and tossed them at O'Brien's feet. "I haven't harmed your little family unit. But if you're not careful, you could."

O'Brien stared at the photos. They were of Tisha and himself out in the parking lot, beside his open car, talking, passionately embracing, hungrily kissing. Suddenly he felt very weak. Rage and helplessness poured in, mixing and swirling together. He barely noticed Murkoski reaching back into his satchel.

"I've been talking to the Board. Riordan, McGovern, all the others."

O'Brien finally looked up.

The kid held a single piece of paper in his hand. "Seems they feel your resignation is in order."

"You—you can't do that."

"I'm afraid it's already done." He shoved the paper toward him. "Not to worry though. Besides a generous severance package, they assure me that you'll be able to keep all of your stock options. Not a bad deal when you consider how our value will skyrocket when this new drug hits the open market. All that plus—and here's the kicker—the Cartel is offering you a cool fifty million. Sort of a thank-you gift, not to mention an assurance of your discretion."

O'Brien's head swam. "And if I don't sign this?"

"Oh, there's no *if*, Phil. You can either resign now or wait until later. In which case, I imagine the offer will be far less generous."

O'Brien stared at him numbly.

Murkoski forced a smile and pulled a pen from his sports coat. "It's a no-brainer, Phil. A win/win."

The kid held the pen out to him, but O'Brien could not yet take it.

"You know, Phil, from what I hear, Beth's not that thrilled with your marriage these days. Something like this could either destroy it, or be the perfect opportunity to bring it together again. All that money. All that time with the family."

O'Brien felt himself weakening.

"Then three, five years from now, who knows—maybe you could start up another company."

O'Brien looked back down at the letter.

"I don't have all day, Phil. We've got sort of a deadline coming up here."

"What type of deadline?"

"Let's just say that, even if you wanted to stop things, it's too late."

O'Brien held his gaze a moment, then looked back at the pictures on the ground.

"You're all set. A lifetime of wealth. Familial bliss. And for what? For just turning your head and doing absolutely nothing." Murkoski shoved the pen closer to him.

O'Brien glanced up from the photos and stared at the pen. It was an expensive Japanese brand. Ceramic. Not all that different from the one Beth had given him for their last anniversary.

# PART THREE

# CHAPTER 13

The glare of the high beams irritates him. He adjusts the mirror. He doesn't know who's behind him; he doesn't care. No one can touch him. The crack has made him invincible.

Flashers behind him; a siren squawking. Cops. He glances at his speedometer: 65. He smiles. A bit fast for downtown Council Bluffs. He thinks of outrunning them. Omaha is just across the river. But he's been careful, he has nothing to hide. He chalks up the paranoia to the coke.

He forces himself to relax. He pulls the Nova over to the side of the road. Gravel crunches and pops under the tires as he comes to a stop.

*He rolls down his window, waits forever, tapping his fingers on the wheel. Anxious. Wanting to get on with it.*

*In the mirror he sees the approaching officers. They split, one to each side. A flashlight blinds his eyes. Cop One's pleasantries are false and insincere. "Sir" this, "Mr." that. "May I see your license, please."*

*On the other side Cop Two shines his light through the passenger window, searching. Coleman smiles. He is a professional. They will find nothing.*

*He hands Cop One his license. It's fake, but too good to tell.*

*"May I also see your registration, please?"*

*Coleman reaches for the glove compartment as Cop Two directs his light to the backseat. He hears words spoken over the roof but cannot make them out. Cop One's flashlight darts to the back. It's the shotgun. Peeking out from under the blanket. Coleman meant to throw it in the trunk, but the Quickie Mart alarm made him nervous, sloppy.*

*"Will you step out of the vehicle, Sir?"*

*Coleman's senses focus razor sharp. He hears his door handle being opened, the hinges groaning, the whoosh of a passing car.*

*"Sir?"*

*His hand is still in the glove compartment. On the surface are crumpled French fry bags with their printed rows of orange, gold, and brown arches. Below that, dozens of lotto tickets, red letters on gray, and of course the candy wrappers. His heart pounds in his ears. He reaches under the trash and pulls out a 9mm Browning High Power, semi-automatic.*

*Cop One goes for his gun. Coleman is too fast. The Browning recoils. Pants and knee cap explode four feet from his face. Coleman squeezes off a second round, but he is distracted by the shattering of the passenger window. Cop Two is trying to be a hero.*

*Cop One is down. Yelling. One more round would silence him, but Cop Two is coming in from the other side.*

Coleman turns. He sees the fear in the eyes. He fires point-blank, feels the bullet as it smashes into Cop Two's chest. He screams. He fires again. He feels the second impact, ripping, searing. Cop Two opens his mouth, but it is Coleman who screams. He fires a third round, again feeling its explosion. But he will not stop, he fires a fourth, a fifth, shrieking in agony, as he tries to kill his own pain.

Now someone is on the roof. Pounding. "Michael . . . Michael!" It's his father's voice. Drunk. Angry. He will kill Coleman.

Coleman rolls onto his back. He fires into the roof again and again, like a madman. There is a pathetic groan as a shape tumbles past the window and to the ground. Coleman hears him crawling and knows he's still alive. He leaps out of the car to finish him off. He races around to the other side, raising his gun. But it is not his father who is crawling on the ground.

It is himself.

The wounded Coleman reaches out to him. "Michael." It is his father's voice, but it is Coleman's body. It has always been his body. Since the beginning it has been Coleman pursuing Coleman.

He fires into the bleeding Coleman, feeling each bullet as it bursts into his chest, his belly. But the wounded Coleman will not give up. He reaches out and clutches Coleman's ankle. Coleman fires at point-blank range. The riddled body jolts with each impact, but the grip will not release.

The wounded Coleman grabs Coleman's knees, pulling himself up. "Michael!"

Coleman staggers under his weight.

"You're mine . . ."

"No!" Coleman tries to break free, but the hold is too strong. "Let me go!"

"You are me . . ."

"No!" He is losing his balance.

"You are mine . . ."

He is falling. "Nooo . . ."

Coleman sat up with a start. As reality forced its way back and his vision cleared, he saw that he was surrounded by marsh grass. Acres and acres of it. He rose stiffly to his knees. The drawbridge lay three hundred yards away. The first signs of rush hour were already beginning to appear on it.

His clothes were soaked from the mist. There was the taste of salt on his lips. But he barely noticed. He was still thinking of his dream. He understood it now, and it terrified him.

He was losing ground.

He had felt it in the hallway with Steiner, with the two thugs at the door, and later in the overturned car. The old man was returning. The rage, the uncontrollable fury, it was all fighting to return, to take over.

*You are mine.*

And with each assault, it grew harder to resist.

*You are me.*

The monster would not stop until it had regained complete control.

Coleman's mind raced. Thoughts spun, whirled. Memories of murders, laughter with Katherine, unspeakable violence in prison, gentle sparrings with Eric, they all tumbled and thundered and cried in his head—along with Katherine's haunting words, "Old things are passed away, behold all things are become new."

He rose to his feet. The mountains were glowing pink and orange as dawn began to spread across their peaks. He recalled the pristine beauty of the snow in the exercise yard, the lonesome wail of the freight train. The exhilaration of breaking bones, smashing cartilage.

*Old things are passed away.*

He saw Katherine's eyes, the vulnerability, the love.

*Behold all things are become new.*

He recalled the Bible, their talks about it.

"This ache inside me—it's like he understands."

"I guess that's why he called himself the Bread of Life."

*He is a new creature.*

"My faith was the only thing that kept me sober."
*Old things are passed away.*
"Like he somehow is able to meet my hunger ..."
*Behold all things are become new.*
*You are mine.*
"I suspect it has more to do with a person's faith ..."
*If any man is in Christ, he is a new creature ...*
*You are mine ...*
*Old things are passed away ...*
*You are me.*
*A new creature ...*
*You are me.*
*Old things are passed ...*
*You are ...*
*All things are ...*
*You ...*
"Noooo!"

Coleman's cry startled a lone crane, causing it to rise up from the marsh and take flight. Its wings beat the air as it rose noisily into the sky.

He took a step. "Please ..." Then another. He raised his head toward heaven and shouted, "Do you hear me? *Do you hear me!*"

There was only silence.

He started to run, but the ground was soft and uneven. He fell. He staggered back up, but only for a few more steps before falling again. He rose and stumbled forward, still trying to run. Where, he wasn't sure. For how long, he didn't know.

"Help me," he gasped, then fell again. And rose again. His vision blurring with hot tears. Three, four, a half-dozen more steps before he fell again. He rose one last time, but his energy was spent, the fight gone. Slowly he sank back down to his knees.

"I can't ..." He fought to breathe. "I need ..." Tears streamed down his cheeks. "Please, I don't want this. Please ... help me ... Whoever you are, whatever you want, I'm yours—take me ... make me yours ..."

Katherine snapped on Eric's computer. She hit a few keys and waited for the modem to connect. She noticed her hands trembling. When she was done, she'd have to have another glass of wine. Across the room the radio alarm glowed 6:39 A.M.

The phone on the other end rang twice before the modem connected with three irritating tones followed by a coffee grinder buzz. It had been a while since her cyber-hacking days. Installing a hard disk or listening to complaints about the configuration of the latest software wasn't quite the same as when she and the guys at NORAD had spent their time fooling around on the Internet. That had been years ago, before the civilians had come in and taken it over. She just hoped they hadn't messed it up too badly. She needed to get in there and do some serious skulking.

The menu popped up, followed by a little red box in the corner of the screen, a sign that Eric had received some electronic mail. Katherine started to skip past it. The last thing she wanted was to read some yick-yack from one of Eric's electronic pen pals. But it was up there, it would only take a moment, and who knows.

She brought it up and gasped.

>MOM
>DONT WORRY. IM OK. THEY TOOK PHONE FROM ROOM BUT LEFT COMPUTER. STUPID HUH? IM READING FILES. LOTS OF SKAREY JUNK. MEET ME IN COMPUTER FORUM LOBY 9:00. ILL HAVE MORE STUFF THEN. DONT WORRY.
> :-) ERIC

Katherine took a long, deep breath. He was alive. Her eyes darted up to the message's time of transmission: 6:14 A.M. He was alive and wherever they were keeping him had taken less than an hour to get to.

She reread the message two more times. Eric had access to a computer and was reading someone's files. She was to meet him on the Internet in an area called the Computer

Forum at 9:00. Immediately she hit the reply command and started typing an answer.

>ERIC
>WHERE ARE YOU? CAN YOU SEE OUT A WINDOW?
ARE THERE ANY LANDMARKS THAT YOU CAN IDENTI

But the modem suddenly clicked and she was disconnected from the Internet. A phone call was coming in. Eric had complained for months about the disadvantages of having only one phone line, and how call waiting always disconnected him. Now she understood. She hit Alt X to escape and picked up the receiver. "Hello?"

"Katherine?" It was Coleman. His voice filled her with a mixture of rage, concern, excitement, guilt.

"Where are you?" she demanded.

"Just north of Everett."

"They took Eric."

No response.

"Did you hear what I said? They kidnapped Eric."

"Yes." Pause. "We've got to ... we've got to get together. We've got to figure things out."

The last thing she wanted was to get together with the monster who'd killed her husband, who'd destroyed her life. And yet—

"Katherine?"

"They said if I stayed quiet for twenty-four hours nothing would happen. They said they'd return him if I just—"

"And you believe that?"

"I–I don't know. No, of course not. I don't know."

Another pause. "It's wearing off, Katherine."

"What?"

"The experiment. It's ..."

She could hear him swallow back the panic.

"Katherine, I'm slipping back to what I used to be."

A cold fear gripped her.

"Katherine?"

At last she found her voice. "But you can fight it, right?"

"I don't know."

Katherine wanted her son back. And, like it or not, she needed Coleman's help. "You *can* fight it," she ordered. "You've *got* to fight it."

The voice responded. Weak and hoarse. "I'm trying. I– I've even been praying. But ..."

Katherine's head spun. She closed her eyes, trying to get her bearings. "Okay, listen—"

"I don't think I can—"

"Listen to me!" He grew quiet and she continued. "You're right—we've got to get together. But not here." She tapped the desk, thinking. It couldn't be public. It had to be somewhere with a computer and access to the Internet, someone who would let her—

And then she saw it. Eric's report card. And on the top line, the name of his teacher: Mr. Thaddeus Paris.

Mr. Paris's cramped twenty-nine-foot Avanti cruiser looked and felt like any other bachelor apartment, including but not limited to the distinct aroma of old socks, old grease, and Old Spice. Katherine knew he'd been picking up the place since she first called, and she kept a cautious eye on the bulging closets lest they fly open and bury her in dirty clothes or empty pizza boxes.

She had arrived with a knapsack of books about the Internet. After enduring the pleasantries and sidestepping the curious questions, she was finally able to scoot behind the computer that sat on his kitchen table and go to work. Several times he offered his assistance, and several times she made it clear that his help was neither needed nor appreciated. Finally, he took the hint and packed up his briefcase for work.

"You sure you don't need anything?" he asked one final time before stepping off the boat.

The keyboard clicked under Katherine's fingers, and she answered without looking up. "I'll be fine."

He stood at the exit, fidgeting. She could tell that this entire scenario was foreign to him. A beautiful woman all alone in his houseboat while he left her behind to go off to work. What was wrong with this picture?

"Well," he cleared his throat, "if you need anything, or just want to talk, my number is next to the phone."

She nodded.

"Oh, and when you leave, make sure you lock the front gate on the dock. Sometimes it sticks open."

"Got it."

Another pause.

"Okay, then."

No response.

"I hope everything works out."

More of the same.

With a shrug, he turned and started to leave.

Then, almost by reflex, Katherine called out, "Thanks again."

He turned back, obviously grateful for the contact.

Realizing she'd have to say more, she continued. "I promise I'll explain all this to you sometime soon. Honest."

"Oh," he said, smiling an idiotic smile, "no need."

She smiled back.

"Well, bye."

"Bye."

He remained standing.

Katherine forced one last smile before returning to the screen. He took the cue and left.

It was 7:30. She had ninety minutes before reconnecting with Eric. Ninety minutes to scour the Internet, to search databases, and maybe squeeze some priority information from old friends.

The first ten minutes were spent finding the street address assigned to the owner of the e-mail account Eric was writing from. It belonged to a Ms. Tisha Youngren of Baltimore, Maryland. A few more clicks of the mouse revealed that Youngren was a biochem grad student who'd recently moved west. Katherine couldn't find the forwarding address.

She tried another route. Any and all information on Genodyne. She'd been at it quite awhile when the boat rocked and she looked up to see Coleman standing on board.

There was the briefest flutter deep inside that she immediately suppressed and berated herself for feeling. Some ridiculous part of her still wanted to race to him, to throw her arms around him. But there was the other part, the part that wanted to tear out his eyes, to beat him, to rip him limb from limb.

"Hi." He tried to smile.

She knew better than to trust her voice and remained silent.

"You find anything?" he asked.

She shook her head. "Nothing. Dead ends. Whoever's running the show is being very, very careful."

He nodded, then with some effort he moved to sit across the table from her. She could tell that he was in pain, probably from the viral leash, but she forced herself to remain matter-of-fact. "I've got all the nonessentials. Everything you'd ever want to know about Genodyne: start-up investments, P and L figures, FDA applications, the works. Even the board members' birth dates and home addresses, but—"

"You got an O'Brien there?" he interrupted.

She glanced up, a little surprised at his abruptness. She looked back at the screen and nodded. "Dr. Philip O'Brien, the CEO?"

"Yeah." Coleman was rubbing his neck. "I met him in November. Pretty decent guy. Maybe we can go straight to the top and call—"

She cut him off. "I hardly think calling their CEO is going to—"

"If you've got another plan, I'm open. But I'm in no mood to sit around here and do nothing."

"*You're* in no mood?" Her voice grew louder. "My son has just been kidnapped, and *you're* in no mood?"

"All right, all right," he said, bringing the conversation back down. "You're right." He closed his eyes, then opened them. "They told you they'd bring him back in twenty-four hours, is that right?"

"That's right."

"Why? Why'd they say that?"

"I don't know—they said if I stayed quiet for twenty-four hours, if I didn't go to the police, he'd be safe and they'd bring him—"

"You can't possibly believe that."

"I don't know! But twenty-four hours isn't that long—"

"I don't *have* twenty-four hours!"

She looked at him.

He rose and began pacing. "Don't you get it? If they have an antidote or something, I need it now. Now! Not in twenty-four hours. *Now!*"

"What about Eric?"

"I'm not talking about Eric, I'm talking about me!"

"But they said he'd be—"

"I need it now!" He hit the paneled wall with his fist. The entire boat shuddered. Katherine stared. Coleman looked at his hand as if it were a foreign object. He turned, not daring to look back at her.

When she finally spoke, it was without anger. "It really is happening, isn't it?"

Without turning, he answered softly, "Yeah." After a moment he crossed back to the table and sat, still careful not to look her in the eyes. He noticed her half-spilled knapsack and poked at it. "What's this?"

"What?"

He reached in and pulled out the Bible she had given him. He gave her a dubious look.

She shrugged. "You're the one who said you were praying. Not that it will do you any good."

Coleman looked to her.

"If it really is wearing off," she said, "I doubt there's anything you can do to stop it. Like Murkoski said, it's all in the genes."

"I'm more than just some kid's chemistry set, Katherine. I've got to be."

"That's right, you're also the murderer of my husband."

It was meant to hurt him, and it did. But he held her gaze. And when he spoke, his voice was quiet and deliberate. "Maybe. Or maybe old things really have passed away."

It took a moment for the phrase to register. When it did, Katherine felt a surge of revulsion. "Please." She rose and crossed to the sink for some water.

He persisted. "You said it yourself, 'If any man is in Christ he is a new creature.' You're the one who taught me that."

"I'm a preacher's kid, what did you expect?"

"Maybe people *can* change, maybe I really can—"

"Save it. I know the routine." She filled a glass and drank the water. It was bitter and brackish.

But Coleman wouldn't let up. "You said it worked for you. Back when you were in AA, you said it was your faith that stopped you from drinking. Isn't that what you said?"

"That was a long time ago."

"But it worked, didn't it?"

"I suppose. When I let it."

"It changed you." His voice was growing urgent. "Didn't you say it changed you?"

She nodded. "It was no cakewalk. But yeah, it broke my dependency."

"So why can't it do the same for me? I've asked for his help. I've given him my life. If I can't get an antidote, why can't that same faith help me?"

She turned and looked at him. His face was full of anything but faith. Desperation, yes. Fear, definitely. But she did not see faith.

"I'm not just chemicals, Katherine. There's got to be a way to beat this."

It was 9:57. For nearly an hour, Katherine had been parked in the lobby of the Computer Forum, staring at the screen, waiting for her son to log on. But so far Eric hadn't shown.

Coleman sat across from her at the table, wearing one of Paris's jackets to fight off a chill, the obvious beginnings of a fever—courtesy of the viral leash. Yet, despite his pain, Katherine sensed a peace settling over him, a peace that grew as he continued staring at the Bible and silently turning its pages.

Peace was the furthest thing from her mind as she sat across from this beast who had destroyed her life—and the saint who had started to revive it. Maybe he was right; maybe they really were two separate creatures. Maybe that old man, the man who'd pulled the trigger that took Gary, really was dead. And maybe he was right on another count. Maybe, with enough faith, that old man would never return.

Katherine glanced back at the screen. Faith. It had been a long time since she'd even thought about the word. But right now, with her baby's life on the line, she would be willing to try just about anything. She had her doubts, but she was no fool. To cover all the bases, Katherine found herself saying a quiet prayer, just in case there was a God out there, just in case he really did care.

Slowly a tiny spark of something began to glow in her. Maybe it was faith, maybe hope, maybe just wishful thinking. Whatever it was, it gave her the strength to leave the lobby and quickly click over to e-mail just in case Eric had written another message.

Nothing.

She reentered the lobby and continued to wait. For the next ninety minutes she waited, refusing the sandwich Coleman had made, the Diet Pepsi he had found, refusing even to speculate on another plan. It wasn't until 11:36 that Katherine Lyon reached up and, with any flicker of faith that might have returned now extinguished, turned off the computer.

She could feel Coleman staring at her. It was obvious that he sensed her hopelessness and wanted to help. But, when he rose to his feet and started to walk around the table to her, she put up her hand. "No," was all she said. As much as she wanted him—needed him—she knew now, more than ever, that some things can never be changed.

# CHAPTER 14

Dr. Philip O'Brien was in the middle of another packing dilemma. This time it had to do with socks. He had none. Well, none that were clean. Ever since Beth had left for Mazatlán, his housekeeping skills, including but not limited to laundry, had steadily gone downhill.

He glanced at the VCR clock in the bedroom. In just a few hours he'd be on the flight to Mazatlán. He doubted that there would be enough time to wash and dry any socks. Of course, he could dig through the dirty clothes hamper and pull out a few of the freshest pairs, but he had been performing that ritual for the last several days and somehow suspected that the socks in there wouldn't survive a third or fourth go-round.

Everything else was ready. The pets were in the kennel, the newspaper had been stopped, the home security folks had been alerted. If he wanted, he could stay down there with his family for months. Or they could head to Asia, or do a photo safari in Africa, or buy a villa in Europe. When it came to time and money, the possibilities were almost limitless.

The phone rang, and he absentmindedly scooped it up. "Hello?"

"Is this Dr. Philip O'Brien?"

The voice seemed strangely familiar, but he couldn't put his finger on it. "Yes."

"Head of Genodyne?"

"Who's calling, please?"

"A friend from Nebraska."

O'Brien went cold. "Where are you? Why are you calling me?"

"Do you know where the boy is?"

"What boy?"

"We need your help."

O'Brien's mind raced. Between the preparations for the trip and disengaging from Genodyne, he'd almost been able to put Coleman out of his mind. Almost. "You must understand, I no longer work for Genodyne. I've—retired."

The pause on the other end seemed interminable. Finally the voice answered. "We need to talk to you."

O'Brien shifted his weight. "There's nothing I can do. If you have a problem, you'll have to take it up with Dr. Murkoski. He's in charge of the program, and I'm sure he's more than willing—"

"Murkoski is killing people. I might be next."

O'Brien felt his face grow warm. "Look, I'm no longer a part of any of this. If you have a problem, I suggest you take it up with—"

"I need to talk to you. I need some answers."

The desperation in the man's voice tugged at O'Brien, but he refused to give in. He had a plane to catch. A new life to begin. "I'm sorry."

"Is there a way to stop this thing? Can I get back to the way I used to be?"

"Even if I knew, there's nothing I can do about it. Genodyne is the only place you can go for help. I recommend that you head up there at once." His palms were damp; he wiped them on his pants. "And if you're worried about safety, you need to know that there's a good chance this call is being monitored."

"I need your help!" The voice suddenly exploded. "Don't you understand? You got me into this, you've got to—"

"Good afternoon, Mr. Coleman."

"Listen to me! Listen, you little—"

O'Brien pressed the off button and slowly placed the phone back into its cradle. He stood for a long moment before turning to the suitcases on the bed. He knew this wouldn't be the last time he'd have to turn a deaf ear. The next months, maybe years, wouldn't be easy. But this was the path he had chosen, and he would hold to it.

Looking again at the clothes hamper, he realized that socks were no longer a problem. He didn't have to wash them. He'd throw them away and buy new ones. Come to think of it, he and Beth could now dispose of their wardrobes and buy new clothes every day of the year if they wanted. He smiled grimly at the prospect and returned to his packing.

Coleman lowered the receiver. The combination of rage and helplessness left him shaking. He could feel Katherine staring at him, and he fought to regain control before turning to her.

"So what's next?" she asked. "Genodyne?"

Coleman thought a moment, then shook his head.

"What other choice is there?"

"Do you have O'Brien's home address on that computer?"

"Right here. But it didn't exactly sound like he was anxious to—"

"There was something in his voice."

"There was what?"

"In his voice," Coleman looked up, trying to explain. "I heard something . . . in his voice."


"What's with that dog?" Murkoski complained as he threw open his office door and stormed into the hallway.

Tisha Youngren looked up from her work. "He's been barking like that all morning."

Murkoski saw Eric sitting frozen on a nearby chair and motioned toward him. "You feed him lunch?"

"I tried. He wouldn't eat."

Murkoski pivoted and crossed the room to Eric. He stuck his face directly into the boy's. "Listen, brat. You hear that dog?"

Eric nodded, wide-eyed.

"Well, he's the size of a bear and he's barking because he's hungry. Unlike you, he doesn't have anything to eat. But if you don't finish that sandwich, we can change all that. I know for a fact that he just loves tender little boys. You catch my meaning, son?"

Eric nodded.

"Good." Murkoski broke into a smile. "By this time tomorrow, we'll have everything shipped and you'll be back home safe and sound with Mommy." Without waiting for a response, he rose and headed down the hall.

Tisha called after him. "You done with the computer?"

He turned. "For now, why?"

"He likes playing the games."

Murkoski looked at the boy a moment, then shrugged. "If it keeps him occupied." He turned and disappeared down the hall.

"You hear that?" Tisha asked, trying too hard to sound cheery. "Just as soon as you finish your sandwich, you can go back in and play some more games. Won't that be fun?"

Eric could tell that this woman was underestimating his age and his intelligence. That was fine with him; maybe he could use it to his advantage. He pretended to nod eagerly, then tore into his cellophane-wrapped turkey sandwich.

"What do you think you're doing? You just can't break into someone's—"

"Sit down."

O'Brien hesitated.

"Sit down!" Coleman headed toward O'Brien, making it clear he meant business. O'Brien understood and immediately sank into the nearest chair—leather, like all the others in this expensive, high-tech family room at the back of his house.

Coleman began to pace, a conflict of compassion, anger, and terror. The battle inside his head raged relentlessly. Still, he had been able to keep most of the anger in check, holding it back like an attack dog straining on a leash. He still had control, he still held the leash, but with each lurch and tug, his grip grew weaker. In a matter of time, the beast would break free—and Coleman knew when that happened it would never allow itself to be chained again.

Katherine was settling down in front of the computer that sat on a large oak desk near the French doors overlooking the pool. "This thing have a modem?" she asked.

O'Brien nodded.

"What's with the bags?" Coleman asked, nodding toward the three suitcases at the bottom of the stairs. "You going somewhere?"

"Yes," O'Brien said. His voice was husky with fear, and he coughed. "As I told you over the phone, I've retired. I'm going down to Mexico to join my family on vacation."

Coleman continued to pace, rubbing his shoulders, the back of his neck. The pain was worse, and he was damp with perspiration from the fever. "What do you know about the kidnapping? Where are they keeping him?"

"Kidnapping?" O'Brien sounded legitimately confused.

"My son," Katherine said as she pulled off the computer's dustcover and turned it on. "Your pals kidnapped my boy."

"They what? What pals?"

The incredulity in O'Brien's voice seemed real, but Coleman wasn't sure. He pressed in. "They said they're only keeping him twenty-four hours—for what, we don't know. But they've already killed two, three other times, so you can see why we might have a little doubt about their credibility."

O'Brien grew pale. "What? Who's killed—how many times?"

Coleman's instincts had been right. The man was honestly concerned. And, for the most part, O'Brien was decent. Frightened, but decent. It was obvious that he knew nothing about Eric, so Coleman moved to the next subject. "What about an antidote?"

O'Brien looked up. There was no mistaking the sorrow filling his face.

Again Coleman had his answer, but he wouldn't accept it. "I'm slipping back. What can I do, how can I stop it?"

"I'm sorry." O'Brien shook his head, then continued. "According to Murkoski, once the process starts to reverse, there's no stopping it."

The sentence hit Coleman hard.

But O'Brien wasn't finished. "I'm afraid ..." Again he cleared his throat. "I'm afraid it will continue to reverse until it leaves you in worse shape than when you first started the treatment."

Katherine slowly stopped her typing.

Coleman swallowed, barely finding his voice. "What?"

O'Brien could no longer look at him. "The chances are high that it will remove any inhibitions you might have previously had toward violence."

"You mean—I'll be worse?"

O'Brien didn't answer. The verdict hung heavy in the room. Coleman had no idea how long the silence lasted before the man continued. "Perhaps in a few months, maybe in a year, they can find—"

Coleman exploded: "I don't have a year! I need it now!"

There was another moment of silence as Coleman took a deep breath and fought for control.

O'Brien waited, then softly repeated. "I'm sorry."

Coleman stood lost, unsure what to do. Finally he moved across the room to the sofa near O'Brien and sank into the cushions.

O'Brien shifted uncomfortably. He glanced at Coleman, then quietly ventured, "Still, I wouldn't give up. Not yet."

Coleman looked at him.

"I mean, you still have a will."

Coleman continued to stare, waiting for more.

"It's true, we all have a proclivity toward certain behaviors, we all inherit programming from our parents. But we're not computers. We still have a will. And in many areas that will has proved stronger than any of our genetic hard wiring."

Coleman frowned. "What about Murkoski's research? What about all those studies he rattles off?"

"There's plenty of evidence to back him up, certainly. But there is other research indicating that how we're raised may carry as much of an influence as our genetic heritage."

"How we're raised?"

O'Brien nodded. "We're not shaped only by the nature of our chemistry, but also by the nurturing of our parents."

Coleman deflated slightly and muttered, "Strike two."

"But there's a third element." Coleman looked to him. O'Brien continued, "Our personal philosophy, what we believe, internally."

"That makes a difference?"

O'Brien nodded. "Absolutely. Take male primates. By nature, they tend to be sexually promiscuous. But through the course of history, we humans have learned the value of fidelity—the emotional values, the social values—so our belief has modified our natural behavior."

Coleman nodded, slowly understanding.

O'Brien continued. "The same can be said about crime, or violence, or addictive behavior. We have learned that the long-term consequences outweigh the momentary gain, so we modify our behavior."

"What about the druggie who can't stop doing drugs, the alcoholic who can't stop drinking—the killer who can't stop killing?" Coleman held O'Brien's eyes, waiting for an answer, but O'Brien faltered. It seemed a simple enough question—if there *was* an answer.

Coleman tried another route. "You said 'belief.' What about faith?"

"Faith?"

"If we can't do it on our own, what about turning to someone we believe can help us?"

O'Brien paused to consider the thought. "It's certainly a consideration. We all know people who have been changed through a religious experience." He looked to Coleman. "You think that's a possibility?"

"I don't know."

O'Brien frowned, thinking it through. "I'm certainly not a theologian, but it would seem—"

"I've got him!" Katherine called from across the room.

Coleman was immediately on his feet, crossing to the desk. O'Brien was right behind, asking, "Who? Who do you have?"

"Her boy."

By the time they arrived, Katherine's hands were flying over the keyboard.

>HONEY ARE YOU OKAY? DID THEY DO ANYTHING TO HURT YOU?

The answer came back tortuously slow.

>IM FINE. CANT TALK LONG. INTERESTING FILES.

Katherine immediately responded:

>WHERE ARE YOU? DO YOU SEE ANY LANDMARKS?
HEAR ANY SOUNDS?
>DONT WORY. I'M COMMING HOME TOMROW MORN-
ING. THEY PROMISE. RIGHT AFTER THE SHIPMENT.
>WHAT SHIPMENT?
>THERE COMING GOTTA GO.
>ERIC, DON'T GO. ERIC?

But there was no answer. She tried again:

>ERIC!

Nothing. All three stared at the screen.

Coleman was the first to speak. "What shipment is he talking about?"

O'Brien didn't answer, but slowly turned and started back to the sofa and chairs. Coleman and Katherine exchanged looks, then followed.

"That explains why they're holding your boy," O'Brien said, almost to himself. "They can't afford any more delays before shipping the drug, so they're holding your son to prevent you from going to the police."

"What drug?" Coleman asked. "What are you talking about?"

O'Brien slowly sat, then looked at his hands a long moment. Finally he began.

"Originally we thought—we thought we were doing so much good. We were going to change the world, change the human race."

Carefully, in painful detail, he told of the death of the mice, the regression of Freddy, the murder of Wolff. He explained how instead of creating a compassionate race, Murkoski had taken over and developed the antisense gene to create conscienceless killing machines. A gene that, according to Eric's newest information, was scheduled for shipment tomorrow morning.

As the minutes dragged on and O'Brien's explanation became increasingly bleak, Coleman found it more and more difficult to contain himself. When he could stand no more, he waved O'Brien into silence. "So, what are you doing to stop it?" he demanded.

O'Brien looked at him sadly, then shook his head. "There's nothing I can do. There's nothing anybody can do."

Coleman was on his feet again, pacing in rage. "What are you saying? There's nothing we can do? I don't believe that. I don't believe it!"

"Coleman . . ." Katherine warned.

"How can you say that, after all you've done?"

"I'm sorry," O'Brien said.

"You're sorry!" Coleman repeated incredulously. "You're *sorry?*"

Katherine rose and moved closer. "Coleman, if he says there's nothing we can do, then—"

"The man creates a drug that can turn us into killers, and he says there's nothing he can do?"

"I—"

"What are you going to do when it falls into the wrong hands? How is 'I'm sorry' going to cut it when some terrorist gets it? Or some crazed third-world dictator?"

"You don't think I've thought of that?" O'Brien answered. "You don't think an hour hasn't gone by without that crossing my mind?"

"And you're doing nothing?"

O'Brien hesitated, then glanced over at his suitcases.

"Of course you're doing something," Coleman said. "You're running away."

O'Brien rose unsteadily to his feet, trying to defend himself. "He shut me out of the company. He's planned this for months. There's nothing I can—"

"What about the truck or whatever they're shipping it in? Couldn't we blow it up?"

"That would just cause a delay. He'd only cultivate and harvest more."

"From what?" Katherine asked.

"The genetic material in the lab."

"And if that was destroyed?" Coleman asked.

"He's got hundreds, thousands of samples; plus, the genetic code is in all of the lab computers."

"What about outside laboratories?"

O'Brien shook his head. "No, we'd never do that. There's too great a potential for a security breach. That's why he's in such a hurry to get it out now, before any leaks occur." He turned to Katherine. "That's why he's holding your son. By preventing you from going to the authorities, he's ensuring that the shipment won't be delayed by some sort of investigation."

"I don't understand," Katherine said. "Why the big rush?"

"Every day he holds this drug, the chances of it being stolen or leaked to others multiply. Today it's worth billions. But as soon as it's duplicated and pirated, it's worth nothing. So you see the risk—if Murkoski is forced to sit on this for a few months, it may become worthless."

"What about patents?" Katherine asked.

O'Brien shook his head. "Nobody will honor patents when it comes to this. Genodyne has a window of months, perhaps a year, to make their fortune before individuals and governments start pirating it."

"You're saying that any Tom, Dick, or Harry will be able to duplicate this stuff?" Coleman demanded.

O'Brien nodded.

Coleman pressed his aching head with both hands. "And you don't think that's worth stopping?"

"I didn't say that. I said there's no way to stop it. Outside of destroying every sample—"

"How would we do that?" Coleman interrupted.

"What?"

"Destroy the samples. How do you kill DNA?"

"Heat, I suppose. It's like any living organism. But you can't just go in and torch a few test tubes."

"Why not?"

"As I said, there are thousands. The entire third floor is dedicated to this study. That's eight separate labs. You'd have to literally go into each laboratory, pull out all the samples, and destroy them."

"That's it?" Coleman asked.

"And the lab animals. The mice, the baboon, you'd have to destroy them all."

"And that would take care of it?"

O'Brien turned to Katherine. "He can't be serious!"

Katherine kept her eyes fixed on Coleman. "Is it possible? Is that something you could do?"

"You can't just burn the place down," O'Brien argued. "You'd have to be sure every single sample is destroyed, nothing overlooked. You'd have to generate a lot of fire in a contained area. You couldn't miss a single sample."

"No problem," Coleman said.

O'Brien stared in disbelief.

"There's plenty you can learn in prison, Doctor—if you take the time to ask the right people the right questions."

Katherine turned back to O'Brien. "What about the computers? You said the map of the gene is in the computers?"

"Yes."

"But nothing outside Genodyne?"

"That's right, that would be far too risky."

Coleman turned to Katherine. "Is that something you could take out, the computers?"

"Maybe." She sounded less sure than Coleman. "If I introduced the right virus I might be able to wipe out the entire system."

"We've got backup disks in the vault," O'Brien said.

"You've got the combination?"

"An old one. Murkoski changes it occasionally."

"It's a steel vault?" Katherine asked.

"Yes."

"Do you have a 220 outlet near by?"

"A 220 outlet?"

"Like for a stove or something."

"There's a lunchroom just down the hall."

"That would help you get into the safe?" Coleman asked.

Katherine shrugged. "In a manner of speaking."

O'Brien shook his head. "I can't believe what you two are saying."

Coleman turned to him. "Tell us everything we would need to know."

"It's impossible."

"If you've got any other suggestions, I'm open."

O'Brien glanced at his watch. "You've got eighteen hours before dawn, before he loads up his shipment. You don't know the layout of the building, you don't know the security—breaking into a place like Genodyne isn't exactly like breaking into the local gas station. This is crazy talk."

Suddenly Coleman sprang at O'Brien, grabbing him by the throat and shoving him against the wall. Katherine cried out, but he barely heard. He was in O'Brien's face, spitting out the words. "I'm crazy? *I'm* crazy? You're talking about turning people into killing machines, and *I'm* crazy!" His grip tightened as he raised O'Brien off the floor a good six inches.

O'Brien coughed and gagged, but Coleman ignored him, his senses tightening, aware only of his own breathing and the pounding of his heart in his ears.

"Coleman!" Katherine screamed, but he heard nothing.

O'Brien kicked and fought to get free, but Coleman's grip was iron.

Then from somewhere far away, he began to hear Katherine's voice. "Coleman! Coleman, you're killing him!"

He felt someone pounding on his back, beating his shoulders. "You're killing him! Stop it!"

Angered at the distraction, he looked back—without letting go of O'Brien—and fixed his rage on her.

It was then he saw the terror in Katherine's eyes. Terror of him. The look hit him hard, shocking his system. Sounds returned. He could hear O'Brien coughing. Turning back again, he saw the deep crimson of the man's face.

Katherine's voice grew louder: "You're killing him, you're killing him!"

Coleman released his grip and O'Brien slid down the wall, coughing and gasping for breath. Coleman looked down, frightened and breathing hard himself. Things were getting worse, no doubt about it. Yet somehow, he suspected that he might have made his point.


At 5:34 that afternoon, O'Brien finally looked up from the blueprints of Genodyne that were spread out across the dining-room table. "That's it," he sighed, taking off his glasses and rubbing his eyes. "That's everything I can think of."

Coleman stared first at the diagram and then at the legal pad of detailed procedures he had carefully written out. Everything was there: security policy and routine, the lab locations, all the storage areas, the location of the vault, the overhead fire extinguisher system, the location of the lab animals—plus any possible areas where Eric might be held, if he was being held there at all. It had been an exhausting afternoon, but Coleman felt confident that they had covered every angle. There was still plenty that could go wrong, but at least they had a plan.

"What time is your flight?" Coleman asked.

O'Brien glanced at his watch. "I can still make it, if I hurry."

Coleman nodded. "Go ahead."

O'Brien hesitated, then scanned the legal pad one last time. "That's everything, I'm sure of it." He glanced up. "But if you need me to stick around . . ."

Coleman shook his head. "No, it's better that you go."

O'Brien nodded, then rose and headed up the stairs.

Coleman closed his eyes, trying by sheer will to force out the relentless pain in his joints and the pounding in his head. The viral leash was definitely doing its job. When he reopened his eyes, Katherine was staring at him from across the table.

"Why are you going through all of this?" she asked.

"What do you mean?"

"If I were you, I'd cut my losses and hightail it into the mountains and disappear forever."

Coleman shrugged, trying to understand it himself. "I guess ... I don't know. All of my life, it's like I've only taken. And now, for once, I just want to ..." His voice trailed away as he realized how inadequate this explanation was. He shook his head. "I'm not sure ..."

Katherine almost smiled. "Sounds like part of that gene is still working."

"What about you? You don't have to do this. Just show me how to knock out those computers and the disks—"

"I would if I could trust you." That slight trace of a smile had disappeared. "But they've got my baby, and I'm not trusting you or anybody else anymore. If he's in that building, I'm going to get him myself."

Coleman nodded, feeling the returning sense of sadness. Things would never again be as they had been. The wall between them would never again come down.

O'Brien headed down the stairs, slipping on a jacket. He tossed a small magnetic card onto the table. "This is my I.D.," he said. "I've got another if you need it."

Coleman shook his head, and O'Brien continued. "With that and the PIN you have written down, you'll be able to enter any room in the building."

"If Murkoski hasn't changed the code," Katherine said.

"I doubt he's had time. Besides, he knows I'm leaving." He turned to Coleman and asked one last time, "You're sure there's nothing else you need from me? We've covered everything?"

"As far as I can tell."

"I could stay behind an extra day, if you think I can help."

Coleman shook his head. "No, go to your family. Do everything just like you planned. There's always the possibility that Murkoski is still watching you."

"If he's watching me, he knows you're here."

"Our car's four blocks away."

O'Brien nodded, then turned and headed for his suitcases. He picked up the three bags and started for the door. Coleman followed.

"So honestly," he asked, as he followed O'Brien into the tiled entry hall. "What do you think our chances are?"

"Honestly?" O'Brien asked. He paused a moment to weigh the question. "Honestly, I hope you're right about this faith thing. Because it looks to me like you're going to need all the help you can get."

# CHAPTER 15

Coleman and Katherine began their shopping spree in the early evening. Most of the stores in the Arlington area were closed, but Coleman was used to shopping at all hours, with or without anyone's permission.

Katherine, on the other hand, insisted on keeping track of each broken window and smashed lock, along with the estimated retail value of every stolen item. Maybe it was the fact that she was a struggling retailer herself, or that she had been married to a cop. For whatever reason, she had promised herself that when it was all over they would eventually pay for whatever they smashed or stole.

The first break-in was at Dr. Tolle's Family Dental Practice. Nothing of real value would be missing. No dental equipment, no computer, no petty cash—nothing but one size E nitrous oxide tank and some surgical tubing.

Then there was the two-hundred-foot roll of ten-gauge Romex electrical house wiring, the five-gallon gas can, the ax, the roll of duct tape, the 220-volt extension cord, the timer, and the hank of #6 white braided cotton clothesline—all courtesy of Burnett's Hardware and Lumber. That left only the large box of Ivory soap flakes and the five gallons of gasoline, both of which Katherine felt obligated to purchase in a more orthodox fashion.

It was 9:42 when their headlights glinted off the perimeter fence that surrounded the Genodyne complex. The six-story building was lit, but blurred by a heavy fog that lay in the parking lot. They turned onto the wet asphalt that followed the fence and drove until they passed the main gate and adjacent security building—a small one-story affair.

Katherine continued down the road until they passed a large stand of firs that momentarily blocked the building's view of them. She pulled into the wet grass, as close to the ditch as she dared.

Coleman climbed out of the car and walked back to the trunk. He was shivering again. The fever was up full. He opened the trunk, which gave a rusty creak. He cringed, hoping the sound would be absorbed by the fog. He reached inside and removed the tank of nitrous oxide as well as the duct tape and clothesline.

O'Brien had explained that Genodyne was not a high-security area. No sweeping video cameras, no state-of-the-art gadgetry. Just a perimeter fence, guards who patrolled the grounds once an hour, and motion detectors near all the doors and windows of the ground floor. Inside, the magnetic ID cards and the six-digit Personal Identification Numbers were the primary source of security. "It's not like we're a nuclear testing facility," he had joked.

Maybe not, Coleman thought, but what was now being housed inside there could be even more dangerous.

As he approached the security building he heard the dull blare of a TV. Some cop show with shouting and shooting. He pressed close to the damp, concrete wall and crept to the nearest window.

He paused there to listen for conversation. He could only make out the voices of two men. There were supposed to be three. The third must still be out on rounds.

Coleman glanced at his watch. 9:52. O'Brien had said the guards began their rounds, which took anywhere from thirty-five to forty-five minutes, on the hour. By arriving this late, Coleman had hoped to catch all three together. No such luck. Guard Three was taking his merry time. If Coleman waited, another guard might leave. If he began, Guard Three might arrive and discover him.

Then again, Guard Three could be dozing or reading the latest *Sports Illustrated* in the john.

Frustration began to boil up inside Coleman. Wasn't it always that way—the greatest plans thwarted by the tiniest detail? For a moment he thought how much easier it would be to just bust in, take the first two out, then pop the third when he arrived.

Of course he knew the source of that thought and immediately pushed it aside. But it resisted more than he had expected, and that fact unnerved him. He wasn't unnerved that such thoughts were present; he knew they were there and growing stronger every hour. He was unnerved because he now realized that he would have to double-guess his every action. A plan like this was hard enough when all of his faculties were at a hundred percent. But if he couldn't trust his own instincts, if he had to double-think his every move, there could very well be trouble.

The security fence surrounding the complex was butted up to the security building. A neat design that saved money and looked sleek, but it had obviously been created by an architect and not a breaking-and-entering expert. In a manner of seconds, Coleman had used the fence to climb onto the roof. A moment later, he had fed the surgical tubing down a sink's air pipe, sealed the pipe with duct tape, and turned on the nitrous oxide.

Within five minutes, both guards were sound asleep.

Coleman dropped to the ground and entered the building through the door, holding his breath as he threw open the windows for ventilation.

He had two minutes before the effects of the gas would start wearing off. He moved quickly and expertly. When the guards woke, they would find themselves locked in the bathroom, bound together, with their mouths securely taped.

>ERIC: WE ARE GOING INTO GENODYNE. IF YOU ARE THERE, LET US KNOW WHERE. DON'T LET THEM CATCH YOU READING THEIR FILES. YOU ARE IN DANGER. TRUST NO ONE. I LOVE YOU, MOM.

Eric read the e-mail twice before clicking the REPLY box. He was about to type in his answer when he heard the door behind him rattle faintly. Someone had just stepped out of the front door of the large cabin, and the difference in air pressure had shaken his own door.

Eric stood and stepped quietly toward his second-story window. Below him Tisha was racing across the driveway toward the idling Mercedes that Murkoski had started up. Eric had heard her answer the other phone line a moment or two earlier. And now, judging by her urgency as she relayed the message to Murkoski and by his angry response, Eric guessed that the news wasn't so good.

He had no idea where he was. Some fancy cabin up in the mountains. Just Murkoski, Tisha, himself, and the two men who had brought him. The older kidnapper was sprawled out on a bed down the hall, nursing his broken nose. The younger guy was downstairs watching TV.

It had been Tisha's job to keep an eye on Eric. But now she was outside.

He looked back at the screen:

YOU ARE IN DANGER. TRUST NO ONE.

He had a choice. Wait until tomorrow and hope that they would release him like they had promised. Or take Mom at her word and get out while the getting was good.

He crossed to the door and carefully pulled it open. No one in sight. He stepped into the hall, moved past the bathroom, and past the closed door where the older man was snoring up a storm. He reached the top of the stairs. Below, he could see the younger guy on the sofa, his back to Eric, engrossed in some karate flick.

It would be tricky, but there was a chance that Eric could make it down the stairs and to the outside door without being spotted. After that—well. Still, between Mom's warning and his own uneasiness, he figured it was better to do something than nothing.

He eased down the steps, one at a time. There was no chance he could be heard. The whirring fan up in the cathedral ceiling and the blaring TV made certain of that. But he had to make sure that his reflection would not be caught on the TV screen.

He had two steps to go when the front door opened. For a millisecond he froze, then leaped the last two steps and ducked behind the sofa just as Tisha entered followed by the ranting Murkoski.

"Incompetent! Why is everybody we hire incompetent?"

As Murkoski stormed toward the kitchen, Eric edged around the far end of the couch. Now the stairs were to his back, the TV straight ahead, and the kitchen on the other side of the sofa.

He heard Murkoski yank up the kitchen phone and demand. "Yeah, what is it?" There was a pause. "What time?"

Tisha headed for the stairs. Eric scrunched low, knowing that, if she looked in his direction, she would spot him.

"What's wrong?" the man on the sofa asked, his voice less than four feet from Eric's head.

"There was a break-in at the lab," she answered.

Eric tensed, expecting to hear his name called, his escape ruined. But there was nothing. Just the simple padding of feet up the stairs. She had never looked toward the sofa.

"No, don't report it!" Murkoski ordered into the phone. "Not yet."

The man on the sofa clicked off the TV remote and rose to his feet. He gave a slight yawn and stretch. He was so close that Eric could have reached around and touched his leg. But he stayed low, afraid even to breathe.

"No, *you* investigate it!" Murkoski yelled. "You're security, that's what we pay you for! Get in there and—"

"Kenneth!" Tisha called from upstairs. "Kenneth, he's gone!"

"What?" Murkoski shouted.

The man at the sofa cursed, headed for the stairs, and took them two at a time to investigate. Murkoski slammed down the receiver and followed. "What do you mean, gone?"

A moment later, the room was empty. It was now or never.

Eric sprang to his feet and raced for the door. He threw it open and bolted into the fog and darkness. The gravel driveway popped and scuffed under his feet, sending the dog in the run beside the house into frenzied barking.

The woods lay thirty feet away. He made it into the first group of trees just as the light from the front door spilled out onto the driveway.

"Kid! Hey, kid!" It was Murkoski. "You out here?"

Eric froze. He could see the man, but there were enough shadows to keep him hidden, as long as he didn't make any sudden moves.

"Hey, kid! I'm talking to you!"

Tisha appeared in the doorway, followed by the younger man, a flashlight in hand.

"He couldn't have gone far," Tisha said. The light came on and swept across the trees, its beam clearly outlined by the night fog. For a moment it caught the edge of Eric's sweatshirt. But it didn't stop.

"Eric?" Tisha called. "Eric, where are you?"

Eric slowly edged toward the nearest tree, a large cedar, to better hide himself. There was no gravel here, only a floor of soft needles and underbrush. There were, however, plenty of sticks, and one of them snapped when he stepped on it.

The beam darted back in his direction, and he ducked from sight.

"Eric?" Tisha called. Apparently she had the flashlight now. He heard the crunching of gravel as she moved across the driveway in his direction.

The dog continued to bark.

"Eric? Eric, you don't want to be out here all alone. Come on now." Her voice sounded gentle and kind, but there was something wrong. She was lying. Under all that kindness he felt a ruthlessness, an ambition ready and willing to do whatever was necessary to have her way.

It was odd. He'd been experiencing these feelings most of the day—knowing from people's tone of voice what they were really saying, seeing in their eyes what they were really thinking. He hadn't thought much about it—until now. Now he needed all the help he could get.

"Come on, kid," Murkoski called. "Just come on back and everything will be okay."

The beam danced on the branches and bushes around him. In a matter of seconds, he would be spotted. He had no choice. He had to move.

Remembering what he'd learned from Coleman's Indian stories, he slowly, and this time soundlessly, worked his way through the undergrowth, watching every step, taking one at a time, keeping at least one tree between himself and the searching beam.

"Eric?" Tisha had entered the undergrowth now too. She was making enough noise to mask any he might make, so he picked up his pace, slowly veering to the left, ducking or freezing whenever the beam came in his direction.

"Come on, now," Tisha called. "It's too scary to be out here all by yourself."

She had that right. But it would be even scarier to trust her. It wasn't just what Mom had said over the Internet. It was also what he now knew, what he somehow sensed in the weird way he'd been sensing things all day.

There was a clanking noise, iron chain against steel fence. The dog barked louder, more frantically.

"What are you doing?" Tisha called back to the house.

Murkoski's voice answered. "We'll let the dog find him."

Chunks of drywall flew in all directions as Coleman chopped into the forest-green wall of the executive office. With each jarring slam of the ax, his head and body exploded in pain. And still he continued. He had tried opening the two-and-a-half-foot-wide Testron safe with the combination O'Brien had given him, but it hadn't responded. Given the short amount of time they had, it would be impossible to drill, torch, or blow the 1,800 pounds of high-tempered stainless steel. There was only one way to destroy the computer backup disks inside, and Katherine was the only one who knew how.

They had dumped all of their stolen items into an old gym bag Katherine had found in her trunk—a remnant of the days when she actually cared how she looked. Knowing that the third guard was still at large, they had carefully made their way through the security gate on foot, then dashed across the parking lot to the entrance of the building. O'Brien's mag card and PIN had opened the door. They had skipped the elevator and taken the stairs. The guard, if he was alert, could have easily keyed off the elevator and trapped them between floors. They had arrived at the executive suites and found the office with the safe exactly as O'Brien had described.

Now, as Coleman swung his ax, chopping out the drywall around the safe, Katherine sat at the executive's desk, exploring the computer system.

"All I need is about eighteen inches around it," Katherine called. "Soon as you get that cleared out, let me know."

Coleman nodded and continued swinging, stopping only to pull out the debris and pieces of wall that fell around the safe.

Katherine couldn't resist the temptation to check her e-mail one last time to see whether Eric had left any messages. She switched to the modem, dialed in the phone number, entered her password, and waited. A moment later she had her answer:

NO NEW MAIL

Katherine's heart sank. Where was her son? Why wasn't he answering her mail? She switched over to the Computer Forum lobby that they had originally met in, just in case.

Not there.

Katherine fought a growing depression and returned to her task. Not only would the backup disks in the safe have to be destroyed, but so would the information stored in the computer system itself.

She reaccessed the mainframe. In just over twenty minutes, she had introduced a virus that she hoped would be destructive enough to eat up any info inside the system—as well as any computer that would log onto that system. Of course, Genodyne's computers were well equipped with virus sniffers and blockers, but her government experience still provided a few tricks that the civilians weren't yet aware of.

At one time, Katherine had been good—the best in her field. Maybe she still was. After all, in the twenty minutes she had just spent, a less-experienced hacker might have been able to introduce a virus equivalent to a bad cold, or maybe even the flu. Katherine had just infected the system with something she hoped to be closer to Ebola.

She paused to double-check her work. Then, holding her breath, she hit ENTER.

She stared at the screen, watching. Slowly, a smile spread across her face as the virus began its work. Within five minutes, there would be no stopping it. The virus would continue to infect and destroy all vital information within the mainframe, up to and including all maps and info on the GOD gene.

"Now what?" Coleman called.

Katherine looked up and saw a two-foot hole cut completely around the safe and running all the way to its back.

Coleman was breathing heavily. "What's next?" he repeated impatiently.

Katherine rose and walked to the gym bag, where she pulled out a roll of heavy Romex wire, the same heavy-duty wiring used inside the walls of most homes. She found one end of the wire and began to twist the three conductive strands together.

Coleman approached, sweating from the fever and obviously fighting through the pain. "So are you going to tell me what's next," he demanded, "or do we turn this into a guessing game?"

She saw such hostility in his eyes that a chill ran through her body. She turned back to the Romex and forced her voice to stay calm and even. "Start wrapping this Romex around the safe. Twenty-five turns."

He lugged the heavy wire over to the hole in the wall. That put him less than a dozen feet away from her, but she was grateful for every foot of that distance. Katherine had been through plenty, and it took a lot to unnerve her, but that last look had done it. She knew that he was struggling with more than just the pain. Coleman was changing. Clearly and irrefutably.

"What's all this supposed to do?" he demanded as he fought the stiff wire, forcing it to bend around the safe.

"I've calculated the inductive reactance that comes from a two-and-a-half-foot-diameter coil wrapped around an 1800-pound steel core."

"Meaning?"

She began stripping one end of the 220 extension cord to connect it to the Romex. "Meaning I'm turning the entire safe into a giant electromagnet."

Coleman nodded. "We can't get to the disks on the inside of the safe, so we're turning the entire safe into a giant magnet and erasing them that way."

"Exactly."

Coleman said nothing. She could feel his eyes on her. Maybe it was approval, maybe it was something else. Whatever it was, it made her uneasy and self-conscious. This was not the man she had known just a few hours earlier.

Once she had connected the extension cord to the Romex, she rose and began stringing the cord into the hall and toward the executive lunchroom, where O'Brien had said a 220 stove outlet would be.

But she had barely entered the hallway when she heard: "Okay, Ma'am. I think you better lay that down and turn around to face me."

Katherine's heart pounded; she dropped the extension cord to the floor and turned around.

It was the third guard, a college kid looking very clean-cut and dapper in his crisp white shirt and blue security uniform. He reminded her of Gary, back when they were first married, back when he had first worn his uniform. The boy was twenty feet away, but even from that distance she could see him sweating as he held the gun on her.

"So, where are your friends?" He motioned toward the office between them. "In there?"

Katherine said nothing as he approached. But with each step he took, she grew more and more apprehensive.

He arrived at the doorway. Keeping his attention divided between Katherine and the room, he called inside. "Okay, it's all over now."

There was no answer.

He was obviously afraid to step inside. "This is Security! I have a gun and I am authorized to use it, so come out now before anybody gets hurt."

There was no movement, no sound.

He looked again at Katherine. Then tentatively, reluctantly, he stepped into the doorway. "Hello? Wherever you are, you'd better—"

Coleman plowed into him like a semi, knocking him back into the hallway. The boy was down on the ground with Coleman on top of him before he knew what hit him. Coleman struck the boy's face once, twice, without mercy. By the time Katherine reached them, his nose was already broken.

"That's enough!" she shouted.

But Coleman continued to hit him. Blood covered the boy's face and stained Coleman's shirt.

"Coleman!"

And still he hit him. Rage had erupted inside him like a volcano, directing all of his fury at this boy.

"Stop it!" Katherine tried to pull him off. "Stop!"

Sounds came from Coleman's throat, grunts maybe, or whimperings, she couldn't tell. She dropped to her knees, pushing against him with all of her weight, crying "Stop it! Stop hitting him!" until she finally got his attention.

His eyes locked onto hers. For a moment, his rage was redirected at her.

Color drained from her face. She felt herself growing numb. She had never experienced such anger, never seen such raw hatred. And the eyes—almost satanic, full of malevolence and fury. But then she saw something else, deeper. Underneath. A flicker. Just a glimmer, way down, deep inside. The Coleman she knew was still there, fighting to resurface and take charge.

His glare softened, then faltered. He blinked once, then again. He looked back down at the boy, at the blood, the pulverized muscle, the broken bone.

"That's enough," she repeated firmly.

His eyes darted back to her.

"That's enough."

Coleman wiped the sweat from his face and rose unsteadily. He looked lost, staring first at the boy, then at Katherine, then back at the boy.

She leaned over and checked the guard. He was still breathing. He had probably lost an eye, and he would definitely need reconstructive surgery.

Coleman coughed. "We've . . ."

She looked up. He was steadying himself against the wall, still staring, still looking confused and frightened. "We've got to get him some help."

She nodded. "How long will it take to destroy all the test tubes?"

"No," he said, shaking his head. "It's over."

"What are you talking about?"

Coleman looked at the blood on his hands. "I can't—"

She slowly rose to her feet. "Yes, you can."

"I almost killed him."

"I know, but—"

"I *was* killing him."

"But you didn't. You were able to stop."

He closed his eyes. She knew that the war inside his head was excruciating.

"You can control this thing," she insisted. "I know you can."

"No."

"Yes you can. I saw it, just now."

"No, I was—"

"You *have* to control it!" she demanded. "This isn't just about you. This is about all of us. You, me, Eric, everybody! You have to control it!"

Her outburst seemed to confuse him. Maybe she was getting through. She couldn't tell.

"Now stay here with this boy. All I have to do is plug in that extension cord, and those disks are history. That only leaves the lab samples and the animals. Then we're out of here. All right?"

Coleman just looked at her. He was starting to shiver again, his face wet with perspiration.

"All right?" she repeated.

He still gave no answer. But no answer was better than a negative one. She picked up the extension cord and headed for the stove outlet in the lunchroom.


The dog raced into the woods, streaks of black and gold in the night. It headed toward Tisha, but Eric knew that it would change course as soon as it spotted him.

He looked at the nearest tree, a huge fir with branches low enough for climbing. But then what? Be treed like some animal? There had to be another way.

He looked back at the driveway. He'd been circling around, moving parallel with it as Tisha had gone deeper into the woods. Three cars were parked there: a van, the car he had been kidnapped in, and the idling Mercedes.

There was no time to think. The dog was already at Tisha's side.

Eric sprang forward. He crashed through the undergrowth, snapping sticks, twigs, and anything else in his path. He no longer cared about the noise. He had only one objective—to reach that idling Mercedes before the dog reached him.

The animal heard him and immediately spun and lunged in pursuit.

Voices shouted.

The car lay twenty feet ahead.

Branches slapped into the boy's face, stinging his eyes, making them blur with tears, but he kept running. He looked over his shoulder. The dog shot through the brush after him—a flash of gold, then shadows, then black and gold, then more shadows. It was huge, bigger than Eric.

The car was fifteen feet away.

He could hear the dog breathing now. Quick grunting gasps with each powerful stride.

Eric flew out of the woods and onto the driveway.

Ten feet to go.

He heard the dog's claws digging into the driveway's gravel.

Six feet.

He reached toward the door handle—just as his left foot caught a chuckhole, buckling his leg and sending him sprawling into the loose gravel. He put out his hands, sliding on them and on his elbows and knees.

He looked over his shoulder. The dog was two strides behind, fangs bared, eyes white and crazed. There was no time to reach up and open the door. Before the slide slowed Eric flattened out and kicked himself forward, continuing the momentum, until he was slipping under the car.

He would have made it if the dog hadn't caught his left leg, sinking its teeth hard into the ankle. Eric screamed and jerked his foot away. He felt the tendons and muscles rip as he heard the thud of the animal's head striking the side of the car.

The impact made the dog release its grip, and Eric scrambled on his belly toward the other side. The animal tried to follow underneath, but could only reach in as far as its chest. Its barks thundered and roared under the car. It gnashed and snapped, fangs just feet from the boy. But the dog was too big to reach him. It pulled out and raced to the other side.

Seeing the move, Eric reversed direction and slid back across the gravel toward the passenger side. He crawled out, scrambled to his knees, and opened the door.

The dog spun around and came back at him.

Eric leaped into the car. But as he reached for the handle to slam the door, the dog lunged for his arm. Eric pulled the door with all of his might. He felt the animal's hot breath against his wrist—just as the car door smashed its head against the car's body. The animal yelped, and Eric opened the door just far enough for it to escape, then slammed it shut. He spun around and hit the locks, gasping for breath, frantically checking for bites. Suddenly there was a pounding on the driver's window.

"Eric!" It was Tisha pounding and shouting. "Eric, open up! Nobody's going to hurt you. Come on now, open up."

It was a lie. Not only could he tell by her voice, but he could see it in her eyes as well. She could not be trusted.

He looked to the ignition. Yes, the keys were there. He was safe. No one could get him. At least for now.


Murkoski had remained just outside the front door of the cabin, watching. The other young man, the kidnapper, joined Tisha at the passenger side of the Mercedes, pounding and pleading. But Eric wouldn't give in. Murkoski knew he was too frightened. The boy would simply stay there in the car until they busted out a window and dragged him out.

Murkoski scowled. The thought of a busted window in his Mercedes SL 600 gave him little pleasure. But what choice did he have? After all, the kid had the keys, so—

Slowly, Murkoski smiled. Well, the kid had one set of keys, anyway.

He turned back toward the cabin, colliding with the older kidnapper, who had just ambled outside. "What's going on?" the man mumbled through his swollen nose.

"Stay here," Murkoski ordered.

Murkoski headed into the house and up the stairs to his office. He pulled open the top desk drawer, and there they were—the spare set of keys.

He scooped them up and started out of the room, then hesitated. Someone had left the computer on. He turned back and looked at the glowing screen. There was a message on it. From the Internet. He slowly approached the monitor and read:

>ERIC: WE ARE GOING INTO GENODYNE. IF YOU ARE THERE, LET US KNOW WHERE. DON'T LET THEM CATCH YOU READING THEIR FILES. YOU ARE IN DANGER. TRUST NO ONE. I LOVE YOU, MOM.

So the kid had been doing more than playing computer games. Grudgingly, Murkoski nodded in admiration, then reread the message. Suddenly he understood the break-in call from Security. It hadn't been a prank or some unknown intruder. It had been the boy's mom, and probably Coleman as well.

Murkoski paused, running through the possible courses of action. If he wasn't careful, things could quickly get out of hand. Gradually, a plan took shape. He would have to beat them to the punch. He would be the one to call the police, to play the victim. After all, Coleman and Katherine were the ones breaking and entering. As for the kid, children wander off all the time. It was their word against his. A broken-down alcoholic and a convicted killer against a world-famous Ph.D.? Not much competition there.

Of course, the boy would have to be disposed of. But Kenneth Murkoski was getting better at that sort of thing all the time.

# CHAPTER 16

More window pounding. This time from the passenger side. Eric spun around to see the younger kidnapper beating on the glass so hard that he thought it would break. Meanwhile, Tisha continued pleading and pounding on the driver's side.

Eric's eyes darted back to the keys in the ignition. He knew that the engine was running, that the car was ready to go. But he also knew he'd never driven before. Still, there was TV and all those movies, and hadn't he seen his mother drive a million times before?

He scooted behind the wheel, which didn't seem to make Tisha and the kidnapper any happier.

The shouting and pounding grew louder. Eric reached his foot down as far as he could and pressed the pedal.

Nothing happened.

Maybe it was the wrong pedal. He stretched until he was able to touch the other pedal with his toe.

The engine revved loudly, but the car still didn't move. He stretched and pushed harder. The car roared even louder, but it didn't budge.

Suddenly the pounding on the passenger window turned to loud, sharp crackings. The man was beating on the glass with the butt of his gun.

In a panic, Eric searched the dash board, then looked to the gearshift. It was on "P." He wasn't sure what that meant but remembered that his mother always fiddled with her gearshift before taking off. Still pushing the accelerator with his toe, making the engine roar, Eric strained to see over the dash. The older kidnapper was walking toward him, shaking his head, saying something that Eric couldn't make out over the revving engine, the barking dog, and all the pounding and yelling.

The passenger window exploded. Eric screamed as fragments of glass showered over him. The younger man reached inside, fumbling for the lock. Eric pushed the accelerator as far as he could reach. Still nothing. In desperation, he grabbed the gearshift and shoved it hard.

The car lunged forward. The man reaching inside had to run to keep up. "Stop the car!" he yelled. "Stop it!"

Eric watched him, terrified.

"Stop the car!" The man began swearing. "Stop the car, stop the—" Suddenly his eyes went wide. "Look out!"

Eric turned forward just in time to see a giant evergreen coming at them. He jerked the wheel hard to the left and the car swerved, barely missing the tree. The man wasn't so lucky. Inertia broke his grip on the car and threw him forward directly into the tree. He gave a loud *OOF!* then dropped from sight.

Eric thought he'd killed him. He let up on the accelerator and craned his neck over the backseat to look out the window. He saw Tisha running over and helping the man to his feet.

He wasn't dead. Good.

Then, before Eric could turn around, headlights of the second car blazed on, blinding him as they glared through the back window.

He spun forward and pushed hard on the accelerator. The car threw gravel and slid as he fought to keep it on the road.


The security guard had regained consciousness. Coleman and Katherine carefully helped him to his feet. They eased him down the hall and into the elevator. They had been able to stop the bleeding, but it was likely that he'd sustained a concussion—perhaps a bad one.

"We'll get you some help," Coleman assured him. "Real soon. Just hang in there."

Katherine could see the kid watching Coleman suspiciously. It may have been their recent history together, or the fact that Coleman was now in possession of his gun. In either case, she understood why the boy might be a bit skeptical of Coleman's goodwill.

The elevator came to a stop on the main floor. They stepped off and headed down the hallway toward the lab division.

"Listen," Katherine asked, as she helped the guard along, "did you happen to see a little boy?"

"Sorry?" The guard's speech was thick from his swollen tongue and broken teeth.

"A little boy. Eight, blondish hair, U of W sweatshirt? Did you see anybody bring a little boy in here?"

The guard shook his head. He talked, but it was obvious that his pain was severe. "FDA forbids children entering a lab."

"What about the offices, could he be in—"

He shook his head. "Every visit recorded."

"And there's nothing on the record in the past twenty-four hours?"

Again he shook his head.

Katherine's disappointment was heavy. Where was her boy? Was he hurt? Was he even alive?

They reached a set of doors. Coleman shoved O'Brien's mag card against the black box and entered his PIN. Katherine noticed his hands were wet and trembling as he hit the numbers. The door buzzed and he pushed it open. They moved through the atrium, walking beside the trickling stream and under the large palm trees until they reached the other elevator. They entered, and Coleman pressed the button to the third floor.

O'Brien had said that the experiment was confined to the third floor. They would have to go through each of the eight laboratories on that floor and clear out all samples of the DNA. It would be an arduous task. She glanced at Coleman, wondering what he was thinking. Did he plan on taking the guard wherever they went? They would be able to move faster without him, but she knew it would be impossible to convince Coleman to leave this kid behind in his battered condition.

It was frustrating—which Coleman was she dealing with, killer or saint? And, as the battle raged inside his head, he seemed to change from minute to minute. Only one thing remained constant: his deterioration. With every passing minute, he seemed to be losing ground.

The elevator doors opened, and to her surprise she saw half a dozen technicians crossing back and forth between labs. Coleman leaned toward her and said, "Must be the shipment. Murkoski has them working overtime to make the morning shipment."

Katherine nodded as technicians noticed the open elevator and slowly ground to a halt. She figured that their shocked expressions had something to do with the guard's bloody face or the way Coleman held the gun or both. She stood watching them, unsure of the next step.

Not Coleman. He quickly moved into action. Brandishing the gun with one hand and motioning to the gym bag with the other, he shouted, "All right everyone, listen up!" He locked the elevator door open and stepped out, pushing the battered guard ahead of him.

He definitely had their attention.

"You've got exactly three-and-a-half minutes to clear the building!"

No one moved.

"I've planted a bomb. It's going off in exactly—" He looked at his watch. "In exactly three minutes and twenty-four seconds."

People stood, stunned. Mouths dropped. Most of all Katherine's.

"If I were you," he continued, voice rising, "I'd quit standing around and get out of here! Do you hear me?" He waved the gun some more. "Get out of here! Now! Move it! Move it!"

Panic swept through the hall. Some of the technicians raced into the labs to warn colleagues, others started for the stairs.

"Three minutes and ten seconds! Move! Let's go, let's go! Three minutes and five!"

Katherine stepped off the elevator, amazed at his performance. Coleman was doing a very convincing imitation of a madman—though she was no longer sure how much of it was imitation.

"Three minutes!"

Coleman motioned the gun toward a couple heading for the stairs. "You," he shouted. "And you!"

They froze.

"Go to the other floors. If there's any other workers, clear them out. Check everywhere, the offices, the johns, everywhere."

They hesitated.

He pointed the gun. "Go!"

They didn't wait to be told again.

"Here!" He shoved the guard at another passing technician. "Take him and get him out of here."

The technician obeyed. "What about the woman?" he asked.

Coleman reached out and grabbed Katherine's arm. He pulled her to him hard. "She's my hostage."

"But—"

"Get out of here before I decide to take more!"

He scurried off, rushing the guard ahead of him.

"Hostage?" Katherine said, angrily ripping her arm free of his grasp.

But with lightning speed he grabbed it again, this time twisting it behind her back. She started to fight, but he yanked it up so hard she cried out. He hissed into her ear, "You want to share the blame for this?"

Again she struggled, and he pulled so hard tears came to her eyes.

"This way they'll only come after me."

"Hey, man, come on—"

Katherine looked up to see a freckle-faced kid protesting. "Can't you see you're hurting her?"

Katherine heard a pistol cocking and turned to see Coleman leveling it directly at the kid. Suddenly she feared that Coleman was no longer acting.

"All right, all right," the kid said as he backed away. "Just take it easy, take it easy."

In a little over a minute, the hallway was clear, and Coleman released Katherine with a shove. She grabbed her arm and rubbed it, wanting to shout at him, to curse him. But when she saw the hate that had returned to his eyes, she forced herself to remain silent. Now that there was just the two of them, she had no idea what he would do.

"You go too," he ordered, wiping the sweat out of his eyes. "Your kid's not here. Get out while you can."

She searched his face for signs of the Coleman she'd once known, once admired. "What about you?" she countered. "You have no stake in this. Why not look out for yourself and get out of here, too?"

He hesitated, and for a split second she saw it. He was still there. Somewhere inside, the Coleman she knew was still there, still struggling, still trying to do right, regardless of the cost.

Holding his gaze, she shook her head. "No, this is too important to let you screw it up on your own. I'm staying as long as you do."

Murkoski stepped back outside the cabin just in time to see his Mercedes disappear down the drive. The older man had climbed into the other car, the Audi, to go after it.

"No!" Murkoski shouted. "Take the van!"

The man rolled down his window. "What?"

"I'm driving this one to the lab."

"Why can't you take the—"

"The van's got a plastic tarp in the back. That way you won't get blood on the carpet. And take a couple shovels so you can put the body somewhere it won't be found." The order had been given, and Murkoski held the man's gaze to make sure there was no misunderstanding.

Coleman and Katherine scoured the labs, emptying every refrigerator of every Eppendorf tube, checking all the centrifuges, the incubators, the sequencers, everything O'Brien had said could contain samples of the GOD gene. They had to be certain. Every sample on the third floor had to be torched.

Katherine wasn't sure why Coleman had chosen to dump all of the tubes into the open elevator. It was getting to be quite a pile, nearly five feet high, and they still had two more labs to go. She wanted to question him on it, but she knew that it was time to keep the arguments to a minimum. He was unstable, a primed bomb ready to explode, and there was no telling what would set it off.

No, she wouldn't question his methods. If there were to be any confrontations, she'd save them for the most critical issues.

She dumped another wastebasket full of tubes into the elevator.

"Hey . . ."

She turned. He stood at the entrance to the last lab, worn and drawn and soaked with perspiration. As threatening and unnerving as it was for her to work with him, she couldn't even imagine what it must be like for him—what type of pain the viral leash was inflicting upon his body, and more importantly, what type of monster he was battling within his mind.

"There's something . . ." He swallowed. "I think you should see this."

She followed him into the laboratory.

It sat on a lab bench across the room. He had just removed it from a freezer. It was a clear, round container, looking very much like a high-tech, Plexiglas humidor. It stood twelve inches high with a base five inches in diameter.

Inside was what looked like a translucent rock. Yellow-brown. But as she moved closer, Katherine realized that it wasn't a rock at all.

It was wax. A small piece of ancient, yellowed wax.

She stooped for a closer look. One end of the wax had been sheered off. And from that end protruded a tiny twig. But she knew it was no twig. She stopped breathing. It was not a twig, but the remains of a vine. And although it was hard to make out through the opaqueness of the wax, there appeared to be the remnant of one, maybe two, long, spindly thorns.

She stared in silent, reverent awe. Of course, she could see no blood through the wax, but she knew it was there. Traces of blood two thousand years old.

As she stared, she couldn't help thinking how those traces of blood on this frail vine were responsible for the unimaginable terror about to be released upon humankind.

No, that wasn't true. The blood wasn't the cause. The blood was holy, pure, good. It wasn't the blood, it was how man had twisted and contorted this goodness, how he had once again found a way to turn holiness into horror.

Coleman cleared his throat. "Better, uh—throw it into the elevator with the rest," he said.

Katherine nodded. But neither moved to touch it. Not yet. They would, of course. But for now they wanted to look upon it just a moment longer. And to quietly wonder.

As soon as Eric's car slid out of the gravel driveway and onto the main road, he knew he'd turned the wrong direction. He was going up the mountain; he wanted to be going down.

Then there was the problem of the accelerator. No matter how hard he pressed, the engine only whined louder—the car never moved faster.

Fortunately, his slower progress made it easier to stay on the road—at least what road he could see. It would have helped if he could have found the switch for the lights, but Eric didn't dare take his hands off the wheel to start exploring.

A pair of high beams bounced onto the road behind him. They quickly closed in, blazing through the back window and into the car. Their approach terrified Eric, and it was all he could do to hold the car in the road. Now the vehicle behind him began honking, long and loud, over and over again.

Eric's anxiety skyrocketed and his driving grew worse, until he was swerving back and forth across the road.

The lights backed off.

It took forever to bring his car back under control. When he did, Eric noticed how hot and damp his hands had become. He wiped them off on his jeans, one at a time.

Once again the headlights approached, flashing from high beams to low and back again, the car horn blaring.

"Stop it!" Eric cried. "Stop it!"

The vehicle pulled directly behind him, so close that he could see it was the van that had been in the driveway, and he could see the faces of both kidnappers.

"Stop it!" Eric screamed.

They eased to his left. Their lights no longer flooded the inside of his car; now they illuminated the road beside him. He knew that they were pulling up. He looked over to see, but lost his bearings and began swerving again.

Once again the lights dropped back.

It was then that Eric noticed a red warning light glowing on the instrument panel. He figured that whatever he was doing wrong, whatever was making the car's engine race without moving, was making the light burn.

He checked the speedometer. Thirty miles an hour. He pressed down on the accelerator as hard as he could. The engine whined louder.

Suddenly the car lurched forward with a loud CRASH.

Eric screamed.

Another crash, another lurch.

The bad guys were ramming him. He had to do something. He looked down at the gearshift. It was on "1." When he had pushed on it the first time, it got him going; maybe it was worth another try. He shoved it into another position. Something labeled "N."

What power he had suddenly vanished, and the engine roared wildly, as if it were going to explode.

They rammed him again.

Eric screamed.

Then again.

But this time they didn't back off. Instead, they kept their bumper pressed hard against his. Suddenly he had more power than he knew what to do with. They were pushing him. They picked up speed. Thirty miles an hour, thirty-five, forty ...

"Knock it off!" Eric shouted, as he fiercely gripped the steering wheel. "Stop it, *Stop it!*"

But they didn't stop.

The shrieks gently subsided as the animal looked first one way, then the other, until his eyes focused on O'Brien.

"Hey, boy."

Freddy cocked his head. He seemed to recognize the voice. It looked as if he were trying to remember something else, something from long ago.

"Freddy, it's me. How are you, boy?"

Freddy whimpered faintly.

"It's me, fellow, remember?" O'Brien stretched his hands out through the rain.

But whatever memory the animal had quickly disappeared. He shrieked again, baring his fangs. Suddenly he jumped on Murkoski's lifeless body, striking him with both fists one, two, three times. Then he leaped to the ground, raced past O'Brien, and disappeared down the stairs, barking and screaming as he ran.

# CHAPTER 18

"Stop it," Coleman growled as he paced back and forth in the hallway. "Stop saying that."

"But it's the truth," O'Brien insisted. "It's over. We've got an entire bomb division waiting outside, a hundred lab animals not yet killed, and—" He glanced at Katherine. "Who knows if we can knock out those gene sequencers."

"I could probably get into their memory," Katherine speculated, "but if they're scattered throughout the building, it'll take time to make sure I get them all."

"And time is the one thing we don't have," O'Brien said.

Coleman nodded as he continued to pace and think. He was slightly stooped now—from the debilitating pain in his body and in his head.

The three of them stood at the other end of the hall, near the window. O'Brien had managed to shut off the main valve to the overhead sprinklers. There was still the sound of water dripping and trickling, but the deafening hiss had finally been stopped.

Katherine looked out the window, down into the parking lot. It was buzzing with the Snohomish County bomb squad and Arlington police. Behind her, at the other end of the hall, sat the elevator with its charred pile in the final stages of smoldering. Directly in front of that, Murkoski's body lay in half an inch of water, covered by O'Brien's jacket.

"I can talk to the authorities," O'Brien offered, "explain what has happened."

"And that will stop it?" Coleman asked. "That will stop the gene from being manufactured, from being sold?" He motioned down the hall toward Murkoski's body. "That will stop something like that from spreading throughout the world?"

Katherine watched as O'Brien said nothing. All three of them knew the answer. Whatever political, military, and financial powers that had enabled Murkoski to go this far would not be stopped until they had their way.

Coleman resumed pacing, then changed the subject. "Everything is contained in this building? The animals, the sequencers?"

O'Brien nodded. "Everything. Why?"

Before Coleman could respond, a light glared through the window. The sound of the approaching helicopter had been registering somewhere in the back of Katherine's mind, but she'd paid little attention, until now. The thumping grew intolerable as the aircraft slowly dropped into view. All three ducked out of its sight, under the window.

*"This is the Snohomish County Bomb Division. You have three minutes to vacate the building or we will come in after you."*

O'Brien turned toward Coleman, who was kneeling beside him. "It's over," he said again. "Let me go out and—"

"No," Coleman said.

It was Katherine's turn to try and reason. "Coleman—"

"No!" he insisted. "It's not over. Not yet."

Katherine and O'Brien exchanged looks.

"Your Shipping and Receiving," he asked. "It's in this building, too, right?"

"That's right," O'Brien said. "First floor, the entire back section."

"What about solvents?"

"I'm sorry, what—"

"For the labs, you guys use solvents, don't you?"

"Of course."

"What type do you have?"

"We use several."

"Toluene?"

"It's one of the more common, certainly."

"You have lots of it?"

"I imagine. But what—"

A second light blazed through the window, striking the ceiling. This one came from ground level. Those outside had obviously located their position. Instinctively, the three pressed closer to the wall under the window.

"Okay," Coleman said, "this is what we'll do. First, you two need to get out of here."

Katherine protested. "Cole—"

He cut her off. "You need to stand up. Let them see you stand up. Then walk down the hall, take the stairs, and head out of the building."

"What about you?" O'Brien asked.

"They want a bomb, I'll give them a bomb."

"Coleman, you can't—"

He threw Katherine a harsh look and she stopped. Then, seeing her fear, he continued more softly. "I don't see any other way. The sequencers have to go, the animals have to be destroyed—"

"Let me stay with you, I can help."

He hesitated—then shook his head. "No."

"But—"

"You've still got to find Eric. If something goes wrong, I don't want to be responsible for killing both of his parents."

She held his look a moment, then asked quietly, "What about you?"

"I'll be okay."

She knew he was lying. He tried to smile, but with little success. He was frightened, and he couldn't hide it. Not from her.

*"You have two minutes and thirty seconds."*

O'Brien shook his head. "It won't work. As soon as we're out of here, as soon as your hostages are gone, they'll come in after you."

"Not if you tell them I have a bomb. Not if you say I've jury-rigged it to go off when they enter."

"Why would they believe me?"

"It used to be your company."

*"Two minutes, fifteen seconds."*

Another pause. "Are you sure you can do it?" O'Brien asked.

"Just don't let them cut the power."

O'Brien nodded.

"Coleman . . ." Katherine's voice was thick with emotion.

He looked at her. He was seeing inside of her again, she knew it. Just as he had so many times before. He was seeing—and understanding—her worry, her heartfelt concern. And when he spoke, it was with the same quiet sensitivity of before. "We talked about faith."

"Yes, but—"

"I don't know if I can pull this off—I don't know if I have the strength, the faith. But if I don't try, who will?"

"You don't have—"

"Katherine, listen to me."

"You don't have to be the one—"

"Listen."

His gentle intensity silenced her.

"There's a lot I don't understand. You're the expert in this field, not me."

"But—"

"And if you don't think it will work, if you don't think I have what it takes, you need to let me know."

"And if you don't?"

He searched her face, looking for the words. "Then . . . I truly am lost."

As she stared into his eyes, realization slowly set in. He wasn't doing this just to destroy the gene. That was important, of course. If the gene, if all record of it, weren't completely destroyed, the powers behind Murkoski would simply retrieve it and continue again. But Coleman wasn't doing this just to stop them. He was also doing it for himself. If he could overcome his old nature, if he could hold it at bay and destroy the project—then he would be winning a much deeper, more important battle.

Moisture welled up in her eyes.

He waited, seeking her assurance, needing to know if she thought his proposal possible.

Finally, slowly, she began to nod.

He smiled. "Go then," he whispered. "Let them see you at the window and go."

Before she knew it, she was reaching out and touching his face. She wanted to say something, to encourage him, to tell him how good he was. She also wanted to tell of her overwhelming fears and doubts. But no words came.

He understood and moved her hand from his cheek to his lips. He gently kissed it. He was trembling again, and her heart swelled so full that she thought it would break.

"Go," he urged.

She closed her eyes and swallowed hard.

*"One minute."*

"Go!"

She nodded. She took a breath to steady herself, then slowly rose to her feet. O'Brien joined her. They stood in front of the window, their bodies glowing eerily white from the intense beam of the helicopter that hovered some thirty feet in front of them.

*"Put your hands on top of your heads and come out of the building."*

They nodded, raised their hands above their heads, and turned to head down the hall.

The dripping of the sprinklers had almost stopped. Now, there was only the sloshing of their feet in the water. The journey took forever. Katherine was crying hard now, but that was okay—Coleman couldn't see.

They passed Murkoski's body. It lay motionless. Beyond that the charred pile of Eppendorf tubes continued to smolder. At the door to the stairway, Katherine hesitated for just a moment and looked back.

Coleman appeared tiny and helpless as he crouched under the window in the shadows of the blinding light. But even through her tears, even in the glare and shadow, she could see him smiling. The new Coleman was still in charge. The thought gave her comfort, at least enough to help her through the doorway, to start her down the stairs.


Toluene, also known as methylbenzene, $C_7H_8$, is one of the Ts in TNT. According to Hector Garcia, the bomber punk Coleman had defended on Nebraska's Death Row, in its liquid form it is highly flammable. In its vapor form, its explosive power is incredible. Forget the fertilizer and diesel fuel. According to Garcia, this stuff, if properly mixed with air, could really do some damage.

On the Row, Coleman had listened to Garcia's stories. Knowing that knowledge is power, and having nothing but time on his hands, he had asked the right questions, challenged the hyperbole, and filed the information away for future reference. If prison is anything, it's a classroom for the hungry to learn. And Coleman had always been hungry. Now it was time to put what he had learned to work.

The anger inside continued to boil and writhe and seethe, looking for the slightest frustration, the slightest crack to rise through and overtake him. But instead of fighting it, Coleman began to use it. Instead of trying to destroy the anger, he focused it toward accomplishing his purposes, using it to push through the sweat and pain and mind-dulling exhaustion that were clouding his thinking.

Still, he was at the edge, and he knew it. He nearly exploded with impatience while cooped up inside the freight elevator, pacing in frustration as it slowly lumbered its way down to Shipping and Receiving.

Then there was the anxiety of trying to locate the toluene. Why hadn't he asked for more specifics? Shipping and Receiving went on forever. It could be anywhere down here. Yet, somehow, through his own tough mental discipline and with whatever understanding he had of faith, he was able to focus and refocus until his efforts paid off.

He found six fifty-five-gallon drums of the solvent. He only needed two.

Getting those drums onto the freight elevator was another matter. He opted for the mini electric forklift sitting outside on the loading dock. But it was too big to bring in through the doorway. He'd have to roll up one of the large loading doors. No problem, except it would rattle and draw the attention of any sheriff's sniper who might be hanging out on that side of the building.

Something about that last thought outraged him. Here he was risking his life to help the very people who were trying to kill him. Why? If they wanted him so badly, maybe he should just run out there and let them fire away. And in six months, a year, maybe two, they could start warring against terrorists without conscience, gunmen without feeling. That would show them.

The thought grew more and more appealing until it was all Coleman could do to fight off the urge to throw open the doors, yell his vengeance at the world, and go out in a blaze of glory.

Instead, barely holding his anger in check, he stole out onto the loading dock. This part of the building was L shaped. What exposed area remained was concealed by a ten-foot-high fence. Still, he moved quickly and quietly to the fork-lift and disconnected it from its charging bay. He climbed on board the machine, backed it up as close to the edge of the dock as possible—and then, finally, he released his rage. He stomped on the accelerator with all of his might. The forklift raced toward the metal door and crashed into it. The impact sent such jarring pain through his body that he let out a sti-fled cry. But when he looked, he found that he'd ripped out only part of the door's bottom seam; he hadn't broken through.

He dropped the forklift into reverse. He expected any minute to feel bullets explode into his back, but he didn't care. In fact, it might be a relief compared to the pain he was already enduring. He ground the gears, found forward, and raced at the door again. This time he broke through, tearing metal and sending brads flying in all directions.

The rush was exhilarating, filling Coleman with such a sense of power that he momentarily lost control. For several seconds he wasn't sure if he wanted to regain it.

But the next task called for concentration and focus, and he fought back to the surface to take charge. Carefully, he maneuvered the forklift, sliding the steel teeth under the first fifty-five-gallon drum. Then he turned, approached the freight elevator, and gently loaded the barrel inside. He repeated the process with the second. When they were in place, he maneu-vered the lift inside between the drums and jumped down. He grabbed the nylon strap and pulled down the heavy steel door. It slammed shut, and he hit the button for the top floor.

Once again, the elevator's slow, lumbering speed irritat-ed him, and once again his anger started to rise. But this time there was nowhere to direct it. He didn't even have room to pace. He pounded his fist into his palm. Again and again. "Help me," he muttered, "help me, help me, help me . . ."

All ten officers and two reserves of the Greater Arlington Police Department had arrived on the scene. They had set up a perimeter around the Sheriff's Bomb Division to hold back the growing crowd. They were successful with the crowd. They weren't so successful with the experienced TV crews arriving from Seattle.

"Excuse me, excuse me!" The camera lights pushed and jockeyed toward Katherine, who was kneeling behind the open door of a sheriff's car. "Were you frightened—where did you meet him—did he threaten you—can you give us any idea of his motives—did he display obvious signs of mental instability—did he tell you . . ."

Katherine stayed low and mostly out of the lights, ignoring the news crews as she gave a detailed description of her son to the deputy. From time to time she looked toward the building. So far, no one was going in. O'Brien was doing his job. For how long she wasn't certain.

"Ms. Lyon, Ms. Lyon?" a policewoman was working her way through the crowd. "Ms. Lyon?"

Katherine looked up, shielding her eyes from the lights. The officer was motioning for her to look across the parking lot toward the crowd at the gate.

Katherine rose, but the reporters blocked her view. She stepped up into the doorway of the car and scanned the crowd. In the distance, toward the back, there was a disturbance. People were parting under the orders of an officer, who slowly made his way through the crowd. An older couple walked with him. And by the way they kept looking down and speaking, it was obvious that there must be somebody much smaller by their side.

Katherine held her breath, straining for a better view. She thought she saw a flash of blonde hair through the crowd.

She hopped down and bolted around the car, sending more than one reporter staggering. She ran across the parking lot and started to wade through the crowd. "Eric, Eric!"

There was no response.

"Eric?"

She caught a glimpse of a purple shirt—maybe his U of W sweatshirt, she couldn't tell.

The crowd was parting faster now.

"Eric?"

There was the hair again, then the sweatshirt, then hair—

And then she saw the face.

"Mom!"

Her heart leaped. She shoved through the crowd, running now, giving no thought to anybody or anything but her son.

"Eric!"

At last she dropped down, and he threw himself at her so hard that she nearly fell.

"Mom!"

They hugged fiercely, burying their faces into one another, neither wanting to let go.

"I'm sorry, Mom, I'm sorry."

She pulled back to look at him. His face had a few small cuts, but other than that he was fine. "Sorry for what?" she asked.

"My glasses. I lost my glasses."

She laughed and pulled him into another embrace. "It's okay, honey. We can get new glasses." She closed her eyes tightly and allowed the waves of love to wash over her.

"He came to our house," the older gentleman was saying, "clothes torn, all cut up like that. And he come right up to the door, knocked as polite as you please."

Katherine looked up at the weathered old man, but before she could respond, somebody in the crowd shouted. "He's on the roof! Look, he's on the roof!"

Heads spun. Hands pointed. Katherine slowly rose to her feet and turned to watch.


With a grunt, Coleman swung his ax into the base of the large intake duct that rose half a dozen feet from the roof. It was part of the building's high-volume air-conditioning unit. The blade easily ripped into the galvanized metal. He swung three more times. When he was certain the hole was large enough, he turned to the toluene drums behind him and began to pry them open.

It had been a little tricky getting the barrels up onto the roof, since the elevator only went as far as the top floor. He'd had to drive the forklift out of the elevator, scoop up a drum, then position it just below one of the frosted skylights. Then he had raised the fork high into the air, busting the barrel through the skylight. When the shards of glass had stopped raining, he had placed the barrel on the roof, then repeated the same procedure with the second one.

Next, he had switched on the giant double fans of the air-conditioning unit. They had begun to beat the air with low, ominous thumps. But as the blades picked up speed, the pounding had quickly blurred to a deafening roar.

Finally, using the forklift as a ladder, he had climbed through the skylight out onto the roof and taken an ax to the duct.

When he had both of the fifty-five-gallon barrels open, he pushed and eased the first onto its side. It fell hard, and the liquid began to chug out. With some minor adjusting, he was able to channel the toluene directly into the gaping hole he had chopped out at the duct's base.

The giant fans below immediately began pumping the explosive fumes through the building. They were strong fumes, reminding him of his younger, glue-sniffing days. Knowing he'd have to keep his wits about him, he turned his head to the side to breathe in as much fresh air as possible.

The first drum finished draining and he kicked it aside, sending it rolling and clattering across the roof. He opened the second barrel just as the helicopter crested the building and blinded him with its spotlight.

*"This is the Snohomish County Sheriff's Department. Exit the building at once."*

He scrambled behind the vent. The glaring light, the beating rotors, and the interruption of his work all helped rekindle his anger. But once again, he was able to channel it. Even though his position behind the duct was awkward, giving him little leverage, he reached out to the open drum and pulled it toward him. He rocked it once, twice, three times before it fell, washing its contents over him, his legs, his waist, before spilling across the roof. It burned and felt cold against his skin, and the fumes made his eyes water, but he fought with the emptying drum until he was able to direct the remaining Toluene down into the duct.

By now the helicopter had crabbed to the right, bringing him into full view, once again blinding him with its light.

*"This is the Snohomish County Sheriff. Cease your activity and exit the building at once. This is your final warning."*

He gave no indication that he'd heard the commands, much less intended to obey them, as the drum continued to empty. Now the fumes were burning his nose. Try as he might, he couldn't avoid inhaling them. Already he could feel his head growing light.

Then he saw it. A little red dot, smaller than a dime, first reflecting off the ductwork to his left, then quickly darting toward him. A sniper in the helicopter was taking aim.

Frantically, he looked over to the broken skylight just fifteen feet away. It was how he'd gotten onto the roof, and now it was his only way off. But a wide pool of toluene lay between him and the skylight. He knew that the fumes hadn't had time to work their way deep into the building. He also knew that, if he ran across that pool and the sniper missed him, hitting a piece of ductwork, there was a good chance a spark would end the show before it even began.

His only hope was to circumvent the toluene—to go around it to the skylight. That would be far more dangerous, and meant an extra thirty or so feet of exposure, but it would have to do.

The drum finally emptied, and he gave it a push across the roof to join the other. His clothes were saturated with toluene, making it impossible to avoid breathing the fumes. Their effects grew stronger. He crouched low, prepared himself, then sprang forward, putting every bit of his concentration, every ounce of strength, into speed.

The first shot missed and thumped into the thick tar.

The helicopter adjusted.

Coleman was nearly there—ten feet, eight, five—when the second shot found its mark. His left leg exploded with pain, sending him crashing onto the roof and sliding across the shattered glass.

But he was there. The skylight was within reach. He grabbed the busted-out frame and dragged himself toward it—the jagged, wire-reinforced glass dug into his arms, then his chest, but he continued to pull. Suddenly the entire frame gave way and he tumbled the twelve feet down to the next floor, missing the steel frame of the forklift by mere inches.

The fumes inside the building and from his own soaked clothes were nearly overwhelming. He ripped off his shirt, found a dry section, and tore it in two, using half as a tourniquet to tie off his bleeding leg, the other half as a filter to breathe through. It did little good. Already his head was spinning, his vision blurring.

It was too early; the fumes hadn't completely spread through the building. But he had no choice. He had to do it now, while he could still think. He reached into his pocket for the matches. When he felt them he went cold. He pulled them out. They were soaked, completely saturated with liquid toluene.

His mind groped. He knew there was another book downstairs in the gym bag. He'd been smart enough to throw in two. But the chances of making it downstairs through these fumes were slim. No way could he stay conscious, let alone remain coherent long enough to make it back to the third floor.

Still, what choice did he have?

With stubborn resolve—and a prayer—he steeled himself and half-limped, half-dragged his body past the roaring air-conditioning fans toward the freight elevator.

The fumes took their toll. His mind was drifting now, starting to float. He entered the elevator and pressed three. The doors rattled shut and the elevator descended.

*Mikey, please . . . It's so cold . . . please don't leave me here.*

Coleman spun around. It was his brother's voice. Was he hallucinating? Yes, of course. No, it sounded too real.

*Mikey . . .*

He clenched his eyes, forcing the voice out of his head.

It took forever for the elevator doors to finally open.

When he stepped out, his vision was worse, colors twisted and blurred into one another. Still, he was able to make out the form of Murkoski's body lying on the floor in front of the burned out passenger elevator. Not far away sat the gym bag.

He staggered forward. Time was distorting, telescoping, moving in painfully slow motion.

He floated down to his knees beside the bag and his unfeeling hands began searching for the matches. He was drifting, high and far away, on automatic pilot. Yet his hands kept working.

They found the second book—just as the footsteps began; construction boots against tile. His father's boots.

*Michael . . . Michael . . .*

He could smell the stench of whisky.

"Help me," he whispered. "Dear God . . . help me . . ."

He pulled out the matchbook. It felt damp. The overhead sprinklers had done their job too well. An alarm bell began ringing. It sounded like the one in the Quickie Mart where he'd shot the clerk. He couldn't tell; it was too far away. The guitar licks from "Hotel California" wafted through his head. So real, so clear, so lovely.

*Michael . . .*

He felt his fingers opening the matchbook cover, more from impulse than from will. He saw them pulling off the first match and dragging it across the striker.

Nothing.

His fingers were wet. They'd soaked the head of the match. He saw his hands wiping themselves on the dry part of his shirt he'd used as a tourniquet. They tried again, this time ripping out a wad of four matches.

*Michael ...*

*You are mine.*

It was time to quit, to give in. To let that lovely music carry him off.

*You are me.*

The euphoria lulled him, lifted him ...

"No! NO!"

His shout cleared his head long enough for him to struggle to his feet. He looked down at his hands. He was still holding the wad of matches. Four of them. He tried striking them all at once.

Too wet. He threw them away.

*You are me.*

*Michael ...*

He tugs at the remaining matches, hands shaking now so badly that he can barely rip them out. He is drifting again, floating, floating ...

The matches tear away.

*Michael ...*

*We are one.*

He drifts back for a moment, long enough to try one.

Nothing.

Another.

Nothing.

*There is only justice.* The sound of Steiner's voice startles him.

"NO!" Coleman cries. His shout brings him back long enough to see that he is holding a match—the last one. He forces his hand to drag it across the striker.

*Michael* ...

Nothing.

He is gone, in another world, no cares, no pain.

*Michael* ...

"Please," he hears himself mumble.

*Michael* ...

His hand starts to strike it again, but it cannot. He is on his knees, his throat knot-tight in emotion.

*You are mine.*

*Justice* ...

*Michael* ...

"Please." The words barely spoken. "Dear God, help me."

Again he feels the match. It is still between his fingers. But it no longer matters, it is time to—

*Michael* ...

Something deep inside him stirs.

*Michael* ...

Again he feels the match between his thumb and forefinger. He tries one last time. He is dragging the sulfur head across the striker. It is sparking, flaming to life ...


A spherical shock wave, consisting of supercompressed air, $CO_2$, and water vapor, forms at the match head. It rapidly expands until it reaches the walls of the hallway; at that point it is traveling at a detonation rate of 4000 feet per second and has a density equal to that of very hard wood. It slams into the walls, demolishing them and continuing to move outward.

But that is only the beginning.

The trail of exploding solvent vapor roars up the air-conditioning ducts at almost four times the speed of sound, rupturing them as it moves through them to involve every room in the building. The shock wave of expanding gas crushes tile and splinters wood. Most importantly, it creates what is referred to by Hector Garcia as "overpressure." In this case, several hundreds of pounds of overpressure per square inch. It disintegrates the concrete walls and twists the steel support girders until they are unrecognizable—until even areas of the building that have not been touched by the blast collapse and tumble under their own weight.

The research building of Genodyne Inc. no longer exists.

*Michael . . . Michael . . .*

*Coleman looks up. At first it is his father's voice, but then it isn't. Unlike the other times, this voice resonates with kindness and compassion. Coleman is awestruck.*

*He's unsure where he is. But there is light, everywhere light. Standing above him is a figure. It is his father, but it isn't. It is inexplicably tender, carved from a light brighter than the other light. It is the source of the light, of all light. But the figure is more than light; it is love, a consuming, all-encompassing love. It reaches down to Coleman, taking his hands, gently helping him to his feet.*

*Unable and unwilling to stop himself, Coleman falls into the light, feeling its arms wrapping about him, its love permeating his body.*

*He hears three words. Spoken yet unspoken. Powerful, roaring like thunder, tender as breath. They thrill him, but he is afraid to believe. They say he will never again be alone. He will never again be a shadow, dancing, searching, aching to belong. He does belong. Completely. Intimately. Eternally. They are only three words, but they tell him all of this and much, much more. They simply say: "Welcome home, son."*

# CHAPTER 19

Katherine rested on the tailgate of the sheriff's van, wrapped in a blanket and sipping some very bad coffee. Eric sat up front, checking out the cool radio equipment. A hundred yards away, on the other side of the police barricade, the media lights glared as reporters filed their stories with the hollowed-out shell of Genodyne Inc. as their backdrop.

Katherine knew that her name had been leaked to the press and that it was just a matter of time before she would have to face them. But for now, it felt awfully good to simply sit and close her eyes.

322

"You doing okay?"

She looked up to see O'Brien standing beside her, trying to drink the same coffee.

"Yeah," she said, scooting over to let him sit. The movement caused the cut in her right cheek to throb slightly, and she reached up to explore the two-inch gash with her fingers.

"You should have them look at that," he said. "You'll probably need stitches."

She said nothing. There was a lot she should do.

"They'll want to talk to you, you know."

She nodded. "What did you tell them?"

"Not much. I don't work here anymore, remember?"

She gave him a look. He shrugged. "I didn't give them a name. I just said he was some friend of Murkoski's. Very angry, very confused, and with a history of mental instability."

Katherine turned away, deeply saddened by the thought. Coleman had given everything he had, everything he was, and he wouldn't even be allowed to have a name. Worse than that, he would be labeled now and forever as some lunatic.

"What about the kidnapping?" she asked.

"That one's up to you. I did suggest he might somehow be responsible for that, as well."

"And they bought that?"

"For now. Keeps everything nice and tidy. Course I'll be in Mazatlán by the time they realize the pieces don't quite fit."

Katherine nodded, wondering where she would be, how her life would ever come back together.

Silence stole over the two as they sat in the damp air, with the bad coffee, staring vacantly at the remains of the building. A handful of investigators were already beginning to scramble over the rubble and sift through the debris. On the horizon, the sky was beginning to glow with the promise of another dawn.

O'Brien took a long, deep breath and slowly let it out. "Poor soul," he muttered. "Poor, poor soul."

Katherine looked to him. "Why do you say that?"

"He came so close to winning."

"You don't think he did? You don't think he won?"

O'Brien glanced at her. "He destroyed the project, sure. In that sense, I suppose. But, dying—" He shook his head. "Not much victory for him in that."

"How can you say that?" Katherine felt herself growing defensive. "All he wanted was to be kind and loving and giving. All he wanted was to defeat the old Coleman with the new, loving one."

"And you think he did that? In the end, do you think he overcame the old Coleman?"

"He gave up his life for us, didn't he?" She motioned to the crowd across the parking lot. "For all of them. You don't get any more loving and giving than that."

O'Brien looked at her.

"'No greater love has a man than he lay down his life for his friends,'" she quoted softly.

O'Brien nodded. "I've heard that."

"Me, too. All of my life. But now ..." Her voice dropped off.

"But now?" O'Brien repeated.

"Now I think I'm finally starting to understand." She paused a moment to look up to the brightening sky. "Coleman won, Dr. O'Brien. Maybe not by your standards, maybe not by mine. But he won."

O'Brien started to answer, but fell silent. He had much to think about.

"Mom! Hey, Mom."

Katherine turned. Eric was standing just outside the van.

"Mom, check it out."

She rose wearily to her feet and walked to him. He was pointing toward a tall pine tree. "Look at that," he said.

At first she saw nothing. "What?"

"There?"

"I don't—"

"Right there."

She kneeled down to his level. It was only then, when her face was beside his, that she saw it. The moon was rising just above the top set of branches.

"Isn't that cool?"

Katherine stared, her throat tightening.

"Isn't it?" he repeated.

He was right; it was cool, very cool. She wanted to tell him so, but she didn't trust her voice. Instead, she wrapped her arms around her son and held him tight. Once again she felt her eyes beginning to burn with tears.

Eric turned to her. "Are you all right?"

She nodded as the tears spilled onto her cheeks. The wetness stung the cut in her face and she winced slightly, raising a hand toward it.

"It's okay, Mom," he said, reaching out to touch her face. "You'll be okay."

The concern in his little eyes and the tender touch of his hand were almost more than she could bear. She reached up and took his fingers. They felt warm, almost on fire as she kissed them. He was right, she would be okay. She had her son, she had her life. And she had something else. A glimpse, a taste of the eternal had started to return. She looked back up to the moon. At that particular moment, it was the most beautiful thing she had ever seen.

"Cool," her son repeated joyfully.

But when she turned to him, he wasn't looking at the moon. He was looking at her, practically beaming as he stared at her cheek.

It was then she noticed how warm her face felt, almost as hot as his fingers. She reached up to touch the cut, but couldn't find it. She ran her fingers over her face, but she couldn't feel it anywhere. Only the heat.

Eric's grin broadened.

"What?" She rubbed her cheek again, searching for it. "What did you do?"

He giggled. "I'm not sure, but it's gone, Mom. It's not there."

She looked at him in rising astonishment. Then spotting the side-view mirror of the van, she moved to it to see.

But there was nothing. The wound was gone.

"How?" she asked. "That's not possible." She turned to him. "How did . . ."

He shrugged, and smiled. "Got me."

She turned back to the mirror.

"But that's not all," he said thoughtfully. "Something else is kinda weird, too."

She turned back to him.

"Lately, when I look at people—real deep and stuff? Well, it's kinda like I know what they're thinking."

Katherine could only stare.

"Isn't that weird?" he said. "That's how I knew those kidnappers were lying. And those old people who brought me here? I could tell that they were good and that they'd help me just by looking at them."

Katherine knelt by her son and held his shoulders. "When," she swallowed, fighting to stay calm, "when did this start to happen?"

"Back when Mr. Michaels and I got all cut up. Remember, with all those blackberry vines and stuff? Remember when we became blood brothers?"

Katherine did remember. She turned back to the mirror, reexamining her face, hoping to find something. She pushed and stretched the skin, searching. There was nothing. Not even a scar.

"Pretty cool, huh?" Eric said.

She turned back to her son, trying to hide the growing panic she was feeling.

"Katherine?" It was O'Brien calling from the tailgate. "Is everything all right?"

She looked at Eric with rising wonder and fear.

"Hey, you two?"

The van rocked slightly as O'Brien rose and started toward them.

"Yeah," she called back. There was a tremor in her voice, but she was able to cover it. "Everything's fine."

She looked at her son another moment, then pulled him into a fierce embrace.

"Mom," he protested. "Mom, I can't breathe."

But she would not let go; she pulled him even tighter. Then, looking up at the pine tree and the moon rising behind it, she blinked back her tears and whispered a quiet prayer.

# Now Available!

## On the heels of *Blood of Heaven*
## From the best-selling author Bill Myers

# THRESHOLD

One of Revelation's "two witnesses" is already among us.
He just doesn't know it.

**Softcover: 0-310–20120-9**
**Audio Pages: 0-310-21571-4**

Some say Brandon Martus has a mysterious ability to see into the future, to experience what scientists refer to as a "higher dimension." Others insist he is simply a troubled Generation-X member who suffers from the accidental killing of his little sister. It isn't until he teams up with Sarah Weintraub, the ambitious but haunted neurobiologist, that the two begin to uncover a far deeper secret.

Utilizing the latest discoveries in brain research and quantum physics, the two wind their way through a treacherous maze of human greed and supernatural encounters that are both real and counterfeit—until they finally discover the astonishing truth about Brandon Martus.

A captivating scientific and supernatural thriller, *Threshold* takes the reader from the mountains of Nepal to the heartland of America, through the deceptions of hell and into the hands of Jesus Christ in a carefully researched and thought-provoking journey.

One of Revelation's Two Witnesses Is Already Among Us.
He Just Doesn't Know It.

THRESHOLD

BILL MYERS

FROM THE AUTHOR OF THE BEST-SELLING BLOOD OF HEAVEN

From the best-selling author
Bill Myers

*Available now at a Christian bookstore near you!*

ZondervanPublishingHouse
*Grand Rapids, Michigan*
http://www.zondervan.com

*A Division of HarperCollinsPublishers*

Coming soon in September 1999!

From the best-selling author Bill Myers

# FIRE OF HEAVEN

Revelation's two witnesses have been chosen. Will their own human weakness undermine the mission?

**Softcover: 0-310–21738-5**

In this sequel to *Blood of Heaven* and *Threshold*, Brandon Martus and Sarah Weintraub have committed their lives to Christ and begin a new life together in marriage.

Brandon's healing powers grow stronger, yet he becomes unsure of his purpose . . . how does God really want to use him? He begins using the healing powers in ways that seem right to him . . . if he has this gift, why shouldn't he heal everyone, instead of just those whom God tells him to heal?

Meanwhile, Sarah is struggling with her identity and how she should relate to Brandon. Following what she believes is her calling, she goes to Nepal and enters the company of a dangerous admirer who'd like nothing better than to take her away from Brandon for good.

Follow Brandon and Sarah as they learn of the importance of their God-given calling and as they struggle to fulfill what they are to do, all the while battling supernatural evil and forces beyond their control.

We want to hear from you. Please send your comments about this book to us in care of the address below. Thank you.

**ZondervanPublishingHouse**
*Grand Rapids, Michigan 49530*
http://www.zondervan.com

Forty-five.

Eric was losing control. He began to swerve.

To his right rose a steep cliff. To his left, the ground fell away in an equally steep drop-off. He played it safe and over-steered to the right. The car scraped, then banged against the cliff, glancing off the protruding boulders. It was a bone-jarring ride. He cringed at the smashing and screeching of sheet metal against granite. He knew that he was making plenty of scratches and dents and figured it would probably get him into lots of trouble. But he also figured that being grounded for life was better than not having a life.

And still the van continued to push.

The road swerved to the right. The rocks and boulders he'd been banging against disappeared, and Eric found himself shooting across the road into the left lane.

"Stop it!" he cried. "Stop it!"

He cranked the wheel to the right, but he was too late. The car crashed through the guardrail and suddenly became airborne.

Eric screamed, taking his hands off the wheel to cover his face. The car glanced off a large tree, than everything went topsy-turvy, like a carnival ride gone berserk. He flew into the roof, then into the doors, then the roof again. It was happening too fast to feel any pain. He figured the pain would come later.

The windshield exploded, spraying glass over his face, his arms, his hands. And then he felt nothing.


When Murkoski arrived at Genodyne, he slowed the car and eased past the dozen or so employees milling outside the security gate in the fog. When he turned and tried to enter the gate, a man with a Greater City of Arlington Police Department uniform stepped from the security building and waved him to a stop.

Murkoski rolled down his window. "It's okay, officer, I'm Dr. Murkoski, head of the—"

"I'm sorry, Sir, no one is allowed inside the parking lot."

"You don't understand. I'm in charge of—"

"I'm sorry, Sir. No one is allowed within a three-hundred-yard perimeter of the building."

"A three-hundred-yard perimeter?"

"Those are my orders, Sir. Now if you'll please back up and—"

"But—"

"I'm sorry, Sir."

Murkoski hated the man's politeness. Underneath all of that courtesy was just some hick who loved to flaunt his authority. Without a word, he threw the car into reverse, spitting just enough dirt and gravel to show his contempt.

He found a level place on the opposite side of the road and parked just as a local TV cable van approached. "Great," he sighed, "a media event." Then he shrugged. It wouldn't be that bad. After all, he was getting quite good at spinning stories and manipulating truth.

He threw open the door, nodded to some of the huddled staff, and strode through the fog toward the gate. The first cop, apparently expecting a confrontation, had already signaled his partner, who was a few years his senior.

Murkoski wasn't concerned. There were only two of them, and from his lofty perspective they were nothing but hayseeds.

"Mr. Murkoski?" the older cop asked.

"*Dr.* Murkoski, that's right."

"I'm Officer Sealy of the Arlington—"

"Did you find them?"

"I'm afraid it's not that simple. Apparently we have a bomb threat here."

"A bomb threat? Why do you say that?"

"Several of your employees were threatened by a man with a gasoline can and other paraphernalia. He claimed to have set a bomb."

"A gasoline can?" There was no hiding the condescending tone in Murkoski's voice. "You don't make a bomb with a can of gasoline."

"It could be a hoax, that's true. His first deadline has already come and gone, but we have to be certain. Fortunately, except for a hostage, everyone else has been cleared from the building."

"A hostage?"

"Yes, a woman."

Murkoski's mind raced. He knew it was Coleman up there. And with him, the boy's mother. But what were they up to? From the e-mail he'd seen on the computer screen, it sounded as if they'd been looking for the boy. But if they'd cleared the building, then they already knew he wasn't there. So why were they still in there? Unless . . .

Sensing a significant danger, Murkoski's thoughts snapped into sharper focus. The e-mail message had also said something about the kid reading computer files. If the kid could open Murkoski's files and navigate the Internet, then he could also transmit those files. And if he had transmitted the wrong file to Coleman and the woman, and if they had read it . . .

Murkoski turned to the cop. "You said he had other paraphernalia?"

"Yes, a gasoline can and a gym bag full of unspecified items. Now we're no experts in this field, but . . ."

The officer continued rattling, but Murkoski didn't listen. Why would Coleman take a can of gasoline into the plant? That's not enough to make a bomb. Enough to start a fire, certainly, but . . .

Destroy all the samples? No, there was far too much material for him to try and destroy on his own. Besides, the new Coleman he'd invented wouldn't be that brazen. Then again, if the old Coleman had returned, the one who'd run Death Row, there was no telling what he was capable of.

". . . a bit out of our league," the officer was saying. "So we'll just sit tight and wait for the Snohomish County Sheriff's Bomb Division to come up from Everett."

"Officer?"

"Yes, sir."

"I know who the man is."

"You do? Are you certain?"

"He is one of my volunteers, a patient."

"Well, then, maybe you could talk to him. If we can establish communication—"

The cable crew had arrived, and a light suddenly blasted into their eyes, momentarily distracting the officer.

"Maybe you could talk to him by phone, I mean, if we set it up."

"It would be better if I talked to him in person." Murkoski flipped the hair out of his eyes and spoke just a little louder for the camera.

The officer looked surprised. "Dr. Murkoski, I don't think that's such a good idea."

"He won't hurt me. He trusts me."

The officer fidgeted. This was obviously not a decision he felt qualified to make, and making it under the glaring light of the camera was even worse.

"Trust me on this, Officer . . . Officer . . .?"

"Sealy."

"Officer Sealy of the Arlington Police Department?"

"Yes."

"Officer Sealy, if you go in there, you'll frighten him, and he may indeed kill his hostage and blow up the entire facility. I'm sure you don't want that."

"Well, no, of course not."

"And if we wait, he may kill her and blow it up anyway. You did say one deadline has already passed."

"That's true, but—"

"If you allow me in there, if you let me reason with him, I'm sure he'll listen."

"But, risking your own life—"

"That's a risk I'm willing to take, Officer." Murkoski knew he sounded a bit melodramatic, but, after all, this was TV. "For his life, for the hostage's life, for the sake of the company, I'll take that risk."

The officer frowned, still undecided. Murkoski knew that he needed a last push. He patted the man's arm and smiled in gratitude as if he had just received permission. Then, without a word, he turned and started across the parking lot for the building.

"Dr. Murkoski. Dr. Murkoski?"

Murkoski pretended not to hear. He was sure the camera was still rolling, and that was good. The cop was out of his league. No way would the hick want to make a public scene now—especially with somebody of Murkoski's position.

Murkoski smiled quietly. Once he got through all of this, he would have to call up the station and ask for a copy of the tape. He always enjoyed seeing himself on TV.

O'Brien sat in the Pizza Hut snack shop at Sea-Tac. He stared out at his Mexicana Flight #142 to Mazatlán. As they had for the past several hours, a half-dozen ground crew members meandered around the 757, trying to look busy.

O'Brien sighed heavily and tore open another pack of Equal. If someone would just take the initiative and cancel the flight, he could go home or grab a hotel room for the night. Instead, every half hour or so, they would announce that the problem was nearly corrected and that they should be boarding shortly.

O'Brien slowly poured a stream of tiny Equal granules into his third cup of decaf. The late news droned on an overhead monitor, but he took little notice—until he heard the name Genodyne. Suddenly his ears perked up:

"... a bomb threat by a man with a hostage. We have a crew en route to this late-breaking story, and we hope to have a full report before the end of the broadcast."

O'Brien stared at the screen in disbelief. He felt numb and guilty and nauseous all at the same time. Coleman had been found out. The plan had failed before it had even begun.

Eric awoke to the sound of voices—thick and blurry and far, far away. His head ached and he wanted to keep his eyes shut, but there was a light flickering against his lids and he knew he should see what it was.

The voices grew clearer.

He pried open his eyes, but his glasses were gone. Without them it was hard to make out the details, but he definitely saw the flames. He sat up. The pounding in his head grew worse. Fifty yards below him, at the bottom of the hill, a car was on fire. There were no explosions, just roaring, lapping flames.

"Eric! Eric, where are you, son?" The men from the van were down below, looking for him. "Eric!"

Across the ravine, maybe a quarter of a mile away, he saw a light. Maybe a farmhouse, maybe a cabin, he couldn't tell. But he knew there were people there. Good people. He wasn't sure how he knew, he just knew.

"Eric!"

Mustering what strength he had, Eric rose to a squatting position. The throbbing in his head grew worse and he wanted to cry, but he couldn't. Instead, he slowly stood up and quietly made his way through the woods toward the light.

# CHAPTER 17

Katherine poured the last of the tubes onto the pile in the elevator. A handful tumbled off, rattling and clinking as they rolled into the hall. She bent over, scooped them up, and tossed them back onto the pile. When she rose, she caught Coleman staring at her. But it was more than a stare. She'd seen that look a thousand times from a thousand different men. It made her feel self-conscious, belittled, and angry. Normally she would have called him on it. But since she no longer knew whom she was dealing with and since they were in such a hurry, she did her best to

ignore it. They had one more job after this. Destroying the lab animals. She didn't want to jeopardize their mission with a confrontation now.

As a reward for her restraint, he flashed her a lascivious grin. "Nice. Very nice."

Knowing he wasn't referring to the pile of Eppendorf tubes, she shot him a glare. His grin only broadened. She turned away.

He changed the subject. "All right," he said, kneeling by the gym bag and pulling out the large box of soap flakes, "move that cute little rear of yours down the hall and start closing the lab doors."

His tone was demanding, condescending, and enough to push Katherine past the point of better judgment. "Why?" she challenged.

There was that smile again. He tore open the box of soap flakes and began sprinkling it over the pile of tubes, pushing and kicking the top layers aside so the flakes would filter down. "The labs here are equipped with automatic Halon fire extinguishers."

"What?"

"Fluorocarbon. They use it instead of water. It puts out the fire by replacing the oxygen. Regular water would short out and destroy all the expensive lab equipment. If you close those doors, we'll have enough oxygen for our weenie roast out here. If you don't, who knows."

"What about these?" She pointed to the overhead sprinklers above them in the hall.

"Just water. That's why everything's going in the elevator. No sprinklers in there."

"And the soap?" Her anger was giving way to curiosity.

"Poor man's napalm. Turns the fire into liquid jelly so it sticks to the tubes and doesn't run off."

She watched as he reached for the can of gasoline and began pouring it over the pile. "Get going," he ordered, "we got lots to do."

Still not fond of taking orders, but knowing it was for the best, Katherine turned and headed down the hall. Even then she could feel his eyes watching her. Angrily, she shut each of the eight doors. When she returned, he had finished pouring most but not all of the five gallons of gas onto the pile. He screwed the lid back onto the gas can.

"What about the rest of it?" she asked.

He grinned. "We save the rest to toast the lab animals downstairs."

She shuddered at the thought—and could tell that he enjoyed it.

He reached into the gym bag, pulled out a packet of matches, and lit one. Without hesitation, he tossed it onto the tubes. The pile ignited with a *whoosh*. Hot air slapped against Katherine's face, and she took a half-step back.

Coleman turned and started for the stairs. "Come on." But Katherine remained, watching the flames melt the soap into a thick, burning goo that stuck to the tubes and dripped further into the pile, cooking all that they touched. What a waste. What an incredible waste. Things could have been so different. So much good could have been accomplished if this had landed in the right hands.

Then again, with the type of money they were talking about, what type of hands *would* be right—or could remain so?

The overhead sprinklers kicked on. Water rained down, soaking her shirt, running down her neck. The cold made her shiver, but she continued standing, watching.

She gave a start when Coleman grabbed her arm. "Come on!" he yelled over the hiss of the sprinklers. "Let's go!"

She pulled away angrily. But instead of releasing her, he grabbed her other shoulder, turning her around. She opened her mouth to shout at him, but stopped. There was that grin again. Only now it had twisted into an obvious leer.

"Let me go," she demanded.

His grip tightened, and his gaze dropped from her eyes to her wet, clinging blouse.

She tried to pull away, but he held tight, looking into her eyes again. Water streamed down his face as his leer broadened, growing more frightening.

She forced herself to sound calm and cold. "I said, let me—"

He pulled her toward him.

"What are you—"

She felt his hand on the back of her head, shoving her mouth toward his. Her resistance was no match for his strength. His mouth covered hers. She tried to turn away, but his grip tightened, preventing it. He pushed harder, his mouth demanding and animal-like.

With a sharp twist, she pulled her head back for a moment and glared at him with venom. But his eyes were mocking, spiteful. The Coleman she had known, the one she had been so deeply drawn to, was not behind those eyes. This was someone else—the old Coleman.

She felt his hand reaching, pulling at her soaked blouse. She tried to raise her own hands to stop him, but she couldn't. They were pinned. "Come on, babe," he said, "You know you want—"

She spat at him.

He stopped and blinked, stunned. For a moment she thought the other Coleman, her Coleman, was returning—until he swung his arm back, clearly intending to smash his hand across her face.

It was the wet floor that saved her. He slipped as he swung, spoiling his aim. She turned and nearly broke away, but not quite. He grabbed her shoulder from behind.

This time she remembered her training. She clenched her left hand over her right fist and sent her elbow flying backwards as hard as she could. It met its mark, catching him in the stomach. He gasped and let go.

She started to run, slipped, and then he had her again. She tried to break free, but suddenly she felt herself lifted off the ground and shoved face-first against the unyielding wall.

Her instincts protected her nose—she turned her head as she saw the wall coming—but her cheekbone hit hard. She fought to retain consciousness as Coleman held her upright, her toes barely touching the ground.

"I like a woman with spirit," he growled, moving closer until his breath was hot in her face.

Tears streamed down her face. She hated herself for them, but couldn't stop. "Coleman, please—"

Suddenly she heard another voice shouting over the sprinklers: "Well, well, well. What do we have here?"

Coleman spun around. Katherine turned, her vision just clear enough to make out the form of a man. Murkoski emerged from the stairwell.

"A little domestic spat?"

Taking advantage of Coleman's distraction and using the wall as support, Katherine slid several feet away from him. She reached up and touched the wetness on her cheek. At first she thought it was water, but water wouldn't be that warm. Then she looked at her fingers and saw the blood.

Murkoski stepped toward her, the sprinklers soaking his sports coat, his hair, making him look like a drowned rat. With a mocking flourish, he handed her a handkerchief. She batted it away. Murkoski chuckled, shrugged, and stuffed it back into his pocket. "You should have that looked at. I'm afraid you'll wind up with a rather unpleasant scar."

"What do you want?" Coleman seethed.

Murkoski flipped his wet hair out of his eyes. "The question is, what do you want?"

As an answer Coleman broke into a wry grin and stepped aside so Murkoski could have a full view of the fire burning in the elevator. "We had a long talk with Dr. O'Brien."

"I see. And you think that's all of it?"

Coleman said nothing.

Murkoski shook his head. "You *are* ignorant, aren't you?"

Katherine glanced nervously at Coleman. She could tell he was straining not to attack.

"You don't think we have that genetic information recorded?" Murkoski asked.

Coleman's voice was low and quiet. "We've destroyed all the computer files, erased all the backups in the safe."

Murkoski registered a trace of surprise, but held his ground. "What about the gene sequencers?"

Coleman hesitated, then looked at Katherine.

"We emptied them," she said, barely hearing herself over the spray of the sprinklers.

"And their memory?" Murkoski asked, unable to contain his mockery.

She stood a moment. A dull, sick feeling began to spread through her body. She'd completely overlooked the independent computers, the ones reading the genes and temporarily storing their data.

"Don't tell me you've already forgotten the features of our expensive gene sequencers," he pretended to scold.

Coleman turned to Katherine. "Which labs are they in?"

Before she could answer, Murkoski motioned grandly to the building. "Why, throughout the entire wing, of course."

"You're lying!" Katherine shouted over the sound of the sprinklers. "O'Brien said everything was limited to the third floor!"

"Yes, well, Dr. O'Brien has been a bit out of the loop lately."

Coleman turned to Katherine. "Can you knock them out?"

She looked at him helplessly.

"If they're computers, can you knock them out?" he repeated impatiently.

She opened her mouth to answer, but Murkoski cut her off. "Don't be stupid. She doesn't have the know-how. Even if she did, you don't have the time. I told the police if we didn't come out in five minutes to come in shooting."

Coleman stared at him. It was obvious he was trying to determine whether Murkoski was bluffing. But whatever discerning ability Coleman had possessed appeared to be gone by now.

"And if you ask me," Murkoski continued, "I think those rednecks out in the parking lot would enjoy a little action, don't you?"

Without missing a beat Coleman turned to Katherine. "Check out the sequencers. I'll go down and start killing the lab animals."

Katherine nodded, and they both started for the stairs.

"Killing—that's what you do best, isn't it?" Murkoski called.

Coleman stopped.

Murkoski seemed to revel in the moment. Standing there with water pouring over him, taunting and baiting like a school-yard bully. "Just like old times, isn't it, Mr. Coleman? That emotional rush of taking another life. All that control. It's the ultimate power trip, isn't it?"

Coleman's breathing slowed as he focused on Murkoski. Katherine had seen this before. She knew what was coming.

"But then, what can we expect? After all, you're just a product of your chemicals, aren't you? This is how you're programmed. You have no other choice. Once a monster, always a monster."

Coleman's body tensed. Katherine reached out and touched his arm. He didn't respond.

"But you see, there's one lab animal you won't be able to kill. One you can't."

Coleman's voice was barely audible over the sprinklers. "Which one is that?"

"You."

Katherine caught her breath.

Murkoski grinned at his little surprise. "You don't think there are remnants of that gene in your blood? You don't think there will always be a remnant that somebody can pull from you to start all of this all over again?"

Doubt and confusion crossed Coleman's face.

"He's lying," Katherine ventured.

"Am I? Everything's been thought out, Mr. Coleman, down to the most minute detail. You see, that's the difference between you and me. I'm at the top of the evolutionary chain. I'm a thinker. In fact, I come from a long line of thinkers. You, on the other hand . . ." His lips curled into a cold smile. "Well, as I've said, we're all products of our genes, no matter how primitive our parentage may be."

Coleman lunged. Katherine screamed as he threw Murkoski into a choke hold, his eyes wild, his face filled with exhilaration.

"Coleman, don't!" She yanked at his arm, but his grip was immovable. "Coleman!"

Murkoski gasped for breath. "That's right," he coughed, water streaming down his face. "Go ahead, prove my point. You're only—" Coleman tightened his grip, choking off the words.

"Coleman!" Katherine cried. "You're killing him! Coleman!" She leaned into his face and shouted. "You're better than this! Stop it!"

"You heard what he said," Coleman sneered. "I'm no more than—"

"You don't have to do this!"

Murkoski kicked and struggled, his eyes bulging grotesquely, as Coleman tightened his grip.

"Listen to me!" she shouted. "Listen to me! He's wrong! You're more than a bunch of genes!"

Coleman shook his head. "It's too late."

"You're a man, not a chemistry set—you've got a will, you've got faith."

The last phrase touched something—in his eyes she saw a fleeting spark. It disappeared as quickly as it had appeared, but she had seen it, and she knew she had found the key. She pressed in.

"'If anyone is in Christ, he is a new person.' Remember? 'Old things have passed away.' Remember that? Do you remember?"

He looked at her. The spark behind his eyes remained a fraction longer this time. There was understanding, a common ground. She had him.

"Let him go. Coleman, let him go."

He shook his head. "I can't."

"Of course you can! You don't have to do this. 'Old things have passed away.'"

"I've tried. All night I've been trying."

"Then maybe you should stop."

Surprise and confusion filled his eyes.

"Stop trying. Stop trying to do it on your own."

He scowled.

"Those are your own words—don't you remember? Stop putting your trust in you. 'If any man is in *Christ* he is a new person.'"

Coleman was listening now. Carefully.

"'Old things have passed away, all things are new.' That's what you said, remember? Stop trusting in you. Put your trust in him, Coleman. Not you. Him, him, Coleman!"

Coleman closed his eyes. Was he praying? Searching for faith? It didn't matter. She didn't care. She didn't even know if she believed it. She just hoped it would work.

"You can't do it on your own. You've tried. Turn it over!"

Coleman hesitated.

"It doesn't have to be forever. Just now. Just one moment at a time. Turn it over to him. Now, Coleman. Turn it over!"

Ever so slowly, Coleman released Murkoski. The kid slumped to the floor, coughing and choking, gasping for breath.

Coleman turned and stepped away; Katherine was right at his side. "You did it," she encouraged. "You did it!"

He shook his head. "Not me," he whispered. "I would have killed him." Looking into her eyes, he repeated in quiet amazement, "It wasn't . . . me."

Katherine searched his face, daring to hope that somehow he was right.

"That's it?" Murkoski said, coughing and struggling to stand in the deepening water. "You beat it one time and you think you've got it conquered? You think you've changed? You'll never change, Coleman. You're chemicals. Chemicals!"

Coleman refused to turn around. Katherine remained at his side, watching him.

"You'll always be this way! You can't keep fighting it, not forever. You'll always be—"

An unearthly shriek echoed through the room. All three spun to see a baboon flying through the rain directly at Murkoski. It hit him in the chest, sending him splashing onto the floor. The animal went straight for the man's throat, tearing, clawing, screeching. Murkoski screamed as he fought and kicked, but his cries bubbled and choked in his own blood.

Quickly, Coleman pulled the guard's gun from his pants and tried to take aim. But they were rolling and thrashing too wildly. As soon as he had a bead on the animal, they'd roll or twist and suddenly Murkoski was in the way. Coleman moved in, searching for a clear shot. But there was only a blur of wet fur and clothes and blood and flesh. He dropped the gun into the water and fell to his knees, trying to grab the animal, to pull him off, to save whatever was left of Murkoski.

"Let him alone!"

O'Brien entered from the stairway.

"Stay back!" he shouted at Coleman. "It's too late—he'll only kill you too."

Coleman looked from O'Brien to Murkoski. The kid was no longer fighting. His body lay in the water, still moving and jerking but only from the animal's ripping and tearing.

"Stay out of his way!" O'Brien warned. "He's a killer now; he'll want to keep killing."

Still on his knees, Coleman reached toward the baboon, one last try. Freddy turned on him, ferocious, shrieking, baring his needlelike fangs, his face covered in blood.

O'Brien slowly knelt in the doorway to the stairs and began to call: "Freddy? Freddy, come here, fellow."